**"I WANT YOU ALL TO PROMISE ME SOMETHING,"
NEELIX FINALLY SAID.**

"Name it," Chakotay replied.

"As long as you're all here in the Delta Quadrant, I want to hear of your progress. Captain Eden has promised to make regular contact, but I want to hear from all of you as well. I have my hands full on New Talax, but even from a distance, I'll always feel a part of this crew."

"Consider it done," Chakotay assured him.

"Do you have any idea where you're headed next?" Neelix asked.

No one did until Chakotay said, "Have you ever heard of a species that call themselves the Children of the Storm?"

Neelix had to confess, he hadn't. "They don't sound terribly friendly," he observed.

"Who are they?" the Doctor asked.

Chakotay sighed. "I don't want to turn this lovely evening into a mission briefing, but I have a feeling we're about to find out."

STAR TREK VOYAGER®

CHILDREN OF THE STORM

KIRSTEN BEYER

Based on *Star Trek*®
created by Gene Roddenberry
and
Star Trek: Voyager
created by Rick Berman & Michael Piller & Jeri Taylor

POCKET BOOKS
New York   London   Toronto   Sydney

Pocket Books
A Division of Simon & Schuster, Inc.
1230 Avenue of the Americas
New York, NY 10020

This book is a work of fiction. Names, characters, places, and incidents either are products of the author's imagination or are used fictitiously. Any resemblance to actual events or locales or persons, living or dead, is entirely coincidental.

First Pocket Books paperback edition June 2011

POCKET and colophon are registered trademarks of Simon & Schuster, Inc.

For information about special discounts for bulk purchases, please contact Simon & Schuster Special Sales at 1-866-506-1949 or business@simonandschuster.com.

The Simon & Schuster Speakers Bureau can bring authors to your live event. For more information or to book an event, contact the Simon & Schuster Speakers Bureau at 1-866-248-3049 or visit our website at www.simonspeakers.com.

Cover design by Alan Dingman; cover art by Michael Stetson

Manufactured in the United States of America

10   9   8   7   6   5   4   3   2   1

ISBN 978-1-4516-0718-5
ISBN 978-1-4516-0722-2 (ebook)

For Anorah . . .
my grace

Your beliefs become your thoughts. Your thoughts become your words. Your words become your actions. Your actions become your habits. Your habits become your values. Your values become your destiny.

—*Mahatma Gandhi*

HISTORIAN'S NOTE

Children of the Storm takes place concurrent with and immediately following the events of *Star Trek Voyager: Unworthy*, from late May to mid-July 2381.

Prologue

Standing just inside what had once been the doorway to the *U.S.S. Quirinal*'s main engineering bay, Captain Regina Farkas felt the adrenaline-fueled tension of the last hour dissipate as a strangely calming thought flitted gently into her mind and found a place to settle.

It's a pity so few of us are allowed to choose the time and manner of our death.

Cold comfort, to be sure, but certainly better than the fate of the billions of Federation citizens who had suddenly found death raining down on an otherwise ordinary day just a few months earlier when the Borg had invaded the Alpha Quadrant.

Though Regina had faced the possibility of death more times than she cared to remember in her forty-nine years of service to Starfleet, she was surprised by the serenity descending upon her now that the die was well and truly cast. If death had once seemed like the unwelcome relation one was forced to invite to major family gatherings, Regina now found herself completely prepared to walk across the room and shake the bastard's hand.

Not that she *wanted* to die. Like those who had worn the weary mantle of command before her, and those who would someday rise to take her place, she had her fair share of regrets. But as she mentally filed them away as "forever undone," she decided that peace was easier to embrace when you didn't doubt for a moment that you had spent the majority of the time you'd been given doing the thing that made you feel alive.

In Regina's case, that had been exploring the vastness of space, leading others on awe-inspiring journeys into the unknown. Though the practical reality certainly came with stretches of the mind-numbingly boring, those were easily eclipsed by the unimagined sights, the exotic tastes and fragrances, and the sheer variety of life, both simple and complex, that thrived within the many systems she had been fortunate enough to visit as she traveled among what had always seemed like the infinite stars of the galaxy.

The hard and basic truth of this moment was that she had no *real* choice. Or, rather, she had made the choice that now brought her such certainty years ago, when she had accepted her first command. And perhaps some small part of her had known even then that in choosing the life of her dreams, she was also choosing her ultimate fate—the probability of it, anyway, if not the finer points.

The acrid tang of the air, which the room's environmental processors were failing to clear, the suffocating heat that rose from the deck, the sweat matting her white bangs to her forehead and trickling down her back, the pulsing ocher glow of the emergency lights, the weight of the compression rifle she cradled in one arm, the glowing panel of the portable beam emitter she had seconds to target, and the uncomfortable itch of the leather band she had just secured around her wrist were the vivid details of a picture that had been drawn the day she'd accepted that her life was to be one of service— a picture that had been hazy and unfocused until these last few precious seconds had finally caught up with her.

Mechanical whines, hisses, clanks, and the occasional grunt behind her were the last symphony she would hear. True, they weren't her beloved Khachaturian, but they would suffice. Focusing on them made it easier to block out the distant intermittent shouts and phaser discharges coming from elsewhere on the deck—nerve-racking reminders that the battle for the lives of her six-hundred-plus crew members would continue even after she was gone.

A crackle of static over the comm system interrupted her reverie, followed by the voice of Lieutenant Psilakis from the bridge.

"Two hostiles and eight escorts are approaching your position, Captain."

Only two?

She smiled grimly before replying with a simple "I know." Her tricorder had told her as much forty-five seconds earlier.

As she imagined the hostiles dancing through the hall toward her, her tight smile widened. They were coming to finish what they had begun. They were hell-bent on destroying her and her ship. But there was still an infinitesimal possibility that they would not succeed. Standing between the Children of the Storm and their ultimate victory was a terrified but ingenious lieutenant junior grade, Phinnegan Bryce. It was still possible that he would succeed in bringing the slipstream drive on line to hurtle her badly damaged vessel far from the peril they now faced. This was a task he alone could perform, and she was duty bound to give him as much time as she could to finish his work, even if it was the last thing she would ever do.

"A few more seconds, Captain," Phinn called, no longer bothering to try to sound brave.

I know.

"Best possible speed, Lieutenant," Farkas shot back, wishing she could inject a little of the absurd hope she had already pinned on him into his lanky frame.

Instead, Phinn's palpable terror caused her to grip her rifle a little more tightly.

Relax, the captain reminded herself, drawing breath from the center of her body. It wouldn't do for the suppression beams to miss their target because she was holding unnecessary tension in her trigger finger. Once they were successfully established around the hostiles, her calm would have to be maintained as she faced the Children's escorts, who would undoubtedly rush into the fray to free them.

Farkas's eyes danced over the heavy pieces of exposed metal framing the doorway. Jagged and twisted into a tangled mass, they were painful reminders of the destructive power of the enemies she was about to face. She could only imagine what the rest of her ship must look like now, given what had transpired in the last hour. En route to engineering, she had glimpsed gaping wounds edged with sharp tritanium spikes and surfaces rotting under the corrosive heat and radioactive power of the Children's ruptured energy shells. By now, almost every deck could have suffered such violence.

There was a shrill *bleep* as Phinn activated the shipwide comm. "All hands, prepare to go to slipstream velocity on my mark."

For the love of the gods, get on with it, Lieutenant, Regina refrained from saying aloud.

"Five . . . four . . . three . . ."

Two.

Two of the alien spheres she had first seen in the logs of Captain Ezri Dax of the *Aventine* rounded the corner of the hall and came into view. If they hadn't been so ominous, Regina might have found them beautiful. Truth be told, the explorer in her heart found them utterly and horribly magnificent.

Inhaling sharply, and holding her last breath, Captain Regina Farkas activated the suppression beams. Orange light shot forth and froze the spheres in place.

A single shot whizzed by her head and sent her rolling to the ground. Coming up, she raised her phaser rifle and with deadly accuracy opened fire on her own people.

Chapter One

STARDATE 58450.2
U.S.S. VOYAGER

"Well, that's just overkill," Harry Kim said glumly as he surveyed the line of cannons dotting the ridge that separated him and his fellow unnamed slave, Tom Paris, from Chaotica's castle.

"Chaotica was never much for subtlety," Tom reminded him, unable to hide his exhaustion.

"Yeah, but this isn't Chaotica," Harry argued. "It's Cambridge."

"You haven't spent enough time with our counselor, Harry," Tom tossed back. "The man makes Chaotica look positively restrained."

Much as he wanted to, Harry couldn't argue with that. Though Hugh Cambridge had joined *Voyager*'s crew almost three years earlier, Harry had never found the time or the inclination to really get close to the man. Even during the last of what Harry remembered as the relatively good times aboard *Voyager*, an extended exploratory mission to the Yaris Nebula, Harry had avoided the counselor. The seemingly ceaseless battles of the year and a half that followed, coupled with the string of losses of those he held dear and his own near death, should have thrown him more regularly into Cambridge's path. Maybe if they had, Harry admitted to himself, he wouldn't feel quite so lost now. Then again, he had always assured himself that he could handle whatever the universe threw at him, right up until he discovered that he simply couldn't.

And this is Cambridge's idea of therapy? Harry thought bitterly. Covered in smelly, tattered rags in a monochrome desert beside the man whom he had once counted as a brother but whose presence now only fired his rage, Harry decided he'd been right not to seek the counselor's services. The sooner he and Tom captured the damn castle, the better. Then he could cross this toilsome exercise off his list, get back to the solitude of his quarters, and figure out what the hell he was going to do with the rest of his life and career.

A grimace of pain Tom failed to hide caught his attention.

"What?" Harry demanded.

"Nothing."

"*What?*"

"It's not your problem," Tom replied tersely.

"Just tell me," Harry insisted without softening his tone. "If you've got an issue that's going to hinder our ability to get over that ridge, I need to know about it now."

"I'm fine," Tom shot back.

"You're not."

"Look, you're not chief of security right now, buddy," Tom reminded him. "You're Unnamed Slave Number Two, and Unnamed Slave Number One can handle a sand flea–bitten, pulled hamstring without your assistance," he added hotly.

Since when are you Unnamed Slave Number One? Harry wanted to ask, but held his peace. They'd been trudging through the desert for what felt like forever, and pulling rank, or forcing Tom to admit that it didn't exist here, wasn't going to solve their mutual problem. *Typical of Tom, anyway.*

He settled for stating the obvious. "This isn't getting us anywhere, is it?"

"Nope," Tom agreed, "but I think I know what would."

Harry doubted it but shrugged anyway. "Let's hear it."

Tom slapped the back of his neck and immediately began scratching at yet another bite as he laid out his plan. "I'm going to head south. The castle's drainage system has an opening just past the walls, and if I can make it inside . . ."

Harry had already found multiple flaws with this suggestion, not the least of which was that getting to the south wall would take hours he was no longer prepared to spend on this exercise in futility.

"Even assuming you get that far, which you won't," Harry assured him, "didn't we destroy that drain in Episode Thirty-nine?"

"'Captain Proton and the Mean, Bad, Dirty, Stinking Robot'?" Tom asked.

"Yeah." Harry nodded, almost cracking a smile.

"Don't worry," Tom said. "I'll find a way in."

"No, you'll die trying," Harry insisted.

Tom paused long enough to offer Harry a cynical grin. "Better me than you."

"Since when?" escaped Harry's lips in surprise.

"Since forever, Harry," Tom said more seriously.

Harry was genuinely taken aback.

"Oh, come on, Harry," Tom answered his unspoken doubt. "You know I'd die for you. It's not a long list, granted. And you're not at the top of it. But right below B'Elanna and Miral, there's you."

"You don't have to . . . I mean . . ." Harry began, but found himself at an uncomfortable loss for words.

"Apparently, I do," Tom went on. "Ever since B'Elanna and Miral got back you seem to have forgotten the years and years of stuff between us that equals me dying for you should the occasion call for it. And even though you don't believe me, that was still true when I wasn't telling you that B'Elanna and Miral were still alive, which, by the way, was as much about protecting you as it was them."

Tom had pleaded his case dozens of times since their "counseling" session had begun the previous morning, but Harry wasn't buying it. He understood the circumstances: a mad Klingon sect wanted Tom's daughter dead. But in Tom's place, Harry could never have lied about his desperate plan to save Miral. He could never have let his best friend believe that two of the people he loved most in the universe were dead. For Harry this betrayal was clear evidence that Tom didn't trust him, which after ten years of friendship was impossible to comprehend. Harry felt adrift in a lonely sea of frustration he could no longer find the energy to attempt to describe.

"Fine," he snapped. "You'd die for me."

"I would."

"Fine."

"I *would*, Harry."

"So you said."

"And I'm going to, right now," Tom added emphatically as he pulled himself up off his belly to begin his southern march.

Harry rose to a seated position, watching Tom trudge away. He knew he should follow. Even with two functioning hamstrings, Tom wasn't going to get within half a kilometer of that drain on his own. But Harry didn't really want to follow anyone anymore. He wanted to find his own road, and somehow reclaim the optimism that had once made him unique among his peers. He used to enjoy his life. He suddenly realized how much of the problem he now grappled with was the fact that he couldn't remember the last time he'd felt anything approaching joy. The hours he and Tom had once spent on this very holodeck used to be the highlight of any given day. A new question caught him by surprise.

"Can you just tell me one thing first?" he called out.

Tom halted but didn't turn around as he answered, "Sure."

"Why isn't this fun anymore?" Harry asked simply.

At this, Tom did turn to face Harry, and the cockiness that had always been his best defense was nowhere to be seen.

"You really have to ask?" Tom said with genuine sympathy.

And then it hit Harry harder than the body blow he'd felt when he'd first read B'Elanna's and Miral's names on that fraudulent casualty list.

"We've been living the real thing for too long, haven't we?" Harry said.

A hint of the cocky returned as Tom brought his forefinger to his nose, tapping it for emphasis. Sighing, Tom retraced his steps and slumped down beside Harry in the sand.

"When we started playing this game, we'd been lost in the Delta Quadrant for a few years and we'd seen a few tough times . . ." Tom reflected.

"I'd already died twice," Harry reminded him.

"And had the exquisite pleasure of being eaten alive by that 8472 virus or whatever it was," Tom added.

"Don't." Harry held up a hand to forestall any recounting of the grisly details of that story.

"But we still hadn't really lost anything that mattered," Tom went on.

"There was Kes," Harry contradicted him. His heart broke a little as he remembered her soft, lovely face and deceptively sweet nature that belied an inner strength he'd never suspected when they'd first met the young Ocampan.

"My mistake," Tom agreed. "But she *evolved*," he added, "which made it a win for her, if not for us."

"True."

"Point is—" Tom began again.

"I get it," Harry cut him off.

I really get it. And though it did not bring him the joy he was seeking, it did diminish the unpleasant burning he'd felt for so long in the center of his chest.

Tom's eyes met his, and Harry was finally able to see the hell of the last few years through someone else's eyes. It had begun for Tom with the near loss of his daughter, followed by the untimely death of Admiral Janeway. Too soon after, the Borg had claimed his father, Admiral Owen Paris, and almost half of *Voyager*'s crew. Something raw and wounded had long ago replaced the careless selfishness that had once defined Tom Paris, and Harry, who had always thought of himself as a true friend, hadn't even noticed. Harry had suffered his own losses, but at the end of the day, they didn't begin to stack up to Tom's. Ashamed, Harry realized what a complete and utter ass he'd been of late.

The first comfortable silence the two had shared in much too long settled between them.

"I'm sorry, Tom," Harry finally said softly.

"You don't have to be," Tom replied. "It killed me to lie to you. I hated every minute of it. But I convinced myself I had no choice and that you'd understand. I didn't stop and think about how you had to be suffering. I thought of myself first. And the truth is you deserved better than that."

"But you've always been so good at putting yourself first," Harry teased, adding, "*Unnamed Slave Number One.*"

A gentle shake of Tom's head acknowledged that he was guilty as charged.

A new and even more troubling thought now rose to Harry's mind.

"You don't suppose this is what getting old feels like, do you?"

Tom feigned shock. "I don't know, Harry. If I ever decide to get old, I'll let you know."

"Right," Harry agreed.

"So what do you say we storm that drain together and let the chips fall where they may?" Tom asked.

A faint spark of mischief glinted to life in Harry's eyes.

"I have a better idea." Harry smiled.

Tom was clearly intrigued. "Tell me."

"Do you remember the time . . ." Harry began.

Captain Chakotay had resumed command of *Voyager* only two days earlier, but already it had begun to feel as if he'd never been away. There were plenty of new names and faces to commit to memory, and the retrofit that had prepared the ship for its current mission to the Delta Quadrant had taken some getting used to, but on the whole, he felt more at home than he had in years. The irony that he had spent his first seven years aboard this ship trying desperately to reach what he'd always thought of as "home," the Alpha Quadrant, was not lost on him.

A soft "Enter" came from the other side of the door, and he stepped inside one of the few rooms aboard his ship he hadn't yet had a chance to see: Fleet Commander Captain Afsarah Eden's personal quarters. He was more than a little shocked by what he saw.

The specs Chakotay had been reviewing since he'd returned to active duty had already told him that the cabin was roughly half the size of the ship's mess hall, which could accommodate up to fifty in relative comfort. But he still hadn't been prepared for the size of it. The thought that so much room would have been set aside for any single person aboard a starship was, quite frankly, disturbing. He knew the quarters had been designed for the personal use of the fleet's original commanding officer, Admiral Willem Batiste. But he also knew that Batiste had only joined the fleet's mission to facilitate his return to his true home. It was still chilling to imagine that a member of Species 8472 had infiltrated the upper echelons of Starfleet Command. He had successfully replaced a highly decorated admiral without anyone knowing the difference until he had led a fleet of ships to the Delta Quadrant and opened a rift to fluidic space, almost killing himself and destroying *Voyager* in the process. Chakotay was still relieved that the creature he had once known as Valerie Archer had been dispatched to deal with the crisis from her people's end, and had believed that the encroachment upon her space was the action of one of their own rather than the opening salvo in a Federation attack. Still, Chakotay found it hard to understand why the admiral's personal quarters should have been so vast.

Maybe he thought he'd be with the fleet a little longer, Chakotay mused, *and that an office where you could land a shuttle would come in handy.*

"Obnoxious, isn't it?" Eden acknowledged.

Chakotay didn't remember anything in Eden's file about her being telepathic, but she probably didn't have to be to read his thoughts at this moment.

"It's definitely . . ."

"Ridiculous," Eden finished for him, rising from behind the large carved mahogany desk embedded with standard data and control panels. Her lithe figure perched with feline grace on the corner as she crossed her long arms over her chest. "There's actually a putting green in the bedroom."

"You're lying," Chakotay replied, stunned.

"Not according to the poor ensign who's been assigned to remove it," Eden assured him.

Chakotay recognized the painting behind her desk, a swirling mass of vivid, impressionistic, heavy impasto strokes in reds, oranges, and blues, as well as a bronze sculpture of a cat balancing its forepaws on a ball on the credenza. They had recently occupied what was now his ready room. That office, along with *Voyager*'s command, had been Eden's only a few weeks earlier when this mission had begun.

"What can I say?" Eden went on, clearly a little embarrassed. "Willem did everything big."

"You would know better than I," Chakotay replied. Several

years before this mission had begun, Eden had been married to Batiste. He imagined she was still reeling from the revelation that Batiste had been sent to spy on the Federation and only married her as part of his cover. But her placid aquiline features and almond-shaped obsidian eyes revealed only a hint of regret.

"I'm actually thinking about reallocating the space until our next refit, when it will be completely demolished," Eden admitted. "The 'fresher could come in handy as an extra cargo bay."

Chakotay paused for a moment. He appreciated her efforts to make light of the situation, but he worried that the defenses she was erecting might keep her at an unhealthy distance from those she was now responsible for leading. Finally, he decided to take a chance.

"You don't have to apologize for him, Captain," he said seriously. "You're not responsible for his choices."

"Right." She nodded. "I only married him, lived with him for years, and somehow managed to miss the fact that he wasn't even human."

"If I hadn't known better, I would have believed I was in San Francisco when we boarded the 8472 simulation they built here a few years ago," Chakotay sympathized. "Their technology, especially their genetic manipulation abilities, were beyond anything I would have thought possible. Not to mention the fact that half the crew of the Maquis vessel I used to command was working for other people."

Eden smiled lightly. "So we've both got blind spots bigger than these quarters? Why doesn't that make me feel any better?"

"I don't know," Chakotay replied. "At least things no longer surprise me like they used to."

"You just expect the worst of everyone you meet?"

"No," he said, shaking his head. "I wait a little longer before I give anyone my complete trust."

"Noted."

Chakotay wasn't sure if they had just begun to bridge the distance between them, or unintentionally made it greater.

"You have a report for me?" Eden asked, returning to business.

"We rendezvoused with *Esquiline, Curie,* and *Achilles,*" he replied. "We're still waiting on *Quirinal, Planck,* and *Demeter.*"

Eden's brow furrowed. "Have we received any word from Captain Farkas?"

"Not yet."

"I want to know the moment they return," Eden said. Chakotay knew that Captain Farkas and *Quirinal* had been dispatched along with *Planck* and *Demeter* to investigate an extremely dangerous species, but he had to assume they were up to the task.

"I'm sure they're fine, Captain," Chakotay attempted to reassure her. "If they're en route, as they should be by now, they wouldn't be able to send a signal from within the slipstream corridor." It troubled him that he kept wanting to address her by something other than her rank, but "Afsarah" or "Eden" felt awkward, like a room he had not yet been invited to enter.

"Have Commander Paris and Lieutenant Kim concluded their temporary *medical* leave and returned to duty?" Eden asked.

"No, ma'am," Chakotay replied with a slight grin.

Eden seemed genuinely surprised. "Have you received a report from Counselor Cambridge as to their progress?"

Chakotay nodded. "I have. And I see no reason to end their session until the counselor is certain their issues have been resolved."

Although Eden shot him a wary smile, she did not press the matter further.

"In the meantime," he continued, "we've got a visitor who is requesting a few minutes of your time."

"Who?" she asked.

Chakotay smirked. "An old friend."

Eden's eyebrows rose to meet the challenge.

"By all means," she said, dropping her arms and rising to straighten her uniform jacket.

"He's waiting in the conference room."

As they headed together for the door, Eden added softly, "You were worried I didn't have room to receive him here?"

"I didn't want to take the liberty of assuming you were available," Chakotay replied.

Eden nodded appreciatively. "Also noted."

As Eden entered the conference room and came face-to-face with Neelix, she decided that the presence she had first come to know through visual files was an accurate if pale representation.

She didn't actually *know* Chakotay's "old friend," but as with most of *Voyager*'s original crew, she felt as if she did. Prior to this assignment she'd headed up Project Full Circle, the Starfleet task force that had reviewed all of the mission logs of *Voyager*'s seven-year journey in the Delta Quadrant. Neelix's logs had been among the most descriptive and oddly personal. It was as if he was constitutionally incapable of hiding his feelings about anything, or anyone.

The slightly portly Talaxian stood almost as high as Eden's

shoulders, but the sheer force of his personality belied his stature. Wisps of sand-colored hair shot out from his mottled head, and though the texture of his skin appeared roughly worn, the hands that took the one she extended to him were both soft and warm. Golden eyes fairly danced with genuine delight as he greeted her, saying, "A pleasure to meet you, Captain Eden. I'm Neelix of New Talax, the Federation's first ambassador to the Delta Quadrant, and if I or my people can ever be of service to you or the fleet, we would consider it an honor."

"The honor would be ours, Mister Ambassador," Eden replied, speaking the absolute truth.

Chakotay stood a few paces behind Neelix, radiating a sense of tranquil happiness. It was understandable. The captain had probably never thought he'd see Neelix again in person, and in his place, Eden felt sure she'd take such an unexpected reunion for the gift of fate that it was.

"You're a long way from home, Mister . . ."

"Please, call me Neelix," the Talaxian insisted.

"Neelix," Eden finished with a smile.

"Not really," he corrected her gently. "Our asteroid colony is only a little over two days from here at high warp. And it was a journey well worth making. I come bearing strange gifts," he added mysteriously.

Eden shot a glance toward Chakotay, who had clearly already heard this part of Neelix's story, then nodded for their guest to continue.

"Are you by any chance missing one of your shuttles, Captain?"

"We are," Eden replied, instantly concerned for Neelix. The shuttle had been stolen by an entity Eden believed to be extremely dangerous. If she had attacked his people . . .

"A few weeks after B'Elanna visited our colony, our long-range sensors picked up another Federation signal," Neelix began. "Naturally, once she had advised me of the Federation's return to the quadrant, I had our systems realigned to maximize our ability to pick up any such signals."

"Naturally," Eden said, unable to believe how touched she was by this simple gesture. She should have expected no less of him, she chided herself.

"Our scouts retrieved the abandoned shuttle, and I have brought it to you today."

Although Eden understood that this would have been his natural inclination, she also marveled at the ease with which he seemed to have come to this conclusion. For people such as his, struggling to eke out an existence in an asteroid field, the shuttle's technology would have come in more than handy.

"I'm deeply grateful," Eden acknowledged sincerely. "Was it abandoned?"

"It was," Neelix replied, bringing a sigh of relief from Eden. "As it was pretty beat-up, I did take the liberty of reviewing the shuttle's logs before I left New Talax. Apparently it had been under the command of a Starfleet medical tech named Meegan McDonnell."

Eden again looked to Chakotay. A shake of his head assured her that he had not briefed Neelix as to the significance of this discovery.

"Are the logs intact?" Eden asked.

Neelix appeared a little flustered. "Actually, they were . . . well . . . it looked as if they were intentionally damaged," he said, unsure of the ground upon which he was now treading. "I was able to restore most of them, however. You don't survive as long as I have without learning a few tricks," he added with a hint of self-deprecation. "It appears that shortly after Miss McDonnell neared our borders, she encountered one of Nacona's mining vessels. I don't know if I mentioned this to you, Chakotay, but his operators have returned to the asteroid field and we've actually established a fairly lucrative trade agreement."

"I'm not at all surprised," Chakotay replied.

Neelix reddened a little at the compliment as he pressed on. "It appears that some weapons fire was exchanged between the two vessels and then McDonnell abandoned the shuttle and . . . well . . . actually stole the mining ship."

"Have you or this Nacona picked up any trace of the stolen mining vessel?" Eden asked.

"No," Neelix replied. "But our search continues."

Chakotay's deep brown eyes were practically boring holes into hers when she raised them to verify her next inclination. She would be well within her rights to simply thank Neelix at this point and send him on his way. She doubted seriously that Meegan would ever darken New Talax's door again, but a few words of warning should insure his people's safety. However, Chakotay's gaze seemed to insist that Neelix deserved more than this, and she had to admit, he had a point. Neelix was a true ally in the Delta Quadrant, and he had been named a Federation ambassador by Captain Kathryn Janeway. It was true that no one other than Janeway had ever taken his appointment seriously, but the unconditional trust he had already demonstrated should be repaid in kind.

"A few weeks ago, we encountered a collection of species known as the Indign," Eden began.

"Hmm," Neelix said, as his eyes searched the ceiling briefly. "Never heard of them."

"Lucky for you," Chakotay said softly.

"Are they hostile?" Neelix asked seriously.

"Not overly," Eden assessed. "They had an unusual reverence for the Borg, which had led them in the past to some rather unpleasant actions."

"Impossible," Neelix stammered.

"We thought so, too," Chakotay agreed.

"One of the Indign species, the Neyser, had developed a means of trapping the consciousnesses of several individuals who had become enemies of their own people. There were eight, and one of them was accidentally transferred into Meegan."

"Oh, dear" was all Neelix could say.

"It gets worse," Chakotay interjected.

"Doesn't it always," Neelix said, turning to him with a knowing glance. It was the first hint of worldliness Eden had seen from him.

"Meegan was actually an incredibly advanced hologram," she went on. "The consciousness that now possesses her should be considered hostile and extremely dangerous. We intend to continue our search for her, but should you pick up even a trace of her trail, I would advise you to contact us immediately but to refrain from pursuing her."

"A wise precaution, Captain," Neelix agreed.

"Please, call me Afsarah," Eden offered, returning his simple courtesy.

"Afsarah," Neelix repeated with genuine warmth.

"Would it be possible for you to spend a little more time with us, Neelix?" Chakotay asked, discomfited for reasons Eden could not place.

"I thought you'd never ask," Neelix replied with a wide grin. "I'd love to check in on B'Elanna and Miral. I assume Miral has recovered?" he asked with a little more concern.

"She has," Chakotay assured him, "and I'm sure they're not the only ones who would love a chance to catch up."

"With your permission, Afsarah," Neelix requested.

"Of course." She smiled. "Welcome aboard, and consider yourself our honored guest for as long as you wish to stay. If you have some time later, I would appreciate receiving a formal briefing about the events in this area since *Voyager* was last here. Although the Federation fleet was sent here to establish new diplomatic relations with any species we may encounter, we will always appreciate the efforts of the first ambassador to the quadrant. I anticipate that this area will frequently be used as a regrouping point for the fleet, and we would very much like to continue to make regular contact with you in the future. I do not doubt that any ongoing intelligence you can provide will be most valuable to our efforts, Mister Ambassador."

The dark spots that lined Neelix's forehead and ran down his neck darkened visibly with what Eden could only assume was happiness.

Lieutenant Nancy Conlon, *Voyager*'s chief engineer, caught up with B'Elanna Torres—the fleet's chief engineer and her new boss—outside the mess hall. She and B'Elanna had been responsible for shanghaiing Harry and Tom for Cambridge's holodeck counseling session a full day earlier. With no word from either of them since, Conlon was beginning to wonder if she'd made a mistake trusting the counselor. Her friendship with Harry was something new and something she hoped wasn't going to end when he emerged from the holodeck.

"Any word?" Conlon asked B'Elanna without preamble. The half-Klingon's slight scowl was the answer she didn't want to see.

"No," B'Elanna replied. "And I told Cambridge that if they're not out today, I'm going in after them. I don't care what he says."

Conlon took some comfort in this thought. Formidable as the counselor might be, she couldn't imagine the consequences of crossing B'Elanna.

"You don't think anything could have happened to them?"

"I've been monitoring their life signs," B'Elanna said. "They're perfectly healthy, and probably still holding tight to their respective grudges. I can't believe I let Cambridge talk me into this ridiculous excuse for counseling."

"I thought you said it was a good idea."

"Sure, yesterday morning," B'Elanna allowed. "But they can both be stubborn as *targ*s."

"Let's hope for the best until we know better," Nancy suggested.

B'Elanna offered a wan smile. "You're not going to get perky on me, are you?"

"Not a chance."

"Good."

"Have *Esquiline*, *Achilles*, and *Curie* begun work yet on their new benamite recrystalization matrices?" Conlon asked, shifting to a safer subject. She knew that B'Elanna had intended to forward them the specs as soon as they were in range. Only days into the mission, the fleet had discovered that the precious crystals that powered their slipstream drives had begun to show microfractures. If the problem had gone unsolved for too long, their supplies would have been diminished well before the end of the fleet's three-year mission. B'Elanna's design of the matrix that solved this problem had confirmed, in Conlon's eyes, *Voyager*'s former chief engineer's fabled ingenuity.

"They have." B'Elanna nodded.

"Commander Drafar will probably have them at maximum capacity by the end of the day," Nancy mused.

"He's that good?" B'Elanna asked.

"Yep," Nancy replied. "The Lendrin work ethic is a sight to see. I'm sure that's part of the reason he was given command of *Achilles*."

"I've never met a Lendrin," B'Elanna mused. "In fact, I don't think I've ever heard of them."

"They joined the Federation while you were, uh, missing," Nancy replied delicately.

"Which time?" B'Elanna asked lightly, probably wondering if Nancy was referring to *Voyager*'s first stint in the Delta Quadrant, or her travels of the last couple of years.

"The first time," Nancy said.

"Well, I guess I'm in for a treat tomorrow morning, then," B'Elanna said. "I'm scheduled to tour *Achilles* first thing."

"Oh," Nancy said, her eyes widening a bit.

"What does that mean?" B'Elanna asked warily.

"Nothing." Conlon tried to shrug it off. "I guess it didn't occur to me that you wouldn't have met Drafar yet, but of course, there's no way you could have."

"What do I need to know about him that you're not telling me?" B'Elanna asked with more concern.

"Nothing," Conlon attempted again, though the smile that was lifting the corners of her mouth was probably not helping her convince B'Elanna. "Just be sure and tell me how it goes," she added, moving toward the mess hall doors.

B'Elanna stared after her, clearly aware that Nancy was enjoying herself immensely. Nancy wondered if B'Elanna was considering pulling rank and demanding to know Nancy's impressions of Drafar. The engineer hurriedly ducked into the busy dining room to avoid the possibility. Much as she had grown to like and respect B'Elanna, Nancy didn't want to poison Drafar's well. If Nancy knew him at all, he'd do just fine on his own, and watching B'Elanna work with him would be well worth the price of admission.

Heaven help her, Nancy thought as she replicated her breakfast. Then, thinking better of it, she revised her assessment.

Heaven help him.

U.S.S. GALEN

"I trust you have experienced no further side effects from your catoms since we left the Indign system?" the Doctor asked Seven of Nine. He assumed if she had, she would not have waited to inform him, but she'd seemed a little distant this morning during her scheduled checkup, and her reticence could be cause for concern.

"No," Seven replied simply, pushing herself off the edge of the biobed, clearly preparing to depart.

"I'm glad to hear it," the Doctor said sincerely. When she had rejoined the fleet, Seven had been deeply troubled by a "voice" in her head. A product of her transformation by the Caeliar, the voice seemed intent on forcing her to abandon her identity as a former Borg. The Doctor had wondered if she would ever again be the calm, confident woman he had known, but ongoing work with Counselor Cambridge and her recent experiences with the Indign appeared to have eliminated the voice, and she seemed completely restored to health.

"Unless there is something else . . ." Seven began somewhat absently.

"Seven?" the Doctor asked in a tone that seemed to bring her more fully into the present moment.

"Yes?"

"You seem somewhat distracted. Is something troubling you?"

"I am fine," she replied with a brisk sigh.

"Seven?"

"I have a great deal of work to complete before assuming care of Miral Paris this afternoon."

The Doctor stepped back a few paces and crossed his arms over his chest. She withered slightly under his knowing stare.

"I do," she attempted.

"I don't doubt it," he replied without relenting.

Finally Seven rested her lower back against the biobed and said, "I honestly don't know why, but for the last few days I can't seem to focus."

"Why don't you tell me what's on your mind?" the Doctor suggested.

"It's difficult to say," Seven said, at something of a loss.

The Doctor registered an uncomfortable twinge in his interpersonal relationship subroutines. He had taken Seven's friendship and trust for granted for so long now, it was impossible to imagine a subject she would be unwilling to discuss.

"Perhaps it's something you would prefer to share with Counselor Cambridge?" he ventured, knowing in advance that he would be crushed were this the case.

"No," Seven insisted immediately, her eyes widening briefly.

The Doctor instantly registered relief. Confusion and deep curiosity, however, quickly replaced that more pleasant sensation.

"Then, I don't understand," he said.

"Neither do I," Seven replied. "I have found it difficult to concentrate for several days now. As soon as I begin a project, my mind begins to wander."

"Down what path?" the Doctor asked gently.

"The past," Seven said thoughtfully.

"It's understandable," the Doctor suggested. "The transformation you endured has started you on a course of deep introspection. You have, no doubt, in your work with the counselor explored many aspects of your past that might have unsettled you. It is quite normal under the circumstances, and will pass in time."

Seven looked at him dubiously. "But the events I seem to return to in my mind are of a decidedly personal nature."

"Personal as in . . . ?" the Doctor asked.

"Interpersonal," Seven finally said.

"Oh," the Doctor said as his eyebrows lifted in surprise.

When it came to Seven's past *interpersonal* relationships, they were relatively few. Seven hadn't made a great deal of time in her life for liaisons of the heart, but as the Doctor well knew, the impression such experiences could leave behind were not a matter of quantity but of quality.

Finally he decided to fish a little. "You did end your relationship with Chakotay rather abruptly. Are you reconsidering that choice?"

"No," Seven replied, her sincerity evident. "Chakotay and I function much more efficiently as friends."

"I hardly think efficiency is the point, Seven."

She flushed faintly. "What I meant to say is that I do not believe Chakotay would be a wise choice in a partner."

"Have you met someone who you believe might be?"

Seven's cheeks grew visibly hotter.

"No," she finally replied.

"Seven?"

"Please excuse me, Doctor. I must return to *Voyager*. I'm sorry to have troubled you," she added as she quickly left the medical bay.

The Doctor found himself smiling faintly once she had gone. Despite her protestations, he did not believe she would have raised the subject had there not been someone that had piqued her interest. He also knew, after his recent experiences with Meegan McDonnell, that passion could flame in unexpected quarters. Given all Seven had been through of late, however, he worried that she might not be ready for any new relationship, and that bothered him. She was an extraordinary individual, and as best the Doctor could tell, the man who could meet her as an equal and stable partner was not on anyone's current sensor readings.

Chapter Two

TWENTY-ONE DAYS EARLIER
U.S.S. QUIRINAL

The swirling miasma of distorted energy that had formed the visual representation of a slipstream corridor looked as if it was going to collapse into itself. Captain Farkas had seen this sight dozens of times already, but it still made her feel ever so slightly like ducking.

As if it would help. She chuckled inwardly.

"Exiting synchronous slipstream flight in five, four, three, two . . ." Ensign Jepel Omar advised the bridge crew from ops.

Like storm clouds suddenly dissipating, the screen before Farkas's eyes cleared, revealing calm, untroubled stars.

"Are we all present and accounted for, Commander Roach?" Farkas asked of her first officer.

Malcolm Roach cleared his throat and replied, "Confirming *Planck* and *Demeter* have safely arrived."

"Excellent," Farkas remarked. "Ensign Hoch, job well done," she commended her helmsman.

Krim Hoch seemed to sit a little straighter in his chair as he acknowledged the captain's compliment with a subtle nod.

Tapping the control panel in the arm of her chair lightly, Farkas opened the shipwide comm. "Attention, all hands. We have arrived at our intended coordinates and will begin implementation of special security protocols immediately. This channel will be kept clear for Commander Roach. Please stand by."

And welcome to a piece of sky only a handful of Federation eyes have ever gazed on before, she thought, unable to repress the tingle of excitement that had always accompanied such moments for her.

"Roach to security, supplemental officers report to stations on decks one and seventeen. Lieutenant Ganley, begin segregation of bio-neural systems. Transporter room one, stand ready to receive incoming crew."

"*Acknowledged,*" the transport officer was the last to reply. *Ensign Genevieve,* Farkas reminded herself, still working hard after only a few weeks commanding *Quirinal* to remember names, faces, ranks, and positions. Like too many of the over six hundred Starfleet personnel now under her command, Farkas had only met Genevieve a handful of times. There were plenty more she had yet to meet. Her ship held the largest crew complement of any in the fleet, with *Esquiline,* the fleet's other *Vesta*-class starship, coming in second.

"Ensign Jepel, please open a channel to *Planck* and *Demeter,*" Roach requested placidly. Her first officer was fastidious and all-business when he was on duty. Farkas sincerely hoped to see him relax a little when the occasion presented itself. Though she appreciated his professionalism and discipline, in her experience, springs wound that tight usually popped at the most inconvenient times.

"Channel open, sir," Jepel indicated.

"Lieutenant Tregart, Commander Fife," Roach called, addressing his counterparts on *Planck* and *Demeter,* respectively. "We are ready to receive designated crewmen."

As both officers acknowledged Roach's instruction, Farkas couldn't help but think that "designated crewmen" was a diplomatic way of phrasing what under normal circumstances might be taken as an alarming example of discrimination. These personnel, who would soon be joined by several of *Quirinal*'s crew, all possessed some form of psionic abilities. Vulcans, Betazoids, Deltans, Cairn, and, if memory served, a Kazarite, were now boarding her ship and in an orderly fashion, *one assumed,* moving to cargo bay three, where they would enter stasis for the duration of this mission. Once they were secured, the bay would be shielded by a newly developed psionic force field. This special protocol, along with several others, was being implemented to protect all of them in the event they encountered the alien species they had come to investigate in this part of the Delta Quadrant.

The first time the Federation had encountered the

Children of the Storm, the *Aventine*'s Ullian helmsman had been briefly and unexpectedly possessed by one of the aliens in order to facilitate communication. Little was known about these "Children." They were noncorporeal, traveled through space in what had been dubbed "thought bubbles"—vessels filled with toxic atmosphere apparently propelled by thought alone—and had managed to destroy thousands of Borg ships without firing a single conventional weapon. Neither Admiral Batiste nor the commanders leading this expedition—Farkas, Captain T'Mar of the *Planck,* and *Demeter*'s Commander O'Donnell—had been willing to risk suddenly losing any of their crew to alien possession. The xenobiologists who had reviewed *Aventine*'s data all concluded that only species with telepathic or empathic abilities were likely to be vulnerable to the Children of the Storm. Farkas had her doubts, but she approached all such situations with a healthy skepticism.

Which reminds me, Farkas thought.

"Farkas to sickbay."

"*Go ahead, Captain,*" the gravelly voice of her chief medical officer, Doctor El'nor Sal replied.

"How is our volunteer doing?"

Doctor Sal considered the petite junior science officer, Ensign Ti'Ana, seated on the biobed before her, looking peaceful as a dead sea, and said, "Why don't you tell the captain yourself, Ensign?"

"I am prepared to do my duty, Captain," Ti'Ana replied with a serenity Sal was certain she had never experienced, let alone would have been able to muster in Ti'Ana's boots.

"*I'm glad to hear that, Ensign,*" Farkas replied. Sal was pretty sure her old friend was smirking and equally sure that Ti'Ana couldn't tell. As was usually the case in Sal's experience with Vulcan hybrids, the ensign's Vulcan half seemed to trump her Betazoid half, so it was hard to tell how much appreciation she had for subtlety. *"You'll be advised when we near the system we are going to study. In the meantime, try and get some rest. Farkas out."*

Sal bit back a smile as Ti'Ana turned disarmingly intense black eyes toward her. "I do not require rest at this time, Doctor, but if you feel it necessary, I will accept a sedative."

Like the captain, Doctor Sal was in her mid-seventies and had probably forgotten more about life than Ti'Ana had yet to learn. *Every year the new kids seem younger than I remember ever being,* she thought a little sadly. Surely there had been a time when she had approached her work with Ti'Ana's earnestness. *Thank heavens that time has long since past.* Both life and work were a great deal more rewarding when you didn't take them quite so seriously.

Sal had served with Farkas on four different vessels and had been one of her closest friends since before Ti'Ana was born. There was simply no way, however, to impart to the ensign the common sense that only came with experience.

"I'm pretty sure the captain meant that as a suggestion, not an order, Ensign," she said evenly. "Now I'm going to step outside and check on the rest of my staff. I'll activate the psionic field around this room, and you just let me know if there's anything you need."

"Thank you, Doctor," Ti'Ana replied, lifting the corners of her mouth a hair, suggesting that perhaps not all of her father's DNA had been wasted on her.

Sal really hoped that was the case. She didn't know—and didn't really want to know—what it would be like to be possessed by an alien life-form, but the presence of another in her mind would have scared the hell out of her. For someone accustomed to telepathic communication, it might be less traumatizing, and the doctor had suggested Ti'Ana for this assignment because of her unique dual heritage. Vulcan discipline combined with Betazoid empathy might ease whatever was to come for the young woman who had volunteered to act as a conduit for the Children of the Storm, should they make contact with *Quirinal*.

Bless her heart, Sal thought sincerely. *And if there's anyone out there listening, hear this: That young woman deserves to live a long and happy life. She's facing this with the temerity of one of my Viking ancestors. Don't let any harm come to her just because the Federation doesn't know how to take no for an answer.*

Shaking her head at one of the hundred misgivings she felt about this mission, Sal returned to the main medical bay and opened Ti'Ana's file to enter a preliminary commendation. It wasn't customary for a doctor to do so, but Sal saw Ti'Ana's choice as one above and beyond the call.

A low hum of activity on the bridge thrummed all around Farkas. She could taste the pleasant tension in the air. It was go time.

For weeks her crew had followed *Voyager*'s lead through the Alpha Quadrant, testing their slipstream engines and streamlining the procedures used during synchronous flight. It was a concentrated shakedown: everyone getting used to a new ship, new crewmates, new commanders, and working the expected and unexpected kinks out of their respective systems. Things hadn't really started to gel, however, until *Quirinal* had made the leap with the rest of the fleet to the terminus of the Beta and Delta Quadrants. This was the farthest she and every member of her crew had journeyed from Federation space, and it was exhilarating.

All of them had seen too much battle in recent years. For her part, Farkas had hoped that the conflict with the Dominion would be the worst she would ever endure. What the Borg had done a few months earlier had made the years of conflict with the changelings seem like a minor inconvenience.

But finally, she and her crew were once again setting out to do what Starfleet did best: explore the unknown. Though the captain had no doubt there were dangers to be faced in the Delta Quadrant—a cursory review of *Voyager*'s logs had made that quite clear—she refused to rein in the sense of possibility that this mission engendered in her.

In some ways it was a shame that her crew—along with T'Mar's and O'Donnell's—had drawn this particular straw for their maiden mission with the fleet. Farkas was never one to run from challenges; indeed, she thrived on them. But she wasn't sure that Sal didn't have a point about this particular mission, a point she'd made repeatedly since their first briefing with Admiral Batiste.

"So these 'Children of the Winds'—"

"The Storm" *Farkas had corrected her.*

"Potato, potahto. They actually told the Aventine *never to return to their space, and that's where we're going?"*

"We're talking about one of the most unusual and potentially dangerous species the Federation has ever encountered, El'nor."

Eying her warily, Sal had continued, "Why can't we just leave well enough alone, Regina? Did I miss a meeting? When an alien species makes contact and then asks you relatively politely to leave . . . you leave. It's been a while since I cracked any of our rule books, but I'm almost certain I read that somewhere once."

Farkas didn't doubt that when the Federation had been formed, it was a good rule, and the vast majority of the time, it remained a good rule. But the warrior in Farkas knew that once in a while, every rule needed a little massaging. Starfleet, with its most advanced technological toys, had barely survived its last encounter with the Borg. Based on Farkas's reading of the classified materials surrounding the final confrontation, without the interference of the Caeliar, Starfleet wouldn't have survived. But somehow the Children of the Storm had managed to clear their system of the Borg forever, leaving a debris ring a light-year wide of Borg pieces. While Farkas didn't really kid herself that her crew was going to discover the means by which the Children of the Storm had accomplished this minor miracle from the distance they intended to keep, anything they could learn would be incredibly useful.

The official word was that the Borg were gone. Farkas hoped with every fiber of her being that this was true. But even if they were, that didn't mean that somewhere out there, another lunatic race bent on galactic domination wasn't waiting to take their shot. For all any of them knew, the Children of the Storm might one day decide to annex a little new real estate. At the end of the day, the Federation could no longer live under the happy illusion that if they left well enough alone, others could be counted on to do the same. They had a responsibility to their citizens to seek out and understand any and all potential threats.

Or so she'd tried to convince Sal. Tried and, as best she could tell, failed.

Daunting as the mission was, however, it was *theirs*. Farkas and her crew were finally out here, far from the watchful gaze of Admiral Batiste, ready to do the Federation proud. It was long past time for someone other than *Voyager*'s crew to make a name for themselves in this part of space.

Lieutenant Commander Atlee Fife's voice rang clearly through the comm. "Demeter *confirms transfer of all personnel complete. We will remain in position until further instructed. Safe travels,* Quirinal."

"We'll see you in fourteen days, Commander," Farkas jumped in before Roach had a chance to close the comm. "Try and stay out of trouble until we get back."

"*Acknowledged,*" Fife replied, signing off.

From the sound of it, Fife and Roach needed to loosen up a little before they strained something.

Time will do the trick, Farkas assured herself.

"Farkas to Captain T'Mar."

"*Morning, Captain,*" his cheery voice replied.

"We're ready to get under way."

"*As are we.*"

"Then let's do this."

"*Indeed,*" T'Mar agreed, sounding every bit as enthused as Farkas felt. "Planck *out.*"

"All right, ladies and gentlemen," Farkas said, addressing her bridge crew. "I know we've all been through the simulations, but we're going to go through this one more time for safety's sake. On my command, Ensign Hoch will set course and engage impulse engines. Our destination is a position two light-years from the system known to be inhabited by the Children of the Storm. Once we've arrived, Ensign Jepel will give our handy dandy new long-range sensor grid its first real test. We're going to gather as much relevant data as we can about the surrounding systems and the debris field without bothering the natives. We're not here to make contact, and we're certainly not here to start trouble. A nice, long look is all we'll be taking. Lieutenant Sienna, I expect regular tactical updates, and at the first sign of trouble we need to be prepared to make tracks. Any questions?"

As expected, there were none.

"All right. This isn't a drill. Ensign Hoch?"

"Setting course one four seven mark three two," Hoch advised.

Farkas took a deep breath, anxious to see what the next few days had in store for all of them.

"Engage."

Chapter Three

STARDATE 58450.8
U.S.S VOYAGER

Captain Parimon Dasht was speechless.

Eden had wondered how he would take the revelation about Admiral Batiste's true nature and agenda. She had already privately briefed Captain Chan and Commander Drafar, and their initial responses had been similar to Parimon's, but neither had taken quite so long to say *something . . . anything* to make the moment less humiliating. Of course, Parimon had known both Willem and Eden casually prior to this mission. If memory served, he'd actually attended a conference or two with Willem.

"That's just . . . not possible," he finally stammered, his normally pale cheeks taking on a ruddy glow.

Eden truly sympathized.

"I know," she offered.

Dasht rose from his seat at the conference table situated in what Eden had taken to calling the "east wing" of her suite and began to pace.

Willem had always seemed to enjoy Parimon's company. A decade younger than either of them—*or at least me,* Eden mentally corrected herself—Parimon Dasht was bright and energetic, with jet-black hair set above vivid green eyes and finely chiseled features. His looks had probably done more than his actual recreational activities to earn him a reputation for cavalier relationships. He was a third-generation Starfleet officer, a passionate defender of Federation ideals, and, Eden suddenly realized, personally offended by what she had just told him.

He might feel worse about this than I do.

Of course, she'd had a few days to let the reality sink in, and he'd had seconds.

"I've known the admiral for years," Dasht finally said, turning his disbelieving face toward hers.

Eden cleared her throat before replying, "As have I, Parimon."

"Of course." He shook his head. "But I mean, I had to have known him before . . ." His voice trailed off.

Eden finally understood.

"Before he was replaced?"

"I was still a lieutenant. I attended a lecture he gave at the Academy, something about first-contact protocols. He was . . . he . . ."

"I'm so sorry, Parimon. I know this is difficult."

Rather than dissipating the tension, Dasht's steps grew more energetic.

"I just don't see how this could happen!" he finally said, raising his voice accusingly.

Taken aback, Eden stiffened in her chair.

"I mean, what are they doing at Command? How exactly does a member of Species 8472 impersonate an admiral for years and nobody has a clue?"

"It's hardly unprecedented," Eden suggested. In truth, the number of aliens who had successfully compromised sensitive command positions over the years was alarming. And that was only considering the ones Eden knew about. Heaven knew there were probably more buried in Starfleet Intelligence's classified files.

Dasht finally deflated a little. After a moment spent collecting himself he asked softly, "Has anyone informed his family?"

At least Eden could offer him this comfort. "Willem was an only child, and his parents passed years before we met. By the time he was compromised, there wouldn't have been a close family member to raise any red flags. And I'm sure Admiral Montgomery will initiate a full investigation. We were advised by Species 8472 when we made contact that the other agents they had planted were now deceased."

"As best we know," Dasht corrected her.

"True, but at least now the threat has been uncovered, and for the present moment, there's nothing more either of us can do about it. I suggest we focus, instead, on the work that is before us."

Dasht stiffened. "Of course, Captain," he acquiesced, resuming his place seated across from her.

"I assume our communications relays are in place and fully functional?"

"Yes, Captain." Dasht nodded. "We've established a time-delay interface with Starfleet Command that should extend almost forty thousand light-years into the Delta Quadrant.

"Excellent job," Eden complimented him. "Anything to report?"

"Our long-range sensors picked up a few inhabited star systems along the way, but we did not deviate from our course to investigate. We did encounter one friendly species, the Urnatal. Nice people. My senior staff held a dinner in honor of their First Minister. He took a liking to the spiced ale," Dasht added, finally smiling faintly in remembrance.

"So we've already made a friend in the Delta Quadrant? That's impressive, Captain."

"It was an easy first contact," Dasht admitted. "They're travelers, a long way from home. I got the sense they'd enjoy any excuse for a party. Their homeworld was a hundred light-years from the position where we encountered them, but they invited us to visit whenever we like and assured me that formal statements of welcome would be forwarded at some point. Oh, and they presented me with a gift, which is rightfully yours now, as our fleet commander."

Eden balked instinctively.

"It was your accomplishment," she began her refusal.

"No, no," Dasht said, shaking his head and hurrying to retrieve a long obsidian staff he'd placed against the wall near the door to her cabin when he'd first entered.

Presenting it formally, he said, "With the compliments of First Minister Scrall, it is my honor to present you with the Staff of Ren."

Eden rose to accept the offering.

"Thank you, Captain," she said, taking it graciously and examining it briefly. "It's lovely," she finally murmured. "Do they manufacture these on the Urnatal homeworld?"

"No." Dasht shook his head. "It was part of the minister's private collection, something he had picked up in his travels. He seemed to set great store by it."

Running her hand along it gently, Eden felt a series of raised ridges and curves. Peering at them more closely, she felt a shock like ice water coursing through her veins.

Noting her reaction, Dasht added, "Scrall said the indentations were believed to be decorative."

Beware those who trespass upon the ground of our ancestors.

Eden didn't know how or why the words entered her mind as clearly as if she'd been reading Federation Standard.

"They never bothered to translate them?" she asked a little defensively.

"They *couldn't*," Dasht corrected her. "Is something wrong, Captain?"

Sensing danger, Eden steadied herself. She set the staff on the table and, composing her face, replied, "Of course not. It's beautiful, and I'm most grateful to the minister, and to you. I'll have your new orders ready by tomorrow. We're waiting to regroup with the rest of the fleet before moving on."

"Of course, Captain."

Clearly sensing dismissal, Dasht rose and moved hesitantly toward the door. When Eden remained rooted to the floor, he turned to add softly, "And may I say, Captain, that I'm sorry for your personal loss. My reaction was unprofessional, but it was also insensitive. Whatever loss I may feel in Admiral Batiste's betrayal certainly cannot compare with yours."

Eden appreciated the sentiment, though at the moment, Willem's many transgressions were the least of her worries.

"Thank you, Parimon," she replied.

"If you ever want to talk, Afsarah," he offered.

"I know where to find you," she assured him.

With a faint nod of acceptance, he left her standing before the table. She waited until she was alone to begin shaking with violent and overwhelming emotion that had nothing at all to do with her ex-husband.

"I'm telling you, Harry, it doesn't get better than this."

"It doesn't," Harry agreed.

Where the desert heat of Chaotica's realm had been stifling, the gentle warmth of the Caribbean sun, particularly after the dip Tom had just taken in the spa pool, was soothing, almost healing.

The resort simulation's bar was deserted. Neither Tom nor Harry had been interested in the scantily clad patrons and staff who usually filled the place. The second thing both had done upon successfully activating the program was to help themselves to margaritas before settling into a pair of partially shaded deck chairs with a stunning view of the ocean.

The first thing hadn't even been in question. After scrounging in the desert sands for the few edible bugs and lizards for the better part of two days, both had ordered and then wolfed down heaping plates of fresh fruit, beef and chicken kabobs, and pitchers of water until their shrunken stomachs had cried out for mercy.

Tom felt better than he had since the first night B'Elanna had lain in his arms a few weeks earlier, and he had known that they would be together from then on. When Miral had crawled into bed between them in the middle of that night,

Tom had felt what he believed was perfect happiness. But the completeness had begun to dissipate the next day when he realized that Harry wasn't going to get over his feelings of betrayal any time soon. The next few weeks, complicated by *Voyager*'s visit to the Indign system and the chaos wrought by Admiral Batiste, had strained Tom to the point where he had convinced himself that he no longer cared what Harry felt. He had tried, time and again, to bridge the distance growing between them, and each time Harry had rebuffed him. Deep down, he'd known that he'd been kidding himself in thinking that he could be happy without Harry in his life. Harry had become his brother, bound to him by ties stronger than blood. The injuries Harry had sustained during the battle at the Azure Nebula had brought Tom literally and emotionally to his knees. He'd spent sleepless days and nights by his bedside while Harry recovered at Starfleet Medical. Like it or not, Harry was a permanent fixture in Tom's heart now. And he hated like hell that it had taken Counselor Cambridge, who Tom rarely wanted to grant *anything,* to bring both of them to this place of renewed harmony.

He hated it, but he'd take it.

"What do you think of Nancy Conlon?" Harry surprised Tom by asking out of the blue.

Tom smiled inwardly before responding. B'Elanna had been trying to set Harry and Nancy up for weeks. But Tom also knew that when it came to Harry's heart, it was necessary to tread lightly.

"I like her," he said as noncommittally as possible.

Harry cast a sidelong glance toward him.

"You don't think it's a good idea?"

Tom took a deep breath.

"I think what I think doesn't matter," Tom said honestly. "I think when you know you've met the right person, you won't give a damn what I or anyone else has to say on the subject. And I think you're actually ready to meet that person. Libby was holding you back, but that's no longer the case. You want to get to know Nancy better, go for it. You could do worse."

"I've done worse," Harry admitted frankly.

"And I've done *way* worse," Tom said with equal certainty.

"You got lucky," Harry observed.

"I did," Tom agreed. "And I took B'Elanna for granted for far too long. I'm still amazed she stuck by me. There's not a day goes by now, though, that I don't thank Chakotay's unnamed gods for her patience and my coming to my senses."

"Chakotay's unnamed gods?" Harry asked a little incredulously.

"I always kind of liked the sound of them," Tom said. "And they beat any other version of a supreme being I've ever come across."

"Didn't we discover that they were just an alien race?" Harry asked.

"I think those were technically the Sky People, weren't they? I don't think—"

"What have we here?" a strident voice interrupted their musings.

Tom turned to see his pristine view blocked by the form of Counselor Hugh Cambridge dressed in a flowing monochrome robe and wearing a black plastic headpiece that accentuated a widow's peak his real hairline would certainly have envied.

"Oh, hey, Counselor," Harry said with a cheeky grin. "Something to drink? It's an open bar."

Cambridge favored both of them with a piercing glare. "I'm on duty," he said curtly.

"We're not." Tom smiled, stretching his arms over his head luxuriously and relocating them comfortably behind his neck.

Crossing his arms over his chest in what Tom sensed was feigned annoyance, Cambridge said, "I don't recall either of you gaining access to my castle in order to destroy my Death Ray."

"Yeah, sorry about that," Harry said without conviction. "Truth is, we got a little . . . what would you say?" he asked Tom.

"Bored?"

"Bored, right," Harry agreed. "Feel free to destroy the galaxy whenever the mood strikes you, your lordliness."

Cambridge considered them both, his eyes darting back and forth in a way that was truly comical given his regalia, and finally said, "That's the first time in weeks I've seen the two of you agree on anything. I hereby pronounce you both cured and return you to active duty."

Tom and Harry sat up simultaneously.

"No—"

"Wait—"

"We're not—"

"He's a jerk—"

"I am—"

"*Tom*—"

"No, I hate him—" both insisted, hopelessly overlapping one another's attempts to refute the counselor.

"I see," Cambridge replied. After a moment he went on, "I might be inclined to reconsider my diagnosis on one condition."

"Name it," Harry pleaded.

"How did you manage to reprogram my simulation?"

"Oh, that was nothing." Harry shrugged.

"Nothing for you," Tom acknowledged.

"True."

"Gentlemen, I'm still waiting," Cambridge interjected.

"I've been mucking around inside the guts of our holo-suites for years," Harry said. "If it wasn't interdimensional aliens crossing over . . ."

"Or the Hirogen," Tom added.

"Don't remind me," Harry said.

"So you're a whiz at overriding the security lockouts?" Cambridge asked.

"Yes, and no," Harry admitted.

"Go on."

"I have a back door," Harry said somewhat sheepishly.

"Do tell, Lieutenant."

Sitting up to explain, Harry went on, "I actually wasn't sure it would still be there, but I guess the folks at Project Full Circle must have missed it."

"Or didn't know what they were looking at," Tom suggested.

"Probably." Harry nodded. "We had a major security breach a few years back when one of our former crewmates, Seska, created a program that was designed to kill the crew."

"Seska was already dead, and she still almost killed us," Tom added.

"There was no way to survive the program and no way to shut it down from the outside," Harry went on. "Once we figured out how to rewrite it, I installed a fail-safe so that I would never again be denied access to the main programming. After our last series of refits, I thought it was a long shot, but turns out my overrides were still there."

Cambridge shook his head. "I never expected to use this

adjective to describe either of you, but I'm afraid I have no choice," he said finally. "Brilliant. Bloody brilliant."

"But that doesn't mean we're cured," Tom insisted.

"Clearly not." Cambridge smirked. "And just how long before you think you might both be willing to behave civilly toward one another?"

"At least a few hours," Harry replied.

"At *least*," Tom agreed.

"Fine," the counselor said, "but I'm not going to explain another night's absence to your wife, Commander Paris."

"Don't worry," Tom said. "I've got your back on this one."

Cambridge stiffened. "I can't tell you how that thought terrifies me."

"You get used to it," Harry assured him.

Nodding, Cambridge said simply, "As you were," and strode out looking positively ridiculous.

"You were saying?" Harry asked without missing a beat.

"I don't remember," Tom admitted.

"Doesn't matter." Harry shrugged. "I think I'm going to ask Conlon out."

Tom smiled as he resettled himself in his lounge chair.

Seven of Nine lay perfectly still on her belly in the dense underbrush. A bead of sweat trickled down her forehead to the tip of her nose, where it itched to the point of distraction. She tried to ignore it, took several slow, shallow breaths, and finally succumbed, shaking her head gingerly.

The faint rustle she created by this action was all it took. A wild shriek of victory was followed by a dull thud that knocked the wind out of her as thirty-five pounds of one-quarter-Klingon joy landed squarely on her back.

"Found you!" Miral shouted at the top of her lungs.

"So you have," Seven acknowledged, turning over and adjusting the child slightly so that she now sat astride her waist. "And for that, you will be tickled."

"Noooo!" Miral wailed, raising her arms, which only made it easier for Seven to run light fingers up the child's ribcage, sending her into a fit of giggles as she impishly struggled to extricate herself from Seven's hands. She finally succeeded in rolling onto the soft earth of the park Seven had selected for their afternoon of play on the secondary holodeck. Seven had been surprised when she arrived at the main holodeck with Miral an hour earlier to find that it was still in use by Commander Paris and Lieutenant Kim. Their "counseling" session had become the worst-kept secret on the ship. Seven had begun to wonder if both of them would make it out in one piece.

"My turn, my turn, my turn," Miral cried out joyfully as she pushed herself to her feet and her plump little legs ran toward the top of a small hill.

"It is your turn to hide," Seven agreed, rising and hurrying after her. "And for that . . ."

"No tickles, no tickles!" Miral ordered, turning on Seven defiantly.

"When I find you, you will be tickled," Seven assured her.

Miral seemed to consider the proposition.

"Tickle you," she decided, rushing at Seven and managing to grab her firmly by one leg, which succeeded in toppling Seven over to one side.

"No, no." Seven pretended to gasp, which only encouraged Miral further. Together they rolled and tickled, laughing and squealing at the top of their lungs until they finally landed side by side on their backs, both struggling to regain their breath beneath a cloudless, bright blue sky.

Seven closed her eyes for a moment, inhaling simple delight, until a shadow fell upon her, blocking the sun. Opening her eyes quickly, she saw a familiar but totally unexpected face grinning at her from above.

"And what do we have here?" Neelix asked.

"Neelix!" Seven said, smiling in astonishment as she pushed herself up off the ground and found herself pulled into a vigorous hug. When the two separated, Seven turned to see Miral staring up at both of them quizzically. Neelix immediately dropped to one knee to bring himself to the child's eye level.

"Hello, Miral," he said warmly. "Do you remember me?"

Miral almost did.

"I'm Neelix. You came to visit my home a little while ago."

"Dexa," Miral said very softly.

"Yes," Neelix said, his smile brightening. "My wife is Dexa. She read you stories when you weren't feeling well. You look much better now."

"Hide!" Miral ordered.

Neelix turned a questioning face to Seven.

"We're playing hide-and-seek," she explained.

"Hide!" Miral insisted again.

"It's your turn to hide, Miral," Seven suggested.

Miral pointed at a nearby tree, which had been designated their "counting" tree for the duration of the game.

"We will count to ten," Seven agreed. "Now hurry up and hide."

Miral needed no further encouragement. She took off like a shot toward a small thicket as Seven and Neelix made their way over to the tree and Seven began to count in a voice loud enough for Miral to hear.

"Seven, you look wonderful," Neelix said once Seven had finished counting.

"As do you," she replied. "What are you doing here?"

"You lost a shuttle," he said simply. "I'm returning it to you."

Seven's face clouded a bit as she realized which shuttle he must be referring to.

"You were not injured when you retrieved it?" she said with hope.

"No," he assured her. "It was abandoned."

"Good," Seven replied with a nod. "B'Elanna said she had seen you and that you and your people are well. I've been meaning to contact you again. I know it has been a long while."

"Too long," Neelix gently chided her. "But this brings back wonderful memories, doesn't it?" he said lightly.

"Naomi is entering the Academy this fall," Seven said, realizing that he could only be referring to the pleasant hours both of them had spent playing with Naomi Wildman years earlier on this very same holodeck.

"I heard," Neelix said. "I can't believe how fast she has grown."

"Time does pass with alarming swiftness," Seven acknowledged. "How long will you be able to stay?"

"Through the night," Neelix replied. "Then I have to get back."

Seven understood, but she had hoped for more.

"Seven!" Miral shouted from the thicket. Clearly she had settled on her hiding place and was anxious for Seven to find her.

"Duty calls." Neelix grinned.

"That it does," Seven replied, rolling her eyes.

"Just tell me," he said quickly, "are you as happy as you look right now?"

Seven gave the question a brief thought. "I am content," she replied. "And sometimes, yes, very happy."

"I've missed you," Neelix admitted.

"And you have been missed," Seven assured him.

Chapter Four

SIXTEEN DAYS EARLIER
U.S.S. PLANCK

Hosc T'Mar had hoped for better things when he had first been briefed about this mission. The opportunity to investigate a noncorporeal species thought to have originated in a gas giant's atmosphere was one no scientist with a passion for xenobiology could resist. And the fact that this species could communicate with humanoids was a bonus. Hosc was in complete agreement with Admiral Batiste that surprise contact such as had been made with *Aventine* would not be in anyone's best interests, but it seemed likely that in the absence of any other possibilities—or telepaths—the Children of the Storm would use their intended "communicator" aboard *Quirinal,* and a real exchange of ideas and information could be established.

Looking back on the past three days since they had finally reached their "safe" distance, however, he felt his hopes sinking. According to the *Aventine*'s logs, the aliens had made contact with the Federation vessels within an hour of their arrival. True, *Planck* and *Quirinal* were keeping a respectful distance, two full light-years from the debris ring that surrounded their system, but he couldn't imagine that the Children didn't possess long-range scanning abilities that should have made the Federation ships visible. It was possible that *Quirinal* and *Planck* had already been written off as non-threatening and, therefore, uninteresting. It was also possible that by entering the area at low speeds, *Planck* and *Quirinal* had gone undetected thus far.

Or maybe Captain Dax made up these mysterious aliens just to have a little fun with us, Hosc thought ungenerously. *This far out in the Delta Quadrant, who was ever going to check?*

Though he doubted this last—it would have been unthinkable coming from a Starfleet officer—he had begun to wonder if he and Captain Farkas were going to return from this mission with anything more to report than the specifics of the five nearest star systems, unremarkable and none of them capable of sustaining intelligent life, and a massive debris field composed entirely of what had once been hundreds of Borg vessels.

Nothing we haven't seen before, Hosc thought wearily, though he had to admit that there was something darkly satisfying in the sight of the Borg graveyard.

In the absence of anything interesting to sink their teeth into, his crew had been debating for three days the possible origins of a few subspace variations they had picked up. Most believed they indicated that long ago, transwarp tunnels had been present in the area. Otherwise, there were no spatial or subspace anomalies present to warrant further comment.

Not much for his first view of the Delta Quadrant. Perhaps their next mission would prove at least a little more stimulating, if not scientifically fascinating.

Hosc was ready to end his day with a review of a few reports from his crew. The most important came from his first officer, Lieutenant Tregart. Shortly after *Quirinal, Planck,* and *Demeter* had left the rest of the fleet behind to begin this mission, *Planck*'s replicator system had gone on the fritz. Apparently there were misalignments that might have occurred during their long slipstream flight, and were proving impossible to fix. The replicators themselves were fine. Their integration with *Planck* was the issue. Fortunately, the problem should be resolved once they rendezvoused with *Achilles* and the system could be dismantled. In the interim, there was nothing more Lieutenant Beldon, his chief engineer, could do. Beldon had been working around the clock to try and coax something edible from the replicators, but nothing had met safety standards. The crew had been restricted to emergency rations and vitamin supplements for the last five days. This was hardly an unendurable hardship for a deep-space mission; however, with nothing more serious to occupy the crew's mind, it was becoming a morale problem, especially since they were looking at another nine days of the same regimen.

Tregart had requested that *Demeter* be called in to provide organic foodstuffs to supplement rations. As this was one of *Demeter*'s primary functions within the fleet, it seemed a reasonable request. Hosc doubted that there were any safety issues at this point. This far from the territory of the Children of the Storm there seemed little to fear.

Hosc made a note to clear the decision with Captain Farkas, a courtesy he felt no compunction observing, and approved Tregart's request before moving on to the other mundane matters requiring his attention.

U.S.S. QUIRINAL

Captain Farkas couldn't sleep. Gamma shift was well under way, and every item on her to-do list had been completed.

By all rights she should have been curled up in her bunk, catching a few hours of relaxation, if not actual rest. But her mind refused to settle. A certainty in her gut had set her walking the decks in the hope that a pleasant stroll would convince her that all was well and that her gut was wrong.

Problem was, her gut was rarely wrong, and she had learned the hard way over the years to ignore it at her peril.

They're watching us.

That was the warning, though the captain had not a single shred of evidence to back it up. None of the multiple scans of the area had resulted in any conclusive readings suggesting the presence of life-forms like the ones described by Captain Dax. Searches matching the exact recorded specifications had all been negative.

This could mean one of three things. The Children of the Storm did not exist. The Children of the Storm were no longer in the system of space they had declared "theirs" and worked for a century to purge of the Borg. Or—and this was by far the most likely as far as Farkas was concerned—the Children of the Storm were right where Dax had left them, but had found a way to shield themselves from the Federation vessel's sensors.

So the next obvious question was: *What are they waiting for?* Again, there were a handful of possibilities. They had not detected *Quirinal* and *Planck*. *Possible, but not terribly likely.* They had detected *Quirinal* and *Planck* and were not interested in making contact. *Not the best of all possible worlds, but certainly preferable to the next option.* They had detected *Quirinal* and *Planck* and were planning an attack on their unwelcome visitors.

Farkas couldn't imagine what kind of attack would take them three days to plan, especially considering their success against the Borg. But it was her job to imagine it, and as the silent hours rolled by she felt the tension in the pit of her stomach ratcheting ever tighter by a sense of impending doom.

Tired of listening to these doubts rattle around in her mind, she turned her steps toward sickbay, where her oldest friend was certainly still working and might at least give her some much-needed perspective.

Doctor Sal heard the faint hiss of the door to sickbay opening and turned from her desk's computer interface to see Regina entering her private office.

"Can't sleep?" Sal diagnosed immediately.

Farkas shook her head. "I'm leading a mission to an unexplored area of space that reportedly contains an extremely dangerous alien race. What's your excuse?"

Sal smiled faintly. "I'm attempting to solve a medical mystery."

Taking the seat opposite Sal and propping her feet up between them on the doctor's desk, Regina stifled a yawn. "You know me. I love a good mystery."

"Oh, I didn't say it was good."

"Tell me anyway."

"It's Ti'Ana."

The wrench in Farkas's stomach clicked one notch tighter.

"Still complaining of headaches?" Farkas asked.

"They've gone from a five on the pain scale to a nine in the last few hours," Sal replied, gently rubbing her temples. "I've sedated her for the time being, but I don't see that as a long-term solution."

"What do her neural scans show?" Farkas asked.

"I assume you want a non-tech answer?"

"Always." Farkas smirked.

"There are chemical imbalances consistent with vaso-constriction—sorry, pain. But nothing that suggests alien interference, which is what I'm sure you're worried about."

Farkas removed her feet from the desk and sat up straight in her chair, releasing a deep, pent-up sigh. "They're out there, El'nor."

"Sensors have finally picked them up?"

"No."

"So this is your telepathy talking? Oh, wait, you don't have that special skill."

"I don't need to be a telepath to know that they're out there and they're watching us."

"Sold," Sal replied, slapping her hand down on the surface of her desk. "When do we leave?"

Farkas favored her with her most withering glare.

"When something other than my overactive imagination confirms that suspicion, or nine more days of unbearable waiting pass, whichever comes first," she replied.

Sal considered her briefly. "You really think you're imagining danger out there?"

"Of course not."

"Good, because I'm not qualified to act as your therapist, and our ship's counselor is in stasis in cargo bay three. Of course, if I were qualified I'd tell you that you are obligated to act in accordance with your experience, and if your gut is telling you we're in danger right now, you should do something about it."

"You don't think I'm crazy?"

"No crazier than I did when you asked me to forgo my well-earned retirement and follow you out here on this fool's errand."

Farkas was truly puzzled. "You think exploring the Delta Quadrant is an insignificant task?"

"I think we haven't even seen all of the Alpha and Beta Quadrants yet, so I'm not sure what the rush is to push our knowledge all the way out here."

"The Borg came from here," Farkas reminded her.

"And the Dominion came from the Gamma Quadrant," Sal replied. "But we've got enemies enough a lot closer to home and plenty of sights unseen to last both of us the rest of our lives without going looking for fights we're probably not prepared to face."

"When did you get so cynical?"

"I've always been this cynical, Regina. It's why we're friends. You need someone to balance the cockeyed adventurer in you," Sal replied with a hint of bitterness.

"If you didn't want to come out here, El'nor, you could have just said so."

"I did," Sal replied dryly. "But you wouldn't take no for an answer."

"Only because I didn't want you to miss all this fun," Farkas said, attempting levity.

"Thanks so much. When I start having some, I'll be sure and let you know."

"Bridge to Captain Farkas."

"Go ahead," Farkas replied after tapping her combadge.

"You have a transmission from Captain T'Mar."

"Patch it through to Doctor Sal's office," Farkas requested, and Sal dutifully turned the screen so that Farkas could see it. The neural scans she'd been studying were replaced by a few wavy lines, and finally the face of the *Planck*'s captain.

"Do we have an epidemic of insomnia going around?" Farkas greeted him by asking.

"I'm just about to turn in," T'Mar replied, *"but I wanted to run this by you. I'm calling in* Demeter *for a supply transfer. Our replicators are still down and the crew is getting a little tired of ration packs."*

Sal shook her head and rolled her eyes and had no doubt Regina would have done the same if not for the fact that T'Mar could see her.

"You think surviving for a few more days on emergency rations is too great a hardship for your crew to bear, Hosc?"

"It's definitely affecting morale," T'Mar replied, sounding a little taken aback by Regina's question.

Children, Sal thought bitterly. *They've sent us out into the unknown leading a pack of children.* It might have been unfair to judge Starfleet too harshly for this, given the number of officers and crewmen they'd lost a few months earlier, but that didn't mollify Sal—or Regina, from the look on her face.

"Obviously it's your call, Captain," Regina said evenly. "But I could more easily send you a few of my people to help repair your replicators."

Because your *people are better than his, Regina?* Sal thought with a shake of her head. Somehow she already knew this conversation wasn't going to end well.

"Beldon has already confirmed that it's a system integration error," Hosc replied sternly. *"I trust his assessment. And I don't think your crew has time to replicate two hundred plus meals a day for my crew, let alone transfer them over."*

Reasonable as the response was, Sal knew what T'Mar was really thinking. He was the younger and less experienced of the two captains, but he couldn't bear the idea that he wasn't in complete control of his own ship. Regina could make suggestions, peer to peer, but he was going to make the final call, right or wrong. A more experienced officer would have taken Regina's suggestion in stride, and accepted it. Good as Starfleet's engineers were, they were hardly interchangeable parts. One might easily see what another had overlooked. T'Mar just didn't have the wisdom or the inclination to see past the offense he was obviously taking from Regina's attitude.

"*My people are really looking forward to a little fresh food,*" T'Mar continued. "*And unless I'm mistaken, that was the point of* Demeter *being out here.*"

Regina shook her head too subtly for T'Mar to notice. "Understood. I would, however, suggest that you instruct *Demeter* to approach at impulse speed. It will take a little longer, of course, but for safety's sake, I think it's worth it."

"*Of course, Captain,*" T'Mar granted her, as if he'd already come to the same conclusion, though Sal was willing to bet he hadn't. He'd already mentally written this mission off, otherwise he never would have considered bringing a ship with minimal defenses into a potentially hazardous area. "*Good night, Captain Farkas.*"

"Night. *Quirinal* out," Regina replied, tapping the controls more strenuously than was necessary before glancing sheepishly toward Sal. "What the hell is he compensating for?" she asked.

"Three guesses," Sal teased. "And the first two don't count."

"If this is all it takes to shake his crew's morale, we're in more trouble than I thought," Farkas said harshly.

"He's young," Sal admonished her. "And he wants to make sure you know that his pips are just as shiny as yours despite the fact that he was still in preschool when you were given your first command. If it weren't for the Borg, he'd still be serving as someone else's energetic first officer for another five years at least. Logic isn't going to get you anywhere with this one. He's going to have to learn these lessons the hard way, just like we did."

Regina dropped her face into the palm of her hand. "What was Command thinking?" she asked softly.

"That this would be fun?" Sal asked wanly.

U.S.S. DEMETER

"*Transcription error,*" the computer's voice said for the hundredth time that night.

Commander Liam O'Donnell had heard these words thousands of times in his career as a botanical geneticist, and they never failed to insult him.

As he still had several hundred samples to test, however, he forged ahead.

"Analysis of sample CR-H-94855-K," O'Donnell requested.

"Wait, don't tell me," he said aloud before the computer could respond.

"Transcription error," they said simultaneously.

Why did I go back to protoplast fusion? O'Donnell asked himself as the next five samples also returned with transcription errors. His work with *Crateva religiosa-Kressari* had begun over twenty years earlier, down a similar and ultimately useless path.

Because everything else you've tried has also failed, Alana answered kindly.

Her presence in his mind was so real that these conversations had long since ceased to disturb him. There was rarely anyone else in the room smart enough to follow his reasoning, let alone step ahead of it and provide sensible suggestions. That privilege had been and always would be hers and hers alone. He resisted the temptation to pull her image up on the lab's viewscreen. There was simply too much work to be done right now for him to indulge in a more lengthy discussion.

"Computer, analysis of sample CR-H-94861-K?"

"Excuse me, Captain?"

O'Donnell actually jumped in his chair and turned to see his first officer, Lieutenant Commander Atlee Fife, his round face and large brown eyes incongruous on his fragile-looking frame, standing at attention at the door to the lab.

"Is something on fire, Commander?" O'Donnell asked seriously.

"Not at this time, sir," Fife replied.

"Are we under attack by an alien species?"

"No, sir."

"Is anyone dead?"

"No, sir."

"Then how can I possibly be of assistance to you, Commander?" O'Donnell asked gently.

O'Donnell thought he'd been perfectly clear with Fife since day one of the mission. Anything that fell into the above categories required his attention. Anything else, he was perfectly content to leave to Fife's obvious good judgment. It was an unusual relationship between a captain and a first officer, but O'Donnell had been made captain of this vessel due to his botanical expertise, despite his limited command experience, and O'Donnell had hand-picked Fife as his XO. Based upon his record and their few interactions to date, it was clear to O'Donnell that Fife lived and breathed to perfect the art of his position. He would likely receive his own command when the fleet returned to the Alpha Quadrant in three years. O'Donnell felt it was a nicely symbiotic relationship that, over time, would provide him with the maximum amount of time he needed to complete his personal projects while still enabling him to do the absolute minimum Starfleet required of him as *Demeter*'s commanding officer. Willem Batiste had promised O'Donnell that this would be more than sufficient when he had pulled him from his research lab for this assignment and offered him his choice of first officers. O'Donnell would have liked to refuse this request, but the admiral hadn't given him the option. Batiste had insisted that O'Donnell was the best in his field—*no argument there*—and all but promised him three years of peace and quiet. O'Donnell had taken him at his word.

"We've received a request from *Planck*," Fife explained.

"Are *they* on fire?" O'Donnell asked.

"No, Captain," Fife replied, "but they have requested that we travel to their position and provide a transfer of organic foodstuffs to supplement their emergency rations. Their replicators . . ."

"Have been on the fritz since we got out here, I know," O'Donnell said, nodding. "They reported as much before we separated."

After an uncomfortable silence, Fife asked, "Shall I inform them that we will comply with their request?"

O'Donnell sat back and scratched the shiny top of his balding head. *You could always look again at the spheroplasts . . . maybe the radiation levels are too low,* Alana suggested.

"Sir?" Fife interrupted his thoughts.

"Whatever you think is best, Commander," O'Donnell replied.

But if the somaclonal variation occurs again . . . Alana continued.

"I am inclined to agree to *Planck*'s request, sir, but they have suggested we approach at sublight speed, which I fear poses unnecessary risks, exposing us to danger for a longer period of time. I believe we should approach at maximum warp and make the transfers as soon as possible. I've asked Ensigns Schiller and Megdal to begin collecting the supplies, and they should be done shortly. The entire mission should take under five hours."

O'Donnell stopped calculating radiation levels in his head long enough to meet Fife's eyes.

"I'll advise you when the mission is complete, Captain," Fife said.

"Very good, Atlee. You're a quick study, I'll give you that." O'Donnell nodded.

Without another word, Fife quickly turned and exited the lab.

Just not learning quickly enough, he decided.

He's young, my darling, Alana reminded him. *Give him time.*

Chapter Five

STARDATE 58451.4
U.S.S. VOYAGER

Neelix looked around the table set in Chakotay's private dining room, a luxury that had been denied Captain Janeway years earlier when Neelix had turned hers into the ship's galley, and marveled at the vicissitudes of destiny. Three years earlier he had bid each of the friends sitting before him a fond farewell, wishing them all the best but knowing in his heart and soul that his future now lay along a path different from theirs. To see them now, Chakotay, Tom, B'Elanna, Harry, Seven, and the Doctor, it was almost as if he were looking at different people.

Chakotay, the man who had once convinced him that life was truly worth living but had always seemed reluctant to embrace that truth to its fullest, was now *Voyager*'s captain. Neelix could only guess at the bittersweet nature of that reality. It would have been one thing assuming command, as he did, upon Captain Janeway's promotion to admiral. But to carry the mantle of command in a universe where Kathryn Janeway no longer lived was not a fate he would have wished on anyone. Something had changed in Chakotay. Neelix couldn't quite put his finger on it. He seemed more at peace than Neelix had expected, more certain of himself, and yet unutterably sad. He had always known that the still waters at the center of Chakotay's soul had run deep, but now they seemed fathomless. Had the two of them been closer, he might have suggested they spend some time by a campfire on the holodeck. As it was, he could only hope that there was someone on *Voyager*'s crew Chakotay could turn to—never to replace Kathryn, but to offer him a little perspective in her absence. Thus far, he hadn't gotten the sense that Captain Eden, who was not present, would ever be that person. And that was just as well, in Neelix's opinion. No reason to repeat the past; better to forge a new future.

B'Elanna and Tom were the picture of marital bliss. Neelix knew well what that looked like, having enjoyed three years of it himself with his beloved Dexa. He knew Tom and

B'Elanna had been separated by circumstance for a number of years, but they seemed to have picked up in a better place than they'd left off. Tom's confidence, once a mirage masking deep insecurities, was now the genuine article. B'Elanna, who had always seemed so young to Neelix, had settled into a more calm and patient version of the fiery warrior he had first met. Her obvious strength was now tempered by darker experiences than he would have wished upon her, but the irreplaceable sense of renewal that a child brought to one's life was also clear in her countenance.

Of all of them, Harry seemed to have aged the most. Perhaps that was simply because he'd had further than any of them to go when *Voyager*'s first mission had begun. Vibrant as ever, but less concerned by the potential of a misstep, he joined his friends in easy conversation. It seemed to Neelix as if he had crossed an invisible border, separating youth from the prime of life. Neelix did not doubt he would make the most of it.

Seven was a puzzle. Though she had spoken of contentment, there was a new restlessness in the woman who had once prided herself on dignified control. Neelix doubted that she knew yet what she was seeking. He'd heard briefly about the discovery of the Caeliar and the transformation, both physical and mental, that the end of the Borg had wrought in Seven. Her physical beauty was as fierce as ever, especially now that it was no longer clouded by Borg technology on her face and hands. But there was a new hesitancy in her that was disarming and brought Neelix's protective nature to the forefront.

Even the Doctor was a new man in some respects. Neelix understood little about the technical aspect of his nature, despite the fact that he had lived with him for seven years.

Neelix had never been able to see the Doctor as anything but a trusted friend. It seemed that the new opportunities presented by his work aboard the *Galen*, an experimental medical vessel he had helped design, and staffed largely by holograms, were stretching the Doctor in ways he had never anticipated. He spoke with great enthusiasm of the challenges presented in his work but—Neelix couldn't help but note—nothing about his personal life. Neelix knew he couldn't leave before taking some time to make sure the Doctor was still placing enough emphasis on his personal relationships, as well as his professional ones. Kes would never have forgiven him otherwise.

As he considered each of them in turn, however, his heart could not help but feel a certain emptiness as well. It was almost grace enough to have been granted this time with so many of his friends. But inevitably his thoughts turned to those whose absence was most keenly felt.

Turning to Chakotay, who was seated at his right, Neelix asked softly, "What has become of our dear Mister Vulcan? B'Elanna mentioned he had accepted a new assignment, but she didn't really know the details."

"When we first got back, he joined the staff at Starfleet Academy," Chakotay replied. "Icheb said he was the hardest teacher he'd had, but I think he appreciated seeing a familiar face on a daily basis."

"I would think the training he received here would have made the Academy a little easier for him," Neelix observed.

"He excelled as a student," Seven said. "He was not in any of my classes, but my fellow instructors always spoke well of him, and his academic record was outstanding. When he graduates at the end of the coming year, he will surely receive a challenging position."

Neelix smiled at the obvious pride with which Seven reported Icheb's progress.

"I think after a while, however," Chakotay went on, returning to Neelix's original question, "Tuvok found he missed life on a starship. He accepted an assignment with Starfleet Intelligence on Romulus and was taken prisoner."

"Oh, no." Neelix's face darkened at the thought.

"He was rescued by the *Starship Titan*," Harry said, relieving Neelix's concern, "and accepted a commission there under Captain Riker."

"And what sort of ship is *Titan*?" Neelix asked.

"Their primary mission is deep-space exploration," Chakotay replied. "I understand, however, that Tuvok's wife was asked to join the crew. I believe he is enjoying his new post tremendously."

"Enjoying?" Tom asked.

"Not that he'd show it," Chakotay agreed.

"I don't know," Harry said softly. "He lost his son when the Borg destroyed Deneva."

Neelix's heart broke anew at this news.

"No," B'Elanna said softly.

"I sent him a message when I saw the casualty report," Harry added. "But I never heard back."

"I'm sure he appreciated it," Neelix offered.

A somber silence descended around the table.

Rising to his feet and taking his glass in his hand, Neelix said, "May I propose a toast?"

Murmurs of assent all around were his response.

"B'Elanna told me several weeks ago of Admiral Janeway's passing. I have to say that even now, the idea is hard to accept. I wish I could have attended the formal ceremony that honored her life, but as that was not possible,

I'd like to say now that I believe in my heart that she would have been proud to see all of you still working together, even in the face of great personal tragedy." The eyes that met his all around began to glisten. "I owe more to her than I can ever say," Neelix went on. "Not the least of which was the opportunity to travel with you for as long as I did. I miss her," he finished simply, further words catching in his throat.

Chakotay lifted his glass a little higher and finished Neelix's toast for him.

"To absent friends."

"Absent friends," the others repeated softly as the Doctor placed a gentle hand on Neelix's shoulder.

Once the clinking of glasses had ended, Tom said, "I'm beginning to think it was a mistake to turn this back into a private dining room."

"And why is that?" Chakotay asked.

Tom shrugged. "I just liked it better when we could cook our own food."

"Don't you mean when Neelix could cook our food?" B'Elanna teased.

"Yeah, I don't remember seeing you slaving over that stove too many times," Harry added.

"Does *Demeter* have a galley?" B'Elanna wondered aloud.

"*Demeter*?" Neelix asked.

"It's one of our mission-specific ships," Chakotay explained. "It's filled with aeroponic and hydroponic bays to grow fresh food for the fleet, and to collect botanical samples as we travel."

"Like the ones Kes designed?" Neelix asked.

Chakotay nodded. "She would have loved it," he added.

Neelix sighed. It seemed no matter how far they traveled,

there would always be empty spaces among them that time would never erase.

Absent friends, Neelix thought again.

"Are you all right, Neelix?" Seven inquired softly.

Neelix nodded in response. "Do you have a new morale officer?" he asked.

"No," Harry replied. "That's one set of shoes no one but you could ever fill on this ship."

Neelix smiled at the compliment and chose not to question its sincerity.

"I want you all to promise me something," he finally said.

"Name it," Chakotay replied.

"As long as you're all here in the Delta Quadrant, I want to hear of your progress. Captain Eden has promised to make regular contact, but I want to hear from all of you as well. I have my hands full on New Talax, but even from a distance, I'll always feel a part of this crew."

"Consider it done," Chakotay assured him.

"Do you have any idea where you're headed next?" Neelix asked.

No one did until Chakotay said, "Have you ever heard of a species that call themselves the Children of the Storm?"

Neelix had to confess he hadn't. "They don't sound terribly friendly," he observed.

"Who are they?" the Doctor asked.

Chakotay sighed. "I don't want to turn this lovely evening into a mission briefing, but I have a feeling we're about to find out."

"Afsarah," Counselor Cambridge greeted the captain as she stepped into his quarters. "To what do I owe this unexpected pleasure?"

Hugh had known her for almost five years. She had come to him as a patient through a referral by Admiral Montgomery shortly after her divorce from Willem Batiste had been finalized. He had seen her through the grief that attends the end of every long-term relationship, whether it had been solemnized before one's gods or not. Once Afsarah and Hugh's professional relationship had ended, a cordial friendship had begun. She referred people his way, and once she had joined Project Full Circle, she had been personally responsible for his posting aboard *Voyager*.

Any first-year counselor could have seen by the deep shadows and puffiness under her eyes and the tension she held at the corners of her full lips that Eden was deeply troubled. And any first-year counselor would probably have jumped to the wrong conclusions about the source.

On the surface, they were easy to catalogue. The stress of her position as fleet commander was the tip of the iceberg. But Hugh knew that Afsarah lived for stress. She slept only a few hours each night, preferring to fill her time with constructive labor, the more intense the better.

Some people would have been terrified by the prospect of returning to starship duty after so many years spent riding a desk on their way to a cozy admiralship, but that wasn't really Eden. She had given up command of the *Hennessy* to marry Willem, and once their marriage had run its course, she made no secret of her desire to return to an active command. Her assignment to *Voyager* was natural after her work with Project Full Circle. Apart from Chakotay, she was the best person for the job.

The only reluctance she might have felt would have come from serving under her ex-husband. But Willem had left her long before his rather unnerving performance of a few days ago, confirming what Hugh had suspected: that the end of their marriage really did have nothing at all to do with Afsarah. Likely it had brought her closure rather than opening the scar tissues Batiste had left in her heart.

Hugh knew that none of these issues had brought her to his door this night.

So what has?

"I think it would be a good idea for us to resume our regular counseling sessions," Afsarah said flatly.

"Then you should see my assistant about scheduling something during regular office hours," Hugh said with a smile.

"You don't have an assistant."

"Yes, pity, that." He nodded as he gestured for her to take a seat in the deep leather chair he reserved for his patients.

The captain took a few restless moments to settle herself while Hugh replicated some warm tea. This late in the evening, anything stronger would have left him sleepless. When Eden had taken a few sips and finally sat in a semblance of comfort, she met his scrutinizing gaze with less certainty than he'd ever seen in her.

"It's your dime, Afsarah," he suggested.

A brief smile, more like a grimace, flashed across her lips.

"You don't think this is a good idea?" she asked.

"I serve at your pleasure," he replied with too much irony to be taken seriously. "I'm wondering now why *you* don't think this is a good idea."

"I didn't say that."

"You didn't have to."

She pulled herself up a little straighter in her chair, placing both feet flat on the deck and entwining her hands around her knees.

"I don't remember much of my childhood, until I was around five years old," she began.

"Shame we don't have a Ullian on board," Hugh quipped. "Isn't memory recovery one of their specialties?"

"I don't need you to help me remember," she went on. "I only wanted you to know."

The counselor nodded for her to continue.

"In my earliest memory, I'm with my uncles, Jobin and Tallar. They were studying some paintings in a cave on a planet in the Beta Quadrant. I was playing in the sand, making pictures of my own. I came across some soft, colored rocks. When I crushed them, they stained my hands. I remember looking at the cave drawings and deciding they were wrong. There were supposed to be colors. So I used what I had on my hands and began defacing a priceless archaeological treasure."

"And how much trouble were you in when your uncles discovered this early tendency toward juvenile delinquency?"

"That's the thing. They weren't mad at all. They made notes about what I had done, catalogued the images, and we were off to the next planet."

"How progressive of them," Hugh decided.

"I don't know . . ." she replied.

Though Hugh was intrigued, he couldn't imagine where this was going. That alone piqued his interest. "Remind me. Were your uncles professional archaeologists?"

Afsarah smiled faintly. "They were 'Renaissance men.' Tallar was a trained geneticist and both were explorers. They'd met in Starfleet, but resigned their commissions before I was born. They collected so many different kinds of information from so many worlds. To this day, I'm not sure exactly what they were looking for. Only that they loved what they did."

"Were they your mother's brothers?" Hugh asked.

Afsarah's eyes thinned. "We weren't related, and they weren't actually brothers."

"Ah." Hugh nodded knowingly. "Then how did you come to be with them?"

"I don't remember," she went on. "They said they rescued me from my homeworld, a planet called Sbonfoyjill. They said my family had died and that one day they would take me home, but they didn't get around to it before the time came to send me to Earth to begin my formal education. I remember being terrified to leave them on their own. I always felt they needed me. But they insisted I go to school, and I did love school once I was there. The last time I saw them I was about to enter the Academy and they were off to the Gamma Quadrant. They never came back," she finished without a trace of self-pity.

"So they died?"

"They must have."

"But you don't know?"

"I know that if they were still alive, I would have heard from them. It didn't matter that we weren't related by blood. If Jobin had had his way, they wouldn't have sent me to Earth. It's the only thing I ever heard them argue about."

"Sending you to school?"

Afsarah nodded.

"So forty-odd years later you find yourself leading a fleet of Starfleet vessels into the unknown. Three of your ships have yet to report in. Your former husband just made a spectacularly humiliating exit from all of our lives. The new captain of your flagship wasn't fit for duty a month ago. Our first first-contact situation was a textbook example of everything you don't want to happen when you introduce yourself to a new species and in the process we've managed to unleash upon the quadrant a powerful and potentially hostile force who escaped with some of our most advanced technology." Hugh paused to let his words sink in before concluding, "And you're worried about two men you last saw when you were fifteen?"

"It's more than that."

"It better be."

"One of the first things I did when I had access to the Federation's databases was to try and locate Sbonfoyjill."

"I've never heard of it," Hugh admitted, and given the amount of work he'd done over the years comparing the mythological beliefs of thousands of species, that was saying something.

"That's because it doesn't exist."

"You're sure? Maybe you misremembered the name."

"They made it up," Afsarah insisted.

"That's quite an assumption."

"It's an anagram. Sbonfoyjill is Jobin's Folly."

Hugh kicked himself mentally for not having seen that one coming.

"So you're losing sleep these days because you don't know where you came from? Is there a reason why a basic fact of your existence that you must have made peace with decades ago is suddenly so important to you?"

"Do you remember the artifact from *Voyager*'s first trip to the Delta Quadrant that I sent to you just before we launched, the one discovered by the Mikhal Travelers?"

Hugh nodded briskly.

"What did you see when you looked at it?" Eden asked, rising and crossing to the large window behind the desk in his work space.

Hugh crossed and recrossed his legs, discomfited and at a bit of a loss.

"It looked like a layman's rendition of a starscape," he replied. "Lovely, and crude. Like something a child, or a civilization not terribly advanced, might produce."

"A cave painting?" Afsarah suggested.

"Maybe. I didn't find any particular comparative pieces that might point to a specific origin. It was too similar to thousands of other images."

Finally she turned. "That's disappointing."

He sat forward.

"How so?"

"It's a map," she replied simply. "Or part of one, anyway."

"Does it correlate to a system in our databases?"

"The Hanara constellation."

Hugh paused, searching his memory. "I've never heard of it."

"Because that's what my people call it," she said, turning to face him and beginning to shake. "I have no idea if anyone from the Federation has ever even laid eyes on it."

Hugh rose. "Your people?"

She nodded.

"You are human," he said.

"According to every Federation doctor who has ever examined me, I am," she replied. "But ever since I learned about Jobin's Folly, I've wondered."

The counselor's astonishment turned to concern.

"And it happened again today," Afsarah went on.

"What happened?"

"Captain Dasht presented me with a gift he'd picked up en route to rendezvous with us, a staff inscribed with a language no one else has ever translated. It was a warning not to trespass 'on my ancestral grounds.'"

"Where is the staff?"

"In my quarters."

Hugh took a deep breath. "I think I understand your problem now," he finally said. "You accepted this mission because command unwittingly offered you a chance to find out who you really are and where you come from. You received confirmation today that there's actually a chance you might succeed. You're worried that the closer you get to the truth, the less interested you'll be in exploring the Delta Quadrant. You've just lived through the havoc Willem caused by making this mission personal, and you're afraid you might do the same."

"Have I come to the right place for help?" she asked.

"Most definitely."

Chapter Six

FIFTEEN DAYS EARLIER
U.S.S. PLANCK

T'Mar stood in his vessel's modest cargo bay, examining the containers of food Lieutenant Commander Fife had personally brought to him. The space was almost completely filled, and the ambient temperature had been lowered to preserve the food's freshness.

"There is enough produce to last ten days," Fife advised him, "assuming each of your crewmen eat only regulation portions at each meal. Naturally, things will go a lot further if you stretch them, perhaps in soups or stews. We've brought a small supply of herbs for seasoning. Most weren't ready to harvest, but we've given you all we have."

T'Mar wasn't sure what a "regulation portion" was, but he assumed it wouldn't be an issue. "We really appreciate your efforts, Commander," he replied.

"Although there is a stock of legumes, you'll want to continue the protein supplements," Fife went on. "Within the next few months, we'll also be able to distribute *kala* eggs, an excellent source of protein, but our production has been slower than we anticipated."

T'Mar didn't know what a *kala* was, but if it needed a little time to get settled in its new home before it started producing eggs, he certainly understood.

"You have livestock on board as well?" he asked.

"The *kala* is a root, native to Kressari. It is a happy coincidence that its fruit bears a striking resemblance in form and consistency to the eggs most birds produce on other worlds."

"Ahh." T'Mar nodded, now happier than he'd been at first that they'd be skipping the "eggs" for now.

"Do you require any additional information about preparing the produce?" Fife asked.

"I've assigned four of my crewmen, who all claim to be skilled chefs, to oversee our food preparation," T'Mar replied. "It should be a nice change of pace for them for the next several days."

Fife nodded.

T'Mar was about to dismiss him for transport back to *Demeter* when Lieutenant Tregart called out over the comm.

"Captain T'Mar, please report to the bridge."

The stress in his voice was unmistakable.

"On my way," T'Mar replied, nodding to Fife as he

matched his steps to his words. "Is there a problem, Lieutenant?"

"Alien vessels have been sighted and are approaching our position."

T'Mar's brisk walk broke into a run. "Transport our guests from *Demeter* back to their ship immediately," he ordered. "How many contacts are there?"

He was stunned by Tregart's answer.

U.S.S. QUIRINAL

Lieutenant Phinnegan Bryce was supposed to be asleep. He'd pulled two extra duty shifts in as many days, working on a special project he'd been assigned by his chief, Lieutenant Ganley.

When the fleet had made their first slipstream jump of any real distance from the Alpha Quadrant to the terminus of the Beta and Delta Quadrants, all vessels had reported the presence of microfractures in the benamite crystals that powered the slipstream drive. *Quirinal*'s weren't initially as severe as some of the others, but their journey deep into the Delta Quadrant had caused the size and quantity of the fractures to increase significantly. Ganley estimated that they might have to tap their benamite reserves before they rejoined the fleet unless the slipstream specialists on Phinn's team could find a solution in the next two weeks. The use of the reserves would shorten *Quirinal*'s stay in the Delta Quadrant by more than eight months, and Phinn was determined to make sure it didn't come to that.

His fellow engineers were focusing on ways to realign the drive to reduce the potential for fractures. But Phinn believed that they needed to find a way to reverse the damage.

He believed benamite could be recrystalized, though the technology to do so didn't exist at this point. With another two weeks to work on it, however, Phinn was certain he could design a matrix to recrystalize the benamite. But as he worked on a sketch of the device's innards, his eyelids stubbornly drooped.

In an instant, the warmth and low light of his cabin were replaced by icy blackness. His stomach heaved as he felt the motion of flight. He was traveling through an unending night at terrifying speed. Anger and fear urged him on.

Phinn jumped as his nervous system shocked him back to alertness. His padd was lying on his lap and a thin strand of saliva was hanging from his open mouth. Running his sleeve across his mouth, he decided he really needed to get some sleep, but his heart was still racing. Fearing that if he let himself drop off again, he might find himself in that unpleasant dream—*he hated flying dreams*—he sat up straight in his bunk and studied his schematic.

Within minutes, another heavy, irresistible wave of weariness flowed over him. His mind refused to succumb, continuing to realign the matrix's magnetic resonators even as he felt himself rising from the solid bunk beneath him.

The blackness was nauseating and disorienting, but the speed was more manageable this time. There was something in front of him—a solid wall of metal. He had to avoid impact. A silent scream stuck in his throat as he continued through the barrier before him, and suddenly, he was still. All around him were long bays filled with something dark—*soil*. He realized that the shoots of green and occasional dazzling color had to be flowers and plants.

As horrifying as the flight to this beautiful garden had been, once he had arrived, he was overwhelmed by the sheer joy of his discovery. The colors seemed to glow ever brighter, and he began to float toward the blossoms nearest him.

He was hovering over a tiny purple bud, tingling with delight, when a shrill sound brought him back to consciousness. Before he was fully awake he had jumped up, banging his head on the bunk above him, where, from the sound of it, his roommate, Ensign Nathan, was stirring.

"Is that . . . ?" Nathan asked groggily.

"Yellow Alert," Phinn confirmed.

Damn it.

He knew he should be looking for his boots in case what was obviously an emergent situation escalated, but he sat again, grabbing his padd, determined to squeeze a few more minutes of work in before he was summoned to less interesting duty. With his free hand he took the now cold cup of coffee from his bedside table and finished it off in two big gulps, relying on the caffeine to eliminate the risk of further dreams.

"Report," Farkas ordered as she stepped onto the bridge. It was both gratifying and unnerving that her suspicions about the Children of the Storm had apparently been proven right.

Lieutenant Psilakis, who'd had command for gamma shift, immediately rose from the bridge's center seat to fill her in.

"Three hundred and forty-seven contacts that conform to the description we have of the Children of the Storm's vessels are approaching our position, Captain."

"Time to intercept?"

"Approximately ten minutes," Psilakis replied unhappily.

"How the hell did three hundred plus ships get this close to us without warning?" Farkas demanded. She knew Jepel had just started his shift at ops, so this wasn't necessarily his fault, but his predecessor, along with gamma tactical, was going to spend the next three years doing waste reclamation unless her question had a really good answer.

"We don't know, Captain," Psilakis replied.

Not good enough.

"Lieutenant Denisov?" Farkas barked at her security chief. "That debris field is two light-years from our position, so it couldn't have masked their signals this long. They're practically right on top of us."

"The debris field must have somehow masked them, Captain," was Denisov's frustrated response. "Sensors show that one minute they weren't there and the next second, they were. And their speed is . . ." His voice trailed off.

"What?" Farkas asked.

"The equivalent of warp 9.9," Denisov replied.

Farkas knew there wasn't time for them to figure this out now. Shifting gears, she ordered Jepel to begin transmitting friendship messages on all channels as her first officer, Commander Roach, hurried to his post at her side.

"You picked a hell of a morning to oversleep, Commander," Farkas warned.

"Apologies, Captain," he replied. "I can't remember the last time I slept that deeply."

"Another time," Farkas cut him off as she assumed her seat and began to analyze data. An unexpected sight tweaked her last available nerve.

"What is *Demeter* doing here?" she spat harshly.

Psilakis stepped into the fray for Roach. "They arrived a few hours ago to provide a supply transfer to *Planck*."

"I knew that was happening, but they shouldn't have been here for another day at least," Farkas replied. "Which part of approach at impulse speed do we think Captain T'Mar didn't understand?" she added in disbelief. It was altogether possible that the abrupt appearance of what seemed to be a hostile alien force was the result of *Demeter*'s hurried arrival. Farkas silently cursed T'Mar before refocusing her attention on the bigger issue.

"Denisov, coordinate with *Planck*. Worse comes to worst, we're going to need to protect *Demeter*," she ordered.

"We've received word from Commander Fife," Denisov replied. "He wants to make a run for it."

Is he viewing a different tactical display than I am? "Tell him to hold position," Farkas shot back. "The last thing we need right now is more area to defend, especially when they've got that many ships. There's no way he can outrun them unless he plots a slipstream jump, and there's not time for that." As fast as the aliens were approaching, Farkas wasn't even sure that would get the job done. "How big are those ships, Gregor?" she asked Denisov.

"That's the only good news, Captain," he replied. "Two of them could fit inside one of our workbees."

"What they lack in size, they more than make up for in numbers," Farkas reminded him.

"Of course, Captain."

Visions of the nearby Borg graveyard danced through Farkas's head. No one had any idea how the Children of the Storm had managed to thrash the Borg so soundly, but the captain silently feared they were about to find out.

"Are our sensors telling us anything about them that we don't already know?" she asked Jepel.

"Not at this distance, Captain," he replied as he studied the ops readouts. "Each vessel is composed of a high-frequency energy field with no discernible means of propulsion and no obvious weapons systems. Atmosphere within the vessels is essentially semifluid liquid metal hydrogen, and each vessel shows hundreds of life-form readings within."

"Any response to our greetings?" she asked, already dreading Jepel's response.

"No, Captain," he replied.

Farkas took a deep breath. "Helm, hold position. Shields to maximum, warm up the phasers and load the torpedo tubes. I don't want to destroy three hundred and forty-seven vessels, each containing hundreds of sentient beings, without so much as a 'how do you do,' but we may not have another option. Prepare firing solutions that maximize our weapons' dispersal and range. At this point we have no reason to believe they're not vulnerable to phaser fire, but everybody feel free to imagine the worst and figure out how we're going to survive it."

"*Sal to Farkas.*"

Breathing a sigh of relief at the thought that the Children of the Storm might just be coming to talk after all, the captain replied, "Go ahead."

"*I'm sure you're busier than an armless dabo girl up there, but you need to report to sickbay immediately.*"

"Is it Ti'Ana?" Farkas asked as she rose from her seat.

"*It used to be. Whoever is speaking through her now didn't give a name, but they asked to speak to the individual in command of this vessel.*"

"I'm on my way," Farkas replied. The captain hated to leave the bridge at a moment like this. "Commander Roach, you have the bridge." En route to the turbolift, she almost plowed into Commander Psilakis.

"You're off duty, Commander," she reminded him.

"Permission to remain on the bridge and observe, Captain?" he requested. He had to feel like hell about this, and she didn't want to deny him the opportunity to redeem himself.

She nodded and turned back to Roach. "Keep a comm signal open to me at all times, Commander. I'll be back as soon as I can."

"Aye, sir," Roach replied.

An unpleasant twinge in her gut made one last recommendation. "And take us to Red Alert."

U.S.S. DEMETER

Commander Fife disagreed with Captain Farkas's assessment of the situation. He had asked Lieutenant Url, *Demeter*'s senior tactical officer, to run multiple simulations to reduce the time required to plot a safe slipstream jump. He knew that, in a pinch, Url could have the ship safely on its way in nine and a half minutes. Of course, he'd already lost more than thirty seconds he'd had once he reached the bridge waiting for Captain Farkas to countermand his decision.

Despite Farkas's orders, Url continued calculating a safe exit vector for the slipstream corridor at Fife's request. There was still a chance that Url might succeed before the alien vessels were in range, and then Fife would have a decision to make. Should he disregard Captain Farkas's order to hold their position, or should he do what he thought best to get his crew to safety?

Most frustrating of all was the knowledge that it wasn't his call to make. On any other Starfleet vessel, the captain would be on the bridge at a moment like this, and Fife would offer counsel but ultimately would leave the final choice to his superior. The conversation he'd had with Admiral Batiste before the fleet launched now haunted him.

"You've been selected to support Commander O'Donnell because he will need the most capable first officer we can possibly provide him. We both know you're on the fast track for a command of your own and this mission might not seem like your best career move, but believe me when I tell you, it is. O'Donnell is the best genetic botanist in the Federation, but he knows ass-all about tactics and weapons. His seniority and experience make him the logical commander of Demeter, but he's been landlocked for most of his career and will need a stellar second-in-command. He won't get in your way, and he'll defer to you if the going should get tough. Be ready to step in, but understand that the commander's rank is not a formality. He'll need your support, and he'll probably annoy the hell out of you, but your job is to make this work."

It was an odd arrangement, but Fife was sure he was up to it. And for the first several weeks of the mission, he'd had no cause to regret his assignment. The few conversations they'd had had been similar enough to the exchange they'd had a few hours ago about *Planck* that Fife wondered if the captain would bother coming to the bridge. *Except this is one of the few instances in which he did ask to be informed.*

Fife watched the aliens moving closer, marveling at their speed in the absence of a visible means of propulsion and knowing he was running out of time.

"Lieutenant Url, what is our best time to engage the slipstream drive?" he asked, steeling his voice so that not a hint of the frustration he felt was evident.

"Seven minutes, sir," Url replied.

We have five at the most, Fife calculated.

Ensign Vincent at ops cleared his throat and asked the obvious question.

"Shouldn't we advise the captain that we're about to encounter alien vessels?"

Normally this wouldn't have been a hard decision.

"I will advise the captain when I see fit, Ensign," Fife replied briskly. "Attend to your station."

"Aye, sir."

By "when I see fit" Fife had meant, *when I think he can actually help us.*

Thus far, O'Donnell couldn't. But if Url completed his calculations sooner, that would change.

Fife would give Url two more minutes. And then, like it or not, he would contact O'Donnell. Right now Fife wasn't sure whom he hated more, his captain or the admiral who had talked him into accepting this impossible commission.

U.S.S. PLANCK

Captain T'Mar stood on his bridge, amazed at how quickly his situation had changed. If anyone had told him when he awakened early to oversee *Demeter*'s supply transfer that within hours he'd come face-to-face with the Children of the Storm, he'd have comfortably bet against them. Now he wondered if he should have requested *Demeter*'s presence at all. It wasn't hard to make a case that the timing of the aliens' arrival and *Demeter*'s probably wasn't coincidence, especially since they had approached the area at high warp, despite Farkas's recommendation. T'Mar had thought Farkas overcautious and chosen not to argue with Fife when he had advised T'Mar that he'd be there in a few hours. In doing so, T'Mar feared he might have damned all three ships.

All he could do now, however, was hope there would be time later to regret his actions. Between now and then, T'Mar vowed, he would follow Captain Farkas's requests to the letter. For now that meant readying all weapons systems and coordinating his helm and tactical with *Quirinal*'s to make sure *Demeter* was adequately protected. Though part of him would have given anything to make contact with this species, he would also leave that to Farkas.

Please let this end well, he prayed.

The sensor readouts of the ships converging on them was stunning. The Children of the Storm moved with a grace and speed that were mind-boggling. The image on the main viewscreen of their approach reminded him of a white-capped wave rolling inexorably forward, seconds away from crashing against a shore. Though it was hard to discern individual ships, it was tempting to perceive these flying spheres as innocuous, so beautiful were they in the abstract. T'Mar knew well enough that the atmosphere inside them was toxic and under extreme pressure, but it was easy to imagine that a child had blown them into existence through a soapy ring.

They entered the area at what appeared to be their top speed and did not slow until they had broken off into three separate groups. Within seconds, given their trajectories, they would surround each of the three Federation ships.

Which cannot be allowed, T'Mar decided.

"Ensign Grim, evasive maneuvers. Keep them off of us and away from *Demeter*."

"Understood," Grim replied as he tapped the helm controls, firing thrusters to move the ship out of direct range of the alien vessels.

Grim succeeded for all of fifteen seconds before the aliens altered course and completely surrounded the ship. T'Mar's display confirmed that *Quirinal* and *Demeter* were in exactly the same predicament. It no longer mattered how he moved his ship. Hundreds of discreet round vessels, only a few meters in diameter each, would surely move with him no matter what. He could only wait until Captain Farkas indicated whether this was going to end with a bang or a whimper.

U.S.S. QUIRINAL

"Come on, Phinn," Nathan shouted as he hurried toward their cabin door.

Phinn had almost completed the algorithm to govern the matrix's harmonics, and he knew if he stopped now, he'd lose his train of thought completely.

"Don't wait on me," he said, waving Nathan off.

"That big flashing red light means we move to battle stations, Phinn."

"I know."

Exhaling in sharp disgust, Nathan exited their cabin.

"Where x is equal to or greater than the coefficient . . ." Phinn said aloud, trying to maintain his concentration through the blaring of the alarm.

Damn it.

Thirty more seconds and he'd have it.

He'd also be bucked back to crewman if he failed to report to his post on time.

Phinn entered the final calculations into his padd and, while he awaited the analysis, hurriedly stuffed his feet into his boots and reached into his drawer. His hand quickly found his secret weapon, a personal site-to-site transporter he'd created at the Academy for just such emergencies. Because it looked so much like an old watch, if anyone ever asked, he said it was his great-grandfather's. He'd only had to use it a few times in his career, but this was going to be another of them. He had to hope whatever chaos was breaking loose on board would cover his tracks when the "watch" tapped into the backup transporters.

Who is ever going to check?

His rationalization firmly in place, Phinn read the analysis he had requested and confirmed that the algorithm was perfect.

Problem solved, he thought with a grin, then lightly tapped his wrist, keying in the transport coordinates for his battle station.

Seconds later he arrived right around the corner from Ensign Sadie Johns, a tall brunette he'd met a few times at this very spot on deck seventeen during drills. He hurried toward her to give the impression that he'd been running all the way from his cabin.

"You'd be late for your own funeral, wouldn't you, Bryce?" Johns demanded, clearly miffed to have been guarding this post alone for the few minutes Phinn had taken to finish his calculations.

"Probably," Phinn agreed. "Did I miss anything?"

Johns gave him a withering glance.

Mentally setting his work of the last several hours aside, Phinn did his best to focus on the task at hand.

"Do you have any idea what all this is about?" he asked.

"The captain didn't check in with me personally, but I'm assuming, what with the Red Alert and all, that it's bad."

"Sure, but there are degrees of bad, Sadie."

"If the captain has called for battle stations, I'm going to go out on a limb and suggest we've probably made contact with the aliens we were sent out here to find and that they're not happy to see us," Johns said.

"Or maybe they are thrilled to see us," Phinn suggested optimistically.

"You go with that if it makes you feel better, Bryce."

As Phinn lived most of his life in the theoretical, he decided that it did, and until he had reason to believe otherwise, he would assume the best.

"What's our status, Commander?" Farkas asked, stopping just short of the sensor that would open the doors of sickbay.

"*All three of our vessels are surrounded, Captain,*" was Roach's unnerving reply. "*They are holding position for now.*"

I'll try to remember and thank someone later for small favors, Farkas decided as she stepped toward the doors.

The tense faces of Sal's staff met her initial questioning gaze. One of the nurses directed her with a glance toward the private room where Ti'Ana had been living behind a psionic force field for the past few days.

Steeling herself, Farkas quickly covered the distance and entered the room. Sal stood with her arms crossed, a tricorder hanging limply in her hand. Ti'Ana lay flat on a biobed, restrained at the shoulders, hands, and feet. Chafing around her wrists suggested she'd struggled against them recently.

"Doctor?" Farkas asked.

Pulling the captain toward a corner of the room, Sal said, "As soon as we went to Yellow Alert, I restrained the ensign and dropped the protective field. Within seconds, she began to thrash about violently. As you can see, she's a little calmer now," she finished softly.

"And we're sure she's not alone in there?" Farkas asked.

Sal shook her head and raised the tricorder for Farkas to see. Though Farkas wasn't an expert in neural analysis, the presence of two distinct patterns was obvious enough.

Nodding, Farkas stepped into Ti'Ana's line of sight.

"I am Captain Regina Farkas of the Federation *Starship*—" she began.

"You were told not to return to our space," a cold voice replied through Ti'Ana's lips.

"I know," Farkas replied, "but you should not misunderstand our presence here. Your species is unlike any we have ever encountered, and we came in hopes that you would reconsider establishing peaceful contact with us."

Ti'Ana's eyes rolled back in her head and her eyelids fluttered momentarily. Disconcerting as this was for Farkas to witness, it paled in comparison to the hard stare that met hers when the ensign's eyes fell back into place.

"Is this why you have brought us the life?" was the alien's inexplicable question.

Chapter Seven

STARDATE 58452.9
U.S.S. GALEN

As the Doctor signed off on the list of supplies he'd requisitioned for Neelix, he noticed the Talaxian gingerly placing his hand against the glass partition separating his office from the main entrance to *Galen*'s medical bay. Neelix pressed firmly, as if testing the wall's strength, before shaking his head.

"I assure you, Neelix, the wall is quite solid."

"You'd think I'd be used to it after so many years on

Voyager's holodecks, wouldn't you?" Neelix replied, looking a little chastened.

Although the Doctor had done his best during their brief tour of his vessel that morning to explain to Neelix that the ship, though equipped throughout with holographic generators, was not, in fact, just one huge holodeck, he feared the distinction had been lost on his old friend. With a smile, he offered Neelix the completed supply list to review.

"I believe that's everything we discussed," he said.

Neelix read through the description of the medical supplies he'd be taking back to New Talax and admonished the Doctor. "This is too much. I'm grateful, of course, but you can't possibly spare all of this."

"We can," the Doctor corrected him gently.

"But if the fleet were to come under attack . . ."

"We have sufficient power reserves to replicate this list a hundred times over, Neelix," the Doctor replied. "I insist you take this, and let me know if you need anything more."

It was clear from Neelix's expression that he'd be returning home a conquering hero with even a fraction of what the Doctor had offered. "Doctor Hestax won't believe his good fortune," Neelix finally said. Then he met the Doctor's eyes firmly. "And neither do I."

Before the Doctor could reply that it was nothing, Neelix had grabbed him and pulled him into a firm hug.

"I've told my people time and time again of the generosity of Starfleet and *Voyager*'s crew. If they ever doubted me before, this should prove my point. Thank you so much."

The Doctor extricated himself gently and responded with a soft pat to Neelix's shoulder. "Happy to be of assistance," he assured Neelix.

"And thank you again for showing me your beautiful

ship," Neelix went on. "You should be very proud of what you've built here."

Though no one who knew him well would have believed it, the Doctor's programming did not actually contain a subroutine for pride. The satisfaction he felt at Neelix's words could only have come from the part of him that had outgrown his initial design, the part that had been nurtured so carefully by his many friends aboard *Voyager*, including Neelix, for many years.

"Doctor Zimmerman had been working on the specifications for years," the Doctor replied, trying to give credit where it was due. "But the modifications I suggested have made all the difference," he added. "The wall color, for example: don't you find it welcoming?"

"I do." Neelix nodded with less enthusiasm than the Doctor might have wished. Of course Neelix's idea of "welcoming" was probably chartreuse flecked with gold and turquoise spots.

It was past time for Neelix's scheduled departure. With genuine regret, the Doctor returned to the seat behind his desk, hoping to avoid a drawn-out farewell.

"We will remain in range with New Talax for quite some time," he said. "Don't hesitate to let us know if we can be of further assistance to you."

Neelix considered the Doctor briefly, then surprised him by taking the seat opposite him rather than moving toward the office door.

"Are you all right?" he asked. The Doctor knew well enough that when Neelix had something caught in his teeth, a skilled surgeon couldn't remove it. Nonetheless, he attempted to brush any concerns aside.

"Of course," he replied. "I've never been better."

Neelix's chin fell and his eyes clearly displayed disbelief.

"What?" the Doctor asked, the testiness that had usually been his default position with Neelix returning as if years had never separated them.

"It's my understanding that the young woman who was taken prisoner by that alien consciousness worked with you," he said kindly, clearly hoping to draw the Doctor out.

"Have you been talking to Reg?" the Doctor asked, miffed.

"Of course not," Neelix replied honestly, "though I was pleased to finally meet him when you introduced us this morning." After a moment he continued, "I must admit, he didn't seem as energetic as I expected."

Though *energetic* might normally have been an apt description of Lieutenant Reginald Barclay, the Doctor knew too well that since the fleet had left the Indign system, he had worked night and day to find a way to track Meegan. When Barclay had received word that Neelix had recovered her shuttle, rather than joining them for Neelix's dinner, he began poring through the shuttle's logs, looking for clues. As far as the Doctor was concerned, he'd earned his penance. Transgressions such as his should weigh heavy on a man's conscience.

"Lieutenant Barclay has a great deal of work to do," the Doctor offered.

"If I had spoken to him, what would he have told me?" Neelix asked gently.

"Hopefully that he's finished meddling in other people's personal lives," the Doctor replied too hotly.

Neelix allowed this to sink in, then asked quietly, "Was this Meegan more than an assistant?"

The Doctor knew when he was beaten. Neelix would remain in his office until he received an answer, even if he reached old age in the process.

"Meegan was a hologram," the Doctor replied with a sigh. "Apparently Reg and Doctor Zimmerman decided that I couldn't select an appropriate romantic partner for myself, so they created one for me. Of course they didn't tell me what they'd done. They didn't tell anyone. And because of that, an incredibly advanced piece of Federation technology is now roaming the galaxy under the influence of a brutish alien consciousness."

Neelix nodded as if he understood.

"Were you in love with her?" he asked simply, deftly avoiding what the Doctor believed to be the source of his current anger and hitting the actual truth on its head.

"I barely knew her."

"But you liked her?"

"I don't know."

Neelix remained perfectly still, as deft a hunter as ever.

"I might have," the Doctor finally said softly.

"Don't worry," Neelix said as comfortingly as possible. "You'll find her again, and you'll free her from the influence of whatever has taken her."

Though the Doctor actually suspected that they would eventually do just that, part of him wasn't sure that he really wanted to.

"It's wrong, Neelix."

"Loving someone else is never wrong," Neelix insisted. "Even when it doesn't end the way we'd like," he added.

"How would you feel if someone else tried to create the perfect woman for you?" the Doctor asked, trying to make him understand.

Neelix's face brightened. "The universe did just that," he replied with a smile. "Twice."

"You don't understand," the Doctor said.

Neelix rose from his chair, not the least bit insulted. "I think both Reg and Doctor Zimmerman are good friends to you," he said. "And I think that even when we disagree with our friends, we owe it to them and to ourselves to forgive them. True friends," he finished, "are too rare to be taken for granted."

Neelix had reached the door before the Doctor had processed his words. Rising, he said softly, "Take care of yourself, Neelix."

"I always do."

"I'm serious," the Doctor said more forcefully. "And promise me that if you hear anything about Meegan, you won't go after her yourself." Somehow the Doctor knew that, given her importance to him, it was exactly the kind of thing Neelix would do. "She's too dangerous."

Neelix nodded. "Take care of our friends," he said as he left the office.

As soon as Neelix was gone, the Doctor made his way to Reg's private lab and found him in exactly the same position he'd left him in hours earlier, his back bent over a data terminal, his eyes bleary.

"I think I owe you an apology," he surprised both of them by saying.

U.S.S. ACHILLES

Commander Tillum Drafar was one of the tallest men B'Elanna had ever met. He stood easily over two meters. Though B'Elanna suspected it was an optical illusion, she got the impression that the top of her head reached barely above his waist.

His features were every bit as bold as the rest of him. A

long mane of fine white hair sat atop his head like a helmet. B'Elanna found herself wondering privately what sort of product he might use to keep every strand of it so perfectly in place, especially working in the often overheated bowels of a starship. A single frontal ridge protruded just above large silver eyes, curving downward in a way that made those eyes his most striking feature. Scores of faint brown spots cascaded over his nose and covered his cheeks. His mouth was small, relatively speaking, but his smile was wide as he welcomed her aboard *Achilles*.

His vessel, like its commanding officer, was massive. The specs put its length at nine hundred sixty meters from stem to stern. Its forward section had a triangular shape that soon gave way to a long, rectangular body. Spaced along its hull at multiple levels were large bay doors that would ease the passage of any large structures that might require ingress or egress. The two largest nacelles B'Elanna had ever laid eyes on emerged from its rear section. What it lacked in elegance, it more than made up for in imposition. There was something comforting in the thought of *Achilles* as a part of the fleet. For the first time in a long time, B'Elanna allowed herself to imagine projects on a scale never known to her in the Delta Quadrant.

"At last we meet," Drafar said cordially as he grasped the hand she extended to him in greeting in two huge six-fingered hands.

"The pleasure is mine, Commander," B'Elanna replied sincerely.

"As you'll see, we run a tight ship here. I personally selected the five hundred sixty-one crew that staff this ship, and all of them are the best in their respective specialties."

"I don't doubt it," B'Elanna replied, though given the

records of the staffs of the other fleet vessels, she thought Drafar might be selling the others short. "I look forward to working with you and your crew," she added, suddenly remembering how displaced and overwhelmed she'd felt the first day she'd taken command of *Voyager*'s engine room. At the time, there had been plenty of Starfleet veterans who doubted both her abilities and Captain Janeway's judgment. It had taken years, in some cases, to put those fears to rest, though like good Starfleet officers, her subordinates had never had the temerity to express their doubts to her face.

Reminding herself that she had earned her position as fleet engineering chief and that her experience in the Delta Quadrant solving complex and often esoteric engineering challenges was on a par with anyone's record, B'Elanna lifted her chin a little higher and said, "Lieutenant Conlon bet me that you'd have the benamite recrystalization matrices up and running by now."

"If you wagered against us, you lost," Drafar replied with obvious pride.

"Shall we start there, then?" B'Elanna asked, ready to get her tour under way.

"Why?" Drafar asked.

Slightly taken aback and concerned that she might have inadvertently offended him, B'Elanna replied, "If there's something else you had in mind, that's not a problem."

"Apologies," Drafar said completely insincerely. "What I meant is that it won't be necessary for you to check our work, Commander . . . I'm sorry, is it Paris or Torres?"

"Torres," B'Elanna shot back quickly. Taking Tom's name when they'd married had been more of a private joke between them than a practical issue. She'd been Lieutenant Torres among *Voyager*'s crew for almost seven years by then, and Tom didn't care one way or the other, though he enjoyed calling her Mrs. Paris when they were alone.

"But you did give your daughter her father's name?" Drafar asked in a way that suggested that to do otherwise would be unthinkable.

"She is Miral Paris, yes," B'Elanna replied. Hoping to find some rapport, she added, "Miral was my mother's name."

Drafar seemed to find this notion puzzling.

"I thought you'd begin by reviewing our mission logs to date," Drafar said. "I've found a spare terminal for you in one of our sub-bays on deck nine. It shouldn't take you long to see that we're at or ahead of schedule on all of our supply and maintenance requests."

And after that I'll just scurry back to Voyager *and leave you to run your ship in peace?* B'Elanna thought. *Not likely.* In her new position as fleet chief B'Elanna was responsible for overseeing the engineering aspects of every ship in the fleet, and she had already concluded that *Achilles* was going to play a big part in her work. Though she hadn't yet discussed it with Tom, she wondered if during missions where *Voyager* and *Achilles* were in the same area, it might be a good idea for her to base her work on *Achilles*. The ship's resources vastly dwarfed *Voyager*'s. Now that she'd met Drafar, however, she wondered if he'd be amenable to such a proposal.

"I'd really like to see as much of *Achilles* as you have time to show me, Commander," B'Elanna said. "I've already reviewed your logs and agree that your crew's work is exemplary. I'm not here to get in the way of that, but as you'll soon learn, I don't take a hands-off approach to my work. Of course, if you have other priorities, you could assign one of your command staff to show me around," she suggested.

"Not at all," Drafar said. "I just assumed you'd be anxious

to get back to your little girl. Children need their mothers so," he added as if it were gospel.

For a moment, B'Elanna was dumbstruck. Though she'd encountered all sorts of race-based prejudices over the years, and struggled privately with her half-human, half-Klingon heritage, sexism of the sort Drafar had just displayed was pretty rare, especially in Starfleet.

He can't mean what I think he means, she hoped.

"Miral is well taken care of," she assured him. In truth, balancing Miral's needs with that of her new job had almost been enough to dissuade her from accepting the position. Some creative scheduling, however, along with the support of Tom, several of her oldest friends, and a certified pre-school education specialist aboard *Esquiline* whom she'd met with early this morning to discuss a curriculum, had lessened her anxieties on this front. Tom was caring for Miral now and, before his shift began, would take her to the holodeck, where Seven had volunteered to give her a morning of rigorous exercise. B'Elanna had been somewhat surprised by Seven's offer but soon remembered the fondness with which Seven had cared for Naomi Wildman and hoped that she might develop a similar bond with Miral. After lunch, the Doctor would take over for a few hours of language arts. B'Elanna would resume Miral's care in the late afternoon, and if the last several days were any indication, she would find her brimming over with stories of what she had learned and done throughout the day. Though it might be unconventional, B'Elanna had no doubt that her daughter would receive an extraordinary education for the duration of their stay with the fleet.

Drafar's eyebrow ridge lifted in what appeared to be disbelief, but he wisely held his peace.

"Well," he said with a put-upon sigh, "this is one of six auxiliary shuttlebays, fairly standard." His long arm gestured for her to take in the large space dotted with a few vessels and crewmen busily tending to them.

As they began to walk toward the interior door, B'Elanna found a question blurting forth before she had the good sense to consider how far she wanted to push Drafar at their first meeting.

"Do you have any children of your own?"

Drafar stopped, as if the thought was offensive to him.

"I'm a Starfleet officer," he replied, as if that settled the matter.

"More officers than I can count have children while serving in Starfleet," B'Elanna replied a little too defensively.

"Of course they do," Drafar agreed too readily. "I am simply not one of them. I meant no offense, of course."

But B'Elanna didn't believe him for a moment.

Throughout the rest of the tour, which took almost an hour, B'Elanna kept her tone and questions purely professional. A gnawing sense lingered throughout that Drafar was humoring her rather than showing proper deference or even respect to her position. Though she was not his superior officer in rank or position, she had expected to find a spirit of kinship with a fellow engineer and at least acknowledgment of her position as fleet chief. While the bridge, main engineering bay, medical facilities, and crew quarters were all quite standard, B'Elanna had never been aboard a ship with the industrial capabilities of *Achilles*. They possessed five replicators large enough to manufacture parts and technology usually reserved for starbases or colonization ships. B'Elanna surmised they could rebuild every ship in the fleet from scratch should the need arise.

Unfortunately, B'Elanna found her estimation of Drafar sinking as they progressed. It wasn't so much what he said as *how* he said it. Few things soured B'Elanna's stomach like condescension, and she swallowed one mouthful of bile after another before she reached the end of her rope.

Drafar's patience seemed to end when they had completed a review of *Achilles'* two largest cargo holds. For now, they were mostly unused, apart from items that were difficult or impossible to replicate, such as benamite crystals and bioneural gel-packs.

The commander ushered her outside the last cargo bay and began to direct their steps back toward the turbolift. Though the wide hallway was dimly lit to conserve power, a modification Drafar had pointed out to her, she couldn't help but note a third large door at the end of the hall that he had not referenced. B'Elanna quickly called up a mental image of the schematics of the vessel and decided that another storage bay must lie beyond those doors, and would have to be at least as large, if not larger, than the two cargo bays she had just seen.

"Excuse me, Commander," she said calmly, "what's back there?"

"More storage." Drafar smiled, though B'Elanna noted that he hastened his steps in the opposite direction.

Instinct rooted B'Elanna's feet to the deck.

"Shall we?" she asked in a tone that was more an order than a request.

Drafar turned to face her, and for the first time, B'Elanna caught a chill in his presence.

"The contents of that bay are classified," he said simply. "For now, our tour is at an end."

Like hell.

"I beg to differ, Commander," she said, standing her ground.

"I mean no disrespect, Commander Torres," Drafar replied amiably. "I was not advised, however, that you were cleared to view the contents of that bay."

"We can fix that," B'Elanna decided. Tapping her combadge, she said, "This is Fleet Chief Torres to the bridge."

"*Go ahead, sir.*"

"Please hail Captain Eden aboard *Voyager*."

"*Just a moment.*"

In the brief seconds that passed until Eden was patched through, B'Elanna's eyes never left Drafar's.

"*This is Eden.*"

"Sorry to trouble you, Captain, but I'm outside what Commander Drafar tells me is a classified storage bay aboard *Achilles* and he is refusing to show me its contents. I assume my position grants me clearance."

After a brief pause, during which B'Elanna believed she heard Eden sigh, the captain replied, "*Of course. Commander Drafar, please escort Chief Torres anywhere she wishes to go. Eden out.*"

Satisfied with this small victory, B'Elanna nodded toward the end of the hall, and Drafar dutifully stepped ahead of her. When he reached the door, he entered a command code and endured a brief biometric scan before the doors hissed open.

B'Elanna stepped inside and discovered a cargo bay as vast as she had anticipated. What she had not suspected, however, was the nature of the bay's contents. The moment she laid eyes on it, her jaw dropped.

U.S.S. VOYAGER

Captain Eden was curious as to what B'Elanna would make of *Achilles*' most sensitive cargo, but she set the thought aside and returned to the much more pressing matter at hand. *Quirinal, Planck,* and *Demeter* were now a full twenty-four hours overdue. The concern she felt for all of them was mirrored back to her in the faces of Captains Chakotay, Dasht, Itak, and Chan.

"All right, gentlemen," Eden said, "we've got three overdue ships. Although our next mission priority once we had regrouped was to continue twenty light-years beyond our present position toward another sector once dominated by the Borg, I'm scrapping that for now. Clearly we need to mount a rescue mission. I'm open to your suggestions as to the complement of that mission, though *Voyager*'s participation is mandatory."

"Why is that?" Chakotay asked, out of seemingly genuine curiosity.

"I intend to lead the rescue mission," Eden replied flatly, suddenly wondering if she was going to face a barrage of reminders that as fleet commander, her duty was to allow everyone else to place themselves in harm's way before herself.

"Fair enough," Chakotay surprised her by replying.

"I suppose the real question is how many ships we want to risk," Dasht said simply. "*Voyager* and *Esquiline* are best equipped to handle themselves in a fight, but I'm not sure you want to leave *Galen* and *Achilles* to fend for themselves out here."

"*Curie* stands ready to defend them, should the need arise," Chan interjected solemnly.

"As does *Hawking,*" added Itak.

"*Curie* and *Hawking* are science vessels, *Merian* class," Chakotay said, treading lightly. "While your vessels and crew are in an excellent position to fight your own battles, defending two other vessels, particularly one as large as *Achilles*, might be too much to ask."

Chan favored Chakotay with a hard stare before replying, "Perhaps. However, if that is Captain Eden's order, I will do my best."

"As we all would," Itak echoed, "but that does not make it the most logical choice."

"Send *Esquiline*," Dasht said decisively.

"Why?" Eden asked, curious to hear his justification.

"We're five times the size of *Voyager*."

"So is the *Quirinal*," Chakotay reminded them.

Dasht's spine stiffened, but he went on, "If we're assuming that any or all of the missing ships are damaged, *Esquiline* is the only ship currently available that could relocate the crews of all three vessels should the need arise."

"But if we assume they were destroyed—" Chan began.

"We're not," Eden cut him off.

Chakotay's eyes darted back and forth between Dasht and Chan.

"The Children of the Storm," Chakotay began. "We know too little about them to guess what may have become of our ships if they encountered them. Naturally, the fact that they were able to handily defeat the Borg is cause for concern, but they did instigate contact with Captain Dax's vessel. It's still conceivable that they did the same with our ships and that our fellow commanders have been delayed by their investigations or cultural exchange."

"Not possible," Eden declared.

"Why not?"

"Their mission parameters were clear. They were given twenty days to complete their studies and rejoin the fleet.

They would not simply have lost track of time or decided on their own to extend their stay."

"If their discoveries were interesting enough . . ." Chakotay argued.

"This isn't *Voyager*'s maiden trek through the Delta Quadrant," Eden insisted too hotly. "We don't alter our plans on a whim. There's too much at stake. and Captain Farkas, Captain T'Mar, and Commander O'Donnell were clear about that before they separated from the rest of the fleet."

Though Chakotay's eyes hardened a little at this ungenerous characterization of *Voyager,* he remained silent.

"The protocol was clear," Eden continued. "Even if they successfully made contact and needed to extend their mission, one or more of the ships should have returned to advise us of that. All three ships are overdue, and we have to assume they are unable to return to our position."

"Without further data to consider, and given your determination to personally assume command of our efforts," Chakotay said evenly, "it seems only logical, then, that *Voyager* should go after them alone. We can get close enough to their intended coordinates to scan for them without disturbing the Children of the Storm. If we find no compelling evidence of their presence or their destruction, we should regroup here and widen our search, utilizing all of the vessels we have at our disposal."

"I'd be happy to have my astrometrics department begin an analysis of what is known of that area so that, should the need arise, we wouldn't lose time expanding the search when you return, Captain," Dasht offered.

"My xenobiologists have prepared a rudimentary analysis of the Children of the Storm, based upon *Aventine*'s logs, and have already calculated that it is unlikely that their territory would extend beyond a radius of five light-years from the system surrounded by the Borg debris," Chan added.

Eden nodded. "I agree with Chakotay. Should the three ships require additional repair or medical assistance, we can call in *Achilles* and *Galen* once they are located. In the interim, I'd rather not risk *Esquiline, Hawking,* or *Curie.* You should make preparations for a wider search, if *Voyager* returns empty-handed."

"And if *Voyager* does not return at all?" Dasht asked delicately.

"We will depart in five hours," Eden replied. "If we have not returned or made contact within the next seventy-two, you should instigate a search pattern that remains well clear of the territory of the Children of the Storm. If that search reveals nothing further within the next seventy-two hours, you should advise Starfleet Command and proceed to our next scheduled coordinates. All of you have our mission priorities for the next four weeks in your databases. Follow them to the letter, and if we haven't caught up with you by then, we're not going to."

"Here's hoping none of that becomes necessary and that we hear from one or all of the three ships in the next five hours," Dasht said as optimistically as possible.

Eden concurred, but wasn't holding her breath. Something bad had happened to three of her ships. The only question in her mind now was *how bad?*

"That's it then," Eden said, rising. Dasht, Itak, and Chan nodded as they headed for the door, but Chakotay remained seated.

"I'll advise you of any changes to these orders before we depart," Eden instructed Dasht, Itak, and Chan, clearly dismissing them. She then turned back to Chakotay but remained on her feet.

"Problem, Captain?"

"No," Chakotay replied. "I asked Seven if she could provide any tactical data regarding the Children of the Storm, and she told me that she has no knowledge of the species at all."

"That's odd, isn't it?"

Chakotay nodded. "Given the age of the debris *Aventine* detected, the Borg's encounters with the Children would have been well before Seven's time, but you would think such a massive defeat would have lived forever in the Collective's memory."

"Or at the very least some directive not to venture too near the Children's territory," Eden added.

"Seven did say that it was possible the memories had been purged from the Collective."

"Why would they do that?" Eden asked.

"The Borg liked to think of themselves as invincible and superior to all other species," Chakotay replied. "Our evidence suggests the Borg were defeated on numerous occasions by the Children of the Storm. That knowledge could have created a cognitive dissonance the Collective might have had trouble reconciling."

"A memory the Borg couldn't live with?"

"An unpleasant thought, isn't it?"

"I'll say," Eden replied, sighing.

"Before we go out there, I'd like to know anything you can tell me about Farkas, T'Mar, and O'Donnell," Chakotay went on.

Eden collected her thoughts, preparing to choose her words carefully. "Farkas has been in command of six different ships in the last forty years. She's as seasoned as they come and one of our most capable diplomats, which is why *Quirinal* was initially chosen to lead the hunt for the Children of the Storm."

Chakotay nodded for her to continue, his face a placid mask.

"T'Mar is young, but good," Eden went on. As much as she wanted to defend all of the choices Command had made in assembling the fleet, she didn't think painting a pretty picture would serve either of them well. "What he lacks in experience, he makes up for with a record of conservative judgments. He's not one to take risks, and with Farkas there to rein him in, he's not my concern."

"That leaves O'Donnell," Chakotay urged her on.

Eden finally settled into her chair.

"As contentious as the choice of who would command *Voyager* in your absence might have been," she said, refusing to ignore any galloping elephants in the room, "it was nothing compared to the spirited debate surrounding Commander O'Donnell's commission."

"Why was that?"

"O'Donnell's background is botanical genetics. There's no one more highly regarded in the field. There was never any question that a ship designed to collect and analyze exotic biological specimens should have him on board."

"But not necessarily in command?" Chakotay rightly surmised.

Eden nodded slowly. "He had seniority, and Willem insisted that after commanding his own research outpost for years, he should be in charge of *Demeter*. But he's not a leader," she finally admitted. "His first officer, Lieutenant Commander Atlee Fife, was selected with the understanding that the lion's share of day-to-day command decisions would rest with him. Both O'Donnell and Fife knew what they were getting into when they accepted their positions, and Willem assured me it would work."

"Do you have reason to believe it's not working?" Chakotay asked warily.

"There were no issues that came to my attention while we were still in contact with *Demeter*," she replied. "Willem led me to believe that everything was proceeding perfectly."

"Would he have lied to you?"

"I can't very well say no, can I?" she replied bitterly.

"Let's assume he didn't, for the moment," Chakotay said. "Although we both want to hope for the best here, if *Demeter* ran into trouble, the only question is, can O'Donnell handle himself in a fight?"

"I don't know," Eden reluctantly admitted. "But Fife could."

Chakotay didn't seem overly enthused by her estimation. "Okay," he finally said, rising to depart.

Eden quickly got to her feet. "I don't want you to think badly of O'Donnell," she said a little defensively. "The man's a genius. And we are lucky to have him with us."

Chakotay stared hard at her. The intensity of his gaze took her slightly aback.

"Permission to speak freely?" he asked.

"Please do," Eden replied, steeling herself.

"I don't think you're worried about my feelings about O'Donnell. I think you're worried that I'm going to judge the rushed and perhaps less than well-thought-out manner in which the entire fleet was assembled so that Willem Batiste could use all of us for his personal agenda."

"This mission was in the planning stages for almost three years," Eden pointed out.

"A lot changed during those years, including the death of billions of people and thousands of Starfleet's best," Chakotay replied, not backing down. "As it stands now, you sent three ships out to make contact with one of the most dangerous species we've ever encountered, and two of the three commanding officers had no business being there. I'm not even sure they're ready to be *here*." After a brief pause, he managed to summon a little self-restraint. "Of course, when I say 'you,' I mean Admiral Batiste. I don't hold you personally responsible for his choices, Captain."

"But I am responsible for cleaning up his messes," Eden finished for him as it dawned on her how arduous a task that would be from this point forward. "And you shouldn't hold yourself back on my account, Chakotay. If there was one person on this ship who might have been in a position to make Willem reconsider his choices, it was me, and I failed spectacularly to do so."

"Forgive me, but based on what little I know of you both, I seriously doubt that," Chakotay replied a little sadly. "And you must not take all of this personally. Sometimes command means letting those under you do their jobs. This fleet needs you, Captain. Your choice to accompany *Voyager* on this mission is starting to feel like a personal quest for redemption. Whatever we're going to find out there, it's probably not going to be pretty, whether you're there or not. If you remain here, and things don't go well out there, at least the fleet won't have lost almost half of its command staff to one questionable call."

Part of Eden knew he was right. She also knew from her readings of his and Kathryn Janeway's personal logs that Chakotay never hesitated to present the big-picture view of the forest, particularly when Janeway found herself obsessed by a particular tree.

"I will take your concerns under advisement, Captain," Eden replied sternly.

"Thank you," he replied, and left without another word.

Once she was alone, Eden did him the courtesy of seriously evaluating what he had said. Though she didn't want to hear it, and his delivery could have been less harsh, he wasn't wrong to raise the issue.

But none of that mattered right now. Almost eight hundred of her people were missing in the Delta Quadrant. She'd be damned before she would send out another hundred and forty and simply hope for the best. Chakotay had experience. He was wise, capable, and for the most part, able to see clearly through his emotions and focus on the task at hand. She didn't doubt his abilities at all. But Eden knew this fleet in a way he couldn't. His choices might be logical, but they would be made in the absence of her level of understanding.

She *had* to go. And she didn't give a damn if he thought she was making this decision for the wrong reasons. Eden knew she was right, and that would have to be enough.

Chapter Eight

FIFTEEN DAYS EARLIER
U.S.S. QUIRINAL

I s this why you have brought us the life?

Farkas knew the universal translator was functioning properly. The first bit of this conversation had made perfect sense. And to keep it on good terms, part of her wanted to simply say yes and figure out later what "life" the alien now inhabiting one of her junior science officers was talking about. But in this case, her word would be taken as a contract, and she couldn't possibly accept terms until she understood exactly what she was being asked.

"The life?" she asked, hoping the alien would clarify.

Instead, the cold, tinny voice said, "The Children of the Storm will accept the life, and you will leave our territory and never return."

"What do you mean by 'the life'?" Farkas tried again.

"The life," the alien replied simply. "Did you not know it would please us?"

"There are hundreds of different species aboard our vessels," Farkas said. "Can you possibly be more specific as to which 'life' pleases you?"

"The simple life."

Farkas could sense frustration growing in the alien's voice, so she opted to try another tack.

"The United Federation of Planets that I represent would be pleased to establish peaceful trade between our peoples, but all life is precious to us, and I cannot agree to leave any life-forms behind until I understand—"

"The Children of the Storm do not negotiate with destroyers of worlds," the alien's voice, sharper now, cut her off.

"I fear you are confusing us with the Borg. Our Federation is based upon peaceful exploration."

"You carry death with you."

Hoping she understood the metaphor, Farkas replied, "We possess weapons and other technology to defend ourselves, should the need arise. But we are not conquerors and we are not destroyers. We do not explore space in the interest of adding to our own resources. We do not take what is not freely given. We respect all life—cherish it, in fact—and seek only to add to our knowledge in a spirit of mutual trust and understanding."

A brief pause from the alien gave Farkas cause to hope that she might have finally made her point.

"We have not misunderstood you or your intentions. We will take the life. You will leave our space or you will cease to exist."

Or not.

"If it is truly your wish that we leave your space, we will do so, and I can assure you that this time, my people will not return. Our only interest was to promote understanding and peace, but if you would rather—"

"*Bridge to Captain Farkas,*" Roach's voice blared over the comm.

"Pardon me for a moment," Farkas said, cursing Roach's lousy timing.

"What is it?" she demanded sharply.

"*You should return to the bridge immediately, Captain.*"

"What's happening?"

"*I'll transfer our visual to the display in your present location.*"

Farkas moved to a nearby screen and watched as a number of the vessels surrounding her ship broke off to add to those that already covered *Planck* and *Demeter,* and moved to within only meters of their shield's outer edge. She entered a command into the panel that would provide a closer view of *Planck.* The individual vessels, dozens of small, deadly, perfect spheres, were now concentrated enough to bump against one another. Where they impacted, they merged, blending into one another. Within seconds it appeared that a solid blanket of energy surrounded *Planck*. The computer also indicated an increase in the power of the resonance field of the new configuration. To the naked eye, the field would have been invisible, but the lights reflected by nearby stars and the three Federation ships made it glimmer with what Farkas could only sense was deadly force.

Restoring the visual so that she could see all three ships, she saw that the vessels surrounding *Demeter* were moving into the same merged energy field. The circle that had surrounded her ship at some distance now showed visible holes, but that hardly comforted Farkas.

Turning back to Ti'Ana, she pleaded, "Please, wait," fearing that diplomacy had already failed.

U.S.S. PLANCK

Only moments ago, the viewscreen before Captain T'Mar had clearly shown the field of what he now believed was a prelude to a battle. *Quirinal* and *Demeter* had been completely surrounded by the small energy spheres, as was his ship. The only disruption to normal operations was the severing of their communications with their sister ships. He knew that Ensign Solonor was trying desperately to restore communications. Before T'Mar could see his way clear to firing on the alien vessels, he needed confirmation from Captain Farkas either that communication with the Children of the Storm had not been established, or that all diplomatic efforts had failed.

Admiral Batiste's orders to all fleet captains on this subject had been crystal clear. *Voyager* had made too many enemies during its first trip to the Delta Quadrant. Precious few of the alien races they encountered ever truly understood the Federation or its principles. T'Mar had heard it privately said that they had acquired the name "ship of death" among many they had never met, but who had heard of the lone ship far from home. Armed conflict was to be a measure of absolute last resort.

As T'Mar's options dwindled, he found a new sympathy for Captain Kathryn Janeway and the crew she had led. Perhaps a bad reputation wasn't so much to risk when the other option was unthinkable.

The image on the viewscreen began to distort. *Quirinal* and *Demeter* against a sea of black were momentarily stretched out into wavy lines before resolving into a field of static.

"Solonor?" T'Mar said, knowing full well the ensign would know the questions that needed to be answered.

"I can't punch through the interference on any channel," he replied distractedly. "We're losing visual as well as communications." Clearly the bulk of his attention was where it should be: on the job at hand.

"There is a change in the configuration of the vessels surrounding us," Lieutenant DeCarlo reported from tactical.

Dread pulled T'Mar to his feet.

"What kind of change?"

"The distinct energy patterns of the individual ships are dissipating, almost as if they are losing coherence."

For a split second, T'Mar wondered if this might not be a sign of weakness and therefore a good thing.

Tregart stood beside DeCarlo, conducting a simultaneous analysis. "The energy field created by the spheres is expanding," he warned.

So . . . not a good thing, then.

"Grim, engage impulse engines," T'Mar ordered. "Let's try and shake them off."

"Helm not responding, Captain," Grim advised.

"Why not?"

"I don't know," Grim replied, clearly frustrated. Like everyone else on the bridge, he was doing two things at once: evaluating an ever changing situation while trying to make their respective stations function properly. "My commands are being accepted, but they aren't producing any results."

"Same here," Solonar echoed, then added, "Our shields are buckling."

"Hull pressure is rising," Tregart added.

T'Mar searched his mind desperately for an alternative.

"DeCarlo, fire all phasers."

"Firing phasers," DeCarlo replied.

"No effect," Tregart reported for him, a few seconds later.

"Bring the warp drive on line," T'Mar ordered. "The formation of our warp bubble might interfere with their energy field."

Grim nodded and shifted his hands to the warp control panel.

His soft "Aye, Captain" were the last words T'Mar heard.

U.S.S. QUIRINAL

Time froze as Farkas caught sight of Ti'Ana's face. It was impassive, unheeding of her plea, and unyielding. A red mote caught in the corner of Farkas's eye, and her face turned automatically back to the display panel. For a moment, the energy field surrounding *Planck* seemed to grow brighter. The computer display of its intensity had registered in crimson digits of warning.

Blood.

And fire.

A low thrum rose into Farkas's ears and her heart began to pound with an intensity that made it feel as if it were looking for a way out of her chest. With each powerful beat, it slowed and the wave of noisy circulation increasing the pressure in her head became a roar of white noise. The image of *Planck* on the screen before her imprinted itself deep into her permanent memory, its pristine white hull wrapped in an angry field of untold power. Farkas wished she could stop her heart, for she knew that with the next beat . . .

Planck vanished, replaced by billions of intensely bright fragments of what looked for a moment like stars. The deck below her feet rocked, almost sending her careening to the floor.

And then the fire was gone, along with the energy field. At least the Federation's people weren't the only dead to be counted. Chunks of wreckage rolled outward in all directions, littering space with horror.

The pounding in her head and chest was joined by warm rage exploding from the center of her body. The waste and senselessness of what she had just witnessed was too much to bear.

"Who the hell do you think you are?" she said, turning back to Ti'Ana savagely. "You just killed seventy people for no reason at all."

"We *will* take the life," was the alien's maddening response. Farkas felt the last of her self-control slipping away.

"Unlike you, we do not take life so lightly. But make no mistake. We do know how to defend ourselves when we have no other choice." After a brief pause, during which she steadied herself, knowing that to act at this moment from the pure fire of her emotions would be unworthy of all who wore the uniform, she called to Commander Roach. "Farkas to the bridge."

With one last glance at Ti'Ana's merciless face, Farkas gave the order she had always dreaded.

"Target all alien vessels and open fire."

Psilakis was still reeling from the sight of *Planck*'s destruction. His stomach turned on him and he feared he would retch. Placing his hands on his knees, he forced himself to swallow the acrid-tasting saliva pouring into his mouth and breathe. The sound of Captain Farkas's voice finally brought him upright again.

"Farkas to the bridge. Target all alien vessels and open fire."

Something small and vengeful in Psilakis shouted with righteous rage.

Damn right.

He had to believe that everyone else on the bridge shared this feeling, inappropriate as it might be. He turned to Denisov at tactical, envious that at this moment he could not be the one to exact reparation from the Children of the Storm. An unexpected shot of adrenaline sickened him again when he realized that Denisov was not responding to the captain's order.

Psilakis scanned the bridge quickly. All the officers stood their posts, and none of them seemed inclined to do their jobs. They all stared passively at the viewscreen, obviously in shock.

"Lieutenant Denisov!" Psilakis shouted to break the spell. "The captain gave you an order."

Denisov remained perfectly still, his hands at his sides.

It took mere seconds for Psilakis to assess the situation. This wasn't shock. This was something else. But for the moment, he didn't care.

Psilakis rushed to Denisov's side, grabbed him by the shoulders, and attempted to force him out of the way. The lieutenant was heavy, but gave ground. Psilakis had barely entered the first targeting solution when an iron arm encircled his neck from behind, constricting his airway.

His hand instinctively fell, reaching for his sidearm. Two more sets of icy hands grabbed his, subduing him.

I'm going to die too, he realized as stars began to flash before his eyes.

But not like this.

With the last burst of energy he could muster, he snapped his head back, meeting what he figured was Denisov's face. The pain of the impact almost finished him, but the move allowed him to gasp one breath. He felt one hand break free and threw his elbow into Denisov's gut just for good measure.

Scuffling of feet told him that reinforcements from the rest of the bridge crew were coming to Denisov's aid. The heel of his palm landed squarely in Jepel's face as Roach's fist met his gut. Psilakis bent forward, and this time, he did lose the contents of his stomach. He barely noticed that it was flecked with blood.

He fought like a wild animal, jerking himself around, landing a punch to Denisov's face that sent him to the ground and barely recovering in time to land a solid kick to Roach's midsection.

In the few seconds he was free, he used one hand to grab his phaser and the other to enter the fire command into the tactical station. Roach was the first to rise, and Psilakis aimed his weapon, set to maximum stun, and fired. Another punch landed in his low back, sending new, unbelievable pain arching up his spine and down his legs, but his hand remained locked around his weapon. He raised it again and began to fire at everything that moved toward him.

Ensign Yuka believed she was dreaming. She remembered dressing for her duty shift half an hour earlier and breaking her fast with a nutrient bar before making her way to the aft shuttlebay. She remembered greeting Mavila as she took over his position at the bay's control panels and configuring the station for her use. She remembered the shipwide announcement of Yellow Alert, followed shortly after by the Red Alert Klaxon.

But all of these memories now felt like someone else's. The lapse of time between them no longer registered in her mind. She couldn't have done them. She must still be asleep in her bunk, imagining that she had started her day but actually stuck in the throes of a dream that would not release her.

It caused her less alarm than perhaps it should have, then, when she watched her right hand move to the shuttlebay door release controls, lower the shields directly outside the bay, and, using her personal security authorization code, open the doors.

These were the actions of someone else. She would never have done this. She had received no orders to open the shuttle bay. She had to be dreaming.

Only when a single sphere filled with brownish gray atmosphere had glided into the bay and come to rest, floating above the deck right before her eyes, did it dawn on her that she had wandered into a nightmare.

Yuka struggled to wake. Her head began to swim and a tingling heaviness almost stilled her breath. Her right hand began to drift toward the interior bay door release. She tried valiantly to hold it back.

But it was no longer her hand.

Someone else had entered her mind unnoticed and locked her away in a small cell from which she could only watch her body's actions.

Watch . . . and fear.

Her attention shifted from the hand she could not control back to the sphere. Where there had been one only moments before, there were now two—no, three. The new spheres were considerably smaller than the first, less than half a meter in diameter. They orbited the larger one like small moons. Soon another joined them, pulling itself off the main sphere with ease.

Her right hand had completed its mutinous task. The doors that would grant the spheres access to the rest of *Quirinal* were now open, and, one by one, the smaller spheres, borne of the single invader Yuka had unwillingly allowed to breach her ship, floated out into the adjacent hallway.

There, the spheres were met by a small contingent of Starfleet personnel. Relief flooded what was left of Yuka's own consciousness. She was certain her people had arrived to deal with the invaders.

Her confusion turned to terror when each sphere was surrounded by a group of officers who calmly led them farther into the ship.

She tried to raise her left hand to alert the bridge of the intruder's presence. The moment she did, a slicing pain shot down her left arm. The more she struggled to move through it, the more it began to blaze.

Trapped in her tiny cell, Yuka began to scream.

U.S.S. DEMETER

Fife had realized he was out of time the moment the alien vessels moved to surround his ship. Url wasn't going to get the slipstream coordinates plotted quickly enough for them to avoid the aliens, and Falto's evasive maneuvers had proved futile. Once they were surrounded by the Children of the Storm, the helm had stopped responding.

He ordered Red Alert and contacted O'Donnell briskly, all but ordering him to the bridge, unwilling to engage in a justification session in front of the rest of the bridge crew. O'Donnell had hesitated when he received Fife's request, but he had agreed to report and was presumably on his way.

Fife could only hope that when the captain arrived, he would at least acknowledge that up to this point his first officer had done exactly what he believed was expected of him. Fife knew his job right now was to remain calm, but between the escalating danger of the situation and the prospect of facing O'Donnell with his failure of judgment—*I should have gone to high warp the minute the aliens were detected and bought us time to make the slipstream jump, Farkas's orders be damned*—he was flush with a heady combination of anger and fear.

The fear had crystallized, however, shoving his rage to one side, the moment the alien's configuration had altered, followed what felt like seconds later by *Planck*'s destruction.

"Status, Ensign Vincent," Fife asked through a throat from which all moisture had fled.

"The ships surrounding ours have merged into a solid energy field," Vincent replied.

There was no room for doubt now. They were about to meet the same ignominious end as *Planck*, and it was Fife's fault.

Unless he could find a way to escape the energy field now holding his ship, he and his crew were going to die, and he presumably had seconds in which to find an impossible solution.

"Commander," Url said.

"What is it?"

"Just before *Planck* was destroyed, the resonance of the energy field surrounding their vessel increased to an extremely high intensity."

"Your point?"

"The energy field surrounding *Demeter* is also shifting, sir, but the frequency is lower."

Fife hardly dared to hope.

"Analysis?"

"We're moving," Ensign Falto reported from the helm, before Url could reply.

"I can see that, Ensign," O'Donnell's voice said softly from behind Fife. "And can we silence that alarm on the bridge? It's an emergency. I get that. But I can't hear myself think."

Fife turned, fully expecting to face the full force of his captain's wrath. O'Donnell would not fail to notice who'd had command of the bridge up to this point and had probably damned them all to destruction.

Instead, O'Donnell stood by the tactical station, one hand at his hip, the other scratching the top of his head as he studied Url's display. Clearly he did not yet appreciate the gravity of the situation. If he had, he would not have looked like a first-year cadet attempting to solve a particularly difficult equation.

Vincent was staring hard at Fife, who nodded in response to his unspoken question. Vincent then silenced the Red Alert Klaxon on the bridge only.

"*Planck* has been destroyed, Captain," Fife began, determined not to display a shred of weakness. There would be plenty of time for guilt and recrimination later if they survived the next few minutes.

O'Donnell's hand left his hip and his forefinger circled a small section of Url's display. "That's the wreckage, I presume?"

"Aye, Captain," Url replied.

"The Children of the Storm approached our position only minutes ago," Fife went on, hating himself for the attempt at justification he heard in the choice of *only* in that statement.

O'Donnell remained silent as he tapped a few commands into Url's station. He then crossed his arms and studied it briefly before finally raising his eyes to meet Fife's.

"Three hundred forty-seven alien ships appeared out of nowhere, at least as far as our sensors are concerned, and we didn't think it might be a good idea to try and leave the area as quickly as possible?" he asked. There was no accusation in his question. He seemed genuinely curious.

"Captain Farkas ordered—that is—" Fife stammered.

"She told you to hold position?" O'Donnell requested clarification.

"She felt it would be too dangerous for the fleet to separate."

"Her estimation of the danger doesn't seem to have been far off," O'Donnell agreed, his eyebrows lifting and his eyes widening briefly. He took a small step down to the center of the bridge and came to rest directly beside Fife.

"The aliens have enveloped our ship in some sort of resonance field, similar to but not exactly the same as the one that destroyed *Planck*," O'Donnell said as if he were reporting on something less serious than the weather. "And we can't break free of this field?"

"That's correct, sir," Fife replied, wondering how it was possible that absolutely no tension registered on the man, "for now. We're working on a solution."

"You might want to take a breath or two, Commander," O'Donnell suggested softly to Fife. Until he said it, Fife didn't realize he'd hadn't inhaled since O'Donnell stepped beside him. "If they wanted us dead, we would be by now," O'Donnell said with a shrug. "The real question is, where are they taking us?"

"We are headed toward the debris field, Captain," Falto reported.

"Do we have some sort of distress buoy?" O'Donnell inquired of Vincent.

"Yes, Captain."

"We should download the logs of the last few hours and drop that here, don't you think?" O'Donnell said in what sounded more like a suggestion than an order. "I mean, I suppose there's a chance we might live to see a few more days and that if we're missed, the rest of the fleet will come looking for all of us."

"*Quirinal* will—" Fife began.

"I don't know, Atlee," O'Donnell cut him off. "From the looks of Url's readings, *Quirinal* has her hands full and might not last as long as we will."

Fife gave a sharp nod.

O'Donnell turned back, his steps directed toward the bridge's exit.

"Launch that buoy, forward every iota of data we have about the Children of the Storm to my lab, and somebody let me know when we get wherever we're going," he tossed over his shoulder. He added, "Good work, everybody. Nice to see you all keeping your heads in a crisis."

"Sir?" Fife asked automatically, certain that O'Donnell must be joking.

"That goes for you too, Commander," O'Donnell replied. At Fife's expression of disbelief, he continued, "The way I see it, we're still alive, and while that may have more to do with the aliens than anything you did, I have no doubt that a more aggressive posture would not have served us well. You did your job. Now keep doing it. And if you think you've found a way to safely free us from this field, I want to know before we commit to anything."

With that, he stepped beyond the doors and they hissed closed behind him.

Fife registered the collective disbelief of the bridge crew. After a silent pause, he took the bridge's center seat and glued his eyes to the main viewscreen.

"Orders, Commander?" Url requested.

"You heard the captain," Fife replied. "Launch the distress buoy, forward the requested data, and continue to monitor the energy field. If it begins to shift at all, I want to be advised immediately. Continue to analyze for weaknesses and actions we might take to free ourselves from it. Falto, report any course alterations."

"Aye, sir," Falto replied.

As Fife's breathing settled, the mass of conflicting emotions writhing within him resolved into numbness. For now, they were still alive. And that was more than he'd hoped for less than five minutes earlier. He found himself absurdly imagining that O'Donnell's casual optimism might be warranted. And he might have been able to accept it, had not the explosion that claimed *Planck* continued to replay in his mind's eye in a terrifying loop.

Chapter Nine

STARDATE 58453.4
U.S.S. VOYAGER

"There you are," Lieutenant Conlon greeted B'Elanna, hurrying to catch up with her in the hall.

B'Elanna turned and practically leveled Nancy with the force of her glare.

"Just back from *Achilles*?" Conlon ventured delicately.

"He's an ass," B'Elanna said without preamble. "He's probably the biggest ass I've ever met, and you didn't think a little fair warning might be in order?"

Conlon tried and failed to hide her smile. This had also been her first assessment of Drafar, but having spent the last three weeks without the need to contact him, she'd almost forgotten the intensity of her initial reaction.

"I try not to speak ill of those who outrank me," she offered.

"I'm scheduled to meet with Waverly aboard *Esquiline* after lunch, and he doesn't outrank you," B'Elanna said. "Anything I should know about him?"

"Waverly's great," Conlon replied without hesitation. "You'll love him. But I still can't put together a complete sentence in front of Captain Dasht."

"Why not?" B'Elanna asked, probably ready to add another officer to her "trouble" list. Not that Dasht or anyone else could possibly beat out Drafar for the top spot, in Conlon's opinion.

"He's gorgeous," Conlon replied. "Like off-the-charts, no-body-should-really-be-that-good-looking gorgeous. Makes me feel like I'm eleven years old just to stand in the same room with him."

Now it was B'Elanna's turn to smile. "I'll see if I can contain myself," she replied wryly.

"I'm sure your husband would appreciate that," Conlon shot back.

"Speaking of . . ." B'Elanna stopped at the door to her quarters. "Tom and I are going to have lunch together before I head over to *Esquiline*."

"I sort of doubt that," Conlon replied more seriously. "Senior staff has been called to the conference room in half an hour."

"See you later," B'Elanna said with a nod, and hurried into her quarters.

To Tom's great frustration, Miral was meticulously smushing all of the peas on her plate when he looked up to see B'Elanna entering.

"It's about time," he remarked before returning his attention to Miral. "No, honey, we're eating the peas, not playing with them."

"She likes them that way," B'Elanna corrected him.

Tom felt an uneasy twinge in his stomach. He'd barely seen Miral in the last two years. How could he possibly be expected to know that? Had he not been counting the seconds until B'Elanna's return, the remark might not have stung so much.

"You ready to take over?" he asked, choosing to let it pass. He didn't have time to exchange fire. The hardening of his wife's face, however, suggested that, like it or not, some fire might be coming.

"I'm sorry I'm a little late," B'Elanna replied, taking her seat and absentmindedly scooping peas onto Miral's spoon without taking her eyes from Tom. "But I didn't think it would be a problem. You could have left Miral with Kula, or just taken her over to *Galen*."

It took even more restraint for Tom to refrain from explaining why neither of those options would have worked; Seven had been late returning Miral for lunch and Tom had already advised the Doctor that Miral would not be coming to *Galen* for the afternoon, given Eden's new orders. Miral had been famished after a full morning of play with Seven, and even though he was running late, he thought he'd chosen well but clearly not well enough. He took a deep breath and tried to rub the tension out of his forehead.

"We've lost three ships, B'Elanna," he explained. "There's a quick briefing and then we're heading off to search for them. Miral's not going to be able to board *Galen,* unless you want to leave her behind with the Doctor for the next few days."

"Absolutely not," B'Elanna replied decisively.

Another deep breath. Tom could have done with a lot less attitude at the moment.

"I assumed as much, which is why I thought we'd just start lunch. But I really do have to go now."

"Because your job is more important than mine?" B'Elanna asked testily.

Tom's restraint met the wall.

"Of course not!" he said, raising his voice, which garnered a look of shock from both his wife and his daughter. Collecting himself a little, he said, "Look, can we do this later?"

"Sure."

In years past Tom might have taken her at her word, but he knew much better now.

"What's the problem?" he asked with as little residual frustration as possible.

"Nothing."

"B'Elanna, this is me trying really hard right now."

The lines around B'Elanna's lips softened. "I know. I'm sorry. I've just spent the last few hours with a man who all but came out and accused me of being a lousy mother because I dare to have a career rather than devoting myself twenty-four/seven to Miral's care."

"Drafar?"

"Drafar," B'Elanna echoed disdainfully. "Eat a little chicken now, honey," she then suggested to Miral.

Tom smiled, glad he'd taken the extra thirty seconds to defuse a tense situation. Watching B'Elanna with Miral, even doing something as mundane as making sure she ate while carrying on a completely separate conversation, was all the evidence he'd ever need of her fitness as a mother. Hell, one look at his daughter was all anyone would need to see that. But he understood B'Elanna's problem.

"You want me to have him killed?" he asked with mock seriousness.

"Yes," B'Elanna replied with real seriousness.

"He's *Lendrin*, honey."

"So?"

"Can I explain later?" he asked.

"Yes." B'Elanna nodded sincerely. "Go."

"And you know I don't think either of our jobs is more important than the other, right?"

"I do."

"It's just a tough day for scheduling."

"Probably won't be the last," B'Elanna said with a shrug.

"We're going to make this work."

"I know. I love you."

"I love you, too," Tom replied, leaning over to give her a quick kiss before planting another on Miral's forehead.

He'd almost made it to the door when B'Elanna called to him again.

"Tom?"

He turned. The tension of the last few minutes had evaporated. B'Elanna seemed suddenly quite composed.

"Hm?"

"You personally oversaw the collection of personnel and materials for the fleet, right?"

"Yes," he replied, a little thrown by the abrupt change of subject.

"Even for *Achilles*?"

"Yeah."

"And you didn't find their cargo unusual in any way?"

Tom thought back. It had been a while, but nothing came to mind.

"No. Are they missing something?"

"No," B'Elanna replied. She smiled and her eyes brightened, as if to assure him that whatever was on her mind was nothing.

"Are you sure?" Tom asked, trying to understand why her face now unsettled him so.

"Absolutely." She nodded too heartily. "Forget I asked. Now don't keep Chakotay waiting."

Tom left their quarters curious. But that was better than angry. He remained curious until he had turned the last moments of the conversation over in his mind a couple more times in the turbolift. Then he got a little angry again.

B'Elanna was lying to him about something.

• • •

Chakotay had discovered a new favorite place in his ready room. Leaning against the rail that separated his desk from a small sitting area, he had a serene view of the stars beyond the long window that ran along the top of the sofa. As he had yet to personalize the space in any way—he hadn't exactly planned on staying when he'd first returned to *Voyager* several weeks ago and had left most of his things back on Earth—the stars were by far the most calming view the room currently afforded.

He wondered if he'd been a little hard on Eden. Not that she couldn't take it, or didn't deserve his complete honesty. However, he might be transferring to her the general, and according to Counselor Cambridge, healthy contempt he'd had for Starfleet Command for years now.

He wished he'd known her longer. Despite the few seemingly open conversations they'd shared, he felt the walls surrounding her were nigh impossible to breach. Of course they didn't need to be close friends in order to work together. But they did need to trust each other, and it was frankly hard for him to do so when Eden held herself at a distance from him.

Trust was a two-way proposition, however, and he considered his words to her in light of the reality that, while open and honest, they'd probably done little to convey the fact that he wanted to trust her, if she would just let him in.

Perhaps if she chose to allow *Voyager* to begin this search alone, it might indicate the seriousness with which she considered his opinions. But he'd known even before he made the suggestion that she would refuse. For all the things he didn't know about her, he could see that she was driven as passionately in her pursuits as everyone he'd ever known who had achieved her rank and status. Problem was, it was hard to tell *what* was driving her, and for reasons he found hard to name, that bothered him.

The door chimed and Chakotay reluctantly turned to meet with Tom, calling out, "Enter."

He was surprised to see Harry standing where he'd expected his first officer to be.

"Harry?" Chakotay said, truly pleased to see him. The last time they'd spoken alone had been days earlier, when Harry had seemed more troubled than Chakotay had ever known him to be. He'd asked for a transfer to *Esquiline* during that conversation, but had agreed to take a few days to think about it. Despite the fact that Tom had indicated that their counseling session with Cambridge had gone well, and Cambridge considered the problem completely solved, Chakotay would not be convinced until he heard it from Harry. The thought of beginning this search-and-rescue mission without the best chief of security he'd known, aside from Tuvok, was not one he relished.

"I know we've got a briefing," Harry began, "but I wondered if I could have a moment?"

"Always," Chakotay said sincerely, stepping down from the sitting area to face him.

Harry seemed unsure of himself, and Chakotay's stomach turned. *How did this distance grow between us in less than a year?* Chakotay knew well that the fault was mostly his, but he didn't know how to begin to bridge it. He had already decided that if Harry still wanted to leave, he owed it to both of them to grant his request.

"I just wanted you to know that I'd like to rescind my transfer request," Harry said, his eyes searching Chakotay's for his reaction.

If he'd expected anything other than relief, he was going to be disappointed.

"Thank you, Harry," Chakotay said, adding warmly, "I simply couldn't imagine this mission without you aboard."

Harry smiled faintly, a little embarrassed.

An uneasy pause followed, which Chakotay hurried to fill. "Do you mind telling me why you changed your mind?"

"I just . . ."

"Obviously, if you'd rather not . . ." Chakotay said, trying to help him out. Small steps in the right direction were a lot better than nothing, and if that was all Harry could give him right now, he'd certainly take it.

"No," Harry said, "it's just that I'm still trying to figure it out."

"Okay."

"It's been a hard year."

"No argument there," Chakotay said, trying to infuse a little lightness into his tone.

"I've felt really out of place, even before the fleet launched."

Chakotay nodded, hoping he would elaborate.

"And I guess I thought a clean slate might solve my problems."

"Sometimes it's good to get a fresh perspective," Chakotay agreed.

"But I think I was really trying to run away from them. And that's not a solution. It's not even me."

It really isn't, Chakotay thought, but remained silent, glad that Harry had come to this realization on his own.

"I've still got stuff to work out, but I think it will be easier if I have my family to help me," Harry finally finished.

"It took you a lot less time to figure that out than it did me," Chakotay offered honestly.

Harry smiled again, not with unrepressed happiness, but with compassion.

"You know," Chakotay continued, "when this part of our mission is over, I'd really like to take some time for you and me to catch up. There's a lot you should know and should really hear from me."

"That would be good," Harry replied.

"Shall we get to work, then?"

"Yes, sir," Harry said, and turned to go with what Chakotay thought was a definite spring in his step. Turning back, he added, "I've studied the pre-mission briefing materials for the three missing vessels, and they initiated some special security protocols in the event they encountered the Children of the Storm. I think we should consider doing the same."

"I've seen those logs as well, and I agree," Chakotay replied. "I've already spoken to Ensign Lasren about remaining on board to facilitate communication, should it be possible or necessary, but Tom should be coordinating our crew transfers of all other known telepaths as we speak."

"How did Gwyn take the news?" Harry asked out of curiosity. *Voyager*'s energetic pilot hated to be left out of anything remotely dangerous.

"Gwyn's a telepath?" Chakotay asked, surprised.

"No, but she's got some empaths in her family tree, and Tom swears she flies by a sixth sense."

"She'll have to stay behind, then."

Harry chuckled, presumably at the thought of Tom breaking the news to her.

As Chakotay followed him out toward the conference room, he decided that he probably didn't deserve the devotion Harry was showing. He'd cut himself off from Harry and the rest of his *Voyager* family for months after Kathryn had died, even while still serving with them. Harry had almost died the last time Chakotay had led him into battle.

Given the gravity of their current mission, Chakotay knew all of them were facing that possibility again. But he would do everything in his power to bring them all through it. Kathryn would have expected no less of him. More important, he expected it of himself.

Seven of Nine stood outside the door to Counselor Cambridge's quarters for a full five minutes before it slid open. Although he had never been one to take personal grooming as seriously as protocol might have demanded, she was shocked by his appearance. His uniform jacket had been discarded and his pants and shirt were rumpled. Dark sweat stains suggested that the shirt was at least a day old. The stubble that peppered his cheeks and chin was longer than she ever remembered seeing, and his eyes were sunken. They displayed a feverish brightness, however, increasing the normal disquieting intensity with which he gazed at her. Though he was clearly seeing her, it almost seemed to Seven that in his mind, he was staring at something else with absolute fierceness.

"Seven?"

She hated to admit it, but in the last few weeks, Seven had grown accustomed to her regular counseling sessions with Cambridge and had begun to look forward to them. His directness could be discomfiting, but she rarely found cause to argue with his analysis. Since they had departed the Indign system, they had begun to discuss at length the dreams she had experienced while the "voice" that the Caeliar left behind when they transformed her Borg implants into a programmable form of matter known as catoms had been trying to convince her that she was only Annika Hansen. These troubling dreams had centered around the figure of a little girl who was part human and part Caeliar, and terrified of the Borg. Although the immediate crisis created by her transformation had passed, and the voice was now silent, Seven believed it would take months if not years of productive discussion before she would be able to make peace with her complicated nature. She had come to the conclusion that Cambridge was well equipped to facilitate this process.

Admitting that she needed help was apparently an indication that she was already better. Accepting help was harder for her.

"I tried to reach you over the comm," she said, "but you did not answer."

Cambridge waited expectantly, probably for her to say something that he felt required a response from him.

Growing unusually tense in his presence, Seven continued, "I will not be able to attend our regular session today as I have been called to a mission briefing." When he only continued to stare, she said, "I assume you are also to attend the briefing, but perhaps you were not notified in time to cancel your appointments."

"I'm not going to the meeting," Cambridge said curtly.

"Oh," Seven said, abashed at his dismissive tone.

"Digesting the sum total of our knowledge of the Children of the Storm is a task requiring mere seconds, and if we find that our missing fellows have escaped an encounter intact, I'm more than prepared to assist with posttraumatic stress issues."

Although some among the crew found the counselor abrupt, Seven usually appreciated this facet of his personality. At this moment, however, she found it rude.

"And our appointment?" she asked pointedly.

Cambridge ran a hand over his stubble and replied, "I forgot."

Seven was dumbfounded. Until this moment Cambridge had always displayed a certain deference to her. He did not coddle her, to be sure; he met her intellect and willfulness head-on. But he had finally made her feel that beneath the rough exterior, he truly cared about her in an entirely professional manner.

Before her now was a side of him she had never seen, and could frankly have lived forever without seeing. Suddenly Seven wondered if he was entirely well.

"You appear to be troubled," she said simply. "Is there anything I can do to assist you?"

"Of course not," he replied. "And I'm not 'troubled.' Just busy."

Seven knew a dismissal when she heard one.

"I apologize for disturbing you," she replied briskly, and turned to make as graceful an exit as she could muster with her heart beginning to pound in her chest and a most unwelcome heat rising in her face.

After too long a pause, he finally called after her.

"Seven?"

She chose to proceed as if she had not heard him.

The briefing had ended and Chakotay was about to leave the conference room and take his place on the bridge when the door slid open and Ensign Aytar Gwyn, his alpha-shift pilot, entered and stood at attention. She was a petite, fiery young woman who wore her hair extremely short and favored a bright blue tint to it.

"Why haven't you reported to *Esquiline* as ordered, Ensign?" he asked abruptly.

"When I was advised of your orders, I asked Doctor Sharak to run a neural scan to confirm what I already knew to be true. While I am half-Kriosian, I've never really shown any strong empathic abilities. According to the doctor, whatever tendencies I have don't even register on the standard PS scale. Given that, I'd like you to reconsider allowing me to participate in this rescue mission."

"We've decided it would be best to err on the side of caution in this case, Ensign, though I do appreciate the initiative you're demonstrating," Chakotay replied in a tone that should have settled the matter.

"But, Captain—"

"You have been advised that we believe the Children of the Storm are capable of compromising humanoids with psionic abilities?" Chakotay asked, cutting her off.

"Yes, Captain."

"You understand the potential risks to yourself and to the rest of us should this prove to be the case?"

"Permission to speak freely, sir?" Gwyn asked with uncharacteristically appropriate deference.

"Go ahead."

"Due respect, I don't think any of us really know what the Children of the Storm are capable of. My understanding is that they chose to communicate through a female telepath. It is possible that this was because of her psionic talents, or because of her gender, or both, or neither. Ensign Lasren is remaining on board to facilitate communication, but if gender is the applicable issue here, that will not be possible. Bottom line, we're assuming we know why the *Aventine*'s Ullian officer was chosen, but that assumption is based on a serious shortage of information. We do know, however, that we will need our best slipstream pilot to navigate our longest journey to date, and that's me. I believe the skills I bring to this mission far outweigh the potential risks." After a moment she added, "Sir."

Chakotay considered her argument. He had to admit, she had a point, both about her abilities, which Tom had already commended in her permanent record, and the reality of what might turn out to be flawed assumptions.

"Very well," Chakotay finally replied.

Each minute that passed as Eden sat to the right of *Voyager*'s center seat seemed like an eternity. The mission briefing with the senior staff had been kept mercifully short. Each department reported ready or nearly ready to depart. Commander Paris was finalizing the last of the crew transfers. Lieutenants Conlon and Kim had settled on the additional security measures they intended to implement, following Captain Farkas's lead, all of which could be accomplished during the eighteen-hour-plus journey they would take to the last known location of *Quirinal, Planck,* and *Demeter.*

Conlon and Kim had returned to their posts and reported ready to get under way. Paris was seated to the left of Chakotay's chair, his eyes glued to the data panel embedded in the arm of his chair. They were only waiting for the arrival of Chakotay.

Eden considered calling to him over the comm. During the briefing, he had not expressed his dissatisfaction with her choice to lead the mission, but Eden felt certain that was for the crew's benefit. She wondered if he was more troubled by concerns for her safety or by the fact that he would have to defer to her for the duration of the mission. Eden had convinced Chakotay to stay on board and resume his command by telling him how much she needed his expertise. Perhaps he now doubted the truth of that or was uncomfortable with the idea of her looking over his shoulder. She did not intend her actions to imply a lack of faith in his abilities, but she could not control how he chose to interpret them.

Finally, Chakotay entered the bridge along with Ensign Gwyn, who took over at the helm. Turning to Paris, he said simply, "Are we ready?"

"Yes, sir," Tom replied, throwing a questioning glance toward Gwyn.

Chakotay softly mouthed the word "Later," then turned his eyes forward, saying, "Let's get out there."

"Aye, Captain."

Eden breathed a silent sigh of relief to be under way.

Chapter Ten

FIFTEEN DAYS EARLIER
U.S.S. QUIRINAL

The delay between Farkas's order to fire on the aliens and its execution seemed to drag on endlessly. Finally, however, she nodded with grim satisfaction as multiple phasers cut through the blackness, destroying several of the Children of the Storm's vessels in one deft stroke. *Demeter* had begun to move out of battle formation, now made irrelevant by *Planck*'s absence, but Farkas couldn't tell if the ship was moving under its own power or courtesy of the energy field that surrounded it.

At least they're still in one piece, she thought, grateful for that much.

Assured that her weapons were as formidable as those arrayed against her, she called out, "Hold fire," and turned again to Ti'Ana.

The young woman's face was contorted with rage.

In a voice so cold she barely recognized it as her own, Farkas said, "It isn't too late to end this. My ship and *Demeter* will leave your space and no one from the Federation will ever return if you will agree to end hostilities now."

The alien speaking through Ti'Ana screeched her response. "You lie! You have shown yourselves to be every bit as destructive as the Borg, and you will meet the same end." She struggled desperately against her restraints, convincing Farkas that if not for them, she would have leaped upon her and tried to rip her limb from limb.

Farkas shook her head sadly and locked eyes with Sal. No words were necessary for the doctor to understand her request. Sal tapped a button on the control panel near the door and a gold force field snapped into existence around the biobed. Confirming the efficacy of the psionic field they had developed, Ti'Ana immediately slumped down, unconscious. Sal then moved quickly to administer a hypo and began to scan her patient.

"It's just her in there," Sal confirmed. "She's going to have a hell of a headache when she wakes up."

If I get all of us out of here in time for her to wake up, Farkas reminded herself.

"Thank you, El'nor," Farkas replied grimly as she exited the room.

Once she had gained the hall outside of sickbay, she called again to the bridge. "Farkas to Roach. We're not out of the woods yet, Commander."

"*Captain, Commander Roach is unconscious,*" came Psilakis's voice in response.

Quickening her steps, Farkas demanded, "What the hell is going on up there?"

"*At this moment, I am the only officer conscious on the bridge. The Children of the Storm can compromise officers who aren't telepaths. Every single officer turned on me when you gave the order to fire on the aliens. I managed to stun them and have control of the situation, but I'd like to transport all of them to our detention cells until the crisis is passed.*"

All of them?

Farkas couldn't believe what she had heard. How could *all of them* have been taken over by the aliens? And, perhaps of greater concern, would Psilakis soon also fall victim?

Farkas's mind reeled as she added this alarming fact to her assessment of her ship's situation. "Make it so," she ordered, then added, "Continue to fire at will upon the aliens' vessels. Take out as many of them as you can. I'm on my way to join you."

"*I could definitely use the company,*" Psilakis replied. "*But be careful, Captain. There's no way to know right now how many of our people—*"

"Aren't *ours* right now," Farkas finished for him. "Understood." She started to turn a corner but immediately stepped back, appalled at the mental snapshot her mind had just taken. At the end of a hallway about twenty meters from her position was the turbolift that would take her to the bridge.

Floating between her and the lift, however, was a small sphere filled with noxious-looking liquid apparently under escort by three of her people.

Oh, no.

"Computer," she said as softly and calmly as possible, "activate emergency force field, deck twenty, section nine." The computer responded instantly, and she peeked around the corner to see that the escort and sphere had been halted behind a wall of blue energy. She then added, "Computer, seal all entrances and exits, deck twenty, section nine." Though she might be locking a few people into their present locations, better that than letting them face this threat unprepared. She tapped her combadge. "Captain Farkas to all hands, intruder alert. Lieutenant Psilakis, scan the ship and contain any alien vessels present behind level-ten force fields."

Hoping that her words were being put into effect immediately, she stepped around the corner. Her officers stood still, their faces blank. Farkas watched as the small transparent sphere floated toward the energy barrier that now divided them. It came right up to the force field, then gently touched it.

She had half hoped that contact with the field would destroy the sphere. Instead, it retreated undamaged, though the murky atmosphere within began to churn. Fear began to gnaw at her insides as the sphere paused. That fear was then justified when the sphere again purposefully touched the force field and held its position through the crackling of energy discharge created by the impact.

She waited until she could see one edge of the sphere begin to breach the field. Without further thought, she turned and began to run, mentally mapping out another route to the bridge and wondering if she would ever actually see it again. Refusing to give in to despair, she tapped her combadge and called out, "Psilakis, our force fields won't hold them, and some of our people are apparently guiding them through the ship. Assemble security forces to engage our people. Phasers set to stun only. We've got to come up with another way to contain them, but do not under any circumstances fire upon any of the alien spheres." Though they were small, the pressure contained within each sphere was immense. The energy shell would be vulnerable to a phaser fired at maximum strength, but the pressure released once the shell was punctured would easily take out half a deck, if not more.

She ducked into an alcove and strained to open a small door that accessed the Jefferies tubes on this level, determined to climb the nineteen decks separating her from the bridge if necessary. The vigor with which she attacked the ladder increased in the seconds that passed without response from the only other officer she knew could help her right now.

"Psilakis!" she grunted as her chest began to heave with exertion and the tops of her thighs started to burn. "Damn it, Lieutenant, what is your status?"

Again, there was no response. Somewhere in the distance, she swore she heard phaser fire.

Throughout the first several minutes of *Quirinal*'s encounter with the Children of the Storm, Engineering Chief Ganley had remained optimistic. His people were keeping their heads, doing their respective jobs with a minimum of chatter. The ship's systems were responding perfectly, and so far, from his position, there was little he could do to aid the captain's efforts beyond maintaining the status quo. It gave him some comfort to know that an armed security detail of ten officers had been positioned at the entrance to engineering, on rotating shifts, for days. As engineering was one of the most sensitive areas of the ship, it made sense, given the number of unknowns they were facing, to have extra precautions in place.

Ganley had begun his own analysis of the alien vessels, however, the moment they had become visible on sensors. Part of this was curiosity, and part of it a desire to find a way to eliminate any threat they might pose without too high a body count on either side.

The computer told him that the energy field that composed the shell of the aliens' vessels was electromagnetic but, at the frequencies displayed, should not have been capable of holding the atmosphere within it in the presence of the high gravimetric fields created by the vessel's motion through space. What was troubling was that the shell obviously did perform this function more than adequately. When he had read the initial reports that concluded that the aliens were traveling through space by the power of thought, he had doubted this premise. It was all good and well in theory, but in practice didn't really seem possible.

He was now being forced to rethink those doubts.

The atmosphere within the spheres obviously maintained the hundreds of life-forms present within them. Clearly those life-forms created the energy shell, but the mechanism by which they did so was unknown. Ganley almost wished there was a way to get a closer look at one of them without venturing out into space. Apart from indicating the existence of hundreds of distinct sentient, noncorporeal beings with high telekinetic powers, the computer was incapable of providing a molecular or submolecular analysis. It seemed that the same energy field that kept them safely contained as they moved through space also effectively shielded them from deep scans. Without knowing more about the actual life-forms, the computer was having a hard time predicting the effects of the numerous hypothetical deterrents Ganley was trying to simulate.

He had begun to toy with the idea of attempting to transport one or more of the aliens on board, should the situation escalate, when the configuration of the alien vessels had shifted. He had recorded every detail of their merging and the destruction of *Planck*. Grim as it was, this should have provided more raw data for the computer to chew on, but apart from recognizing the shifts in resonance frequencies, the computer still could not tell him *how* the Children of the Storm were doing what they did.

Ganley had been absorbed in a number of new theoretical premises when the captain ordered the bridge to open fire. He noted that the aliens were susceptible to phaser fire, even at relatively low power settings, but the sheer number of them and the alacrity with which they adjusted their courses meant that destroying all of them with phasers alone was going to take longer than *Demeter*, which was also completely surrounded, probably had. It seemed, however, that any threat they posed to *Quirinal* could be mitigated.

He had believed this right up until the moment the captain had notified the crew that they had been boarded.

The relative silence in engineering had been replaced by an outbreak of concerned conversations coming from all of his people.

"Everybody stay focused," he called out, as much to buoy their confidence as anything. Federation ships had survived boarding and near assimilation by the Borg. Surely they could handle a few telekinetic spheres.

He quickly began reading the internal scans and analyzing the location and trajectory of each of the intruders. The largest sphere was located in the rear shuttlebay, and six others now moved throughout the ship. They didn't seem to be approaching any particularly sensitive areas, except for . . .

"*Lieutenant Ganley,*" Lieutenant Sanchez's voice sounded over the comm. "*Intruder approaching engineering.*"

"I see that, Sanchez," Ganley replied softly. "I trust you'll hold them off."

"*We'll do our best, sir. Sanchez out.*"

Ganley reconsidered his options. He wanted to hope for the best but prepare for the worst. A few seconds later, he transferred all essential engineering commands to his station and ordered the eleven crewmen he was currently supervising to leave their posts and arm themselves to stand as reinforcements to Sanchez's team.

His people moved swiftly and efficiently into position as Ganley threw every single spare bit of power he had into an emergency field around the warp and slipstream drives, knowing full well that his people were sitting on the closest thing any starship had to a bomb. Should the matter/antimatter core be breached, that would effectively be the end of the story.

Steadying himself and working as fast as possible, he constructed a simulated suppression beam. He'd already heard the captain report that a level-ten force field couldn't hold them. If he was going to protect his core, he had only minutes to create something that would.

"Hold your positions until I say otherwise," Sanchez advised his team. "Take out the sphere's escorts, stun setting only, but do not under any circumstances hit that sphere."

His team knew better than to question his orders, and settled for brisk acknowledgment.

Moments later, two officers stepped into view ahead of a small floating sphere. There was something so serene in its motion, it seemed almost impossible that it was approaching with deadly force.

"Rivin?" Sanchez said softly.

"I've got the one on the left," Rivin barely whispered.

And I've got the other, Sanchez thought. They fired simultaneously, and the sphere's escorts fell to the deck.

The sphere paused briefly, then resumed its forward motion. Sanchez had no idea what it intended to do. There was no way it was getting through the tritanium doors now closed over the entrance to engineering.

"Sanchez to Psilakis. We've got a single sphere approaching engineering. Have you found a way to contain it?"

"*You can't fire on it. Fall back,*" Psilakis ordered briskly.

Sanchez knew Psilakis was right, but he couldn't stomach abandoning his post or Ganley and his people. Still, an order was an order.

"Break off!" Sanchez said. "Move to section twelve."

Everyone began to move, double quick, as Sanchez kept his eyes trained on the sphere. He watched as it came to rest just outside the door to engineering and the atmosphere inside it began to churn.

He had no idea what to make of this development, but every cell in his body told him that it wasn't good. His team was eighty meters down the hall, and he suddenly wondered if that would be far enough.

"Ganley, get all of your people away from the main door," Sanchez ordered, then turned to run.

He had just reached his team when an explosive force struck him from behind and sent him face forward onto the deck.

He inhaled sharply on impact and immediately felt his lungs begin to burn.

Phinn hadn't started to worry until he'd heard the captain's announcement that the ship had been boarded. Ever since he'd been a cadet he had used boring tasks like guard duty as an opportunity to force his mind to solve complex problems. Having completed the harmonics algorithms for his matrix, he was busy mapping circuits when the captain's voice had alerted him to the fact that he really should be paying attention to the task at hand.

A sharp inhalation from Sadie caused him to turn.

"What?" he asked.

Her wide eyes were glued to her tricorder. She nodded for him to look. A single sphere and two crewmen were approaching two hundred meters from their present position.

Phinn immediately tightened his grip on his phaser and turned in the direction from which the sphere would approach. After a moment's consideration, however, he turned back to Sadie.

"They're not coming for us," he whispered, hoping to calm her. Her face had gone white and telltale beads of perspiration trickled down her forehead.

"You can't know that!" she hissed back.

"Between us and them is engineering," Phinn replied calmly. "If you were an alien trying to take the ship, what would you target, a couple of junior crewmen or the heart of the ship's power?"

Phinn noted that after considering his words, her breath was coming in a longer, deeper rhythm.

"They don't know we're junior crewmen," she offered.

"Just calm down, Johns," Phinn suggested as soothingly as possible. "There's a team of Starfleet's finest security officers ready to engage them at the doors to engineering right now. They don't stand a chance."

Sadie's eyes narrowed. "We should move into position to back them up."

Phinn knew she was right, though he honestly believed he was of more use to *Quirinal* alive and continuing to build his matrix than risking a suicidal run toward the aliens. Still, he knew his duty.

"On three then?" he said.

Sadie nodded.

"One," she said.

"Two," Phinn added.

"Wait," Sadie said sharply.

Angling her tricorder for Phinn to see, both noted the security team retreating from the area.

They exchanged puzzled glances.

Phinn then returned his eyes to the tricorder, studying the team's movements. When they had come to rest, he asked, "What's in section twelve?"

"Weapons and emergency supply storage," Sadie replied.

Phinn hadn't heard a single shot fired, so it was hard to imagine what other weapons they might need. He was, however, willing to grant the security team the benefit of the doubt. Still, since they were armed only with their phasers, the chances that he and Sadie could do much good had just gone from slim to none.

What the—

An earsplitting concussive burst made it impossible for Phinn to finish that thought.

• • •

Farkas knew she needed to get to the bridge, but the sound of weapons discharging inside her ship made that a secondary concern.

She stepped out of the Jefferies tube on deck seventeen, section one, and moved as swiftly as she could toward the sounds of conflict.

Rounding a corner, she noted that at the end of the hall, a group of security officers were standing with their backs to her. She hurried toward them, but they were so focused, none of them noticed her approach. She had almost reached them when she caught sight of Sanchez running for all he was worth toward them.

A riotous, violent explosion shook the deck, sending Sanchez down and pulling Farkas's feet out from under her. The captain landed hard on her back, and for a moment, the pounding and ringing in her ears made her head swim and her stomach churn.

An acrid smell assaulted her nose as a wave of intense heat washed over her. She pulled herself up off the deck and held her breath until she had gained the supply locker and grabbed an emergency rebreathing mask. She noted that the others were assisting Sanchez into a mask of his own, though he coughed blood and writhed in agony.

"What was that?" Farkas wheezed through her mask to the nearest officer.

When he turned to reply, she saw the naked fear on his boyish face.

"They've accessed engineering, sir," he replied.

The thought terrified Farkas as she paused to prioritize the dangers she and her crew now faced. If one of the spheres had detonated, and nothing else could account for such an explosion, there would be massive damage to the area directly around engineering and possibly to the decks immediately above and below. The captain forced her mind to focus on the noxious odor that had sent her instinctively reaching for a mask. It was more than burned conduit and melting deck plates. *Coolant,* she realized . . . which meant engineering had been breached, but clearly not destroyed. If it had been, all of them would be dead right now. Her exposed flesh felt as if the heat still rolling down the corridor was searing it.

She grabbed the boyish officer by the arm and said, "Get Sanchez to sickbay and regroup at the nearest designated safety zone. Wait for further orders from Psilakis before you proceed."

Farkas then turned back to the locker and saw three pressure suits remaining. She grabbed one and struggled to pull it on, worried that each second she lost now was one her ship could not spare—not if the aliens had reached the heart of her ship.

Chapter Eleven

STARDATE 58454.5
U.S.S. VOYAGER

The ground beneath Chakotay's feet had been rising steadily for the last half kilometer. He slowed his steps to gather a few longer, deeper breaths before starting up the steep hill face that marked the center of this trail. His climb would continue once he'd reached its peak, but the rises would once again become more gradual. He quickened his pace, breaking into a light jog as he attacked the hill. Loose dirt shifted beneath his steps, so he began to reach for the sturdier rocks jutting out of the ground. As his breath began to come in quick bursts, he mentally pictured the view that would soon be his reward. From the top of the hill a lush green valley dotted with waterfalls should provide both beauty and peace, as well as a calm place to collect his thoughts before tomorrow's work would begin.

Voyager was en route to the last known coordinates of the three missing ships. Nine hours had passed since they had engaged the slipstream drive, and nine more were required before they would reach their destination. Chakotay had decided a few hours on the holodeck would help him clear his mind before he tried to sleep.

A sharp spasm caught in his side as he considered how much shorter his first trip to the Delta Quadrant would have been if they'd had a slipstream drive. Still, even with all of its difficulties, Chakotay knew now that he wouldn't have traded a minute of that journey. The memories he kept in his heart of the long days and nights forming some of the most meaningful relationships of his life with his crew and, of course, Kathryn, were tended like the treasures they truly were. On this night, he would have wished more than anything to see his former captain just a few steps ahead of him, racing him to the top where they could share a few moments of quiet reflection and perhaps strategize about the mission he was now facing.

Kathryn was so real in his thoughts as he took the last long strides, reaching out for a large boulder that signaled the peak, that when he saw two black boots jutting out from the hill's edge, he almost stopped short. His momentum carried him up, however, and he gained the crest to find Captain

Eden standing above him, hands on her hips, staring out at the magnificent landscape below.

Breathing heavily, Chakotay took a few steps past her to allow his breath to calm before turning to see why she had interrupted his last waking hour this night.

"You actually find this relaxing?" she asked when their eyes finally met.

Chakotay dropped his hands to his knees and raised his shoulders to give his diaphragm a little more room to work before replying, "I do."

"Seems to me the best part is standing right here," she said thoughtfully.

"No," he decided. "The view's hardly worth it if you haven't earned it."

Eden nodded, considering this. "To each his own."

"Of course." Chakotay nodded, rising back to his full height. "Was there something you needed, Captain?"

Eden began to pace around the edge of the peak, her eyes glued firmly to the ground, though Chakotay sensed this was less to keep her footing than to collect her thoughts.

Finally she said, "I can't sleep."

"It's understandable," Chakotay replied patiently. "Tomorrow's a big day."

Eden favored him with a quizzical glance. "Actually, I can rarely sleep," she admitted.

"Even when you haven't lost three ships in the Delta Quadrant?"

"Especially then. My mind just won't settle. I've tried various relaxation techniques, strenuous exercise, even a few medications, but nothing seems to work."

Although Eden wouldn't have been his first choice for company right now, he could easily recognize when a fellow officer needed to think out loud. Eden's burden was a lonely one, and it wouldn't cost him much to offer to share it.

"Walk with me," he suggested before turning his steps toward a long, narrow path that led to the next short climb.

"I don't want to slow you down," she began to demur.

"You won't," he promised her.

Eden fell into line behind him, stepping gingerly down the path.

"What do you think we're going to find tomorrow?" Chakotay asked, cutting right to the heart of their shared fears.

"Worst case, debris," Eden said bluntly.

"How likely do you believe that to be?"

"The Children of the Storm stated that we were *not* to violate their territory again," Eden said. "And they did manage to destroy thousands of Borg cubes, so it's not outside the realm of possibility that our ships were detected and met the same fate."

"If that's the case," Chakotay said stoically, "then we'll accept it and move on."

"You say that like it will be easy."

"There's nothing easy about it," he assured her, his voice hardening a bit. "But it's all there is when that is the reality you are facing."

Eden's silence suggested she knew this to be all too true.

"There's something I think you should know, Chakotay," Eden said. Chakotay noted that even though this path wasn't particularly demanding, she was already becoming a little winded.

"What's that?" he asked, not turning back, but slackening his pace a little.

"Willem was the one who originally concocted this mission, over Kathryn Janeway's strenuous objections, I might add. But he did it with my full support."

No one had ever confirmed this; however, Chakotay had always assumed it to be true. He remained silent, hoping she would come to the point quickly. He wasn't sure why Eden would bring this up now, and frankly, he wasn't in the mood to pick at the scars of a wound that were so recently healed.

"Looking back, Willem was right to fear what the Borg might do, though his obsession with them is certainly easier to understand knowing that he was a member of Species 8472."

"You didn't have to be an alien spy to know that the Borg were a threat," Chakotay said flatly.

"The thing is, the more I think about tomorrow, the more I begin to believe that Admiral Janeway was right too."

This stopped Chakotay in his tracks. Inhaling sharply, he turned to face Eden. Twilight was gathering around them. He had designed the program so that he would reach the hike's end at sunset. With Eden along, it appeared he was going to miss that.

"How so?" he asked as evenly as possible.

Eden stopped, her ebony skin turning her face to an unreadable mask in the fading light.

"With or without the Borg, maybe there are some parts of the galaxy that are just too dangerous for us to explore right now."

"Kathryn said that?" Chakotay asked, taken aback. It didn't sound like her.

"Why else would she have been so dead set against this mission?" Eden wondered aloud. "It had to have been more than sparing her former crew another extended tour of the area. She gave her life in an attempt to prevent it," Eden finally said, her voice heavy with trepidation.

Chakotay knew this, though the knowledge had been given him in confidence. The thought suddenly struck him that Eden might somehow blame herself for Kathryn's fate.

"Permission to speak—" Chakotay began, but she cut him off before he could finish the request.

"Don't ever ask me that again," she said testily.

"I was simply—" he tried again.

"No," she admonished him. "I appreciate the courtesy, but somehow every time you ask permission to speak, I get the feeling you just want me to prepare myself to hear something unpleasant. You and I are leading this mission for the next three years. I trust that whatever you have to say is worth hearing. I have to, because apart from you and Counselor Cambridge, there's really no one else for me to confide in. So can we drop a little of the formality going forward?"

Chakotay was actually relieved to hear this.

"Of course," he said, stopping short of calling her by her given name. Taking a deep breath he went on, "I just wanted you to know that though Kathryn went out to investigate that cube ostensibly to assess its potential threat and the necessity for this mission, a pack of ravenous weasels couldn't have kept her away from it."

Eden chuckled in spite of herself. "Really?"

"You had to know her," Chakotay said with a nod. "The Borg have driven more than a few of Starfleet's finest to recklessness. Even after we'd managed to escape them the first time we encountered them in the Delta Quadrant, she couldn't leave well enough alone. There were times she almost seemed to go out of her way to antagonize them, despite the risks to herself and the crew. She always had her reasons, mind you. She wasn't totally irrational on the subject. But the minute that cube appeared in the Alpha Quadrant, I could have told you she'd be on her way to see it for herself."

"You know this how?" Eden asked sincerely.

Chakotay paused. He'd never shared this much personal information with Eden, and wasn't sure he was ready to start. But she was right that they were going to have to begin to build some bridges between them for the next three years to work. *Probably for the next three days to work*, he admitted. There was no time like the present to begin.

"For months after Kathryn died I blamed myself for her death. I convinced myself that if I'd been there, she never would have taken such a foolhardy risk. But that was my pain, lying to me. Kathryn always did exactly what she wanted to do, never more nor less. She would never have been satisfied with anyone else's reports about that cube. She would have known in her gut that somebody had missed something, and short of its destruction, nothing could have assured her that it truly posed no threat. Taking her choices on myself was wrong. It was disrespectful of the woman she was. And what's more, had she survived the Borg attack and witnessed the devastation firsthand, and Command still decided to launch this fleet, she would have been first in line asking for the right to lead it."

He paused to see if his words were sinking in. Eden's face was inscrutable in the gathering gloom.

"Kathryn didn't make decisions from a place of fear. She knew too well that most things worth doing came with their fair share of risks, and she met those dangers with her head held high. She might have questioned Command's choice to launch this fleet with so many other pressing priorities in terms of rebuilding the Federation after the attack, but once the determination was made, she would never have shrunk from it. Just as the people she led all those years didn't shrink from it when they were ordered on this mission."

Eden stepped toward him into a patch of light cast by the waning sun. Free of the shadows, he saw a new sense of relief on her face.

"I wish I'd known her better," she said softly.

Chakotay nodded.

"Would she have been able to sleep tonight?" Eden asked.

"She'd be on her third pot of coffee by now," Chakotay replied honestly. "But, you never know. We might find our three ships with damaged drive systems, just waiting for us to show up."

Eden tried this thought on for size.

"Possibly," she agreed. "Was Kathryn also an eternal optimist?"

"She tried to live in hope," Chakotay replied. "She had to." *And taught me to do the same,* he refrained from sharing.

Eden looked for a moment as if something else had come to her mind that she wanted to say. Chakotay watched as she intentionally raised her internal shields and pulled away from him.

"Computer, arch," she said softly as a doorway appeared out of thin air hanging over the side of the trail.

"Thank you, Chakotay," she said sincerely. "I think I will try and get a little sleep now. But it will be less troubled than it might have been," she added.

"Good night, Captain," he replied.

Once she had gone, he continued to the top of the last hill, wondering as he walked less about what she had shared with him, and more about what she was clearly still hiding.

"Daddy, read!" Miral shouted petulantly.

"Daddy is still working, my love," B'Elanna replied

firmly. "Harry is going to read you your bedtime story tonight."

Harry had actually been looking forward to spending a little time with B'Elanna and Miral once he went off duty, and had enjoyed watching Miral climb all over the furniture with her last burst of energy, clearly fighting sleep for all she was worth.

"Which story do you want?" B'Elanna asked in a tone that would brook no refusal.

Miral huffed a little, eyeing Harry like the enemy before saying softly, "Timmy Targ."

"*Timmy and the Targ* it is," B'Elanna agreed readily, selecting an aged and tattered book from a small box of Miral's toys. "Now let's get you tucked in."

Miral fell in line behind her mother and actually accepted being put to bed rather gracefully. Once she was under her covers and had had three good-night kisses from her mother, Harry set himself opposite her and gingerly opened the book. It was a story he'd never seen before, and the copy was so ragged he worried it would fall to pieces in his hands.

"He's doing it wrong!" Miral called to her mother, who had almost made it out of the room before this outburst. Harry, who had yet to read a word, only looked up at B'Elanna with chagrin.

B'Elanna turned back and obviously saw the problem. "You have to sit next to her, Harry, so she can turn the pages," she advised him seriously.

"Oh," Harry said quickly, moving to settle himself beside the little girl. "Is this better?"

"Read," Miral ordered with a yawn.

B'Elanna was clearly stifling a giggle as she left the room

and Harry dutifully did as ordered. He was only three pages into Timmy's adventures when Miral yawned again with what looked like her entire face, turned away from him, and closed her eyes. Harry remained beside her for a few more minutes, basking in the sight of innocent slumber, before quietly rising and returning to the living room, where B'Elanna sat studying a stack of padds.

"Did she make it through Timmy saving little Tusk?"

"No," Harry replied, suddenly wondering what danger was going to befall poor Tusk. "Timmy was just taking Tusk for a walk when she fell asleep."

"Figures," B'Elanna said with a smile. "She was totally wiped out."

Harry allowed the last hour to replay in his mind, trying to match B'Elanna's description with the child who had been scaling the walls fifteen minutes earlier.

"She doesn't get that testy unless she's *really* tired," B'Elanna assured his dubious gaze.

Harry settled himself next to B'Elanna, putting his feet up on the small table that sat before the couch and leafing through the book to quickly learn Timmy's fate. As he did so he said, "Can I replicate another copy of this book for you? I think this one is pretty much done for."

B'Elanna shook her head, taking the book from him. "Thanks, but no." She spent a few moments gently turning pages, then said, "You won't find it in our databases anyway. It's one of a kind."

"An antique?" Harry asked.

"Not quite yet." B'Elanna smiled. "My father wrote it for me when I was about Miral's age. There weren't a lot of Klingon books for children, and none that featured a human character with a Klingon pet. So he created this. I think he was hoping it would help me understand that I wasn't so unusual."

"Did it?"

"I don't remember," B'Elanna replied, her eyes misting up a bit. "I'd actually forgotten all about it until we got back to Earth. My dad really wanted me to get in touch with him, and he sent a package for me to Owen and Julia's with a letter. This was part of it."

"Wow," was all Harry could think to say. He knew B'Elanna's relationship with both of her parents had been difficult. He took a moment to realize how lucky he'd been to have his own adoring mother and father.

"Miral loves it," B'Elanna said wistfully.

"Does she know where it came from?"

"Not yet," B'Elanna replied. "I think she's a little young to hear about my tortured family history."

"She really is a beautiful little girl, B'Elanna."

B'Elanna smiled more openly now. "Thanks."

"So what's it like being fleet chief?" Harry asked to direct the conversation to more neutral territory.

"Fantastic," B'Elanna replied, setting her own work aside and taking a long sip of *raktajino*. After a moment, she added, "For the most part."

"For the most part?"

"It's going to be the hardest job I've ever done," B'Elanna said, "except for one, of course."

"It should be harder than running *Voyager*'s engine room," Harry said. "But you'll have access to a lot more resources than you used to."

"I wasn't actually talking about *Voyager*," B'Elanna chided him gently. Seeing Harry's blank face, she added, "I was talking about being a mother."

"Oh, right," Harry said, his face reddening a bit.

"It's okay, Harry," B'Elanna said lightly. "You can't really understand it until you do it. Someday it'll be your turn."

"You think?"

"I know," B'Elanna assured him. "You have 'potential great father' written all over you."

"And that's something that's attractive to a woman?" Harry teased.

"To the right woman, yes."

Harry wondered silently if she was talking about Nancy Conlon. He hadn't yet had a chance to ask her out, but he'd noticed B'Elanna's ham-handed attempts to bring the two of them together. He'd already decided that he and Nancy should figure out on their own if there was really anything there before doing too many "couples" things with B'Elanna and Tom. Much as it sucked to break up with one person, it was a lot harder when too many others felt they had a stake in the game.

"Tell me something," B'Elanna interrupted his thoughts.

"Shoot," he replied evenly, hoping it wasn't a question about Conlon.

"What are we really doing out here?"

Harry paused, unsure of what she was asking.

"You mean the fleet?"

B'Elanna nodded solemnly.

"You heard the admiral," Harry began, then remembered that B'Elanna hadn't actually been aboard when the fleet launched. "Oh, no, you didn't."

"Let me guess," B'Elanna said. "We're exploring the unknown and hoping to make lots of new friends?"

"Sort of," Harry replied. "We're also trying to make sure that the Borg are really gone."

"Eden granted me access to the files we have on the Caeliar. Seems to me they were pretty clear about their intentions."

"Yes," Harry agreed, "but it's not the kind of thing Starfleet is going to take their word for. The Borg killed billions of people in their last attack. We can't risk another, now or ever."

"But it seems like a lot of resources to risk on an intelligence gathering mission," B'Elanna argued. "The devastation in the Alpha Quadrant and Starfleet's losses were massive. You'd think we might be more useful closer to home, helping with the rebuilding efforts."

"We're not the last nine ships the Federation has, B'Elanna."

"Nine," B'Elanna said softly.

"We're going to find the other three," Harry said assuredly.

B'Elanna stared ahead, lost in thought.

"What are you worried about?" Harry finally asked.

"I don't know," B'Elanna replied. "I just think there's more to it than either of us knows right now."

"Why?"

B'Elanna shook her head, but did not meet Harry's eyes. "I can't say."

Something in her tone made Harry wonder if she really *couldn't* or *wouldn't*.

Lieutenant Devi Patel, *Voyager*'s chief science officer and resident xenobiologist, had never been inside Counselor Hugh Cambridge's quarters. She'd never actually had cause to seek out his services, and looking about her now, she wondered if she would ever want to. Though she didn't think of herself as overly fastidious, the current state of the counselor's quarters made her wonder how anyone could possibly think, let alone help people, in the middle of such a mess.

Padds, bits of stone and parchment, odd relics and statues, large astrological maps, and what looked like scraps of ancient texts were strewn everywhere. She didn't bother to try and pick her way across the room when she entered. Instead, she stood placidly in the doorway waiting for the counselor, who was currently on his hands and knees poring over some sort of diagram and making careless notes with a heavy black chalk of some kind, to address her.

After a few moments he looked up and seemed almost surprised to see her there. His eyes glowed with feverish intensity, and he looked like he hadn't changed his uniform or shaved in days.

"Ah, Lieutenant," he greeted her brightly. "Come in, come in." He rose and crossed to her, stepping over the detritus in his way.

"You wished to see me?" Patel asked, remaining firmly where she was.

"I did," Cambridge replied, nodding several times. "You are our xenobiological specialist, yes?"

"I am." Patel didn't know what unnerved her more, the utter disarray of the room or the almost manic frenzy of the man whose job it was to keep the rest of the crew on an even keel.

"Excellent," Cambridge said, clearly oblivious to her reticence. "And you did your thesis on the most ancient known humanoid species."

"The Progenitors, yes," Patel said, nodding warily. That thesis was over a decade old, and she couldn't begin to imagine his interest in it now.

"Why did you conclude that they are not the common ancestor they stated themselves to be?" he asked.

"You read my thesis?" Patel asked, shocked.

"In less than ten minutes," Cambridge replied. "Probably not your best writing, but you were young," he added. "As it is, however, you stand among only a handful of other scientists in your conviction that many of our galaxy's humanoid species do not, in fact, share this mutual ancestor."

Patel tried and failed to hide her shock. The paper she had written was hundreds of pages in length, and she doubted seriously it could be fully digested by anyone in less than a few hours. Searching her memory, she finally replied, "As I said, deeper analysis of the various strands of DNA encoded into their message don't sustain that argument. There are obvious similarities, but there are also vast differences which, to my mind, cannot be accounted for by simple evolutionary or environmental factors. To me this suggests that no single species could possibly have been the predecessor of all humanoids."

Cambridge stared so hard at Patel that she almost wanted to take a few steps back. Only the door behind her prevented her from doing so.

"And you still stand by this claim?"

"May I ask why you need to know, Counselor?" Patel summoned the courage to ask.

"You may not."

His response was so sharp, Patel almost felt she had been slapped across the face.

"I admit, it's a charming notion, this idea that a single species gave rise to us all," Patel said evenly. "But we do not possess a single example of this ancient DNA. Working backward from the DNA of various humanoid species, there are too many missing links to state unequivocally that we all arose from the efforts of a single species. I agree it is possible that some may have, but we will never be able to prove it, given only what the Progenitors left for us in their computer code."

"I think you might be wrong about that."

Equal parts annoyed and curious, Patel replied, "What is your evidence?"

Cambridge smiled broadly. "Glad you asked."

Returning to his desk, he tossed several padds aside before selecting one and offering it to her. Patel took it, feeling a small tingle of excitement at the prospect of reviewing data that might actually settle a debate that had been raging ever since Captain Jean-Luc Picard had followed a trail of DNA evidence that led to a message from the supposed Progenitor race.

Patel studied the padd for a few moments. It contained a single genome of an unnamed female, and at first glance, the sequences that must have aroused Cambridge's curiosity and caused him to seek out a more expert opinion were quite interesting. Naturally, a great deal of the diversity among these sequences was attributable to the fact that they were distinct to each individual, but taken as a whole, it was immediately obvious to Patel that there was something unique about this particular genome. But almost as quickly as her enthusiasm elevated, another unexplainable gut reaction tamped it down. There were few fields as unequivocal as science, particularly genetic studies, but the truly great members of the field had followed their instincts to new discoveries as much as the facts of the evidence before them. Patel had never experienced a moment like this, but the more she looked at the relevant sequences, the more they struck her as somehow unbelievable.

Cambridge was waiting expectantly for an analysis, and Patel did not wish to disappoint him, but she didn't want to lie to him either.

"May I ask where you obtained this sample?" she asked as neutrally as possible.

"You may not," he replied.

Patel lifted her eyes to his. "I'm sorry, Counselor," she finally said, "but there is no way this is a sample of Progenitor DNA."

"I didn't say that it was."

"No, but you implied it," Patel began.

"Would I be correct in stating that these particular sequences suggest a common humanoid ancestry that predates similar comparative sequences?"

Patel hesitated, but only a moment. "No, Counselor, you would not."

"Explain," Cambridge demanded.

"I can't."

Cambridge appeared to be genuinely shocked. "Why not?"

"Because while on the surface what you are saying could be true, there is something wrong here."

"What?"

"I don't know. I just don't believe what I'm seeing could possibly have been part of natural selection. It's too perfect, if that makes sense."

"Hardly."

"I'm sorry," she went on. "It's like looking at a really good copy of an ancient sculpture. Everything about it seems right, but taken as a whole, it's wrong."

"Are you saying that this sample could not be that of a living human being?"

"No," Patel replied. "But I have a hard time believing it's one that evolved naturally."

"Thank you, Lieutenant," Cambridge said, clearly dismissing her.

"If I can assist you in any way, Counselor . . ." Patel began hesitantly.

"Your thesis showed a spark of original thinking, Lieutenant," Cambridge seemed to commend her. "I see now, however, that the spark did not, in fact, ignite a flame."

With that, he turned away and retreated to a large stack of padds, which he unceremoniously swept from the surface of his desk before seating himself and setting to work on his main data terminal.

When Patel hesitated, he added, without looking up, "You may go."

Devi Patel could not remember ever having been so insulted.

Commander Tom Paris stared at the main viewscreen, the constant pulsing and regular gyrations of the slipstream corridor before him lulling him into a more relaxed state than he usually enjoyed while on duty. He had agreed to take the watch for Chakotay, knowing it would cost him precious sleep and more precious time with B'Elanna and Miral, but neither he nor the captain were comfortable with the idea of leaving the command to a less senior officer on this night. Harry was set to relieve him in a few hours, after which Chakotay would begin his shift a little early as well.

Tom spared a glance at the two empty seats on either side of him. After serving aboard *Voyager* for ten years with only two command seats in the bridge's center, it was still a little odd to see that third seat. It had been added for the admiral of the fleet or mission specialist's use and now belonged to Captain Eden.

As there was absolutely nothing else to focus on for the moment, Tom's mind began to wander, traipsing through memories of the years that had led him to this moment. A padd on the arm of his chair contained a letter he was constantly updating: a letter to his mother that would only ever be sent in the event of his and/or Miral's death. In some ways it felt like tempting fate to write it, but the one thing Tom had sworn to himself when he agreed to allow B'Elanna to fake her and Miral's death in order to end the quest of the Warriors of Gre'thor was that he could lie to his mother in the short term, but not forever.

His heart broke when he imagined her rambling about his family home alone. The death of his father had taken something from her nothing would ever replace. A light had gone out forever, and the only thing that might have soothed her was the presence of her only granddaughter. But fate, dressed as a sect of Klingon lunatics, had decreed that Julia Paris must also be denied this comfort for now, for her own safety and Miral's.

Tom had decided then that he would create a history of all the things Julia was now missing and that, should she outlive them, she would at least one day know the truth of Miral's life, as best he could tell it.

The first part of the letter was an apology for the lengths to which he and B'Elanna had gone to protect Miral. He had been truly happy the day he'd been able to add to it the news that despite their earlier intentions, B'Elanna had elected to remain with Tom and Miral on *Voyager* for the duration of their mission in the Delta Quadrant. Where any of them would go once the mission had ended, he still did not know. But he didn't trouble himself worrying about it now. Tom knew too well that the best laid plans often went awry, and he was content to allow the future to unfold, rather than trying to bend it to his all too fallible will.

I learned today that your granddaughter prefers her peas to be smushed, Tom wrote, smiling at the recollection. Nearly everything Miral did was a tiny treasure to him now, after missing so much of her early years. *I also learned that no amount of patience is too much for a three-year-old. She has to do everything for herself. Especially things that would go a lot quicker if she'd just let you do them for her. She crinkles her nose when she's working particularly hard on any task, like mashing up the aforementioned peas.*

I was so worried when B'Elanna and Miral finally got to Voyager that Miral wouldn't remember me at all. Now it almost feels like we were never apart. She's commandeered me for bedtime story reading, and between you and me, it is my favorite part of the day.

We're about to begin a search-and-rescue mission. B'Elanna and Miral are here, of course. Now I'm wondering, though, if I wouldn't feel better if I'd left them behind for this one. I think these decisions are only going to get harder as we go. There's nothing I wouldn't do to protect them, but am I being selfish in wanting to do that in person? I don't know what we're going to find tomorrow, but if it managed to destroy our three missing ships and we meet the same fate . . .

Here, Tom paused and finally closed the file for the time being. He tried to keep his words light, knowing that they were meant to offer his mother glimpses into his happiness, but more often than not these days, they drifted into darker territory. He had made the choice to leave everything but his wife and daughter behind, and only now understood the price of that choice. Worse, when he considered that by bringing his daughter into this quadrant, he might be exposing her to greater danger, a terrible sense of anxiety welled within him. The fleet had been out here for a little more than three weeks, and it was possible that their numbers had already been reduced by a third. Had he been risking only his own life now in continuing this mission, he would have been able to justify his choice. But he was also risking Miral's.

Should he ever have cause to send this letter while he still lived, he wondered now if he would be able to find for himself the forgiveness he would surely be asking of his mother.

In his heart of hearts, he doubted it.

Chapter Twelve

FIFTEEN DAYS EARLIER
U.S.S. QUIRINAL

A harsh, bitter stinging sensation brought Ganley to consciousness. He coughed automatically, gasping for fresh air, only to choke on his next inhalation. Forcing himself to hold his breath, he crawled through a wasteland of chunks of metal and past various bodies, many of which were also struggling to move, until he reached the emergency masks that lined the wall behind the core. His hands felt like lead and stars were dancing before his eyes, yet he managed to strap a mask in place and finally take a full breath of clean air. His lungs revolted, sending up brownish sputum, but after a few deep breaths, he found himself able to take in the wreckage that had once been main engineering.

The most obvious alteration was the absence of the large doors that separated the room from the outer hall. Those doors had been reinforced with tritanium. It was hard to believe that the explosion that had turned them into roiling debris had not destroyed the entire ship. The computer interface panels and workstations nearest the doors that were not engulfed in flames were now littered with debris and flashing intermittently. He was relieved to see, however, that the emergency field he had erected around the core had held.

If it hadn't, none of us would know the difference, Ganley thought grimly.

Only then did he realize how incredibly hot it was. The few scattered chemical fires could not account for it. It had to be a result of the explosion that had just occurred, but its intensity was alarming.

He grabbed as many masks as his arms would hold and immediately began distributing them among his people. A few appeared to be trapped under large pieces of metal, but they were already being assisted by those who had been farthest from the door when the explosion happened. He then hurried to the nearest undamaged console and called up an environmental display. Added to his list of immediate problems were a number of small coolant leaks saturating the air with noxious fumes. The air processors had already detected the presence of toxic atmosphere and were straining to clear the air.

"Ganley to sickbay," he called. "Prepare to receive incoming wounded."

"I'll handle that, Chief," a voice called from behind him, barely piercing the ringing in his ears and sounding kilometers away.

Turning, Ganley saw Riggs, one hand held over a gash to the side of his blackened and charred face, and the other holding a mask in place over his mouth and nose.

"I'm getting you out of here," Ganley replied.

"Bigger problem, sir," Riggs said, pointing to a tricorder he held in his hand.

There Ganley saw a single sphere, fifteen centimeters in diameter, approaching engineering.

"Get everyone out!" Ganley shouted.

"Aye, sir," Riggs replied as Ganley turned his attention to the calculations he had been working on just prior to the explosion. He called up the program he'd written to create a suppression beam. Half of the emitters in the room had been blown to hell, and it took him over a minute to find a portable field emitter, which he stationed as near as he dared to the core. With shaking hands he coded the beam. His initial intent had simply been to stop the sphere's progress, but now he realized he had to do more than that. No one, least of all he, had understood that the Children's most destructive weapons were the Children themselves. The small sphere approaching his position contained a blast yield powerful enough to destroy the entire ship if it took the core with it. Less than ten, properly positioned throughout the ship and detonating simultaneously, would have the same result.

His job now was not only to contain the sphere but to alter the harmonics of the energy shell surrounding it so that it could not detonate.

Another cough racked his body. He could only hope that Doctor Sal would be able to reverse the damage his lungs had already sustained.

Eventually, he decided. For now, his duty was to stay put

and do whatever it took to keep that sphere from doing to the core what its companion had done to the door. A few moments more, and his program was complete. Now all that remained was to see if it would work.

"Ganley to Psilakis."

"*Good . . . hear . . . voice, Chief,*" came Psilakis's voice over a garbled channel.

"I could use some help down here," Ganley said.

"*Already on . . . way,*" Psilakis replied.

"I've created a suppression beam for the sphere approaching engineering. It's got a triaxilating frequency that should disrupt the sphere's energy shell without allowing it to destabilize. We've got to keep the rest of these things intact until we can clear them into space."

"*That much I'd already figured out, Chief,*" Psilakis replied.

"I'm sending you the specs now. If it works, you should be able to use portable emitters to establish similar beams wherever you need them."

Before he could continue, a single sphere floated into engineering and came to rest only a few meters from the core. His hands continued to rebel, refusing to calm themselves. It took every ounce of his remaining strength to target the beam and activate it.

A bright orange light shot forth from the emitter, enveloping the sphere and, to Ganley's relief, freezing it in its tracks. A quick scan confirmed that the pressure contained within the beam, coupled with the harmonics with which it resonated, had effectively rendered the sphere inert.

Choking on a sigh, Ganley felt his legs give out. He'd made it this far on adrenaline, but even that was beginning to fail him. His hands resting on the base of the emitter and his eyes glued to the sphere it was now holding in place, Ganley hoped that whoever was coming would hurry.

Phinn was brought back to consciousness by the sound of a regular deep whoosh.

". . . to Sal. Two more wounded, deck seventeen, section twenty-six."

"I'll find room for them."

"There's no way for me to tell if they've been compromised, El'nor."

"We'll transport them in behind a force field until we can determine—"

"Wait," Phinn heard himself say as he gingerly pulled himself to his knees. "I'm okay, I'm okay," he insisted.

Instantly his face was being covered by an emergency respirator. It was hard to tell who was assisting him, as the person slipping the mask's strap behind his head was wearing a full pressure suit.

"Make that one to transport."

Phinn suddenly recognized the captain's voice. He turned to see the unconscious figure of Sadie disappear in a shimmer of light.

"What's your name?" Farkas asked. Her voice had a sharp, barking quality through the suit's comm system.

Phinn rose to address her, suddenly conscious of a number of aching bones and muscles that had been fine only a few moments earlier, as well as the fact that his entire body was soaked with sweat. He suddenly realized how unseasonably warm the corridor had become. "Lieutenant Junior Grade Phinnegan Bryce, Captain," he replied.

"Are you security?"

"Engineering," Phinn corrected her. "Slipstream specialist, ma'am."

"Are you injured?"

Phinn did a mental check but found nothing beyond the bruises he'd sustained upon meeting the deck at a relatively high rate of speed.

"I don't think so."

"Good," the captain replied. "I have a feeling a slipstream specialist might come in handy right now. You're with me," she ordered.

"Aye, Captain," Phinn replied automatically. As they headed toward engineering, he added, "It's nice to meet you, Captain Farkas."

The captain paused for a moment and turned to face him. Though it was hard to tell for sure, he thought her eyes were a little misty.

"You too, Bryce," she replied.

Phinn nodded, then tensed as Farkas's eyes grew wide. Sensing danger, he started to turn, but Farkas pushed him roughly to the deck as a burst of phaser fire barely missed the spot where his head had been seconds earlier. Phinn rolled to his back to see where this new threat was coming from. Two crewmen were rushing toward him, phasers raised. One of them was his roommate, Nathan.

As Phinn struggled to process the sight of his friend pointing a weapon at him, another shot whizzed past and Nathan fell to the deck. Phinn automatically raised his weapon, and though it was an eerie sensation to fire on his own, he managed to hit the other crewman as his last shot when wild, pinging off the deck over Phinn's shoulder.

"Was that phaser set to stun?" the captain asked.

"Yes," Phinn replied.

"Good," she said, helping him to his feet. "You still okay?"

"Absolutely," he said. "Though I wouldn't mind knowing who decided this would be a good time for a mutiny." *And how they got Nathan on their side.*

"Some of our people have been compromised by the Children of the Storm. Given the fact that they were firing on us, I think it was a safe bet they were among them. I'm hoping that when we put enough distance between us and the aliens, our people will recover. I want to avoid killing any of them."

"Of course," Phinn replied, checking again over his shoulder before he fell into line behind her as she jogged down the hall.

It suddenly struck Phinn that she had just saved his life twice in the last few minutes. Starfleet captains were usually shrouded in a certain mystique, but this woman seemed more real and human than he'd ever imagined. He couldn't stop thinking about the way she'd turned to reply to his offhand greeting a moment earlier. He didn't know why this simple gesture—half a second to meet his eyes—touched him so. In the middle of an emergency, he doubted most other senior officers, let alone captains, would have taken the time. But because she had, she'd saved both of them from being shot ignobly in the back.

She'd had his loyalty from the minute he joined her crew, but Phinn decided then and there that he owed her more than that. He'd follow her anywhere.

Starfleet officers were taught to multitask, but Psilakis couldn't remember ever trying to focus on so many things simultaneously. He had sealed off the bridge to prevent further attacks from any of his fellow crewmen who had been compromised and had transferred the rest of the bridge crew to detention cells after notifying Doctor Sal that she should activate Emergency Medical Holograms to tend to them should they awaken. Sal sounded as busy as he was but promised to get to it.

The helm, operations, and tactical were all routed to his console. Of the three, the helm was the least of his troubles. In a conventional space battle there would be enemy fire to contend with, and no autopilot system would be as effective as a living, breathing crewman at evading it. As the Children of the Storm did not possess conventional weapons, the auto program needed only to adjust course in order to target the alien spheres, and in that regard it was performing optimally.

Psilakis had also successfully created a targeting sub-routine that had already destroyed dozens of the alien vessels. Could he have given his full attention to this task, the battle might already have been won. But right now, the greatest danger to his ship by far was the presence of the intruding spheres. He was tracking the movement of seven of them through the ship and thus far had not managed to slow their progress at all. He had observed the destruction of a few taken out by errant phaser fire. Huge sections of decks three, four, and eleven were now destroyed, and the survivors were executing emergency evacuations. Apart from the single sphere that had been headed for engineering after the initial explosion, he was struggling to find a pattern—any rhyme or reason—to the movements of the others. None of them seemed to be headed for particularly sensitive areas, but he doubted their intent was as benign as it currently appeared.

He was simultaneously taking reports from crew members who had been engaged by fellow personnel. As they were identified, he adjusted the display of their comm signals to indicate that they were, for the moment, considered hostiles. As of now, he counted forty-nine confirmed, in addition to the eight that had been manning the bridge when the battle had begun. Though he wasn't overly concerned at present with figuring out why these particular officers had been compromised, he had noted that all of them were alpha shift personnel and would have just been coming on duty when the Children of the Storm were first encountered.

Setting this fact aside for his subconscious to chew on, he continued to attempt to devise a strategy that would rid the ship of the intruding spheres. Nonessential crew had been ordered to congregate in designated emergency areas, as far from the paths of the floating bombs now moving through the ship as possible. Ganley's beam appeared to be effective, and Psilakis had dispatched security teams to take out the spheres' escorts and try to contain them with suppression beams. The next major problem was eliminating the source—the single large sphere that still hung in one of the shuttlebays. Though it had not shed any new spheres in the last few minutes, it probably still had the ability to do so. To attempt to destroy it would destroy most of the ship. The blast yield of the smaller vessels was immense, but it was nothing compared to the capacity of the single, much bigger vessel. Part of him wondered why it had not simply detonated already. It seemed the quickest way for the Children to secure their victory.

He struggled to focus, but balancing his efforts between keeping those who could not safely fight the aliens out of harm's way and dealing with the continuing threat of the larger sphere was pushing his concentration beyond the breaking point.

"Lieutenant Narv to Psilakis."

"Tell me you've come up with something, Narv," Psilakis replied as he simultaneously slammed his fist down on the console. A massive phaser barrage had just resulted in the destruction of only one sphere outside the ship. It seemed the Children of the Storm were getting better at evading his firing patterns.

Narv had been sealed in one of deck fourteen's science labs since the attack had begun and was working out contingencies for destroying the spheres.

"We have to neutralize the main sphere. It's just released another two small vessels."

"Agreed."

"Stanton is taking a security team to the shuttlebay."

Psilakis took a moment to study his display.

"There are two spheres and nine of our people blocking his path," he replied, displeased.

"It's not a suicide run," Narv assured him. *"They're taking the long way. Once they get there, the objective is to manually seal the interior bay doors. You need to restore the atmospheric field. Once the door is sealed, increase the pressure within the bay to tolerance plus ten percent."*

"That'll destroy the shuttlebay and probably take half the deck with it," Psilakis said, the strain obvious in his tone.

"Not according to my simulations," Narv replied. *"But it will make the environment incredibly uncomfortable for the sphere."*

"We're not trying to piss it off," Psilakis warned.

"At the same time, we need to flood the bay with harmonic bursts to destabilize the energy shell."

"If that sphere blows—" Psilakis began.

"If it stays put, five minutes will destabilize it," Narv agreed, *"but that's not the point. Give the harmonics a couple*

of minutes to work and then open the shuttlebay doors and drop the force field. If the thing has any sense of self-preservation at all, it will take the escape route we're offering it."

"Damn it." Psilakis didn't like the idea, but he didn't have a ready alternative.

Stanton's team was closing on the shuttlebay, avoiding the spheres and their escorts by traveling through a series of Jefferies tubes. Psilakis checked the shuttlebay and noted the emergence of an additional sphere, bringing his count to ten targets apart from the main sphere. Much as he hated Narv's plan, he could hope against hope that his math was wrong and that the destruction of the main sphere would take out less than ten of the adjacent decks.

Psilakis noted the presence of one of his crew still in the bay, Ensign Yuka. Her life signs were weak. He transported her to the detention area just as Stanton's team reached the shuttlebay.

He entered a new firing solution into the tactical controls as he watched Stanton's team fan out and begin to struggle with the manual overrides for the interior door. Fifty seconds later, the door was closed.

Psilakis activated an additional force field outside the bay doors, then restored the atmospheric field, preventing the sphere from escaping into open space until he was good and ready. Hands trembling, he manually increased the pressure in the shuttlebay beyond the tolerance of any organic life-form. The sphere began to shrink, then elongate as it attempted to compensate for the pressure change.

He then added the harmonic bursts Narv had requested and glued one of his eyes to the sensors displaying the integrity of the sphere's energy shell.

He watched the pressure bar climb past 100 percent of

tolerance and forced himself to allow the pressure to increase. It had barely reached 111 percent when the energy shell integrity began to destabilize. Taking a deep breath, Psilakis opened the shuttlebay doors and dropped the force field. He watched in satisfaction as the sphere darted immediately through the doors, evacuating the ship and heading into open space.

For good measure, Psilakis manually targeted the sphere with the ship's phasers, and seconds later, it exploded.

Sounds of celebration came over the comm as Narv said, "*We're showing the sphere has been destroyed.*"

"Confirmed." Psilakis sighed in relief as he slowly restored normal pressure to the bay.

"*If we can trap the others with Ganley's triaxilating containment modules, that should hold them long enough for us to clear them off the ship.*"

"Good work, Narv," Psilakis replied. "I'll send three more teams after the last of the spheres."

He was about to contact the captain when the computer alerted him to a new threat.

A hundred new spheres had been detected, approaching *Quirinal*'s position. When they arrived, they would undoubtedly join with those he had not yet destroyed in open space and attempt to do to *Quirinal* what they had already done to *Planck*. He also noted that *Demeter* was now several thousand kilometers from its original position, still on course for the debris field. It was possible the new spheres were approaching for *Demeter*, but Psilakis doubted it. Given the numbers required to destroy *Planck*, he thought that more than enough currently made up the field surrounding *Demeter* to destroy it, were that their aim.

Damn it all, he thought.

"Bridge to Captain Farkas."

"*Go ahead, Psilakis,*" the captain replied.

"I've got good news and bad news, ma'am."

After a pause the captain said, "Give me the bad news first."

Farkas hurried to engineering with Phinn at her heels as she listened to Psilakis's report.

"We have to get the hell out of here," she said as soon as he'd finished.

"*What about* Demeter?" Psilakis asked.

"Assuming we survive this, we'll come back for them," Farkas replied through gritted teeth. The thought of abandoning *Demeter* to the whims of the Children of the Storm galled her, but she had to see her own ship to safety first and trust the officers aboard *Demeter* to do the job for which they'd been trained. She tried not to think about the fact that most of *Demeter*'s crew were scientists. Their tactical staff could have fit in one of *Quirinal*'s escape pods. But Farkas knew that to give in to that concern would likely damn them all.

"*We know they can keep up with us at high warp,*" Psilakis said, apparently agreeing with her estimation of their priorities.

"Can you bring the slipstream drive on line from the bridge?" Farkas asked.

After a brief pause, Psilakis replied, "*Negative. The computer indicates that the navigational circuits were damaged in the explosion in engineering.*"

"I can fix that, Captain," came Phinn's tinny voice from behind her.

Farkas turned to see the eager young man staring at her

with fervent certainty. She then turned her attention to her tricorder to take a reading of engineering's interior before entering. The temperature was over a hundred and twenty degrees, and the environmental processors indicated the air was not safe to breath. Multiple chemical fires, coupled with coolant leaks, overpowered their ability to clear the area. Phinn had only minutes to complete his repairs, but she doubted his body could survive that long.

Nodding to Phinn, she said, "Double back to section twelve and get a pressure suit."

"We don't have time, Captain," Phinn argued. "I can do this with the rebreather."

"The temperature in there—" she began.

"Is really hot, I know," Phinn replied. "But I can take it for the couple of minutes we have."

Farkas didn't know why her gut screamed at her to take the extra minutes she agreed they didn't have. Calculating the odds that Phinn could repair the slipstream drive before the other spheres reached her ship and surrounded it, she decided to stow her fears and replied, "All right. Psilakis, we're going to get the drive back on line. Be ready to go to slipstream velocity as soon as the board goes green."

"*Understood.*"

The entrance to engineering was a gaping wound. Curled, jagged metal framed the opening, testifying to the severity of the explosion. Farkas was amazed it hadn't taken the rest of the deck with it, but she chalked it up to the size of the sphere.

Farkas slowed her steps as they approached, and gestured for Phinn to do the same. Rounding the corner into engineering with her phaser rifle raised, she took in the destruction before her in a heart-stopping glance.

The captain's attention was immediately drawn to the sight of a single sphere, trapped inside a field emanating from a portable emitter. At the base of the emitter, her chief engineer, Lieutenant Ganley, lay unconscious, the skin of his face and hands blistered and bright red.

"Farkas to emergency transport. Get Lieutenant Ganley to sickbay immediately."

Seconds later, Ganley disappeared in a shimmer of light, and Farkas hoped that she had not been too late.

Phinn was rooted to the floor, staring at the trapped sphere.

"Is that going to hold?" he asked, the terror obvious in his voice.

"You let me worry about that," Farkas replied briskly. "Focus on the slipstream drive, Lieutenant."

"Aye," Phinn said, attempting to shake off his fear. With a nod, he disappeared into the bowels of engineering, stepping cautiously through the debris that littered every surface of the room, his face already beginning to drip with sweat.

Farkas moved to the emitter and did a quick analysis of Ganley's work. The field was constructed of rotating harmonics, similar to the shield frequency adjustments that had once been an effective countermeasure against the Borg. Setting aside the irony, Farkas studied the sensor readings and determined that the field had effectively neutralized the sphere. Her sense of relief was almost overpowering.

"I've found the damaged circuits, Captain," Phinn announced.

"Good work," Farkas said, hoping she sounded more enthusiastic than she felt.

"*Captain?*" Psilakis's voice cut through the comm system.

"What is it?"

"*Two spheres are moving toward your position,*" Psilakis reported grimly. "*And they are accompanied by nine of our people. Our internal transporters are now down, so I can't clear them for you. I have a team moving to intercept, but I'm not sure they'll—*"

"Understood," Farkas cut him off.

Assuming they would arrive before Phinn had finished his work, Farkas's options were limited to one. The approaching spheres would have to be contained in the same manner as the one Ganley had trapped. The personnel sent to allow the spheres to get close enough to do their job would have to be subdued as well. Firing a phaser rifle in the toxic atmosphere of engineering was likely to set off additional explosions. She could survive them, safe in her pressure suit, but Phinn would not. Though his mask would protect his lungs, nothing would protect his flesh from the heat or shrapnel.

She knew what she had to do.

It took less than two minutes for her to find two functioning emitters and load them with the appropriate containment field settings. She positioned them so that the beams would activate and hold the spheres just outside of engineering.

Farkas then set her rifle on the floor, and keeping one eye glued to her tricorder, she began to remove her pressure suit.

Phinn had been carrying around a mental map of *Quirinal*'s slipstream drive for weeks. Finding the damaged navigational circuits took seconds. Finding the replacement parts he needed was more of a challenge, but he'd cobbled them together faster than he would have believed possible. Turned out, terror was a fantastic motivator.

He was so focused on rerouting damaged circuits and

creating hasty patches for the minimally damaged ones before him that he jerked in alarm when Captain Farkas tapped his shoulder.

The first thing he realized was that she was no longer wearing her pressure suit, but holding it in her hand and gesturing urgently for him to put it on.

Confused, Phinn thought, *Didn't we already cover this?*

He waited for her to explain until he realized that she was holding her breath. Phinn took a long, deep inhalation, then passed his mask to the captain.

Farkas took a grateful breath before saying, "We're about to have company."

Phinn only shook his head and pointed to her as he grabbed the suit she tossed to him.

"Put it on. That's a direct order!" Farkas shouted.

"But, I'm almost—" he spluttered, wasting what little oxygen he had left.

"Look, Bryce," Farkas said coldly, "right now only one person on this ship can get us to safety and it's not me, it's you. My only job right now is to keep you alive long enough to do that. End of discussion."

Phinn hurried to do her bidding as she turned away, her eyes glued to the entrance from where, presumably, the attack would come. Distant phaser fire sliced through the air, only adding to his anxiety as he finally locked the suit's helmet in place with shaking hands and took several deep breaths.

Once Farkas was satisfied he was secure, she started back toward the entrance.

"Captain, wait!" Phinn called, quickly unlocking one glove and removing his personal transporter.

Farkas turned. Phinn stumbled over to her, unaccustomed to the ungainly suit, and fastened the leather strap around the wrist that held the body of her phaser rifle.

"What the—" Farkas began.

"It's a personal transporter," Phinn explained. "I know it's not regulation, but just toggle this switch and it will take you back to my quarters." At Farkas's bemused shock, he added, "I know. I'm reprimanded. Write it up later."

"Get back to work," Farkas replied. Phinn couldn't tell for sure, but he thought he caught a smile before she resumed her post at the entrance to engineering.

All he could do now was prove himself worthy of her faith and sacrifice. He had the rest of his life to make it happen.

Psilakis estimated that the additional alien vessels would be upon the ship in less than two minutes. Allowing his auto-targeting program to eliminate as many of their comrades as possible, he was focusing exclusively on the team headed for engineering. Thirty of his people were converging on deck seventeen, but from the looks of it, they weren't going to be able to reach the spheres or their escorts in time. It would be an unacceptable irony indeed if the captain were to succeed in getting the slipstream drive on line, only to have the effort wasted as the remaining intruders exploded near enough the core to breach it.

With Narv's assistance, they had trapped all of the seven spheres located throughout the rest of the ship. Psilakis had finally realized, once they were subdued, that had they traveled much farther, they would have formed a perfect line every five decks and that, had they detonated simultaneously, they would have easily destroyed the entire ship. It was a nice bullet to have dodged, but the two remaining spheres would reach engineering in less than thirty seconds.

Sweat drenched the back of his neck. The blows he had sustained during the initial attack made his body a mass of aches and sharp spiking pains.

Psilakis didn't care. All he knew now was that his ship would survive or would be destroyed in less than one minute.

It was the loneliest minute he had ever known.

"Two hostiles and eight escorts are approaching your position, Captain."

Phinn ignored the report. Two circuits remained to be tested before he could safely bring the drive on line. He had preloaded terminal coordinates approximately twenty light-years from their present position. It would be a short jump, but he couldn't safely plot a longer one without additional astrometric data he did not currently have time to feed into the navigational array.

"I know," he heard the captain reply to Psilakis's report.

"A few more seconds, Captain," Phinn called, worrying that he didn't have them.

"Best possible speed, Lieutenant," she replied.

A warning sensor sounded, and Phinn took a precious second to see the emergency force field Ganley had erected around the core begin to overload. It would fail within seconds. He forced himself to ignore it as the computer confirmed that the navigational circuits were finally functional.

Phinn activated the shipwide comm. "All hands, prepare to go to slipstream velocity on my mark."

"Five . . . four . . . three . . ."

Phaser fire erupted from the main entrance. Captain Farkas had clearly engaged the approaching hostile force.

Two spheres darted into Phinn's peripheral vision,

followed instantaneously by the bright flash of suppression beams.

"Two . . . one . . ."

Consoles near the entrance began to explode and debris rained down all around him.

"Mark."

Phinn felt the deck leave his feet and his back hit a wall with enough force to send a flurry of stars exploding before his eyes.

Wondering at their brightness, he thought he saw another shimmer of light and had time to pray it was Captain Farkas making her escape before darkness finally took him.

Chapter Thirteen

STARDATE 58455.5
U.S.S. VOYAGER

Chakotay's stomach tensed as Ensign Gwyn brought *Voyager* out of slipstream velocity. He honestly didn't know what he hoped most to find. It would have been overly optimistic to believe they'd simply arrive and see all three ships waiting there. Though much of his internal sense of order and peace had been restored in the last month, he knew he couldn't rely on the universe to make anything that easy for him.

Traveling through a slipstream corridor, it was impossible to engage long-range sensors, which at least would have given him a sense of what to expect. The biggest disadvantage of this marvelous technology, at least from a tactical perspective, was that you reentered normal space effectively blind.

In the event that whatever had befallen *Quirinal, Planck,* and *Demeter* had occurred this far from the known territory of the Children of the Storm, Chakotay had ordered the ship to Yellow Alert in anticipation of their arrival. As the slipstream tunnel dispersed, revealing calm open space, one part of Chakotay relaxed as the rest of him realized that the hard work was about to begin.

"Ensign Lasren, engage long-range sensors," Eden ordered before Chakotay had the chance. As she technically outranked him, this was her prerogative, though he wondered if in her place he would have so quickly asserted his authority.

"Aye," Lasren replied.

"Lieutenant Kim?" Chakotay asked, knowing Harry would already be compiling a tactical report.

"There are no alien contacts present," Harry began. "Slight gravimetric variances suggest the presence of slipstream distortions."

"Other than ours?" Eden asked.

"Yes, ma'am," Harry replied. "The variances diminish over time, and the ones created by our arrival are distinctly higher than the traces I'm reading."

"So they made it this far," Eden directed toward Chakotay.

"It would appear so."

Eden rose from her seat and moved to the upper ring of the bridge to stand beside Harry. Chakotay doubted she questioned his findings; rather, her pent-up anticipation needed a little release, but pacing openly before the bridge crew wasn't going to do much for anyone's nerves.

"According to their mission profile, they were to group here and then *Quirinal* and *Planck* would move approximately two light-years from the debris ring surrounding the Children's system to begin their investigations," Eden went on. "But *Demeter* was supposed to remain here for the duration of their stay in this sector."

"Captain?" Lasren said, his voice low.

"Yes?" Eden and Chakotay replied in unison.

"Sorry," Lasren said immediately. Until a few days ago, Eden had been the only captain on the bridge, and whatever he had found had clearly thrown him far enough off his pins to forget to address Eden as Fleet Commander.

"It's all right, Ensign," Eden said evenly. "What is your report?"

"I'm picking up debris approximately two light-years from the debris ring."

Chakotay's heart sank, and a familiar heat began to rise to his face.

"What kind of debris?" he asked, forcing his voice to remain calm.

"It's definitely of Federation origin," Lasren replied with unmistakable regret.

"Can you be more specific?" Eden queried.

"From this distance, all I can confirm is its presence, but there isn't enough of it to account for all three ships, ma'am."

A heavy sigh caught in Chakotay chest.

"Is there any sign of the Children of the Storm in the vicinity of the debris?"

After a moment Lasren confirmed that there was not.

Eden looked to Chakotay, but it was clear her mind was already made up.

"I suggest we move closer to the debris at low warp,"

Chakotay said. He shared her burning curiosity, but it would avail them nothing if they attracted the attention of the probable destroyers of one of their ships en route. "If there was a battle at those coordinates," he continued, "it's possible there are still scouts monitoring the area for the arrival of reinforcements."

"Agreed," Eden said firmly, though the pain in her eyes indicated how much this cost her.

"Seven of Nine to the bridge."

Chakotay's heart rate increased slightly. Seven would have been monitoring their arrival from astrometrics and probably would have had a clearer picture of what they were facing than Lasren, given the advanced capabilities of the tools at her disposal and the skill with which she wielded them.

"Go ahead," Chakotay replied.

"I have located a Federation distress buoy a hundred thousand kilometers from the debris I do not doubt Ensign Lasren has already detected."

Chakotay smiled slightly. It was a comfort to have Seven back and performing near her peak. Of course, her report complicated his initial assessment.

"What's the vessel signature of the buoy?" Eden asked.

"It's from Demeter," Seven replied.

"I can take the *Delta Flyer* to retrieve it and be back in seven hours," Tom offered.

Three weeks later, Chakotay wondered if seven hours would make a difference. Dangerous as it might be to move that close to the wreckage, he was no longer content to waste another second.

"That won't be necessary, Commander," Eden replied, obviously on the same page. "Ensign Gwyn, plot an intercept course to the coordinates of the buoy at maximum warp as well as our return vector. I want us in and out of the area in less than three minutes. Lieutenant Kim, prepare to transport the buoy into our shuttlebay as soon as we're in range."

"Aye, Fleet Commander," Gwyn replied.

"I'd like to oversee the recovery from the shuttlebay," Harry added.

"Make it so," Eden said with a nod, and Harry quickly exited the bridge as Tom rose to take his place at tactical.

Chakotay had spent the past eighteen hours mentally preparing himself for the worst. Now that those fears had been at least partially realized, he decided that eighteen years wouldn't have been enough. Though the fleet wasn't his to command, he felt that every member of it was part of him. Just because they weren't serving on his ship, that didn't make them any less significant to him.

Depending upon the contents of the buoy, he would soon learn exactly how many of them had lost their lives and by whose hand. He would then try very hard not to take pleasure in seeing that those responsible were made to account for their actions. It wasn't revenge he was seeking. He already knew too well the bitterness of succumbing to wrath. But the warrior inside him demanded that whatever losses they had just sustained should not have been in vain.

As Eden returned to her seat beside him, her face was inscrutable. He took a moment to wonder how it was possible that she appeared to be taking this news better than he was.

Or maybe she's just better than I am at hiding her emotions.

He wasn't sure which idea disturbed him more.

The conference room was silent, and it was clear to Eden that all of the senior staff officers—Chakotay, Paris, Torres,

Conlon, Patel, and Lasren—were sharing the same anxious thoughts. Finally, Kim entered with Seven of Nine and presented her and Chakotay with padds containing the logs they had downloaded from the buoy. Eden counted herself lucky that the retrieval mission had gone off without incident. In the few minutes they were there, Seven had used the astrometric sensors to take the widest possible reading of the area, and Eden hoped that once she'd had a chance to study them, they might reveal the location of two ships still counted as missing.

Kim began to speak.

"The buoy was launched on Stardate 58409.9," he began.

"Two weeks ago?" B'Elanna asked.

Kim nodded and continued. "For the first several days of the mission, *Demeter* held position at these coordinates as planned. They then received a request from *Planck* to rendezvous in order to transfer food supplies. Up to that point and for several hours after they arrived, there had been no contact with the Children of the Storm, and apparently Captain T'Mar did not believe it likely that the ships would make contact."

Chakotay said something softly under his breath. Though Eden didn't catch the words, she doubted they were complimentary of T'Mar.

"Shortly after the supply transfer was complete, hundreds of contacts were detected approaching the three ships. Sensors didn't pick them up until they were almost right on top of them."

"What?" B'Elanna asked, obviously stunned.

"Without confirmation of this report from either *Planck* or *Quirinal,* I would hesitate to accept this as factual," Seven said evenly. So many had spoken of Seven's cool and placid demeanor, particularly under pressure, but until now, Eden hadn't witnessed it firsthand. During the early weeks following Seven's arrival, she had been wrestling with a personal issue that had clearly affected her deportment. Eden took her appearance now as further evidence that no permanent damage had been sustained by Seven in her transformation by the Caeliar.

"Why would *Demeter*'s computer report this but the others indicate something different?" B'Elanna asked of Seven.

"The fact that the sensors did not pick up the approaching vessels farther out suggests only that *Demeter*'s sensors were malfunctioning," Seven replied simply.

"Or that the Children of the Storm are even more formidable than we first suspected," Paris added. "They might be able to shield themselves from our sensors in ways we don't yet understand."

Seven favored Paris with a hard glance, but said nothing further on the subject.

Kim cleared his throat lightly and continued. "Without *Quirinal*'s or *Planck*'s logs, it's hard to say exactly how they chose to respond to the threat. *Demeter* reports that Captain Farkas ordered them to remain in formation to make protecting them easier. Though *Demeter*'s first officer notes that he disagreed with this assessment, he was not able to successfully plot a slipstream jump that would have moved them to safety between the time that the aliens were first detected and the moment they surrounded each of the three vessels."

"Surely they fought back," Paris said, as if offended on their behalf.

"It had been Captain Farkas's intention to try and make contact with the Children of the Storm. Communications were lost between the three ships the moment they were surrounded, however, and *Demeter* could not confirm whether or not this contact ever took place."

Kim paused, obviously struggling with intense emotions before he collected himself and continued.

"Approximately twelve minutes after the alien vessels arrived, those surrounding *Planck* and *Demeter* shifted their formation. The individual vessels merged, creating a massive single energy field around each ship. The resonance signatures of the field shifted, and less than one minute later, *Planck* was destroyed."

"By an energy field?" Eden asked, seeking confirmation.

"It will take us several hours to examine *Demeter*'s readings and hopefully ascertain the exact mechanism of the attack," Seven said, "but the short answer is yes.'"

"Is that how they destroyed the Borg?" Tom interjected.

"Possibly," Seven replied, "though after one or two such attacks, I presume the Borg would have adapted their defenses accordingly. I find it hard to believe the same tactic would have destroyed so many Borg cubes."

"If this energy field is that powerful, I can't imagine we're going to find an effective countermeasure," B'Elanna offered tensely.

"One issue at a time," Eden advised. "Lieutenant Kim?"

"Naturally *Demeter* expected to suffer the same fate within seconds of *Planck*'s destruction, but at the time the buoy was launched, all they could report was that the field surrounding their vessel was effectively locking them out of helm control but setting them on a course away from *Quirinal* and toward the debris field surrounding the system that we believe to be their territory. The last thing the log notes was that *Quirinal* was engaging the alien vessels with phasers and that for all of their obvious power, the alien vessels were vulnerable to phasers, even at relatively low settings," Harry finished.

"Then *Quirinal* survived as well," Tom said, the relief clear in his voice.

"Possibly," Chakotay said, obviously unwilling to allow his hopes to be raised. Turning to Eden, he added, "We should begin analysis of the readings we took when we retrieved the buoy, as well as deeper study of these logs before we settle on our next move. In the meantime, we should consider a run at high warp to retrieve *Planck*'s remains. They might provide further necessary evidence."

"Am I correct in assuming that there are no escape pods or life signs present in the debris of *Planck*?" Eden asked of Lasren.

"You are," Lasren replied.

"Then while I agree that those remains might be instructive, I believe we should wait before endangering ourselves further in a retrieval mission," Eden said, noting that Chakotay's head jerked sharply in her direction when she countermanded his suggestion.

"You're going to leave them out there?" he asked in disbelief.

"For now, Captain," Eden said, emphasizing his rank. Cordial respect among senior officers was important, but she wasn't going to argue right now about who had the last word.

Chakotay held her firm gaze for a moment before turning to Lasren. "Harry said *Demeter* was heading for the Borg debris field. If they made it that far and were subsequently destroyed, would you be able to detect their wreckage among the thousands of cubes?"

"Yes," Lasren replied, "but given the volume of debris, it would take a while."

"Like looking for a needle in a haystack," Kim said, obviously not relishing the thought.

"Well, start looking," Chakotay ordered. "Seven, return to astrometrics and get to work on our latest readings. See if you can find any trace of *Demeter* or *Quirinal*. Tom and Harry, you're responsible for *Demeter*'s logs. I want to know everything we can possibly glean from them about the Children of the Storm's tactics as soon as you have it."

Harry nodded as Tom replied, "Understood, sir."

"I'd like a copy of the logs as well," Conlon said. "I'd like to focus on the possible sensor malfunction, if there aren't any objections."

"I'm with you on that," B'Elanna added. "The fact is, if it's true, they could be closer to us right now than we're aware, and I'm not going to feel safe within ten light-years of that system until we can detect them."

"You're not going to find evidence of a sensor glitch in a log," Seven chided her gently.

"You'd be surprised," B'Elanna replied, a note of challenge in her voice.

"That's fine," Chakotay said, ending discussion. "Patel, I'd like you to work with Doctor Sharak. We have more data now than *Aventine* collected to add to our profile of this species. I want your best analysis as soon as possible."

"Yes, Captain." Patel nodded dutifully.

Chakotay then turned to Eden. "Do you have any further orders?" he asked.

She couldn't argue with his thoroughness or the assignments. But she did have one thing to add.

"We'll remain here for eight hours. If no new information surfaces in that time about the whereabouts of *Quirinal* or *Demeter,* we will retreat to a safer distance before determining our next move."

Chakotay clearly bit back his response, but his disapproval

of her choice to limit their time was obvious. Addressing the group, he said only, "You have your orders. Dismissed."

Eden expected a full-throated complaint once the others had left, but he surprised her by following the others out, leaving her alone with her copy of *Demeter*'s logs in the conference room.

The silence that was her companion was no less tense than that which had permeated the room before she had learned of *Planck*'s fate. She took a moment to scroll through the list of the names and ranks of all hands lost aboard *Planck*, and a few minutes more to begin to grieve their loss. Seventy deaths were on her head, and each one left a bitter wound in her heart. She refused to add the weight of *Quirinal*'s or *Demeter*'s crews for now, though how they could possibly have escaped intact was hard to imagine.

Eight hours from now, she might not have a choice, but she'd be damned if *Voyager*'s crew or the rest of the fleet would also be lost in a vain attempt to bring closure to this incident. She understood Starfleet's curiosity about this species, but absolute truth often came at a price that was simply too high to pay. Thinking back over the last few minutes, she knew she could make peace with that eventually, but she doubted seriously that Chakotay would.

"Damn you, Willem," she said softly before retreating to her office.

It took Seven nearly an hour to create a search subroutine for the astrometric sensors that could pinpoint Federation debris within the field comprised otherwise of Borg wreckage. Her initial review of the snapshot the sensors had taken during their all too brief mission to retrieve the buoy hadn't revealed anything, but given the fact that a truly accurate reading would have taken at least an hour to render, she was not disheartened by her initial inability to find what she was seeking. The astrometric sensors were amazing things, but they were not designed to function best under time limits. They extended the power of long-range sensors dramatically, assuming they had sufficient time to extrapolate the data they were receiving. The three-minute glimpse she had to work with was almost useless, but even from this distance, she could align the sensors to study the debris field and search for alloys unique to Federation starship construction.

All she needed was time, which was precisely the thing she did not have.

She had also enhanced the astrometrics array's subspace receivers. They had detected the buoy's signal almost immediately upon *Voyager*'s emergence from slipstream velocity. The more she considered *Quirinal*'s predicament, however—at least as best she understood it from the fragments logged by *Demeter*—the more certain she was that the only chance they would have had to escape would have been by using their slipstream engines to put greater distance between themselves and the Children of the Storm than would allow for pursuit.

This meant that the search grid for a signal from *Quirinal* needed to be much wider than the array's receivers could possibly detect under normal circumstances.

For all I know, they could have made it back to the Alpha Quadrant in the last two weeks, Seven thought morosely.

This thought, however, suddenly sparked another, and sent her searching all available data for something else. Within minutes, she had found it.

She immediately turned her attention to the deflector array and, to her consternation, found that access to the controls she required had been restricted. Given Admiral Batiste's recent use of the deflector for his own dangerous purposes, Seven understood the increased security, though understanding made it no less irritating.

"Seven of Nine to Lieutenant Conlon," she said briskly. Her mind was racing, already calculating field densities and gravimetric wavelengths in preparation for putting her plan into effect.

"*This is Conlon,*" the chief engineer replied.

"Please release deflector controls to me at once," Seven requested; though, because she was Seven, it sounded more like an order than a request.

After a brief pause, B'Elanna's voice answered her. "*Why do you need deflector control, Seven?*"

"I have detected a class-A magnetar and intend to use the deflector to target it with a tachyon pulse in order to collapse it into a micro-singularity."

Another long pause suggested that her response was not being met with appropriate enthusiasm.

Confirmation of this suspicion came when B'Elanna charged into astrometrics a few minutes later, almost seething. Without preamble she launched into an entirely unnecessary history lesson.

"Seven, do I need to remind you what happened the last time you tried to use the deflector to emit tachyons? Because as I recall, it ended with me stranded in space trying to recover the warp core we had to eject when the deflector overloaded."

"I remember the incident perfectly well, Commander," Seven replied flatly. "And while I realize the events of that day were traumatic, didn't they also result in the profession of feelings for Commander Paris that ultimately led to your union in marital bliss?"

The lightness of Seven's tone had the intended effect. B'Elanna's wrath deflated as quickly as it had asserted itself and she sighed, though she fell short of breaking into a full smile.

"If I had it to do over again, I'd have found less extreme circumstances under which to begin my relationship with Tom," B'Elanna said.

"Would you?" Seven asked. Thankfully, both of them knew she was teasing.

"What do you need a micro-singularity for? What did that poor magnetar ever do to deserve destruction? I mean, I'd like to leave as much of space as possible the way we found it," B'Elanna said, returning to the subject at hand.

"I intend to use it to expand our subspace receiver's range."

Seven watched as B'Elanna mentally calculated the risks and rewards of her plan.

"You think one or both of the ships might have used their slipstream drives to escape and are now too far out of range—"

"I do," Seven cut her off.

B'Elanna turned away to stare at the large wall, which displayed the several searches the astrometrics array was currently undertaking, including the grid that showed the location of the magnetar Seven had discovered, less than a light-year from their present location. After a moment, she shook her head. "I hate it when you're right."

"One would think after all these years, you'd have grown accustomed to it," Seven replied.

Finally, B'Elanna did smile. "You contact Chakotay. I'll return to engineering to walk Conlon through this. And we're going to go really slowly this time. If we end up needing to dump the core again, I'm going to blame you. And then I'm going to make sure you're the one who has to go out there and get it."

"Understood." Seven smiled back. "Though you should also add Reg Barclay to your list of targets. I would never have considered it had he not so successfully used similar technology to reach *Voyager* years ago."

"Yeah, remind me to thank him again for that the next time I see him," B'Elanna said with appropriate sarcasm.

Five hours later, and without damage to the deflector or core, Seven had successfully expanded the range of *Voyager*'s subspace receivers by approximately thirty thousand light-years.

It would be another hour and forty minutes, however, until Seven's efforts were rewarded.

"You have to talk to her," Tom said.

He was seated at Chakotay's left and had been quietly insisting for the last several minutes that whether or not their search results bore fruit, they were honor-bound to return to the scene of the battle to retrieve *Planck*'s remains and more thoroughly analyze the debris field for remnants of their other ships.

"I know," Chakotay replied.

"Between the two ships we're talking about over seven hundred people. That's too many families back home to leave wondering what happened to their loved ones."

Chakotay hadn't considered it from this point of view; he was more worried about the seven hundred plus crewmen and officers that might still be in need of rescue. But Tom was right.

"I know," Chakotay said again.

Tom paused, clearly not satisfied with Chakotay's acknowledgment.

"It's not that I don't understand the risks," Tom went on. "But I can't believe she'd just abandon them without knowing for sure that they were destroyed."

Chakotay met Tom's eyes. "I get it," he said intently. "But I'd like to see her come to that conclusion on her own before—"

"Captain," Ensign Lasren interrupted from ops.

"Yes, Ensign?" Chakotay replied, turning to see the young Betazoid's face alight with relief.

"I think I've found our needle," Lasren said.

"On-screen," Chakotay ordered as he turned back to the main viewscreen.

A dark, grainy image filled the screen, replacing the star field. At first, Chakotay couldn't see what had Lasren so excited.

"I know it's not much to look at, but this is the best image I can pull from the astrometric sensors," Lasren said. After a moment, a subtle blue flash emerged and then disappeared so quickly Chakotay almost thought he had imagined it. "The debris field conceals the image but for that tenth of a second. It appears that the Federation contact is located well within the system." When no one hurried to congratulate him, Lasren continued, "It's faint, but I'm almost sure it's them."

"Who?" Chakotay asked.

The wind left some of Lasren's sails as he replied, "I can't say for sure."

"Could it be debris?" Tom asked.

"Yes," Lasren reluctantly admitted. "But as it's the only

contact visible, I'm thinking it's an intact vessel, probably *Demeter.*"

Chakotay stared hard at the image that Lasren had running in a recurring loop. Every few seconds, the blue flash appeared, almost daring him to come closer.

"I agree with Lasren," Harry piped up from tactical. "It's definitely a Federation signature. I'd estimate approximately six hundred thousand kilometers from the system's fourth planet. It's also a viable trajectory from *Demeter*'s last known course."

Before Chakotay could contact Eden to inform her of this development, she hurried onto the bridge, her face aglow.

"Ensign Gwyn, you should be receiving new coordinates from astrometrics at any moment. Plot a slipstream jump and let me know the moment you are prepared to execute."

"What happened?" Chakotay asked, rising as she approached the seat to his right.

"Seven has picked up *Quirinal*'s distress call. They're approximately twenty-two thousand light-years from our present position."

"They survived," Chakotay said, briefly sharing the intensity of her relief.

"It's an automated signal. It doesn't tell us anything about their condition. But we know where they are and we're going after them," Eden said.

"Ensign Lasren believes he has detected *Demeter,*" Chakotay advised her.

"Explain," Eden requested.

Chakotay directed her attention to the viewscreen and the sensor loop. When she didn't immediately respond, he said, "Lieutenant Kim concurs with Lasren's hypothesis."

Eden's initial enthusiasm began to dim. After a moment

she turned to Chakotay and, rising, said, "Your ready room."

Chakotay followed her through the bridge doors that accessed his private office. When the doors were closed behind him, she said, "My inclination is to go after *Quirinal*. Our evidence of their survival is more compelling than what Lasren has presented."

Chakotay took a moment to consider both sides of the unhappy equation.

"Frankly, neither evidence is terribly conclusive, and if we go after *Quirinal* now, we risk losing *Demeter*."

"Let's say Lasren is right," Eden said, clearly unmoved. "Two weeks ago the Children of the Storm took *Demeter* into the heart of their territory, and the ship has survived this long in one piece."

"Without a lot more information we can't assume that their condition is stable."

"Nor can we begin to mount a rescue mission without a lot more information about what we're up against," Eden countered. "We know *Quirinal* engaged the enemy. Before we risk going after *Demeter*, we need to know a hell of a lot more than we do right now about their tactics and destructive capabilities."

Chakotay massaged his forehead with the heel of his palm. "We could return to the fleet and send *Esquiline, Achilles,* and *Galen* after *Quirinal*," he suggested.

"And lose another two days in the process."

"Or we could send the *Delta Flyer* in to aid *Demeter* while we go after *Quirinal*."

"After what they did to *Planck*, you really think the *Delta Flyer* is going to be much help?"

She was right, and he knew it, but he still couldn't justify abandoning that flashing blue signal. After a brief pause

Chakotay finally admitted, "There's no good answer to this one, is there?"

Eden shook her head. After another tense moment she made her decision.

Chapter Fourteen

SIXTEEN DAYS EARLIER
U.S.S. DEMETER

As Commander Liam O'Donnell exited the bridge, his hands were already beginning to shake. The calm veneer he had just displayed for his crew was a performance he had perfected over the years. It was easier to do in the presence of a genuine problem as intriguing as the Children of the Storm because at least part of his mind could focus on that. The moment he was alone, however, he was forced to acknowledge the gravity of the situation, and to add this to the list of things at which he had failed in his life.

Anyone looking at O'Donnell's file would have had a hard time seeing those failures. His record was a collection of one amazing and usually impossible accomplishment after another. Only Liam counted the lives lost in the days, weeks, months, and years leading up to his breakthroughs. Only Liam knew that the most important thing he had ever attempted had ended in abject failure and two deaths he could never accept.

Only Liam knew that he had eschewed active command

of a vessel for years because he doubted his ability to function under the stress of a situation exactly like the one he now found himself in. Every life aboard *Demeter* was now his to save or lose, and if lost, he doubted he would ever recover.

"Alana," he whispered, placing one slow and steady foot in front of the other, trying as best he could not to allow the familiar panic that was the prelude to failure to engulf him.

As the seconds dragged with no response, a cascade of shadows began to crowd in around him.

This isn't my fault, Alana, he pleaded with her. *Please, answer me. Everyone is doing the best they can. No one is going to die. I'll go back to the lab and get to work. These aliens have a weakness and I'll find it before anyone else does. You'll see. I won't fail you again.*

Every time he repeated this thought, he believed it less.

Alana, please . . .

A vaguely familiar darkness asserted itself. A nauseating wave swept over him, beginning in his toes and leaving him sweating and breathless within seconds. A hand lifted to his head came down drenched.

No . . . nobody has died yet.

It's been years.

Years since the walls had fallen.

Years spent patiently rebuilding them with Alana's help.

Years since he had risked anything more disastrous than the failure of one of his experiments.

Damn you to hell, Willem Batiste. Damn the Children of the Storm, the Borg, the Delta Quadrant. Damn the entire Federation.

Placing one hand against the hallway wall to steady himself, the commander wondered how long his stomach would continue to hold its contents.

He forced his eyes to focus on a single joint on the wall, but with each breath he attempted, the sourness in his stomach ratcheted upward and a pool of tinny saliva gathered in his mouth.

Looking up, he saw a ghost standing before him. Obsidian eyes glared at him, far more menacing than the brown, rough-scaled flesh of Kressari's Quorum Minister Genov-see.

"The land in question has been privately held for nineteen generations," the minister thundered.

O'Donnell hadn't laid eyes on the man in twenty-four years, and he damn sure wasn't in the Delta Quadrant right now.

"You were brought here to help us solve this problem, Lieutenant O'Donnell," Genov-see went on vehemently. *"You promised us yields would quadruple within the first three planting seasons. Are you really the best the Federation can do?"*

O'Donnell felt his knees buckle, but he caught himself with both hands against the wall before hitting the floor.

I won't . . . go . . . back . . . there! he shouted in his mind.

The vision disappeared, and he got his first fresh breath in minutes. Swallowing bile, O'Donnell righted himself and staggered toward the turbolift.

Where the minister stood patiently waiting for him.

"The fate of my people is in your hands. Children will go hungry . . ."

"Stop it!" O'Donnell shouted, this time aloud. "They're already dead!"

Children.

Hungry children.

Starving children.

Emaciated faces racked with helplessness.

Memories of the Kressari he had once been sent to save crowded into his mind's eye, each more horrifying than the last.

So many children.

O'Donnell knew what was happening to him, and he wasn't going to meet it on his knees.

It took every ounce of strength he possessed to walk the few meters from the turbolift to his cabin. As soon as he reached it a terrifying new thought struck him.

She's gone, he assured himself.

Dead.

She's abandoned you and she won't return until you do your job. You have to solve this. You have to make this right. You have to make her proud.

But despite his certainty, he hesitated to open the door. Behind it, Alana was surely waiting for him, her face wrenched in inexplicable agony, her hands dripping blood as they reached out to him in supplication.

"No!" he shouted, forcing the image from his mind and stumbling into his mercifully empty lab.

"Computer," O'Donnell rasped through his parched throat. "Continue sample analysis."

"*Please specify sample designation,*" replied the maddeningly patient voice of the ship's computer.

"CR-H-94978-K," O'Donnell replied, not caring where in the sequence the analysis began.

"*Sample CR-H-94978-K fusion failed. Transcription error detected.*"

"Continue in chronological order," O'Donnell requested, as his head began to clear.

"*Sample CR-H-94979-K fusion failed. Transcription error*"

detected. Sample CR-H-94980-K fusion failed. Transcription error detected."

By the time the computer reached sample CR-H-94991-K, the darkness had begun to recede. His hands were clammy and his breath still came too quickly, but he knew the worst of it had passed.

I can fix this, Alana, he promised her. *You'll see.*

He seated himself on his stool before his data terminal as the computer droned on, reporting error after error in his latest batch of samples, until its voice took on the quality of white noise.

He was standing before Genov-see's burled-wood desk before he knew what had hit him.

"*The land in question has been privately held for nineteen generations,*" the minister thundered.

"*And if the quorum doesn't see fit to nationalize it now, tens of thousands of residents in Neshan and Plaro will starve come winter,*" Liam replied just as forcefully.

"*You were brought here to help us solve this problem, Lieutenant O'Donnell,*" Genov-see went on vehemently.

"*You've seen the estimated yields for the land we currently have under cultivation, and you seem to have at least a rudimentary grasp of mathematics. What is your alternative?*" Liam fired back.

"*You promised us yields would quadruple within the first three planting seasons. Are you really the best the Federation can do?*"

"*And the yields would have if your quaint notions of botanical purity hadn't restricted several of our hybridization schedules, Minister,*" Liam said.

"*The health of our people is my only concern. For thousands of years the Kressari have thrived by providing the* quadrant with the most structurally pure botanical lines."

"Spare me the history lesson. And spare me your sanc-timonious lies. You don't need to select for purity anymore, you need to select for yield volume. You'd rather allow thousands of your people to starve than disappoint the an-cestral elite that put you in power. The end of the famine cycles is within your grasp, but you won't risk your seat on the quorum by redistributing land lying fallow because it's owned by the lazy, self-serving bastards who put you in office."

"Minister, I am sorry to interrupt, but there is an urgent message for Lieutenant O'Donnell."

"It can wait," O'Donnell spat, unwilling to allow his anger with Genov-see to cool, even for a moment.

"I am assured it cannot," the page replied.

"Captain?" Fife's voice brought him immediately to con-sciousness, if not alertness.

O'Donnell turned sharply.

"What is it?" he demanded.

A faint glimmer of hope in Fife's eyes extinguished in-stantly.

"We have just entered the debris field. Our captors seem adept at avoiding contact with the largest pieces that might damage us during our progress."

"Our captors?" O'Donnell asked, trying to clear his head.

"The Children of the Storm," Fife reminded him dubi-ously.

"Aren't all children borne of chaos?" O'Donnell spat harshly. "It is only our desire to exert some sense of useless control over the madness all around us that permits anyone the arrogance of trying to continue their genetic line."

Fife seemed genuinely confused.

"Are you all right, Captain?"

In a sickening flash O'Donnell remembered where he was and, more important, what Fife was talking about.

"It's their debris field," O'Donnell said, steadying his voice. "They must be masters at navigating it by now."

Fife nodded, a little relieved. "I thought you'd want to know that *Quirinal* is gone."

O'Donnell's chin fell to his chest.

"Destroyed?" he finally asked.

"We monitored a battle for several minutes and then *Quirinal* vanished. Vincent believes they successfully brought their slipstream drive on line and escaped."

O'Donnell didn't bother to hide his surprise.

"Good for them," he said.

"Url is searching for a way to weaken the field surrounding us. He should have something in the next hour."

"Fine."

"In the meantime, Falto believes we are on course for the heart of the system that lies beyond the field. There's nothing particularly notable about it, as best we can tell for now. There are no planets capable of sustaining humanoid life."

"Keep me apprised of our progress," O'Donnell said, dismissing him.

"Captain?"

"Yes?"

"Who were you talking to when I arrived?"

O'Donnell's eyes narrowed.

"What did you hear?"

"Something about land lying fallow and self-serving bastards," Fife ventured.

"I was talking to myself," O'Donnell tried to toss back casually.

"I only ask because . . . that is . . ." Fife struggled a moment to summon up his courage. "We know the Children of the Storm are capable of possessing the bodies of telepaths."

"Then it's a good thing I'm not telepathic, isn't it?" O'Donnell shot back.

"What I was going to say, Captain, is that Url suspects their telekinetic abilities might allow them to infiltrate the minds of nontelepaths as well. He's studying the sensor readings we first took of the aliens. He hasn't finished his work, but—"

"Order him to finish it as quickly as he can, Commander," O'Donnell interrupted him. "Obviously, if that's true, we need to know. But you're not going to find evidence of it in my lab."

"Of course not, sir."

"Keep me informed."

"Aye, sir." Fife nodded and exited briskly.

After a moment, O'Donnell turned his attention to the files now waiting on his terminal; they contained all available data on the Children of the Storm.

Don't worry, Alana. I will not let this madness have its way.

He knew in his heart, however, that the madness usually did just that in the end.

Determined to slacken its pace, however, he began to analyze those who had captured his ship and could easily, within seconds, end the lives of everyone aboard.

Even without Alana's help, the mental exertion had its usual calming effect.

Chapter Fifteen

STARDATE 58456.9
U.S.S. VOYAGER

Tom Paris could hardly believe his eyes. In the ten hours it had taken *Voyager* to reach the source of *Quirinal*'s distress signal, he had imagined dozens of versions of what they might find. None of them came close to the real thing.

The main viewscreen displayed an image of *Quirinal*, or what had once been the massive ship, resting at an angle against a range of mountains, capped a few hundred meters above the top of the saucer section with the last of the winter's snow.

Among the many breaks *Quirinal* had apparently caught in their mad rush to escape the Children of the Storm was exiting the slipstream corridor near a system containing a Class-M planet. The planet was devoid of humanoid life, though it was home to a vast variety of plants, and thousands of different animal species roamed its plains and filled its skies and oceans.

Dotting the valley that lay at the base of the mountain, several kilometers of which had been cleared by the ship's obviously rough emergency landing, an encampment had been created where the ship's survivors had taken to living for the past two and a half weeks. Several large chunks of the ship's hull were missing, and the result reminded Tom of a scarred carcass whose innards have been plucked out by scavenging vultures.

Soon enough, the visual of the ship was replaced by the face of an officer Tom remembered from several of the pre-launch mission briefings, Lieutenant Psilakis. Sharp brown eyes greeted them, though several yellowing bruises dotted his face, mingling with dirt covering his cheeks, hands, and ragged uniform.

"*I've never a seen a more beautiful sight than* Voyager, *Captain Eden,*" Psilakis said cheerily. Tom could well imagine his relief.

The image on the screen began to distort, and Eden turned sharply to Lasren.

"What's the problem, Ensign?"

"Interference on their end, Fleet Commander," Lasren replied. "Their power is fluctuating."

"*We're on the last of our emergency backup modules,*" Psilakis grinned. "*You didn't arrive a moment too soon.*"

"Where is Captain Farkas?" Eden inquired.

"*She's alive, but in critical condition,*" Psilakis replied. "*She faced down several . . . um . . . intruders before we got the slipstream drive running. Doctor Sal has been watching her day and night. She thinks it'll take more time, but the captain will pull through. The rest of the senior staff is still undergoing evaluations. They were compromised during the attack. I've assumed command in the meantime.*"

"Sounds like you've been through hell," Eden rightly surmised.

"*I've had better weeks,*" Psilakis agreed.

"We'll get emergency teams down to you as soon as possible," Eden advised him. "And I'd like to begin my review in sickbay."

"*Understood,*" Psilakis said, nodding. "*Pardon me, but is the admiral with you?*"

"We've had our own challenges the last few weeks, as well," Eden said dryly. "I'm in command of the fleet now. I'll be happy to explain when we see you."

"*Looking forward to it,*" Psilakis said. "Quirinal *out.*"

As his face disappeared, Eden turned to Chakotay. "Can Seven of Nine repeat the trick she did to locate *Quirinal*'s signal?"

"Possibly," he said.

"We have to contact the rest of the fleet as soon as possible. They're over forty thousand light-years from our present position, but we need *Achilles* out here yesterday."

"And *Galen*," Chakotay added.

"But I'm not going to leave these people alone one day longer to make that happen."

"I'll speak to her, and then join you in the transporter room."

With a nod, Eden turned again to the viewscreen.

"It could have been worse," Paris offered.

"But not much," Eden replied.

U.S.S. QUIRINAL

"Well, if you aren't a sight for sore eyes," Doctor Sal said congenially as Eden and Chakotay entered sickbay. *Voyager*'s CMO, Doctor Sharak, had already been dispatched to the valley to attend to the medical needs of those in less critical condition. One of the few blessings *Quirinal* could count was that the location of sickbay had prevented it from suffering too much damage in either the attack or the "landing" they had made on the planet's surface. Every ounce of power the ship could spare was being routed to sickbay, and thanks to Sal and her staff's efforts, an amazing number of wounded had been moved out of critical care in the last few weeks. Only two now remained under constant evaluation: Captain Farkas and Chief Ganley.

"Hello, El'nor," Eden greeting Sal warmly.

Chakotay was busy trying to adjust his feet to a comfortable position. Though the deck was solid beneath him, it sat at a slight angle thanks to the ship's resting position.

"And who might this tall drink of water be?" Sal said, extending her hand to Chakotay.

"Captain Chakotay." He grinned, not at all offended by her forward manner.

Sal raised a quizzical eyebrow. "The same Captain Chakotay who used to command *Voyager*?" she asked.

"Yes."

"Huh," Sal said, considering him a little more carefully now. "Nice tattoo."

"Thank you." He smiled again.

"And Psilakis tells me you're now commanding the fleet?" Sal demanded of Eden.

"It's a long story," Eden replied.

"I can't wait to hear it," Sal replied. Turning to Chakotay, she added, "You get used to the list, Captain. I swear my left leg is going to be permanently shorter than my right if we ever get this ship in space again. And I'll probably have a constant crick in my neck."

"Sounds like that is the least of your problems right now," Eden suggested.

Sal replied with a gallows laugh. "You want them in alphabetical or chronological order?"

"I understand Captain Farkas remains in critical condition," Eden said.

All traces of mirth fled from Sal's face. "She was exposed

to the heat and atmospheric toxicity of dozens of explosions before she transported out. I've placed her in a coma until the damage to her lungs has time to repair itself. I'll let her tell me when she wakes up how much cosmetic work she wants done on the rest."

Gesturing them toward a single room surrounded by a transparent wall, Chakotay caught his first glimpse of Regina Farkas. She rested peacefully enough beneath a sheet, but her visible bare arms and chest were covered with surgical bandages, and a neural monitor was affixed to her forehead.

"How were the Children of the Storm able to board the ship?" Eden asked.

"Remember how we were worried that they could possess the bodies of telepaths?" Sal said, and Eden nodded in response. "Turns out we should have thought bigger."

"What do you mean?" Chakotay asked.

"The psionic force field we devised works like a charm, but everybody not protected by it is a potential victim," Sal said grimly. "As best we can tell, of the hundred and sixteen crewmen they compromised once the attack began, none of them have any psionic abilities at all. But all of them were alpha shift officers, and almost all of them have reported odd dreams just before they went on duty. We think that's how the Children of the Storm accessed their minds."

"While they were asleep?" Eden sought to clarify.

Sal nodded. "They all remember attacking their fellow crewmen and, as you can imagine, they feel like hell about it. But the consensus is that they couldn't control their bodies. It was like they were watching themselves and were unable to resist, no matter how hard they tried.

"All of their neural scans have been clean for weeks now, but Psilakis still doesn't want to return them to duty. Given that he fought eight of them personally before single-handedly taking control of the bridge, getting us this far and then landing the ship, I can't say I'm willing to fight him too hard on it for now. Commander Roach is spitting nails, he's so mad, though. He's dying to get back on duty."

Eden and Chakotay shared an uneasy glance. "We'll look into it," Eden assured Sal.

"So in answer to your original question, one of the ensigns in our shuttlebay basically welcomed a single sphere on board. From there— Psilakis can explain it better than I can, but a number of smaller spheres broke off from the main one and infiltrated the ship. We had a hell of a time containing them, and a couple hundred of our crew members were injured or killed in the battle to do so."

"Were you able to make contact with the Children of the Storm during the attack?" was Eden's next question.

"Oh, yes." Sal nodded. "Regina followed first-contact protocols to the letter, for all the good it did her. All they kept saying was that they would take what they called 'the life' and that we were destroyers of worlds." Sal lowered her voice. "They fired first, though, Captain. They destroyed *Planck* without warning, and after that, Regina fought back to defend the rest of us."

"I'm sure she did everything she could, El'nor," Eden readily agreed.

After a moment, Sal asked, "Did *Demeter* make it?"

"We don't know yet," Eden replied. "But we're going to find out."

•   •   •

After the first ten minutes spent examining Phinn's work, both B'Elanna and Conlon were dumbstruck, partially by his ingenuity but more by how determined he was to remain cheerful in the face of catastrophe.

"What's my option?" he asked, when Conlon had voiced this compliment.

Neither she nor B'Elanna had a good answer for him.

That said, from the moment she stepped into what remained of main engineering, B'Elanna had doubted that *Quirinal* would ever fly again. What was traditionally an ordered space was a tangled mass of conduits and power distribution nodes, arranged in what initially appeared to be a completely random and haphazard way, though in time the method to Phinn's madness became clear enough. Massive chunks of debris had been piled in corners. Most consoles had been removed, exposing the circuitry within, and deck and wall plates had been tossed aside to allow for direct access to functioning components. Fine particulate matter sat atop every surface save Phinn's command station. Most of the engineers working in the area had developed chronic coughs in the absence of functioning environmental controls.

The slipstream drive had been completely fried during the single jump *Quirinal* had made to safety. The warp core was in one piece, but had been disconnected for the time being.

"Job one," Phinn explained, "is to keep what little power we have flowing to our most sensitive areas. The bridge has been dark since we landed, except for sensor checks every few hours. The crew has been relocated outside the ship. The weather has held, which has helped tremendously, though our remaining crew quarters wouldn't have housed half of them, even if I could keep them warm and lit. We have fifteen functioning replicators, and all of our emergency foodstuffs are rationed daily."

"So where is your power going?" Conlon asked.

"Sickbay," Phinn replied. "We would have lost a third of the crew without Doctor Sal," he went on. "I don't think she's slept in two weeks."

"Doesn't she have an EMH?" B'Elanna asked.

"Our hologrid pulls way too much power," Phinn replied. "It was that, or our emergency containment field on deck thirty."

"What are you containing on deck thirty?" B'Elanna asked.

Phinn's face fell into the most serious lines B'Elanna had yet seen. "Psilakis didn't tell you?"

"No."

Phinn rubbed his nose, then shook his head. "I guess you'll find out soon enough anyway. We captured and contained ten of the alien spheres. Their destructive capability is too intense to risk freeing them, so we secured them in a containment beam. It's held in cargo bay eleven behind our last functioning psionic force field. Weird thing was, as soon as we put them in the same room, they merged of their own accord into a single larger sphere. Truth be told, I thought Psilakis should try and find a way to destroy it safely, but he thought it might come in handy."

B'Elanna took a moment to study Phinn's board. "You're diverting fifty-eight percent of your power reserves to that cargo bay. That seems like an awfully high price to pay."

"You'll have to take it up with Psilakis," Phinn replied.

B'Elanna decided she would, the first chance she had.

Chapter Sixteen

FOURTEEN DAYS EARLIER
U.S.S. DEMETER

Fife stood beside Url's tactical station, speaking under his breath. *Demeter*'s forward motion had ceased nineteen minutes earlier, but the field surrounding it hadn't wavered in formation or intensity.

They held position five hundred thousand kilometers from the system's fourth planet, a little over a hundred and seventy-five million kilometers from the star at the system's heart.

"I'm telling you, something's not right," Fife insisted.

"We have no control over our ship. We just watched one of our sister ships destroyed by a power we barely comprehend and the other barely escape. It'll be weeks at best before anyone might come to our aid. *Nothing* is right about any of this, sir," Url replied.

Though Url wouldn't necessarily have been his choice in a confidant—Fife had never really had much use for close interpersonal relationships with his crewmates—he needed to talk to someone, and thus far, Url seemed to possess the steadiest hands and head around.

"I'm saying if his behavior becomes more erratic, I might have to relieve him," Fife said bluntly.

"I'm reasonably sure none of us, including Captain O'Donnell, are at our best right now," Url said evenly. "But if his behavior should become dangerous, I would, of course, support that decision, Commander."

It wasn't the resounding clamor of support Fife had wanted, but it would do for now.

Fife inhaled sharply as O'Donnell ambled onto the bridge. It had been five hours since they had last talked, and the captain had actually expressed something like enthusiasm when he had learned that after almost two days the ship had finally reached its apparent destination.

Perhaps he got some rest, Fife thought bitterly. He was trained to believe that a captain put his crew's needs before his own. His crew ate, then he ate. They slept, then he slept. Whatever the cause of his incomprehensible temperament, O'Donnell was more than the eccentric genius Admiral Batiste had described to him. He was, in Fife's estimation, borderline unstable.

And he had absolutely no place commanding a starship, regardless of his rank and experience.

"You have a report for me?" O'Donnell asked with considerably less hostility than he had displayed the last time he and Fife had spoken at length.

"We appear to have arrived at our destination," Fife said briskly.

O'Donnell turned to study the main viewscreen, which at the moment displayed a calm, star-filled sky.

"What's special about this location?" he asked of no one in particular.

"We don't know," Fife was first to answer.

"The closest planetary body is Class-K, approximately five hundred thousand kilometers from our position," Url expanded for him. "The system contains seven planets surrounding a common G-type star."

When O'Donnell turned a quizzical face to Url, he continued. "None of the planets are currently capable of sustaining life of any kind. The Class-K might once have, but there is evidence of some sort of natural catastrophe that would have rendered it uninhabitable, probably hundreds of years ago."

"Do any of the planets appear to be the home of the Children?" O'Donnell asked.

"No, sir," Url replied. "There are two gas giants present, and it has been hypothesized that the Children of the Storm originated in a gas giant, but neither of them possess compatible atmospheric conditions."

"So why do they live here?" O'Donnell asked.

"Forgive me, Captain," Url said, "but we don't know that they do."

"They must have brought us here for a reason," O'Donnell suggested.

"That reason remains a mystery," Url said.

"I see," O'Donnell said as he took the center seat, which rotated on its base, and turned to face his tactical officer. "But for how long?" he asked.

When no one answered, he said, "Computer, display file O'Donnell COS Alpha on the main viewscreen. If something more interesting comes up, you'll let us know, Lieutenant," he said, nodding to Url, "but in the meantime, I want to go over what I've learned about our captors in the last few days. Unless anyone has a better suggestion, of course," he directed toward Fife.

"Of course not, sir," Fife answered automatically.

Clearing his throat, O'Donnell began, "This sphere is typical of those which first approached our position." The image of the sphere was suddenly filled with hundreds of tiny multicolored points of light. "The computer confirms that each sphere contains hundreds of distinct sentient life-forms, encased in an energy shell, source unknown. The atmosphere within each shell is composed of superhot liquid metal hydrogen and other trace metals. None of them are necessary for life as we know it to exist, so we're clearly dealing with some form of extremophile."

After a moment spent studying the bridge crew's faces for a perceptible reaction, he said, "Am I the only one who finds that amazing?"

"It might be more amazing if we weren't at their mercy right now," Fife said.

"Fair enough," O'Donnell agreed. "Moving on. Clearly they possess extraordinary telekinetic abilities. I have not been able to detect a distinct means of propulsion either in the spheres or in their conjoined formation. I have also studied our sensor logs to better understand the incredible speeds we have witnessed from the spheres, given that they lack obvious propulsion systems, as well as their ability to fool our sensors."

"And?" Url asked.

"I believe the energy shell is organized and sustained by the individual thoughts of the life-forms. I also believe they might be capable of traveling great distances by 'thinking' their way there."

"You're saying one minute they're one place and they can just decide to be somewhere else and that's where they appear next?" Fife asked in disbelief.

"More or less."

"That's impossible," Fife decided.

"When you have a better working hypothesis, Commander, I'll be all ears," O'Donnell replied.

"Actually, if you imagine a ship like ours with impulse, warp, and slipstream propulsion capabilities, it's not all that different," Url said.

"No," O'Donnell agreed. "We use our engines to bend space. They use their telekinetic abilities to do so."

"So why don't they do that all the time?" Url asked.

"Perhaps, as with us, it takes an enormous amount of energy to achieve that result. Linear travel would be less demanding. They might use their high-speed abilities only in situations of great need or danger."

Url seemed to consider the possibility, then nodded.

O'Donnell continued, "The computer can also accurately read several distinct resonance frequencies among the individual life-forms within each sphere. The only time the frequencies resonate in harmony are in the highest bands, those that show as violet in the example before you. The field that destroyed *Planck* was composed entirely of violet-hued life-forms. In the individual spheres, however, dozens of different frequencies are present."

"Which suggests what?" Fife asked, finally legitimately intrigued.

"If we think of each sphere like one of our starships," O'Donnell suggested, "it is possible that the different hues represent different functions within the sphere."

"So they have command officers, helmsmen, tactical, positions?" Fife asked.

"Possibly," O'Donnell said. "There is no way for me to classify the distinct frequencies, but their existence suggests some sort of necessary specialization."

"I agree," Url said.

"Thank you," O'Donnell replied amiably. "The formation currently surrounding *Demeter* has resonated in the orange range as we have traveled."

"Can an individual life-form change its frequency?" Fife asked. "Have we observed a tactical officer assume command, for instance?" he almost teased, eliciting nervous laughter from everyone on the bridge short of O'Donnell.

"No," the captain replied with a faint smirk. "I think that's why it was necessary for so many spheres to merge when they surrounded *Planck* and *Demeter*. The individuals inhabiting the merged spheres that did not resonate at the necessary frequency actually seemed to disappear as the spheres merged. They either escaped undetected, which I doubt, or they sacrificed themselves for the greater good. As seen from their point of view, of course," he added with emphasis.

Silence enveloped the bridge as everyone began to digest the captain's findings. Finally Fife asked, "How much of this is supposition, Captain?"

O'Donnell appeared almost offended by the suggestion. When he didn't respond immediately, Fife said, "I mean, you've had days while Starfleet's finest xenobiologists had months to examine *Aventine*'s data before our mission was launched."

"Those scientists had data on two spheres that were within sensor range for minutes. I've been able to study hundreds of spheres visible to our sensors for hours, along with new observations about their propulsion capabilities and destructive potential," O'Donnell replied evenly. After a moment he added, "And I am, after all, me."

This elicited a welcome round of light laughter from the bridge crew, as Fife felt his face growing red.

"Captain," Url interrupted, "hundreds of signals are incoming."

"Here ends the lesson." O'Donnell nodded. "On-screen."

Just as Url had indicated, masses of spheres were approaching *Demeter*. Fife found the sight absolutely terrifying.

"Url, would it be possible to program the computer to display the resonance frequencies of the individuals contained in each of the spheres approaching?" O'Donnell asked.

Before he could respond, Fife cut him off. "Belay that. Captain, if the spheres that brought us here did not contain enough of the destructive individuals, these could be their reinforcements."

"In which case, we're all about to die, Commander," O'Donnell said flatly. "But even if that's true, we might at least see it coming."

"The program is complete, and now visible on-screen, Captain," Url said, ending debate and casting a harsh glance at Fife.

The spheres continued their approach, now speeding toward them filled with bright variations all along the color spectrum.

"Beautiful, aren't they?" O'Donnell asked of no one in particular.

"And deadly," Fife reminded him.

"Goes without saying," O'Donnell noted.

At last, they came to rest several thousand meters short of *Demeter*.

"They have surrounded us, Captain, but they are holding their distance for now," Url reported.

"*Brill to the bridge,*" a gravely voice called over the comm.

"Go ahead," O'Donnell sighed.

"*Captain, I'm in aeroponics bay one and I think you should see this.*"

O'Donnell rose. "On my way. Atlee, the bridge is yours. Everybody enjoy the view until I get back."

As he exited the bridge, Url turned to Fife, who was already moving to take the center seat. In a low voice he said,

"I don't know about you, but I see nothing at all unstable about the man. It took him all of a day and a half to give us more information about this species than the rest of Starfleet could come up with in the months they had before this mission started."

Fife nodded compliantly, but all he could think was, *For now.* The only thing he wanted to know about the Children of the Storm was how to destroy them, and on that point, Captain O'Donnell had been entirely silent.

O'Donnell met no ghosts on the short trip to the aeroponics bay. His mind was focused on his analysis of the aliens; there was simply no room for the darkness to find purchase.

All he had to do now was keep it that way until Alana graced him with her return. In the interim, he would do all he could to prove himself worthy of her attention.

Ensign Brill, one of his botanical specialists, was waiting for him at the door to the bay, a long room lined with hanging aeroponics vessels stationed above tracks of humidifiers.

O'Donnell actually gasped at his first sight of the vessels.

"This is—" he began.

"Impossible, I know," Brill replied.

As late as yesterday morning, every one of the dozens of vessels had held seedlings and plants with bare branches that optimistically wouldn't have been expected to flower, let alone bear fruit for at least another two weeks. The first harvest of this bay had been completed a little early to provide *Planck* with the resources they requested.

But now, O'Donnell stared open-mouthed at vibrant ornamental blooms pouring out of the first two tracks, and plump, ripe fruit bursting from branches and vines along the rest. It might have been his imagination, but he believed several of the tomatoes, grapes, and figs were growing larger before his very eyes.

Brill stepped in to answer his unspoken question.

"The increase in growth rate was detected several hours ago. I just came back to check on them, and this is what I found."

"You're telling me we went from seeds to fruit in hours?"

"Yes, Captain."

O'Donnell's mind immediately began to spin hypotheses to explain this disturbing development. Only one seemed to have any merit at all. He'd never seen growth affected by telekinesis, but then again, he'd never seen anything else faintly resembling the Children of the Storm.

"Why would they do this?" he asked aloud.

"Who, sir?" Brill asked.

"The Children, obviously," O'Donnell replied, moving briskly to the nearest data terminal, where the growth rates of the last several hours were prominently displayed.

"O'Donnell to the bridge," he called.

"Fife here, sir."

"Give me a current image of the spheres that have surrounded us. Patch it through to the main terminal in aeroponics one."

"Aye, sir."

Moments later, O'Donnell watched as the spheres began to spin and gyrate along their individual axes. The various colors within them—oranges, reds, yellows, lavenders—all increased in vibrancy with the motion, and within minutes they had begun to move gracefully among each other, gliding, diving, spinning upward with ever increasing speed and intensity.

He could almost feel their delight.

He looked again at the vessels to see tendrils begin to droop under the weight of the fruit and blooms they bore.

"*Captain, as you can see, their configuration is changing, but we can't determine a cause,*" came Url's tense voice over the comm.

"I can," O'Donnell replied.

"*Sir?*"

"They're dancing, Ensign. For joy, unless I'm mistaken."

A memory, so vivid that the event might have occurred yesterday, shot to the forefront of O'Donnell's mind. When he was seventeen, he had first learned of the *Goldroni kurnit.* This staple of the Goldronians' diet had refused to yield a third of normal quantities, due primarily to a series of prolonged rainy seasons. The inhabitants had come to the Federation seeking aid. Liam had worked tirelessly for a year, creating tens of thousands of hybrid varieties until he found one that could endure the rain. The day he had presented his hybrid to the Goldronian prefect, he had been hailed as a hero and secured his place forever among elite botanical geneticists. More important, his work had ignited the passion that would drive him to this very day—a passion that had only dimmed in the years he spent on Kressari.

The pure happiness he had felt when genetic analysis confirmed the stability of the hybrid had been rivaled only by the serenity he'd known the day he and Alana had been sealed before Kressari's High Anointed.

He somehow doubted that these, the most powerful moments of his past, could rival what the Children of the Storm seemed to be experiencing in their current revels.

It was at that moment that the most alien species he had ever encountered became something more than a dangerous curiosity, or a problem to be solved.

It was at that moment that Liam O'Donnell learned that he shared with these strange dancing spheres a small shred of common ground.

The spectacle lasted for less than an hour. During that time, O'Donnell moved through each of *Demeter*'s labs, confirming the exponential growth of thousands of seeds, including dozens of exotic ornamentals that only now proved their viability.

Finally, spurred by a sense of heady elation, he entered his private lab, where several of his experimental samples of *Crateva religiosa-Kressari* waited in growth solutions. To his dismay, none of them showed the same growth as the rest of *Demeter*'s stocks.

As he chided himself internally for expecting a miracle where none was warranted, Fife's voice called to him over the comm.

"*Captain, the intensity of the resonance signatures of the spheres has begun to diminish.*"

"What about their movement?" O'Donnell shouted as he left his lab at a run to return to aeroponics one.

"*It is slowing,*" Fife replied.

As soon as O'Donnell reached the bay, he understood the reason. The few flowers that remained on stems were dried brown and black. Most of the blooms had already fallen into the humidifiers below them. Likewise, the unharvested fruits and vegetables were rotting on their vines.

Brill had begun along the first track and was methodically clearing vessels.

"All hands, this is the captain," O'Donnell called urgently. "Everyone who isn't flying the ship or standing post on the bridge is to report to their designated labs immediately. Fill every available receptacle with fresh sod or solution and seed them with whatever is handy. Forget about growth schedules. Plant anything you can find, and be prepared to continue planting around the clock until otherwise notified."

Assuming that his orders would be followed, and pleased that within minutes, six crewmen assigned to aeroponics one hurried into the lab and began clearing the dead specimens as if their lives depended on it, O'Donnell joined them, pulling as many spare vessels as he could carry to the first vacant row.

When he turned to grab his first set of seeds, he realized there might be a long-term problem with his plan. Desperation told him to throw as many seeds as each vessel could hold into the solution containers, but a little math reminded him that their seed stocks were not endless, nor easily replenished.

Of course, all of the specimens that had just gone through a growth cycle would have produced seeds that were automatically harvested. O'Donnell hurried to the seed receptacles that lay beneath the first row of vessels. There he found only a few of the dozens of seeds they should have contained. Those present were dark and coarse and clearly not viable.

They're moving through the life cycle too quickly, O'Donnell realized. Or something about the Children's influence over them was destroying the seeds.

Either way, it didn't matter.

"Limit your plantings to a single seed per vessel," he called to those working hurriedly around him. "And be careful with the seeds. We can't afford to waste a single one. Brill, pass the order along to the supervisors of each bay. We're going to have to make our current seed stocks last as long as possible."

With a nod, Brill hurried out of the bay to do as

O'Donnell ordered. Before he had finished seeding his first ten vessels, O'Donnell noted with satisfaction that tiny green shoots were already visible. Fifteen minutes later, Url confirmed from the bridge that the Children's "joy" seemed to be returning. O'Donnell was truthfully less concerned with their emotional state than the opportunity it provided him to keep his crew alive and his ship intact until a long-term solution could be found.

"Keep me advised," O'Donnell ordered as he dug both of his hands into a fresh container of seeds and realized that he probably had less than two weeks to come up with that solution.

Fife entered aeroponics one and paused, taken aback at the flurry of activity all around him. In the weeks he had spent aboard *Demeter,* he had avoided the growth bays. They were simply outside his area of expertise and were filled with quiet scientists who usually spent more time talking to their specimens than to each other.

He quickly spotted O'Donnell standing on an antigrav lift, hanging a series of vessels from a track that ran overhead.

"Captain," he said, crossing to him.

"What is it, Atlee?"

"Am I to understand that your entire plan for dealing with our current crisis is to placate our captors indefinitely?"

O'Donnell didn't stop working as he replied, "I wouldn't call it my entire plan, but it's definitely the first part."

"We need to find a way to escape the energy field," Fife insisted.

"Feel free to work on it, but if you're not on the bridge, you need to get your hands dirty, Commander," O'Donnell replied briskly.

Fife didn't bother to tell him that he was constitutionally incapable of making things grow. Though he had made a point of studying all of the species *Demeter* stocked, as well as their uses, he had killed every single plant or flower that had ever been given into his care, usually out of negligence.

"Sir," he said, unable to believe that the anyone, least of all a Starfleet officer, could so vastly underestimate the danger they were in. "Have you forgotten that these creatures destroyed one of our ships, killing seventy of our people?"

O'Donnell brushed the sweat from his brow with his forearm and turned to face Fife.

"Of course not," he said sincerely.

"Then why are you appeasing them?" Fife spat. "It seems to me that if we've actually discovered something that makes them happy, we should use it to negotiate our release."

"How?" O'Donnell demanded.

"We should begin by withholding it from them, and force them to make contact with us."

O'Donnell stared at him as if he were the stupidest person he'd ever encountered.

"The few telepathic crewmen we had were transferred to *Quirinal* before this mess began. Without anyone capable of conversation, how the hell do you propose we engage in negotiations?"

"I'm not sure," Fife allowed, "but we can't just go on providing them with entertainment until our supplies run out."

"I quite agree," O'Donnell said. "But we need to buy ourselves a little time to find a more permanent solution, and in the interim, I think keeping them happy is exactly what we ought to be doing."

"They're monsters, Captain," Fife finally said, releasing more hostility than he realized he'd been holding back.

"Hardly," O'Donnell replied. "We found them, they asked us to leave their space and never return, and we decided to come back anyway. It's not hard to argue that we are the aggressors here and that they have only acted to defend themselves and their territory."

"The destruction of *Planck* was completely unwarranted," Fife argued.

"From our point of view, sure," O'Donnell agreed, "but I'm not sure we should be judging them too harshly until we have a chance to get to know them a lot better. We've found a way to do that, and in the interest of keeping all of us alive a few more days, I'm ordering us to go with what we know until a better solution becomes available."

Fife started to open his mouth again, but O'Donnell cut him off. "Dismissed, Commander."

"Yes, sir," he replied.

Before he made it back to the door, O'Donnell called after him. "One more thing, Atlee. We need to reschedule all personnel to ensure that every growth lab is fully stocked around the clock. And you should restrict all hands to replicated foods only until ordered otherwise."

"Aye, Captain," Fife replied, though he was reluctant to obey the last. To accomplish what O'Donnell was asking would limit every member of *Demeter*'s crew to less than four hours of sleep per day. Assuming they kept this schedule up for the next two weeks, which was the earliest any rescue attempt might be expected from the rest of the fleet, they were all going to be bone tired. One of the few perks of working aboard *Demeter,* at least as Fife saw it, was the almost constant access to fresh food. Restricting everyone to the comparatively tasteless replicator fare wasn't going to help morale.

He decided to address the issue again the next time he spoke with O'Donnell. It was no use getting into another pointless argument right now.

In the meantime, he needed to find a way to make obeying that order unnecessary. He appreciated the fact that O'Donnell had stumbled upon a way to keep the Children of the Storm distracted for the time being, only because it might buy him the time he needed to find a tactical advantage that might grant *Demeter* her freedom.

Chapter Seventeen

STARDATE 58458.5
SURFACE OF UNNAMED PLANET

B'Elanna found Captain Eden in the makeshift outdoor mess that had been set up a few hundred meters from what had once been *Quirinal*'s deflector array. Given all they were facing, she was surprised to see the fleet commander distributing hot meals to a long line of crewmen. It was likely the first warm food any of them had enjoyed in weeks, and it was possible thanks to a pair of replicators Conlon's people had managed to rig in just a few hours.

B'Elanna was about to take issue with Eden's command priorities when she paused long enough to notice the looks on the faces of those who were accepting food, and in most cases, a few moments of conversation or a simple handshake from her. Their relief was palpable, as was their obvious pleasure in seeing the fleet commander cheerily pulling a duty shift none of them would have envied.

Hesitant as she was to take Eden away from work that was clearly more important than it appeared at first glance, B'Elanna decided she must. And it would be better if what she had to say went unheard by *Quirinal*'s crew.

"Captain, a word?" she asked, stepping beside Eden.

The captain turned and acknowledged her with a faint nod. Minutes later, they were walking slowly away from the mess toward the valley's command post.

"You have a report for me?" Eden asked.

"I've been through every centimeter of the ship that's accessible," B'Elanna replied, "and frankly I'm amazed it survived the landing."

"Let's just be glad it did," Eden offered.

B'Elanna swallowed hard before continuing. "I know *Achilles* has many of the parts we'll need to reconstruct her, and what they don't have, they can replicate, but I'm still not convinced she'll ever fly again."

Eden's head snapped toward B'Elanna and she stopped dead in her tracks.

"Why not?"

"The structural damage is immense. A space port could probably make all of the needed repairs, but with her lying here like this, I don't see how we can do it. Plus, it's not like she just needs to be in good enough shape to get to the nearest starbase. She's going to have to survive slipstream flight to rejoin the rest of the fleet, let alone ever see the Alpha Quadrant again. The effort alone is going to cost the rest of the fleet dearly in terms of supplies, personnel, and power. At the end of the day, I'm not sure it's worth it."

Eden considered B'Elanna silently, her face settling into hard lines.

"I don't care what it costs," she finally replied. "Seven was able to make contact with *Esquiline*. *Achilles* and *Galen* are on their way here right now and should arrive inside of twenty-four hours. Between now and then your orders are to prepare a complete list of supplies and personnel required to completely restore *Quirinal*."

"Understood," B'Elanna replied. "But you do realize, this project is going to take weeks, even with all of our people working around the clock."

"How many weeks?"

"Four, maybe five."

"You have three, Chief."

B'Elanna shook her head. She couldn't believe she was about to have *this* conversation again. "Four is a minimum, Captain. I know a lot of engineers like to overestimate their timelines, but I'm not one of them. When I say I need four weeks, that's exactly what I mean, and no amount of wishing or pushing or prodding is going to change that."

A quick smile flashed over Eden's lips.

"Very well. Four it is."

U.S.S. QUIRINAL

Harry, Seven, and Patel had spent the last hour submitting the single sphere *Quirinal* now contained to every analysis possible, using portable scanners they'd brought from *Voyager*. As it was unsafe to enter the cargo bay, they had stationed themselves just outside it, but they could view the sphere through a small transparent window embedded in the titranium-reinforced walls. While they had successfully scanned the sphere more thoroughly than any other individuals up to this point, the energy shell of the sphere and the psionic field keeping those inside it from projecting their will onto any nearby humanoid made a complete analysis difficult. Still, they were making progress.

Seven had been the first to point out that the sphere contained two distinct resonance frequencies of the life-forms and to hypothesize that these distinctions might indicate particular specialized functions of the individuals. Patel had argued that the distinctions could as easily indicate age, gender, or mood. Harry had decided they should agree to disagree until they were able to actually ask their captives about the frequencies' significance, if that ever happened. They had then worked to construct a harmonic scan that could pierce the energy shell without puncturing it. Watching Patel and Seven try to solve a problem together reminded Harry of the early days of contention between Seven and B'Elanna. He was happy to referee, but he wondered if that job might not be better accomplished by Counselor Cambridge, who had also been ordered to join their team but had yet to report for duty. Harry had only been assigned to provide security while they worked.

"That's it," Patel said triumphantly.

After a moment, Seven apparently agreed, though with considerably less enthusiasm.

"Lieutenant Kim," Seven said, "we have managed to get a clear scan of a single life-form's DNA."

"That's great, you two," Harry said, quick to divide the praise between them. He moved to the data terminal to glance at the DNA, but had to admit that he didn't really understand exactly what he was seeing. The structure didn't even vaguely remind him of the humanoid DNA he had seen countless examples of.

Patel worked quickly, feeding the data they had retrieved into *Voyager*'s computer and requesting further analysis. For her part, Seven watched, staring at the various images on the screen before her as if they had some private message meant for her alone.

Finally she said, "This can't be right."

Patel nodded. "I know. I think our harmonics were off slightly."

"They were not," Seven countered.

"They had to be, Seven. There isn't enough here to account for consciousness, let alone sentience."

"This does explain their resilience, however," Seven noted.

"Definitely."

Harry raised his hand. "Could one of you possibly explain what you're talking about to the member of this team who is not a xenobiologist or former Borg?"

Patel turned away from her screen and placed a hand on her hip, shooting Harry a weary smile.

"The first question is: how do these life-forms survive in the atmosphere that sustains them?" Patel said.

"I'm with you so far," Harry replied.

"To have life, you have to have metabolism, but there's nothing in the atmosphere inside the sphere that any life-forms I've ever seen would metabolize."

"Other than these trace heavy metals," Seven said.

"Exactly." Patel nodded. "Which are more likely to be waste products than a nutrient source."

"So that leaves the hydrogen," Seven finished for her.

"And the hard radiation they'd have plenty of access to in open space."

"So the quantity of available food is what makes them so resilient?" Harry asked.

"No, this part of their DNA does," Patel explained, indicating a particular sequence on the display. "I think they actually use radiant energy to repair their DNA."

"They appear to be virtually indestructible," Seven added, "as long as their atmosphere remains relatively constant."

"But none of this explains their telekinetic abilities, which have to be a product of consciousness," Patel went on. "These are microscopic organisms, not single cells, but no more than a couple hundred thousand each."

"What if we're looking at two life-forms?" Seven suggested.

"Go on," Patel replied dubiously.

"There are examples of species that have evolved as pure consciousness. Perhaps at some point, likely thousands of years ago, one such species encountered these hardy extremophiles and infected them."

"Like a virus," Patel said, obviously warming to the theory.

"Exactly." Seven nodded. "These sequences," she said, pointing to the screen, "could have been formed by the merging of a distinct genome with a parasitic consciousness."

"And they evolved together," Patel agreed. "That's entirely possible."

"Can they reproduce?" Counselor Cambridge asked.

All three turned to see him standing at the entrance to their makeshift lab.

"Good of you to join us, Counselor," Harry said with a light dollop of sarcasm.

"Of course," Cambridge replied as if he hadn't noticed. Turning to Patel and Seven, he asked again, "Well, can they?"

"Not in their present form . . ." Seven began.

"They're lacking key enzymes necessary for procreation," Patel finished for her.

Harry crossed his arms and considered them both.

"What?" Seven asked.

"I'm just not sure I'm ready for another pair of crewmen on *Voyager* who can complete each other's sentences," Harry said wryly.

"But the upside is that it should make our scientific briefings considerably shorter in the future," Cambridge said.

Striding toward them, he continued, "It seems you three have made short work of this without me. Unless there's something apart from the obvious you think you've missed."

Harry noticed Patel stiffen, while Seven settled for staring at the counselor with a gaze that could have melted the deck plates.

"The obvious, Counselor?" Harry decided to ask, as both of his teammates seemed content to allow the uncomfortable silence to drag on indefinitely.

"Yes." Cambridge nodded. "We may now know what makes these extraordinary creatures thrive, but the fact that they can't reproduce shouldn't surprise anyone."

At the blank or hostile stares of the others, Cambridge asked, "Don't they call themselves the *Children of the Storm*?"

"Yes," Harry replied.

"So where in the universe are their parents?" Cambridge asked.

U.S.S. VOYAGER

Chakotay found Seven and Patel's briefing fascinating, as usual, but at the end of fifteen minutes was less convinced than Counselor Cambridge that the most significant issue now before them was to discover the source from which the aliens had originated.

Captain Eden, on the other hand, was taking a more serious interest in the question.

"Are we certain that there are no likely candidates for the Children's 'mother' in the system surrounded by the debris field?" she asked.

"We are," Seven replied. "Even the cursory scan we were able to run while retrieving the buoy gave us complete readings of the seven planets contained in that system. Neither of the gas giants located there contains similar atmospheres to the one that sustains the Children."

"And we're looking for a gas giant because . . . ?" Eden asked.

"The contents of the atmosphere contained within the individual spheres most closely resembles that of a gas giant," Patel answered.

"If we wanted to find their mother, do we know what we need to be looking for?" was Eden's next question.

"Yes." Seven nodded. "But I believe our odds of finding this 'mother' may be slim."

"Why?"

"We cannot precisely determine the age of the Children, but given their resilience, it is possible that they have survived for thousands of years. The creature or creatures that gave rise to them could easily have died out during that time," Seven said.

"Which might also have been a factor in their migration to the system which they now consider their own," Patel added.

"Their age, then, apparently has little correlation to their maturity," Cambridge noted.

"You believe they are behaving like the children they call themselves?" Chakotay asked.

"I confess, I find myself at something of a loss to explain their choice of a designation, but if, as Seven suggests, they have existed for centuries, one does wonder if they even have a concept for maturation. Consider the single-mindedness with which they approach their work. Clearing their space of the Borg cannot have been easy, but clearly they persevered. Any experience gained in the process, however, did little to engender in them even the most basic curiosity about other species. They demand to be left alone, and when their demands aren't met, they throw a tantrum. I don't care how long they've lived, from a developmental point of view, they are, in fact, children. Unfortunately, it is often true that wisdom does not always follow on the heels of age."

"And the best person to tend to an unruly child is usually its parent, isn't it?" Eden asked.

"Unless the parent is psychotic," Cambridge agreed.

"We could waste a lot of time looking for this 'mother,'" Chakotay noted pointedly.

"We do have another option," Seven added.

"What's that?" Eden asked.

"We are holding several hundred captives. Perhaps we could trade them for the safe release of *Demeter*."

As Eden considered this, Chakotay asked, "Do we have any idea why *Demeter* might have been spared in the first place?"

When no one ventured a guess, Cambridge spoke up. "They said they wanted 'the life.'"

"All three vessels contained numerous life-forms," Eden said.

"Pardon me," the counselor replied, "I meant the simple life."

"You're referring to the botanical specimens contained aboard *Demeter*?" Chakotay asked. "What use does a non-corporeal life-form have for plants and flowers?"

Cambridge shrugged. "I'm not sure, but we would do well to take them at their word. They wanted *Demeter* badly enough to destroy *Planck* and all but destroy *Quirinal*. Clearly there was some value there."

"That's quite a leap, Counselor," Chakotay observed.

"Not really," Seven said, though it clearly caused her pain to find herself in accord with Cambridge.

"How so, Seven?" the counselor asked, smiling congenially.

"We know the Children first encountered the Borg centuries ago. My memories from the Collective do not include the system or species, but it is likely that the Borg entered their territory in order to extract raw materials from it."

"The Children would have been of no interest to the Borg," Cambridge said, nodding as if a light switch had just been thrown in his head.

"They were not candidates for assimilation," Seven went on. "But the system must once have contained resources the Borg found desirable enough to send thousands of cubes to capture."

"If, centuries ago, any of the system's planets were capable of sustaining simple life-forms, and the Borg came along to strip-mine them, the Children might have found their actions contemptible enough to wage war on the scale we've witnessed," Cambridge said. "They obviously have a disdain for complex life-forms."

"They called us 'destroyers of worlds,'" Eden said thoughtfully.

"But perhaps they found some sort of intrinsic value in more simple life-forms."

"Any planet where flora and fauna thrive would also have contained countless microbial life-forms which would have shared some common traits with the Children," Patel agreed.

"You think they were friends?" Chakotay asked.

"Probably more like curiosities," Patel replied. "The Children may not understand themselves to be conjoined life-forms. They might not even remember how they came to be. But if they do, and they detected other single-cell or basic life-forms, they might have tried to make contact with them or find a way to instill them with sentience, in the same way the organism first joined with the parasitic consciousness."

"Until the Borg came along and destroyed the worlds on which those life-forms thrived," Cambridge said.

After a moment, Patel noted, "It's still hard to believe this species so savagely destroyed the Borg."

"But we forget it at our peril," Eden said decisively.

"Captain?" Chakotay asked, sensing with considerable unease where Eden's thoughts were headed.

"Apart from the psionic force field, which would only protect our crew, we have no defense ready for that merged energy field that destroyed *Planck*. Attempting a rescue of *Demeter*, even with our hostages, which they may or may not be willing to bargain for, still seems impossible."

"We don't know right now if *Demeter* is still intact, but if it is, we can't let the crew struggle on alone indefinitely," Chakotay said.

"And we can't simply sacrifice ourselves on a mission we could not possibly hope to survive," Eden countered.

"They are vulnerable to our phasers," Chakotay reminded her. "We could make it worth their while to consider an alternative to further hostilities."

"The Borg had phasers and torpedoes and likely dozens of other conventional weapons they must have used against the Children," Eden shot back. "For all the good it did them."

When no one seemed inclined to argue further, Eden said, "Seven, begin long-range scans for any possible planets that could contain the Children's mother. In the meantime, I think we should ask Ensign Lasren to attempt to make contact with our captives. Unless anyone thinks we can learn any more about them without their input?" she asked of everyone present.

As the silence in the room stretched out, it was clear to Chakotay that no one did. He just wished he could offer a more compelling reason to throw caution to the wind and go after *Demeter* immediately, as he believed Kathryn would have done when faced with the choices before them. The only justification he had at the moment was his gut instinct that if *Demeter* was still in one piece, she was living on borrowed time.

U.S.S. QUIRINAL

Ensign Kenth Lasren stood completely still as Doctor Sharak, *Voyager*'s CMO, placed the neurological scanner in the center of his forehead and activated it. After studying its various bleeps and flashing lights for a few more seconds, he said in his low, pleasantly melodic voice, "The device is functioning at best possible configuration."

At which point Lasren's nervous system completely betrayed him and he broke into a nervous, cold sweat.

Doctor Sal shot a questioning glance toward Captain Eden. "Does he mean it's working?" she said softly.

"He does," Eden replied. "Doctor Sharak is the first member of the Tamarian species to accept a commission with Starfleet, as well as the first to master Federation Standard. We are lucky to have him serving with us."

Though Sal raised a dubious eyebrow at Eden's suggestion that he had "mastered" the language, she extended her hand to greet her fellow doctor.

"It's a pleasure to meet you," she said congenially.

"It is," Sharak replied, just as graciously, then added, "To meet you, of course." Turning to Eden, he said, "I will monitor the ensign's neurological stability while he attempts to speak with the aliens."

"Excellent. Thank you, Doctor," Eden replied.

All four of them stood outside the cargo bay where hours earlier, Seven, Harry, and Patel had analyzed the sphere. Lasren was honored by the confidence of the fleet's commander in asking him to undertake this mission. His past study of other telepathic species, as well as the actions of the Children of the Storm up to this point, however, left him more than a little frightened at the prospect of opening his mind to them.

As a Betazoid, he doubted his ability to communicate directly with the Children, unless they were able to initiate it. Though he could easily share his thoughts with other Betazoids, direct telepathy outside his species had never been one of his strong points. Should the Children possess strong enough emotions, he would be able to translate them fairly clearly.

And should they be as angry as I would at being held prisoner, they might just enter my mind and destroy as many brain cells as possible before I can be transported to safety, Lasren worried silently.

"Are you ready, Ensign?" Eden asked.

"Absolutely, Captain," Lasren replied, hoping that apart

from the beads of perspiration rolling down his forehead, Eden would find no reason to doubt him. Reaching out a little, he sensed only concern for him, along with a steadying dose of faith in his abilities.

"We'll be keeping a close eye on you, young man," Sal offered. "At the first sign of trouble, we'll have you out in no time."

Lasren offered Doctor Sal a faint smile. The concern rolling off her in waves eclipsed that of Captain Eden, but her experiences to date with the Children had traumatized her in ways she was not yet admitting to herself. Still, Lasren was grateful to have her there. He had no reason to doubt Sharak's abilities, but a split second lost while *Voyager*'s doctor translated his readings into the words that would convey an emergent problem might be more than his mind could handle. It didn't help that Tamarians were harder for him to read than many other humanoid species. The only thing he got from Sharak at the moment was faint anticipation tinged with curiosity and excitement.

Eden placed a steadying hand on Lasren's shoulder, then tapped her combadge. "Eden to transporter room one," she called to *Voyager*. "Transport Ensign Lasren inside the cargo bay."

"Acknowledged."

Sal had deemed it absolutely unsafe for the psionic field surrounding the bay to be lowered even for the moment it would take Lasren to cross the room's threshold. Transporting him directly inside would eliminate the risk to everyone but him. He took a deep breath as he felt the transporter take hold of him.

The moment he was released into the room, the pain slicing into his head dropped him to his knees. He felt his arms lifting from his sides of their own accord, but quickly regained enough control of them to bring them to the sides of his head. His only coherent thought was to keep his brain in place, though a sticky fluid meeting his fingers suggested it might be attempting to escape through his ears.

A low wail sounded all around him. Several seconds later, he realized it was coming from his mouth. The sensations bombarding him were so powerful as to be completely overwhelming, but through the anger he could clearly perceive came another, more powerful feeling.

Despair.

A few moments more, and the excruciating physical and emotional torment had vanished. He was vaguely aware of strong arms lifting him onto a biobed. His vision cleared long enough for him to recognize the ceiling of *Voyager*'s sickbay and Doctor Sharak's face over him as the neurological scanner was removed and a cool hypospray hissed into his neck.

Around him, soft voices floated in and out of his consciousness as the experience he had just endured unraveled itself in his mind.

U.S.S. VOYAGER

"I told you it was too dangerous," Sal chastised Captain Eden. Doctor Sharak had been capably tending to Lasren from the moment the emergency transport to *Voyager*'s sickbay had been completed.

"We had to try," Eden replied tensely.

"Those things don't understand anything but destruction," Sal went on, clearly not mollified.

Eden understood Sal's frustration. The last few weeks would have driven anyone in her position to the brink. And

Lasren's still, pale face, marred by drying blood that had oozed from his ears almost as soon as he'd entered the cargo bay, had her questioning her decision to try to communicate with the inhabitants of the sphere.

But more was at stake here than Lasren's life, and she knew it.

Doctor Sharak moved quietly to join them.

"He will thrive," he said simply.

"There is no permanent damage?" Eden asked, noting a faint huff of disgust from Sal.

"No," Sharak confirmed. Turning to Sal, he asked, "Are you in need of wellness?"

"I'd say we could all use a little wellness right now, Doctor," Sal replied.

Sharak considered her for a moment. His mottled face betrayed no expression, but his eyes were filled with compassion.

"Do not fear, Doctor," he said softly. "To attempt to communicate with a species so different from your own brings risk. But once the distance is bridged, it can also bring great reward."

Sal softened a little at his words.

"I'm sorry," she finally said. "I've lived long enough to know you're right, and to know better. Sometimes the reward is never worth the risk."

"I disagree," Sharak replied. "As did Ensign Lasren."

"That poor kid was ordered to take the risk," Sal corrected him, "and he was terrified to enter that room, or didn't either of you notice?"

"But that is the definition of courage," Sharak countered. "He accepted the order even with his fear."

"I'm not saying he wasn't brave," Sal replied. "Just that he didn't really have a choice."

"He chose to serve among the stars," Sharak said, bristling.

"And was probably hoping to serve with senior officers who would protect him," Sal said flatly.

"Sadly, that is not always the first concern of a captain," Sharak replied. "Sometimes for all to thrive, one must risk."

"Spare me the 'needs of the many' argument," Sal shot back. "I've seen too many people die in the last few weeks and months to find it terribly compelling."

"One of our greatest captains died to bring understanding between our people and yours," Sharak said sternly. "He did not think his sacrifice vain or unwarranted. There is no greater calling."

Sal was about to continue arguing the point when Lasren began to stir. Eden moved instantly to his side and automatically took his hand in hers as she spoke to him.

"Gently, Ensign," she said softly.

His eyes fluttered open and finally met hers.

"Wow," was his first word.

Eden smiled automatically. "How do you feel?"

"Actually, fine," Lasren replied, clearly surprised. After taking a quick physical inventory, he attempted to push himself up to a seated position.

"Doctor?" Eden turned to Sharak, concerned.

Sharak returned to Lasren's side and ran a tricorder over his body. "As I said, he thrives," he assured Eden.

Lasren's next question took Eden by complete surprise.

"Is there a way to modulate the psionic field?"

"Why?" Eden asked.

"Is it possible?" Lasren asked again more intently.

"Sure," Sal said, moving closer. "But it's not like we've tested the thing completely. It would be hard to know if there is a safer setting than maximum, and I can't imagine that you'd volunteer to be a guinea pig again."

"We have to try, Captain," Lasren practically implored Eden.

"What happened to you in there?" the captain asked.

"It hurt," Lasren replied. "I guess that was obvious. But I did get one very strong impression though the pain."

"Which was?"

"I think they're dying, Captain."

Chapter Eighteen

ELEVEN DAYS EARLIER
U.S.S. DEMETER

*I*t's going to have to be some version of Paspalidium constrictum, *probably crossed with* Festuca ovina, *given the temperatures. What do you think, Alana?*

Liam had been working his new puzzle for four days with barely a few hours sleep, but having finally settled on what he believed was the best possible solution, he half hoped to hear a little encouragement.

Alana remained stubbornly silent.

That's all right, darling. Whenever you're ready, Liam replied to the silence. Although the loneliness of the hours without her was palpably painful, he would endure. He'd suffered worse on her behalf in the hours leading up to her death.

His one-sided discussion was interrupted by Fife's requesting entrance to his private lab.

"What is our status?" O'Donnell asked briskly. He'd kept a casual eye on hourly status reports since the continuous planting regimen had begun, and though the Children were cycling through their supplies even more quickly than he'd first estimated, he was finally nearing the light at the end of the tunnel.

"There is no change in the formation or emotional state of our captors," Fife replied tonelessly. "Several hours ago, two additional spheres merged with those currently composing the energy field, but they did not disrupt or strengthen the field in any measurable way."

O'Donnell looked up to see Fife's eyes glued resolutely to the floor.

"What's the matter?"

Fife sighed deeply and stared, stone-faced, at O'Donnell. "Crewman Bell and Ensign Lamoth were found dead an hour ago in hydroponics four," he said stoically.

O'Donnell rose to his feet in alarm. "What happened?" he demanded.

"Doctor Peyman has just completed the autopsy. Apparently they suffered acute, instantaneous neurological damage."

"Cause?"

"Isn't it obvious?" Fife asked with open hostility.

O'Donnell ran his hands over what had once been a mass of dark, thick curls. To this day it surprised him when his fingers found only the hard, cold skin covering his head where his hair used to be.

"Why those two?" O'Donnell asked as evenly as possible. "We've been 'captive,' as you put it, for over a week, and this is the first sign of violence from the Children directed at us."

"Maybe they've just been biding their time," Fife suggested. "Or maybe they wanted to encourage us to work faster."

O'Donnell couldn't shake the feeling that Fife was holding something back. Eyeing him warily, he replied, "Somehow I doubt it."

Fife's eyes again hit the floor. "The doctor did find a fair amount of undigested tomatoes in their digestive tracts."

Finally O'Donnell found his anger.

"Damn it all to hell. I gave the order—" he shouted.

"And although I disagreed with it, I did pass it along," Fife shouted back.

O'Donnell's breath came in rapid spurts. "You don't have the luxury of disagreeing with my orders, Commander. And if you passed it along as a suggestion, so help me you'll spend the rest of this mission—"

"I gave the order, Captain," Fife said again, this time with greater control over his emotions. "I didn't understand it—"

"The only thing, the *only thing* we know for sure about these creatures is that the presence of living, growing botanical organisms fills them with absolute delight," O'Donnell replied, aghast. "By eating the thing they hold dear, we could be perceived as destroying it."

"They were hungry," Fife replied, struggling again with his anger. "They couldn't have known."

"I gave the order that no one was to eat anything that wasn't replicated, Fife!" O'Donnell bellowed. "And you should know me well enough by now to understand that when I trouble myself to give an order, I have good reason. You don't have to understand it. You just have to follow it. That's one thing I didn't think you would have a problem grasping."

"It won't happen again, Captain," Fife replied.

"*Are you really the best Starfleet can do?*" Genov-see thundered in Liam's mind.

"Not now!" O'Donnell shouted.

Strained silence filled the room.

After a moment, Fife ventured, "I beg your pardon, sir?"

"Assemble the command staff in the briefing room in one hour," O'Donnell replied, his rage finally spent.

Fife looked like he had never been so happy to be dismissed as he hurried from the room.

Url watched anxiously as the other bridge officers took seats around the small rectangular table that was the briefing room's only furnishing. He paid special attention to Commander Fife, who appeared to be showing the strain of their predicament more than the rest of them. His initial impression of his XO was that he was efficient and demanding; not unusual in young officers who clearly aspired to one day command a ship of their own. He'd had no reason to doubt Fife's abilities until this crisis had begun. Though he had been initially inclined to share Fife's concerns about their captain, once O'Donnell had begun to interact more regularly with the crew, Url had decided that though he was eccentric, he certainly seemed to know what he was doing. Url would gladly follow the smartest person in the room before the strictest. As the last few days had unfolded, however, he'd seen Fife's hackles arranged in a permanently raised position. What had at first appeared to be concern about O'Donnell might now more generously be described as contempt. Url was third in *Demeter*'s command structure and did not relish the idea of constant tension between his two superiors, especially now, when every moment they lived was the apparent gift of a mercurial alien species.

Fife said nothing as he took the seat to Url's left. Vincent and Falto both studied the table's surface in a clear attempt to avoid addressing Fife. After what seemed like an eternity, Captain O'Donnell finally entered and distributed a set of padds to each of the officers present.

"Though I'm sure you've all enjoyed our little detour into the territory of the Children of the Storm as much as I have," O'Donnell began, "I believe we've stayed here long enough."

Fife's eyes shot up and fixated on O'Donnell. They were filled with dubious hope. Faint smiles played over the lips of Vincent and Falto. Url found the captain's light tone refreshing, given the obvious tension that was in need of regular fracturing.

Settling into his chair, the captain continued, "The good news is, we have discovered a means of distracting the Children. It appears that as long as we provide them with objects of constant interest, they will allow us to go on living. But this is clearly not a permanent solution. Nor was it ever meant to be," he directed toward Fife.

"Ensign Brill has just confirmed my estimate that we will run through our supply of seeds inside of the next fifteen days. He's managed to prolong our supplies, but they are not infinite."

Url inhaled sharply. They were at least nine days away from being missed by the rest of the fleet. Heaven only knew how many days beyond that they might require to locate *Demeter* and prepare a rescue operation.

"But there is no cause for alarm," O'Donnell said patiently. "The fourth planet of this system holds the key to our freedom."

Seeing the confused stares whipping around the table, Url asked, "How so, Captain?"

"It is my belief that if we could provide the Children with a constant source of amusement, they might lose interest in us."

"But the fourth planet isn't capable of sustaining life, sir," Url interjected.

"Never mind that," Fife added. "How can we possibly seed the fourth planet without helm control?"

"Both good questions," O'Donnell continued, unfazed. "The fourth planet isn't capable of sustaining humanoid life, nor most botanical species which thrive in oxygen/nitrogen atmospheres. I have successfully created a hybrid grass, however, along with six different strains of bacteria to help it along, that has shown itself to be compatible with the planet's atmosphere. Naturally it will take years for it to spread beyond any initial planting, but I believe if the Children's actions thus far are typical, they might be able to help our little plants along their way."

Url was impressed. He'd known O'Donnell only by reputation before joining *Demeter*'s crew. He was best remembered as the man who single-handedly saved Kressari from decades of famine that threatened to eradicate a large portion of their population. He doubted that most other Starfleet captains would have been able to provide this kind of solution, though some of their science officers would certainly have possessed the requisite skills.

"That still doesn't explain—" Fife began.

"How to get the seeds to the surface," O'Donnell finished for him. "Yes, Commander." Turning to Url, he asked, "We were able to successfully launch our message buoy through the energy field, weren't we?"

"Yes, Captain," Url replied. "It penetrated the field without disrupting it."

"As I suspect one of our robotic planter drones will as well," O'Donnell said, smiling. "But just in case the Children doubt our intentions, I intend to fill a portion of the drone's storage hold with a few of our seedlings. I don't know how else to make the drone nonthreatening enough for them to allow it to pass all the way to the planet's surface," O'Donnell admitted.

"How long will it take the drone to do its work once it reaches the surface?" Fife asked.

"Ten hours at least," O'Donnell replied. "And without the Children's help it will be days, if not weeks, before the first buds might be visible. I'm hoping we'll be able to access the drone's command systems from the bridge in case adjustments need to be made once it actually samples the surface soil. I've programmed it with every variation I can think of, but that won't matter if there's one I've missed."

Vincent had been following the captain's words enthusiastically, but seemed to deflate a little. "Captain, during the first twelve minutes of our battle with the Children, while we were still in range of *Quirinal* and *Planck,* we were never able to establish communications. If that was intentional on the Children's part, and not simply a by-product of the energy field, I doubt that we'll be able to sustain a communications link with the drone."

O'Donnell nodded. "I agree. But I'm hoping the Children will see what we're trying to do. We've already gained a little of their trust. All we need is a little more for this to work."

"Url," Fife asked, "when you say our buoy penetrated the field without disrupting it, do you mean that the field was dispersed around it?"

"I'd have to go back and study the readings," Url replied honestly. "But in theory, I suppose it must have."

Fife smiled for the first time in days. "That might be all we need, Captain."

O'Donnell turned a quizzical gaze toward Fife. "I don't follow," he said.

"The launch of the drone might distract the Children, even for a few seconds. If sustaining the energy field surrounding our ship requires their full concentration, it might waver enough for those seconds for us to regain helm control."

"And go where?" O'Donnell asked.

Fife's eyes began to blaze. "Wherever we want."

Falto seemed to catch some of Fife's fire. "I've been studying the field for several days now," he said. "It has remained constant, despite the motion of the life-forms within it. There have been a few noticeable variances, however, that seem to correspond to our planting cycles."

"How so?" O'Donnell inquired.

"Whenever our specimens reach the peak of their life cycle, the field decreases slightly in intensity."

"They're busy enjoying the view," Fife interjected, clearly pleased.

"So what exactly are you suggesting?" O'Donnell demanded of Fife.

"We should plot a slipstream jump, coordinated with our planting cycle and the drone's launch. If there is a fraction of a second during which the Children are sufficiently distracted that gives us helm control, we might be able to execute the jump before they realize we're gone."

"Or they might decide to destroy us," O'Donnell countered.

Url could see that it would take more than this to dim Fife's resolve.

"I think that's a risk worth taking."

O'Donnell heaved a deep sigh, then studied the faces of Url, Vincent, and Falto. Url could see that he was torn. The scientist in him probably wanted to see the fruits of his labor. But the captain in him couldn't deny that Fife's suggestion was worth considering.

After a few moments' thought, the captain in him clearly won out.

"Very well," O'Donnell decided. "But I'd feel better about this if we could give it a test run."

"How do you propose we do that?" Fife asked.

"We could launch a drone, coordinated with a growth cycle, and study the readings. If the window we're hoping for appears, we could launch another a few hours later. If, by then, the Children see what we're trying to accomplish on the fourth planet, we might get an even wider space of time during which to establish helm control."

Fife gave the captain's argument its due, then shook his head. "There's no way to know for sure that we'll get more than one shot at this. For all we know, the Children will destroy the drone before it reaches the surface. They might think it's a weapon of some sort. Or the drone could fail to do its job. There are simply too many variables, in my opinion, Captain."

O'Donnell ran a hand over the top of his head, a gesture Url now associated with contemplation on his part.

Finally O'Donnell shrugged. "You may be right."

Fife rose from his seat. "We'll prepare the necessary calculations and be ready at the peak of the next growth cycle."

O'Donnell nodded faintly as the rest of the staff stood to follow Fife out. Url paused for a moment to note the disappointment clear on O'Donnell's face. The captain in him may have won the argument, but the scientist clearly bristled at having his work relegated to the status of a tactical distraction.

The scientist had Url's sympathy, but he found himself increasingly grateful that the command officer in O'Donnell was every bit as fierce as its counterpart. He returned to his station, wondering if Fife had appreciated the subtlety of the battle that had just been waged, or how much his victory had cost Captain O'Donnell.

Chapter Nineteen

STARDATE 58461.9
U.S.S. QUIRINAL

Chakotay watched anxiously as Ensign Lasren reentered the cargo bay aboard *Quirinal* that housed the captive sphere. B'Elanna and Conlon had spent the morning working with Lieutenant Bryce to modulate the psionic field to clear a small corner of the bay, from which Lasren would try again to reach the inhabitants of the sphere. They had also successfully realigned the field's intensity so that it could be lowered at intervals to make it safer for Lasren. Despite Doctor Sharak's confirmation that the ensign had suffered no permanent damage from his first encounter, Chakotay was not convinced that the risk Lasren was about to undertake could be justified. When he'd shared these concerns with Lasren, all but offering to support him should he wish to demur, the ensign had insisted that he wanted to try again. Apparently his first contact with the Children had filled him with concern that extended beyond himself, or the rest of the crew. Lasren seemed convinced that the Children needed him, though he couldn't explain exactly how he knew this.

Chakotay had seen and personally experienced enough esoteric mental journeys to trust Lasren's instincts, but that didn't lessen his fears for the young man's safety.

Eden stood by Chakotay's side. Doctor Sharak waited a few paces behind, studying the tricorder that was linked to the neural scanner affixed to Lasren's forehead. Apparently Doctor Sal had chosen not to continue to monitor their efforts to communicate with the Children, and from Eden's report of the first round, Chakotay got the impression that Sal was less than thrilled by their continuing efforts.

Lasren's combadge was set to an open channel linked to B'Elanna's in what was left of *Quirinal*'s engine room. On his instructions, B'Elanna would adjust the field intensity until they found a level with which he could work.

Chakotay watched as the ensign calmly seated himself cross-legged on the floor of the bay and heard him ask B'Elanna to reduce the field's intensity by one degree.

Eden tensed as soon as Lasren spoke, adding to Chakotay's discomfort. Despite all of the precautions being taken, she clearly did not trust the situation. Chakotay wondered why, if it bothered her this much, she had agreed to allow it at all, despite Lasren's obvious determination.

Lasren appeared to be fine, however, and progressed

through three further field reductions before signaling for B'Elanna to hold the intensity.

Half an hour later, he rose calmly from his place and advised B'Elanna to restore the field. He emerged from the bay pale and clearly exhausted by his efforts.

"What have you learned, Ensign?" Eden asked, as soon as he joined them.

Lasren took a moment to collect his thoughts, then said, "They don't understand that their lives will ever be different than they are right now."

"So they are dying?"

Lasren nodded. "They've never experienced captivity like this. They have no context for it. It fills them with rage, but there is no outlet for that rage, given the strength of the psionic field. Many of them have fallen into despair. Some have already been lost."

"They told you all this?" Chakotay asked.

"No." Lasren shook his head. "They are, in some ways, the purest beings I have ever encountered. Their feelings are simple. No, they're single, if that makes any sense. There are two distinct emotional states present. The aggressive, rage-filled few, and many more who are simply seeking a way out. But none of them could speak directly with me. I gathered what I could from their emotions. I actually think some of them might have sensed me, but they could not or would not respond."

Chakotay turned to Eden. "Seven and Patel have suggested that the different resonance frequencies present in each of the spheres might indicate a differentiation of function. This sphere currently has two distinct frequencies."

"That is exactly what I gathered, Captain," Lasren said. "If I had to assign 'duties,' I'd suggest weapons and navigation, which, given what they were doing aboard *Quirinal,* might be all they would need."

"Maybe this sphere doesn't have any 'communicators,'" Eden suggested.

"That doesn't bode well for our efforts here," Chakotay replied.

"With your permission, I'd like to keep working with them," Lasren requested of Eden.

"What more do you hope to learn?" she asked.

"If we intend to use them to bargain for *Demeter*'s return, they need to survive awhile longer," Lasren said. "Given enough time, I might be able to do more than sense them. I might be able to establish some form of indirect communication. Or at the very least, I might be able to comfort them a little. If I can make them understand that we don't intend to hold them forever, it might raise their spirits long enough for them to survive until we locate *Demeter.*"

"We can't risk freeing them, even if it means they all die," Eden said softly.

"Agreed," Chakotay offered, amazed that she would even consider it.

"Thank you, Ensign." She nodded to Lasren. "Continue your efforts, but don't exhaust yourself."

"Aye," Lasren said.

"I will stay with him," Doctor Sharak offered.

"Keep me advised," Eden replied.

Turning to Chakotay, she said, "*Achilles* and *Galen* should be here in the next five hours. Once they arrive, we will leave orbit and begin our search for the Children's mother."

"Captain, if Lasren can't reach them, we might not have the luxury of taking that much time."

"Then we have to hope he does," Eden said firmly.

She exited the bay without another word.

U.S.S. VOYAGER

B'Elanna was well and truly spent when she finally entered her cabin. The lights in the living area had been dimmed and the remnants of Miral's dinner still lay on the table.

She tiptoed toward the bedroom and crooked her neck around the doorway to peak inside. Her heart was immediately suffused with a pleasant, warm tingling at the sight of Miral cuddled in her father's arms. Their mouths were open, and Tom snored softly. *Timmy and the Targ* lay open on Miral's lap, obviously unfinished for the night.

No other sight could have filled B'Elanna with more certainty that she was one of the luckiest women alive. To share her life with a man she loved and a daughter who brought the amazement and simple joy of discovery to each day was a gift. B'Elanna vowed to remember to be grateful that the universe had granted her this much.

As she began a silent retreat from the doorway, Tom stirred and opened his eyes wide. Seeing B'Elanna, he relaxed and gently extricated himself from Miral's arms, laying her delicately on her back and creeping softly from the room to join his wife.

"Good bedtime?" B'Elanna asked when they were well clear of the door.

Tom replied by taking her in his arms and kissing her tenderly. "The best," he whispered in her ear.

B'Elanna pulled back to caress Tom's cheek with the back of her hand and lose herself for a few moments in his deep blue eyes.

"I love you so," she said softly.

"Glad to hear it," Tom teased. "You hungry?"

"Starved," B'Elanna admitted. She couldn't remember eating since breakfast, but at the moment she really didn't care.

Reading her thoughts, Tom pulled her toward the sofa. The need to avoid waking their daughter had brought a new tenderness to their intimacy. Though part of B'Elanna longed for the careless, more tempestuous passions of earlier years, what she and Tom now shared was every bit as satisfying for all of its restraint.

An hour later, the spell woven between them remained powerful as they sat over the remnants of their dinner, laughing and chatting quietly by candlelight.

Soon enough it was time to go to bed, but Tom clearly sensed B'Elanna's reluctance.

"What is it?" he asked as she played her fork over the last few bites of pasta on her plate.

"Nothing," she said softly and unconvincingly.

Tom gathered the plates and recycled them as B'Elanna tried unsuccessfully to let go of her concerns about the coming day. He returned from the replicator with a small parfait dish containing banana pudding topped with whipped cream.

"This would have really come in handy an hour ago," B'Elanna mused with a wistful smile.

"Hey, I'm game for anything that includes you, me, and chilled dessert toppings," Tom teased.

B'Elanna smiled appreciatively, but didn't even pick up her spoon.

"Sweetheart," Tom began, "whatever it is, you know you can tell me, right?"

"Of course," she replied sincerely. "I just hate how quickly my mind goes from total happiness back to work."

Tom shrugged. "Right now you have one of the hardest jobs in the fleet. I'd be surprised if it didn't weigh pretty heavy on those gorgeous shoulders."

"I'm just not looking forward to tomorrow," B'Elanna finally admitted.

"Why not?"

"*Achilles* will be here by then."

"Ah," Tom remembered. "Commander Drafar?"

"What were you going to tell me before about Lendrins?" B'Elanna asked.

Tom leaned back in his chair, wrapping his hands around the back of his neck. "Sadly, male Lendrins are denied what I have discovered to be one of the great pleasures of life."

"What's that?"

"Raising their young."

B'Elanna was both surprised and intrigued.

"You mean the men don't help at all?" she asked.

"They *can't*," Tom clarified. "It's biology, not sociology. When Lendrin children are born, they live the first year in a small pouch attached to the mother's abdomen. No one but the mother can have any physical contact with the infants or they die. For the next few years after that, the mothers also have to continue to nourish the child from their bodies. Their culture has evolved in such a way that the women tend to join together in small groups when they've borne children close in age, and these female clans provide all necessary care until the children are old enough to begin school. Most couples aren't even reunited until that happens."

B'Elanna was truly shocked. While it made biological sense, it also sounded like the sheer demands on a Lendrin woman would overwhelm most other females.

"That does explain Drafar's behavior," B'Elanna was forced to admit.

"It actually makes me kind of sad for him," Tom added.

With this, too, B'Elanna had to agree. She remembered vividly the years she and Tom had spent apart by necessity. Having now enjoyed, even for a few weeks, the sight of Tom and Miral bonding and Tom's complete devotion to her, she realized how much joy all three of them had sacrificed on the long road to their present happiness.

As soon as this realization hit her, so did an idea so elegant in its simplicity, she couldn't believe she hadn't thought of it earlier.

Tom sat back and considered her carefully.

"Why are you smiling like that?" he asked.

"Was I smiling?"

"Yes. Reminds me of the time you and Seska decided to break in Chakotay's new pilot by rigging the helm to only make port turns."

At this B'Elanna's smile widened. "That was a lifetime ago. I can't believe you remember it."

Tom's face fell a bit, as if a darker memory had suddenly intruded.

"We've come a long way since then, haven't we?" B'Elanna gently prodded.

Tom nodded slightly, but remained silent.

"You ready for bed?"

Tom reached for B'Elanna's hand and grasped it lightly.

"Something else has been bothering you the last few days," he finally said. "I'm wondering when you'll be ready to tell me what it is."

Damn it.

B'Elanna knew she couldn't keep anything from Tom for

long, but she'd never actually been in a position where duty forbade her from doing so.

"Not yet," she said seriously. "But it has nothing to do with you or Miral, and I promise, as soon as I can, I will share it with you."

Tom squeezed her hand and offered a faint smile.

"Okay," he said. "Then let's go to bed."

When the door to Counselor Cambridge's quarters slid open, Chakotay wondered if an ion storm had moved through the ship without anyone bothering to mention it to him. Stepping gingerly over two large carved stone blocks and around a stack of astrometrics charts, he found the counselor seated in the only empty chair in the room: the one he usually reserved for his patients.

Hugh sat deep in thought, though he did give a slight nod of acknowledgment when Chakotay stepped into his line of sight. Waving a hand listlessly, he said, "Neatness is the hobgoblin of little minds."

"I thought that was consistency," Chakotay replied, gathering up a few padds from what was normally the counselor's chair and placing them on the floor among the rest of the collective mess.

Hugh brought his hand to his chin before he replied, "Maybe it was *accuracy*."

Chakotay smiled in relief. Though clearly Hugh was in the throes of something deeply troubling, he obviously wasn't completely lost.

"I'd offer you a drink, but I haven't seen my replicator in days." Cambridge smirked.

"I'm fine," Chakotay said. "Do you want to tell me what all this is about?"

"No."

A little taken aback, Chakotay continued, "Seven said you canceled your counseling sessions."

"The first was postponed by necessity," Hugh corrected him. "She canceled the rest."

"And you're okay with that?"

"If she feels our work is at an end, who am I to argue? You know counseling is only useful when the patient is a willing participant."

"That's not exactly how I remember our first sessions," Chakotay half joked.

"Well, you were particularly stubborn," Hugh replied.

"I think Seven is concerned about you," Chakotay said, deciding to pry a bit.

"No, she's angry with me," Hugh countered. "She'll get over it. She's hardly the first woman I've disappointed." After a moment, he added, "But you are concerned about me, and you needn't be. I'm in the middle of a project that has become a little consuming, but I assure you, I will emerge victorious shortly."

"If this is victory, I'd hate to see defeat," Chakotay mused.

Finally Hugh smiled wryly. "Why don't we talk about whatever's bothering you?"

Now that he had the counselor's full attention, Chakotay saw little use in dissembling.

"I'm concerned about Captain Eden."

Hugh's head cocked to one side as he considered this.

"How so?" he asked.

"She's wasting time looking for a creature the odds are long at best we'll find, and in the meantime, *Demeter* has been lost for weeks."

"So you disagree with her orders?"

"I think she's afraid to face the possibility that we've lost two ships on this mission. But on the small chance *Demeter* is still intact, we're wasting time they probably don't have."

"So you want to throw caution to the wind and just charge in after them, phasers blazing?"

Chakotay shrugged. "It sounds less like a plan and more ridiculous when you put it like that."

"That's because it is ridiculous."

Glancing around the cluttered disaster that was currently Hugh's quarters, Chakotay wondered a little at the confidence in that last statement.

"Hugh—" he began, but the counselor briskly cut him off.

"I'm not kidding. This isn't the Maquis. It isn't even *Voyager* lost and alone in the Delta Quadrant. Afsarah isn't treading lightly because she's wedded to the Starfleet procedural manual or because she's afraid to face loss head-on. She's guided by a healthy sense of self-preservation, coupled with her acceptance of the fact that she is responsible for eight ships right now, not one."

"So we sacrifice *Demeter* as well as *Planck*?" Chakotay felt his ire rising. "On a mission Starfleet was foolhardy to contemplate, let alone send a group of ill-prepared ships to face?"

"I'll grant you the second part," Hugh admitted. "I could have lived the rest of my life in peace without knowing what makes the Children of the Storm tick. But we're talking about a species that single-handedly trounced the Borg when we lost billions to them in their last attack."

"The Borg are gone."

"Seven certainly believes that they are, and thus far we've seen little to convince me otherwise," Hugh acknowledged.

"And it's doubtful a race as xenophobic as the Children of the Storm would have come looking for us sixty-thousand-odd light-years from their territory," Chakotay added.

"Possibly," Hugh agreed, "but you're missing the point."

Chakotay found himself hating the fact that Hugh was generally right about his blind spots.

"And what would that be?"

"This is who we are," Hugh replied simply. "This is what we do. Zefram Cochrane may have strapped a modified nuclear warhead to his ship out of boredom or a more fundamental desire to see if it could be done, but he's hardly the first human being who was willing to risk his life in the name of discovery. Our race is defined by our bone-headed curiosity. Thousands of years ago, when we were still thanking the sun god for showing up each morning, we were also looking just beyond the next ridge and wondering, 'What's over there?'"

"But surely we've evolved past the point where every single whim of our curiosity must be satisfied," Chakotay argued, "especially when the risks so far outweigh any potential reward."

"You don't know yet what reward may lie at the end of this road. And even if it's nothing beyond the deaths of a hundred of our fellows, I don't think either of us really wants to live in a universe where we keep only to the safe corners of our existence."

"If that is so, why not go back to my original plan?" Chakotay asked. "You've just said there's no point in playing it safe."

Hugh shook his head. "Because your plan, while satisfying in the short term, would likely only add to the death toll, while Afsarah's may not."

"That doesn't sound much like a vote of confidence in our fleet commander."

"Doesn't make it any less true," Hugh replied. "What I find curious is the fact that four years ago, you and I would never have been having this conversation."

"We didn't know each other four years ago."

"No, but if you were still serving under Kathryn Janeway, and she was the one ready to charge in where anyone else might tread more carefully, I guarantee that you'd be the one trying to slow her thrusters."

Chakotay sighed. "The thought had occurred to me."

"It's not a bad instinct, the desire to act now and decisively," Hugh advised. "It's an important position to consider. But if it were the only voice heard in the conversation, *Voyager* would never have made it home the first time. Afsarah honestly hasn't faced loss on the scale you've lived through only recently. But I'm not sure she's the one who's afraid of it now."

Chakotay paused as this sank in. "You think I am?"

Hugh shrugged. "I think if there is the slightest doubt in your mind, you'd do well to focus on your job, and let the fleet commander do hers."

Chakotay considered his point. Finally he said, "It's going to be a long three years, isn't it?"

"I sure hope so," Cambridge replied.

Chapter Twenty

TEN DAYS EARLIER
U.S.S. DEMETER

Forty hours after the briefing had ended, Fife stood on the bridge next to O'Donnell, who was seated in the center chair. The planter drone had been programmed and stocked with seeds and nutrients destined for the system's fourth planet, as well as a small group of buds designed to convey the importance and benign intention of the drone to the Children of the Storm. Naturally, Fife couldn't have given a damn whether or not the Children accepted the drone or its mission. As far as he was concerned, it was useful only as a tactical distraction.

Falto and Url had worked diligently, studying the field strength readings both from the launch of the distress buoy and throughout the growth cycles aboard *Demeter,* and had carefully plotted the small window during which they believed the field might weaken enough to grant Falto helm control. The slipstream drive had been brought on line, and if all went well, within the next five minutes *Demeter* should be on her way back to the rendezvous point of the rest of the fleet a little earlier than their mission parameters had intended.

The only niggling doubt in the back of Fife's brain was O'Donnell. Although the captain had agreed in principle to prioritize the escape attempt above the success of his drone, Fife wondered if he would lose heart at the last minute. When the critical moment came, it would be O'Donnell's place to give the appropriate order, and if he hesitated even a few seconds, all might be lost. Fife could only hope that Falto and Url would execute their orders as they already understood them.

O'Donnell was uncharacteristically silent as one section of the viewscreen monitored the loading of the drone into the tube that would eject it into space. The rest of the screen was divided between a display of the field surrounding the ship and a view of the aliens, still spinning and weaving gracefully in and out among each other. To think of them as happy, even now, soured Fife's stomach. He felt it should have fired the same anger in everyone aboard *Demeter* to see the enemy glorying in their triumph.

Thankfully, they'll have less to celebrate shortly, Fife thought grimly.

"The drone is prepared for launch, Captain," Url reported.

"Hold launch until the growth cycle peaks," O'Donnell replied flatly. "Falto, confirm slipstream jump plotted and ready to initiate."

"Confirmed," Falto replied.

"Growth cycle peak in thirty seconds," Vincent advised.

Fife's eyes were glued to the schematic of the field intensity. As predicted, the resonance frequencies had begun to diminish ever so slightly.

"Twenty seconds," Vincent said.

"Prepare to launch drone on my mark," O'Donnell ordered.

Though Fife's gut tensed, he was certain this was going to work.

"Ten seconds," Vincent said.

"Prepare to initiate slipstream corridor," O'Donnell ordered.

"Peak in five . . . four . . . three . . . two . . . one."

"Launch drone," O'Donnell said firmly.

As the drone was shot into space, Fife saw the resonance frequency diminish further and the instantaneous response of the dancing spheres. Their motion grew suddenly chaotic, lacking its previous fluid grace.

For a few seconds, the frequency dropped even lower than their simulations had foreseen. Fife waited breathlessly for O'Donnell to order Falto to initiate the slipstream drive.

When he could bear it no longer, Fife said tensely, "Captain?"

"Initiate slipstream corridor," O'Donnell ordered.

The deck plates beneath Fife's feet rumbled.

"Drive on line," Falto reported. "Helm responding."

For the first time in days, *Demeter* moved under the power of its engines rather than its captors. During those few glorious seconds, Fife could actually taste freedom.

An instant later, the ship lurched forward and was brutally pulled back. Fife was thrown to the deck as he heard the captain say softly, "No, don't."

Pulling himself upright on hands and knees, Fife watched on the viewscreen as a group of spheres detached from the formation, intercepted the drone speeding toward the planet, merged around it and blew it to pieces.

For the next several seconds, the ship shook and shuddered violently.

"Falto, report!" O'Donnell shouted.

"I've lost helm control," Falto replied frantically.

"Field frequency is increasing," came Url's strained voice from behind Fife.

"Take the drive off line immediately," O'Donnell ordered.

Fife watched in horror as several more spheres broke from their formation and headed straight for *Demeter*.

"O'Donnell to aeroponics one, three, five, and nine," the captain called. "Reseed all available pods."

The spheres continued their inexorable approach. Fife knew O'Donnell's efforts would be too little too late.

"What is the status of the energy field, Url?" O'Donnell demanded.

"Intensity continues to increase."

The approaching spheres moved beyond the range of the viewscreen as the rattling all around Fife reached its peak.

Fife held his breath, awaiting oblivion.

Then, as suddenly as the storm had begun, it ceased.

Through the disbelieving silence Url called out, "Field intensity has stabilized."

Fife hoped against hope that was a good thing. Turning again to the viewscreen, the computer translated the frequency as the pale violet to which the commander had become accustomed over the last several days.

At last, O'Donnell turned to Fife. His utter disdain was palpable. "Congratulations, Commander. We've just blown our last, best hope of establishing some form of accord with these creatures."

Without another word, O'Donnell rose from his seat and left the bridge.

For a moment, Fife was stung. Then he remembered that he didn't care. As long as they were still alive, there was still a chance that they could escape this mess.

Every face on the bridge was turned toward his.

"Stations," Fife ordered briskly.

Eyes were lowered all around as Fife slid into O'Donnell's seat. Only once the danger was completely past did he begin to shake.

O'Donnell charged into his quarters, his anger and disappointment writhing within him.

"It would have worked!" he shouted to the emptiness around him.

His workspace was littered with the tools he had used to construct the hybrid capable of thriving on the fourth planet. With both hands he swept all of them from the table's surface. The clattering of nutrient dishes, samples, and padds hitting the floor was momentarily satisfying, but his rage was hardly slaked.

Turning, he saw a slight Kressari male standing behind him.

"Minister, I am sorry to interrupt, but there is an urgent message for Lieutenant O'Donnell."

"It can wait," O'Donnell replied to one of his worst memories.

"I am assured it cannot," the page replied.

With every bone in his body, O'Donnell wished he had ignored the page.

Of course, he hadn't.

"This conversation is not over, Minister," O'Donnell warned as he hurried toward the door.

Outside the quorum chamber, Alana stood patiently, dressed in a peat-colored tunic. The eyes that met his were a vibrant violet, but he didn't need to understand the subtle shifts in iris patination characteristic of the Kressari to know she had good news. Absolute happiness lit her entire face.

"Liam," she said, taking both his hands in hers and pulling him close.

"I'm trying to save two cities, Alana," O'Donnell said petulantly.

"And I'm trying to save you," she replied without giving an inch.

O'Donnell bit back further argument. Her implacable nature had been the first thing that had attracted him to her, and countless futile disagreements over the last three years had taught him that she was the only person in the universe more accustomed than he to getting her own way.

"It's going to take more than you to do that," he said, though the softness with which the words escaped his lips belied them.

"I don't think so," she replied with a knowing look. *"I just came from Nurel's office. We did it."*

Liam felt his heart begin to race in his chest as her hands tightened around his.

"Is he sure?"

Alana nodded, unable to repress her joy.

"It's a girl."

For the next few seconds, the residents of Neshan and Plaro were the furthest thing from Liam's mind. He and Alana had been sealed before the High Anointed almost two years earlier, and over a dozen subsequent attempts to conceive had only solidified Nurel's firm belief that human and Kressari DNA were genetically incompatible.

"Nurel owes me a drink." Liam smiled.

"It was a bet he is only too happy to lose."

"You have to get home and off your feet," Liam chided her. There was nothing delicate about his wife, but for the next ten months she would pretend that there was. "I'll be done here shortly and I'll meet you—"

"You have to get to Nurel's office now," Alana corrected him. "He wants new samples, and if he can process them to-night he'll be able to formulate my next series of injections for tomorrow."

"Genov-see is stonewalling. He'd rather let his people starve than disappoint the ancestral elite that put him in office."

"And given the amount of money they all spent to put him on the quorum, that's not going to change this afternoon," Alana replied knowingly.

"You want this as much as I do, Alana. The eradication of the famine cycles is within our grasp now. And I'll be damned if politics is going to stand in our way."

"Right now, I want to see the face of our daughter," Alana said.

"I'll get to Nurel's office. I promise."

"Don't fail me, Liam."

"Never, my love."

The next fourteen weeks had been the happiest of Liam O'Donnell's life. Regular hormonal injections had successfully prevented Alana's body from rejecting the fetus. The baby was growing and developing perfectly. O'Donnell had even managed to convince Genov-see to reallocate hundreds of acres desperately needed to feed his people.

And then, one evening, Liam had returned home, flushed with excitement at the news that the yields he had promised the quorum would likely be double what they had anticipated, and found Alana standing in the doorway of their bedroom, her hands covered with blood.

Their daughter was dead, and three days later a combination of hemorrhaging and grief had taken Alana's life as well.

Liam stood in the midst of his latest loss, overwhelmed by the speed with which rage could transform itself into mind-numbing emptiness.

His dream—Alana's dream—had been so simple. All they had wanted to do was to prove the gods wrong; to meddle where science told them they could, but some inexorable power of greater magnitude demanded they should not.

"I will prove you wrong one day," Liam said aloud to the gloom.

He knelt on the floor and carelessly picked up a few shards of a shattered dish that hours earlier had held the beginnings of another life-form never meant to exist.

But his daughter had *lived once. For fourteen brief weeks, she had lived inside Alana's womb, where the gods had said nothing borne of human and Kressari cells should ever live.*

Fourteen weeks.

As he chuckled at the absurd limits of his formidable abilities, a new thought flickered through his mind.

He caught it just before it disappeared, turned it over a few times, and a faint smile creased his lips.

It wouldn't even have to survive that long.

"Why not?" he said.

Url couldn't believe that he was still alive. The moment those spheres had broken formation and flown toward *Demeter* in fury, he knew for certain that they had finally pushed the Children of the Storm too far.

Why did they spare us?

The question didn't intrigue him so much as plague him.

In his short life, Url had never wanted anything as much as the Children of the Storm appeared to want to witness the birth, life, and death of the simple life-forms housed aboard *Demeter*. Their focus on this process, the energy they expended aiding it along, had almost been enough for them to lose their hold on the ship. But the speed with which they had recovered their attention had brought all Url's hopes to naught.

No.

The beings that composed the field surrounding *Demeter* had not recovered in time. They had required the assistance of several dozen more spheres to regain their hold.

Url quickly scanned the sector and counted the number of spheres in the immediate area.

Four hundred sixty-three.

That was more than enough to destroy *Demeter* several times over.

Or was it?

He estimated that a little over a hundred merged spheres

composed the field around them. If, as O'Donnell had theorized, only some of the inhabitants of each sphere resonated at the proper frequency to hold or move or destroy a ship, then perhaps only a fraction of the number of lifeforms contained in each sphere were capable of destroying anything. And if they wanted *Demeter* intact badly enough to sacrifice their own to reinforce the field strength, then perhaps . . .

"Commander Fife?" Url said.

"What is it, Lieutenant?"

"I have an idea."

Fife turned an expectant face toward him.

"Let's hear it," Fife replied.

Chapter Twenty-one

STARDATE 58463.8
U.S.S. VOYAGER

"Boy, you never get the easy jobs, do you?" Harry asked Lieutenant Conlon once he had appeared on the transporter pad.

"I'm starting to think it should be part of the job description for *Voyager*'s chief engineer," Conlon replied without looking up from the transporter controls.

Harry stepped off the pad and moved to Conlon's side, saying, "Patel confirms they are ready for transport."

Conlon took a moment to glance at Harry, but it was clear

from her face that her mind was light-years away, aboard *Quirinal* on the planet below.

The previous afternoon, Eden had ordered Harry to oversee the transfer of the alien sphere from *Quirinal*'s cargo bay to one of *Voyager*'s. Whether or not they succeeded in locating the "mother," they were going to attempt a rescue of *Demeter,* and for that Eden wanted the sphere on board.

Conlon's people had been working to install a psionic force field shipwide. Harry had begun by asking Seven and Patel to find a way to transport the sphere. They had quickly informed him that it was impossible to get a transporter lock on the alien vessel's energy shell, though they did believe they could get a lock on the individual life-forms within the sphere. Unfortunately, they would have to destroy the shell to do it, which created a bigger problem in that they could not precisely reproduce the atmosphere within the sphere.

Harry had left them to try and find a better solution, but it had been Nancy Conlon who had hit upon it, almost as soon as he asked.

"Why don't we just transport the entire cargo bay?" had been her suggestion.

"I'm not kidding," Harry had said, believing that she was joking.

"Neither am I," Conlon had replied. "Come to think of it, we don't need the whole room. We could build a containment box for the thing and just bring it up."

"I don't get how that helps," Harry had said.

"The box gives the transporter a focal point beyond the sphere. Anything within the box will remain intact because it will be protected by the box, so even if the energy shell is disrupted by transport, it can be reestablished instantly once it rematerializes."

If Harry hadn't been so conscious of his attraction to Conlon, he would have hugged her right then out of sheer relief. As it was, he had settled for a congratulatory pat on the arm and his profuse thanks.

"Don't thank me," Conlon said. "Thank the Koas."

"Who are they?"

A faint smile flashed across Conlon's face. "Remind me to tell you the story one day. It's a good one. They put their whole planet in a box."

Now Harry was certain she was teasing, but he had been too pleased by the thought of her wanting to tell him a long story someday to care.

He watched her fingers slide gingerly over the transporter controls. Seconds later, a sigh of relief came from her lips.

"Done," she said, nodding officiously.

"You made that look really easy," Harry offered.

She started to shrug off the compliment, but Harry added, "You know, you're doing a great job."

"Thanks," she replied, unconvinced. "Now I have to get down to the cargo bay and make sure we get that sphere unloaded so that Lasren can continue his work."

"Hey," Harry said, moving to prevent her from leaving the room. "You okay?"

"Sure."

Now Harry was the one who needed convincing.

"Eight hours ago two of the smartest people on this ship told me what you just did couldn't be done," he said.

Conlon's eyebrows lifted in surprise. "Who?"

"Seven and Patel."

"That's your problem. You needed an engineer, not a scientist or whatever the heck Seven's designation is for this one."

"I'll keep that in mind in the future," Harry said, nodding. "But you don't seem . . . I don't know . . . happy."

Conlon paused to consider Harry's words.

"It's tough to be really happy right now," she finally said. "*Quirinal* was a thing of utter beauty, and now she's lying in pieces on that planet down there." Raising a hand to forestall argument, she went on, "And we don't even have the pieces of *Planck*. I just . . . I guess you never really get used to . . . I mean, this is the part of the job that's tough."

Harry sympathized. Actually, her feelings were so similar to his own, it was a little scary.

When he didn't respond, she took a quick breath and tried to shake it off. "I'm sorry. I just remember when I joined Starfleet I had this crazy, stupid idea in my head that we were the good guys. We would go charging around space, saving the day wherever we were needed."

"But some days we can't," Harry said.

"I hate those days," Conlon admitted.

"I do too," Harry agreed. "But this one isn't over yet, and so far, we've done pretty good."

"Yeah," Conlon replied, and with a faint smile stepped around Harry and moved to the door.

"Nancy?" Harry called after her.

She stopped and turned back.

"You still owe me a workout on the holodeck."

Her eyes widened a bit. "You're not angry with me?"

"For what?"

"For setting you up with Cambridge last time."

Harry shook his head. "Not at all."

This time, Conlon's smile was genuine.

"I'm glad. How about we set a time when all this is over?"

"Sounds good."

As she left, Harry decided that this mission couldn't possibly end soon enough.

Miral squirmed mercilessly on Tom's lap while he tried to pull her small boots onto her wriggling feet.

"Come on, honey. Help your daddy out," Tom pleaded.

B'Elanna emerged from the bedroom, a duffel bag draped over her shoulder.

"You all packed?" Tom asked as the second boot slid up to Miral's heel and refused to budge another centimeter.

"Yep. Miral, you know how to put your shoes on," she added as she crossed to the table and downed the last of her *raktajino*.

Miral threw a sneaky glance at her father and then threw her arms around his neck in apology before settling the wayward boot firmly in place.

Tom thought he loved Miral as much as a human could. He realized then that the feeling of his heart breaking that had become so common since Miral had once again become part of his daily life was actually his heart growing larger to accommodate all the love it held for her.

As Miral pulled away and rushed to join her mother at the table, clambering up on a chair to grab the last piece of toast from his plate, Tom tried to feel good about the fact that he was about to say good-bye to his family again, if only for a short while. He rose from the sofa, knowing he was about to be late for the start of his shift but unable to tear his eyes away from his wife and daughter.

Perhaps feeling the intensity of his gaze, B'Elanna turned and offered him a knowing smile. She crossed silently to him and took him in her arms.

"You take care of yourself," she said firmly.

"You too" was all he could manage through his tightening throat.

A chime sounded at their door, and B'Elanna pulled away as she called out, "Come in."

The door slid open and the Doctor stepped in. "Commanders," he greeted Tom and B'Elanna with a barely repressed grin. Turning to Miral, he said, "Where is my new roommate?"

Miral jerked around to see him, slid quickly off her chair to run over to him, and raised her arms for him to pick her up. "Are you ready to have some fun today, Miral?"

Miral nodded with a smile that held the unchewed portions of her toast.

Tom crossed to the Doctor and said, "I can't thank you enough for making room for my girls."

"It's not a problem at all," the Doctor tried to toss back casually, though his obvious delight in Miral suggested how excited he truly was by the prospect of B'Elanna and Miral bunking with him on *Galen* while *Voyager* went in search of the "mother" and *Demeter*. "Are you certain, B'Elanna, that it wouldn't be more convenient for you to oversee repairs of *Quirinal* from *Achilles*? I'm sure they could accommodate you both."

"Positive," B'Elanna replied.

She gave Tom a quick kiss and said, "See you in a few days."

Tom wanted to pull her back to him, but knew he didn't dare. Part of him couldn't believe he was letting them go, but the realities of duty made any other choice impossible.

He didn't seriously consider resigning his position, however, until Miral reached for him from the Doctor's arms.

Pulling her into a last embrace and whispering softly, "Be

a good girl for your mommy and the Doctor," he realized just how much of himself he would be leaving behind. His only solace was his belief that B'Elanna and Miral would be infinitely safer where they were than where he and *Voyager* were headed.

Eden stood in astrometrics as Seven briefed her on the five planetary bodies she had discovered that in her opinion were the best candidates for the Children of the Storm's "mother." They were scattered across the five nearest star systems beyond the debris field and spanned a range of ten light-years.

"We'll start there," Eden decided, choosing the closest system.

"I will forward the coordinates to the bridge," Seven replied without comment.

As Eden turned to head for the bridge, the doors slid open to reveal Doctor Sal and a petite ensign Eden had never met. The young woman's features were perfectly placid, though there was a hint of tension in her eyes.

"Captain Eden," Sal began in introduction, "I'd like you to meet Ensign Ti'Ana, one of our science officers."

Eden immediately extended her hand. "It's my understanding that you were able to establish communication between your captain and the Children of the Storm," Eden said graciously. "On behalf of the entire fleet, I offer my thanks for your services."

Ti'Ana's face flushed slightly as she said, "Is there someplace we could speak privately, Captain?"

"Of course," Eden replied, glancing quizzically at Sal.

"I'll be getting back to my ship," Sal informed Eden. "Safe travels, Captain."

"Thank you, Doctor," Eden said as she led Ti'Ana from the room.

Ti'Ana kept her eyes glued straight ahead as they traveled the short distance to the turbolift. Eden ushered her into her office and offered Ti'Ana a seat before her desk as she perched on its edge to hear whatever the young woman had to say. Her reticence suggested Eden wasn't going to like it, but the captain hoped that was only evidence of her Vulcan restraint.

"How can I help you, Ensign?" Eden asked, attempting to begin the conversation.

"Permission to speak freely, Captain?" Ti'Ana asked.

Eden nodded for her to continue.

"In the days since the crash, I have begun to remember what it was like to be invaded by the consciousness of one of the Children of the Storm."

"I am certain it was a very difficult experience," Eden offered.

"I also understand that you have another officer attempting to communicate with them now and that he has developed a sort of sympathy for them."

"Perhaps *concern* would be a better word, but yes," Eden granted her.

"You must believe me when I tell you that these creatures do not deserve our mercy. They are beings of rage and hatred, and there is no common ground to be forged between them and us."

The young woman's tone chilled Eden, but she tried to remember how painful Ti'Ana's only encounter with the aliens must have been.

"We are talking about an entire race, Ensign," Eden reminded her gently. "While it is possible that you are appropriately characterizing the individual with whom you were in contact, I hesitate to judge the entire species by a single entity."

"Then judge them by their actions, Captain," Ti'Ana insisted. "The being that spoke through me directed the others to destroy *Planck*. They killed with no hesitation, no thought, and no emotion beyond pleasure at the ease of their success."

"Again—" Eden began.

"I'm sorry, Captain," Ti'Ana interjected. "Your crewman may have the best of intentions, but if he thinks he has found any redeeming qualities in these creatures, he is mistaken and he is leading you toward your destruction."

"Ensign Lasren has spent days trying to reach the inhabitants of the sphere your ship captured," Eden answered evenly. "He has sensed their anger and rage, but also more subtle emotions. We may not be able to reach all of them, but we don't have to in order to forge some kind of understanding. We may only need to find one who is sympathetic toward our cause. And if that helps us rescue *Demeter*, it is certainly worth the effort."

"You don't understand," Ti'Ana said, clearly growing more frustrated. "They will never release *Demeter*."

"How could you possibly know that?" Eden asked.

"Their need for *the life* as they called it was absolute. I have never been near death, but the force of their desire made me feel that without it, they would die. They would never destroy it, but they would absolutely kill anyone or anything that tried to come between them and it."

Eden rose, and Ti'Ana took this as her cue to stand as well.

"Thank you for your analysis, Ensign," Eden said firmly. "I will take your words into consideration as we proceed."

"But you will not reconsider returning to their space?"

"I believe the *Demeter* is still intact, and I cannot leave them behind, no matter how strenuously you or the Children of the Storm might wish otherwise."

Ti'Ana nodded, the grief at her failure to persuade Eden clear on her face.

Once Ti'Ana had gone, Eden sank into the chair the ensign had briefly occupied. One thing she hadn't considered was the possibility that the Children of the Storm had captured the ship but killed its crew. If all they needed were the simple life-forms aboard her, they might have opted to rid themselves early on of the humanoid "destroyers" that were part of the package.

Of course, none of this changed the fact that Eden had to know for certain that her people were beyond hope before she continued on without them.

But at what price?

Weighing the needs of the many over the needs of the few was the most difficult lesson every Starfleet captain learned. It was so ingrained as to be reflexive in nature. Eden was about to lead over a hundred to rescue a handful, and it wasn't supposed to matter that *Demeter*'s forty-seven crewmen and officers were the least prepared of any in the fleet to face sustained battle with a hostile alien force.

But it does matter.

She had just received intelligence that should have given her pause about the entire operation, as if she needed more than *Quirinal*'s shredded hull to remind her of the dangers inherent in their mission. *Demeter* was a crew of scientists, led by a young commander and an eccentric captain who would no doubt struggle valiantly to survive, but simply did not have the resources to overcome a force as powerful and single-minded as the Children of the Storm.

Am I wasting time trying to find the origins of these creatures in order to prevent Demeter's *destruction, or will my actions insure it?*

If she thought *Voyager* stood a chance against the Children now, Eden would have set course for *Demeter* at once, but something in her gut told her that they were still missing a vital piece of this puzzle. Perhaps the true history of the Children of the Storm was unknowable. Perhaps it didn't matter. Most troubling of all was the thought that the researcher in her needed completion when the reality of space exploration was that there were mysteries out there that were never going to be solved.

As these dispiriting thoughts raced through her mind, Eden realized she had never felt so alone in her entire life. For all that she had loved and hated Willem, and would argue a point with him until it had disintegrated into dust, there had been something comforting in the knowledge that in the end, the hard choices were his to make. Had she not accepted this command, Starfleet might have recalled the entire fleet and Eden might have lost the chance forever to discover the truth about her own elusive past. Was that chance really all that had brought her to this moment, and more important, was it worth it?

Stop it, a voice chided her.

With a twinge of regret, she recognized it as Willem's. Though he had lied to her with every breath for years, he had valiantly imitated a Starfleet admiral and pretended to uphold the Federation's values. He had privately believed that those values would damn the Federation to destruction.

But his voice was right to halt her racing thoughts. Fear, hope, regret, doubt—they meant nothing. Her motives in choosing to join and then lead the fleet meant less than nothing. All that mattered was her determination to do right by her people, and the greater good here was learning what she must to safely bring as many of her people home as possible. It might be easier, and more satisfying in a way, to throw all of their weapons against a foe that had shown them nothing but hostility up to this point, but it would not further the cause to which she had dedicated her life when she had joined Starfleet.

Peace is born of mutual understanding.

If there was one thing the Federation could not afford, it was the luxury of solutions made easy by the sheer force they could bring to most difficult situations. War had its place, but it had to be the last resort.

Ti'Ana had learned in one brief encounter to hate the Children of the Storm. Eden could not allow her heart to succumb to that most powerful of emotions. She must seek out the dim and troubled path that might lead to understanding.

And if it cost Eden the lives of *Demeter*'s crew, so be it. She would never forgive herself, but she would accept responsibility for her choices, and take comfort from the certainty that she was at the forefront of a new age. The Children of the Storm had called them "destroyers of worlds," and had demonstrated on a vast scale that they knew how to conquer those who came to destroy.

Eden knew now that what she wanted most of all was to prove them wrong.

No matter what the cost.

Chapter Twenty-two

NINE DAYS EARLIER
U.S.S. DEMETER

Fife had never been so anxious to see Liam O'Donnell's face. He and Url had worked through a full four duty shifts, running dozens of simulations born of Url's idea, and Fife was chomping at the bit to put their plan into action.

The captain's eyes were heavy and surrounded by dark circles as he took his place at the head of the briefing room table. Fife and Url were seated on either side of him, and when he settled himself and turned toward Fife, the commander took the initiative and began.

"Lieutenant Url and I have come up with a new plan, based largely on your analysis of the Children of the Storm," Fife said, hoping O'Donnell might warm to the notion if he felt his work had been its foundation.

O'Donnell's face remained inscrutable as he glanced at Url. Clearing his throat, Url explained.

"There are currently four hundred and sixty-three alien vessels in this system. The inhabitants of perhaps a hundred more form the energy field surrounding *Demeter*."

O'Donnell nodded faintly. Fife refused to believe he was genuinely as disinterested as he appeared.

"You have already discovered that each sphere contains hundreds of life-forms that resonate with a handful of distinct frequencies. If, as you suspect, each frequency determines that individual's function among the group, then at best, only a fraction of each sphere's inhabitants would reso- nate at the frequency required to destroy our ship."

When O'Donnell remained impassive, Fife picked up where Url had left off.

"We believe that the aliens currently holding *Demeter* are not capable of destroying it," he said.

"What makes you think that?" O'Donnell finally seemed interested enough to ask.

"Two things," Fife replied. "The first is that they do not resonate with the same frequency as those that surrounded *Planck* just prior to its destruction. The second is actually based upon the deaths of Bell and Lamoth."

O'Donnell tensed as if struck by the unpleasant memory, but said nothing.

"Two spheres merged with the field just before their deaths. We believe those spheres must have contained the life-forms that killed our crewmen."

"But perhaps the best evidence that they can't destroy us, Captain," Url interrupted, "is that they haven't."

"Yet," O'Donnell said.

"Of course," Url replied.

"But that doesn't mean the hypothesis is totally without merit," O'Donnell allowed.

Encouraged, Fife continued, "If we're right, it might take as many as a hundred of the remaining spheres to engulf and destroy *Demeter*. But we've already learned, thanks to our at- tempt to launch the drone, that they can be distracted."

"Surely you're not going to suggest—" O'Donnell began.

"That we try to escape again?" Fife finished for him. "Not exactly."

"Then what *exactly* are you proposing?"

"We could rig another three drones with enough ordnance to take out at least a hundred of the spheres each currently holding position around the ship. At the same time, we could program our phasers for wide dispersal and with some luck take out fifty or sixty more before they could converge on our position and create their destructive field."

O'Donnell's mouth fell open.

"You want to destroy hundreds of thousands of them in a matter of minutes?" he asked, aghast.

"If we succeed in destroying half that many, it may be enough to distract them long enough to escape," Fife said.

"Or it might eliminate the possibility that enough of them still exist to destroy us, Captain," Url added.

O'Donnell took a deep breath and rose from the table.

"Captain?" Fife asked.

"No," he said simply.

"May I ask why not?" Fife said.

"I can't believe you have to," O'Donnell replied sharply.

"Captain—" Url began.

"End of discussion, gentlemen," O'Donnell said clearly. "You are contemplating death on a scale I am unprepared to even consider."

"Death of our enemies, Captain," Fife reminded him.

"Death of countless sentient life-forms," O'Donnell said, raising his voice to silence further debate. "I didn't come out here to kill. We're not murderers. We were sent here to make peaceful contact with alien races, and that's exactly what we're going to do."

"What's peaceful about being held against our will?" Fife asked.

"Nothing, but that's not our doing, it's theirs," O'Donnell replied. "For our part, we're going to behave like Starfleet officers, damn it all."

"How?" Url asked incredulously.

"We're going to help them," O'Donnell replied before storming out of the room, leaving both Url and Fife momentarily speechless.

A few moments after O'Donnell had stormed out, Url rose to return to his station. Though he agreed that the attack they had planned might come with an unusually high casualty rate, he had been unprepared for the captain's flat rejection of the idea. As to "helping" them, he was also at a loss to imagine in what way they could possibly assist these creatures, beyond continuing to plant endless specimens for their amusement. If O'Donnell was truly unwilling to consider any alternative . . . But Url hesitated to even allow his thoughts to go further in that direction.

"Lieutenant, please keep your seat," Fife instructed.

Curious, Url did as ordered.

Fife appeared to consider his next words extremely carefully. Finally he said, "I never intended to discuss what I'm about to share with you with any member of this crew. I do so now only because I believe all of our lives may depend upon it."

"I'm listening, Commander."

"When I was assigned to my post, Admiral Batiste called me in for a private meeting. He essentially told me that Commander O'Donnell was only given command of *Demeter* because of his seniority and scientific expertise. At the time, given *Demeter*'s purpose within the fleet and the likelihood that we would be kept far from any field of battle, the admiral did not believe this assignment posed any risk. But he told me that I was to provide tactical support to O'Donnell should the need arise, and he assured me that the commander would defer to my judgment in any such matters."

Fife paused to search Url's face for a response before continuing. "I assumed he and the commander had a similar discussion and that the understanding of our respective roles would not become a point of contention. I believe that Commander O'Donnell has just indicated, however, that he does not intend to honor the admiral's orders."

Url couldn't help but note Fife's continued use of O'Donnell's actual rank rather than the title *captain,* indicating his function aboard *Demeter,* which had gone essentially unquestioned by the crew up to this point.

"Are you attempting to justify your desire to assume command of this vessel?" Url asked evenly.

"If the commander is unwilling to act in the best interests of this crew, I don't believe I have any choice," Fife replied.

Url shook his head. "I'd feel a lot better about this if you hadn't already questioned his fitness to command over a week ago. Last time you tried to convince me he was mentally unbalanced."

"At the time, that was a greater concern, and I'm not entirely sure that's not part of it as well. I've had a number of discussions with him that made me feel like I wasn't the only person in the room he was talking to."

"He's eccentric," Url conceded, "but he's also one of the smartest people I've ever met. I don't want to throw the word *genius* around casually, but if he actually created a species of plant that would thrive on the system's fourth planet in a couple of days, the shoe might just fit."

"We'll never know if he did or not."

"But that's not his fault."

Fife paused, his face unreadable. "Then should I assume you do not concur with my assessment?"

This time Url took a few moments of silence. Finally he said reluctantly, "I didn't say that."

"Thank you, Lieutenant."

Unable to believe he was actually contemplating mutiny, Url asked, "How do you intend to proceed?"

"By my estimation, we have a minimum of five more days until we are missed by the fleet. They will, no doubt, come looking for us, but without our help, I don't believe any rescue mission will succeed. We saw what the Children did to *Quirinal* and *Planck*. Even if *Voyager* and *Esquiline* both come to our aid, there's no way to tell for sure that they will be successful. There is also no way for us to be certain that the spheres currently visible on our scanners comprise the entirety of the force arrayed against us.

"I believe we should prepare the drones, as we discussed, along with the phaser targeting solutions. I will speak with Vincent and Falto. If, or more precisely, *when* we detect any other Federation vessels, we should proceed with our plan and attempt to free ourselves. Any other ship present would then be able to aid in our efforts and hopefully effect escape for all of us."

"And what are your intentions for the captain?" Url asked.

"I will relieve him of command and secure him in his quarters."

Url nodded faintly. "One thing, Commander?"

"Yes?" Fife asked.

"If in the interim Captain O'Donnell does come up with an alternate plan that might convince our captors to release us, he will have my full support."

"Along with mine," Fife assured him.

Url wanted to take him at his word, but in his heart, he didn't believe Fife for a moment. Faintly nauseated by what had just transpired between them, Url rose and returned to his post. He was in no hurry to die, and Fife's might truly be the only chance he had to avoid that. But somehow, even considering betraying the captain felt worse than death. It went against the oath he had taken such pride in swearing when he joined Starfleet. To stand with Fife was to become something less than he had promised to be.

Silently he prayed that O'Donnell would find a better solution before he was forced to take an action he never believed he would have to contemplate.

O'Donnell's lab was a mess. One corner of his worktable had been reserved for his latest attempts to coax his beloved *Crateva religiosa-K* into existence. The rest was filled with fresh specimen containers all containing the noxious semifluid equivalent of the atmosphere contained within the energy shell inhabited by the Children of the Storm.

Glancing at them, he decided he could forgo the computer's analysis. Small black specks dotted each of the containers, clearly indicating his failure.

So far, he reminded himself.

What he was now attempting made his work on the *Goldroni kurnit* and all he had achieved on Kressari look like child's play. Even his most recent hybrid grass specimen had been nothing compared to what he now contemplated.

It was exactly the kind of problem on which Liam O'Donnell thrived.

Turning away from the lifeless specimens, he took a moment to examine his latest group of CRK attempts. He methodically transferred one after another to the tray of his microspectrometer and scanned quickly through each of his failures.

The third to the last sample, however, gave him pause. He should have been looking at a single, dead cell. Instead, he found himself peering at two dead cells.

You divided?

The thrill of possibility quickened his pulse. In twenty years of work, he had never achieved the level of metabolism required for cellular division in a single sample. He hurried to his data terminal and called up the second-by-second analysis of the sample's progress. Nineteen hours into the experiment, he watched in awe as the single cell duplicated itself.

Of course, this sent him searching for the potential cause. It, too, was relatively easy to find. The sample's growth medium had been contaminated. An unusually high level of metallic hydrogen was present in the dish. He would have chided himself for his carelessness; clearly he had used one of the specimen containers meant for the Children's project. But that happy accident had shown him the path to what he was now convinced would lead to ultimate success.

When he had imagined the life of a single flowering *Crateva religiosa-K,* he had always seen himself returning to Kressari to plant it atop Alana's grave. It almost broke his heart to realize that now, he would likely never see it bloom there. It seemed this creation was only meant to thrive in the most inhospitable of environments.

A single tear slid down his face.

We're almost there, Alana.

Chapter Twenty-three

STARDATE 58464.3
U.S.S. VOYAGER

Ensign Gwyn didn't think she needed to wait for Seven's analysis from astrometrics to confirm what was plain to the naked eye. The gas giant *Voyager* was now orbiting, the second they had scanned in search of an ancient alien life-form, was not the one they sought.

As the captain and fleet commander conferred quietly behind her, she studied the next set of coordinates. She didn't think it would do any harm to key them into the navigational array.

Save time where you can, Aytar, she thought.

As she began to enter them, however, her index finger betrayed her and missed two digits. Just as an error in typing into a padd registered in her unconscious before she could read the mistake, her brain automatically paused and told her to look again at what she was doing.

She saw the error immediately, but also noted that the coordinates weren't exactly wrong, they were simply farther down on the list of their intended targets.

Anxious for this to be over? she teased her own mind. But the longer she stared at the coordinate she had entered, the more something in her stomach tickled.

Gwyn knew this feeling all too well. When she had been a child, she had promised her mother that she would restrict her play to the yard, but sheer naughtiness had called her to explore beyond the fence to the far more interesting creek that ran through a valley beyond their home. Whenever she did so, she had felt the same tickle. She had initially mistaken it for the thrill of misbehaving. In time, however, she had realized that it was a sign of her mother's psionic connection to her only daughter. It wasn't that Yasim Gwyn hadn't trusted Aytar. There was simply no severing the bond between a Kriosian female and her offspring.

Her mother was over fifty thousand light-years from her present location and could not possibly have known that her daughter was again contemplating mischief. But something in that tickle convinced Gwyn that she had not, in fact, erred in entering the coordinates.

"Helm," came Captain Chakotay's voice from behind her. "Enter our next scheduled coordinates and report when we are ready to proceed."

"Captain, if I may?" Gwyn asked.

"What is it, Ensign?"

"I have already entered the coordinates for one of our targets, but it is the last one we were scheduled to investigate."

Silently Gwyn searched for a way to explain her instinct that they should proceed according to her mistake and, unfortunately, came up short.

"Rectify the mistake, Ensign," Eden ordered.

Gwyn sighed, then turned in her seat to face her commanding officers.

"I'm not trying to be difficult, I promise," she began, noting a faint smirk from Lieutenant Kim, who was stationed just above Captain Chakotay. "But we're not really going to lose any time by altering the schedule, and, well, I have a hunch."

"A hunch?" Chakotay said, requesting clarification.

"It's hard to explain, Captain, but I just feel like this is our best bet."

Chakotay exchanged a glance with Eden.

"The planet she is suggesting we head for next is the farthest from the known territory of the Children of the Storm," Kim advised from tactical.

Gee, thanks for the vote of confidence, Gwyn thought, until Kim added, "Which in some ways does make it more likely to be the one we're looking for."

"How do you figure?" Paris piped up to ask.

"It's also part of a system whose star has almost reached the end of its life," Kim added. "We are looking for something pretty old, right?"

Chakotay again looked to Eden, who simply shrugged.

"All right," Chakotay replied. "We'll go with our helmsman's hunch on this one," he said lightly.

"Thank you, Captain," Gwyn said, and hurried to complete the navigational computer calculations.

A few moments later she reported that they were ready to proceed.

"Engage," Chakotay ordered.

In his mind, Kenth Lasren was climbing a narrow path surrounded by a riot of lush, green vegetation. The Muoni canyon was one of Betazed's most beautiful landscapes, and his family had spent summers there when he was a boy. Every morning had begun with this hike, which wound lazily through dense brush before opening into verdant hills topped with a spectacular waterfall.

Although the scenery was magnificent, Kenth spent less time fixating on its beauty and more recapturing the sense of utter freedom he'd felt as he made his way ever upward toward the falls. Everything about the path had been an invitation, and his heart had pounded with excitement with each step, anticipating the release at the trail's peak.

He continued the remembered climb, reaching out gently to the inhabitants of the sphere, hoping against hope that even if they did not understand the context of the vision he was sending, they could at least relate to the joyous and wondrous abandon the memory brought him.

Finally he reached the peak, the sound of crashing water filling his ears. He stepped gingerly into the river, careful to keep his footing until he reached the large rock in the center of the river from which he would launch himself. With the fearlessness of the child he had been, he climbed atop the rock, opened his arms, and inhaled deeply.

Come with me, he pleaded with the Children.

Bending his knees, Lasren sprang upward and for a split second was weightless. Bringing his arms forward, he allowed gravity to catch him, pulling him with dizzying speed over the edge of the falls until he split the chilly water below with a slight splash.

He came to the surface and began treading water, still tingling with the thrill of the flight. As he reached out again to the sphere, the complete desolation of its inhabitants threatened to pull him under the surface.

A single thought kept him floating. It wasn't the connection he had been hoping for, nor was it particularly enthusiastic. But it felt like curiosity—an entirely new sensation after days spent in similar exercises.

It passed so quickly, Lasren almost hesitated to believe he had felt it at all. Pushing all thoughts of failure aside, he began again at the head of the trail, running along with all the speed his little legs could muster.

●　　●　　●

Seven stood placidly at the astrometrics station. By her calculations, *Voyager* would arrive at the next gas giant in less than six minutes. She had already filed away the sensor logs of their previous investigations. While she waited, she called up the long-range scans that had caused her to include this particular gas giant among the list of potential planets of origin for the "mother" of the Children of the Storm. Of the five, its atmospheric balance, unusual size, and age had made it promising, but the age of the system's star had concerned her. She could not conceive of a life span beyond a few thousand years for the Children, and given that this would have been the blink of an eye in the life of the star in question, it had been practically as near death then as it was now and unlikely to have been capable of providing the necessary radiant energy to sustain any life-forms in the system.

Her thoughts were interrupted by the sound of the door opening behind her. Turning, she saw Counselor Cambridge enter and walk toward her with long, loping strides that, like everything else about him right now, annoyed her intently.

"How goes the hunt?" he asked cheerily.

"Our efforts until now have been unsuccessful," she reported evenly.

Cambridge crossed his arms and leaned against the station, his back to the huge wall upon which the scans were displayed and easily the most interesting sight in the room at any given time.

"I know how you feel," he remarked.

Seven recognized this as an invitation to inquire further into his current status, but she refused to show the slightest bit of interest.

"I was wondering," Cambridge continued as if he hadn't noticed, "whether or not in all of your travels you ever came across a species known as the Meguti?"

"I haven't," Seven replied.

"What about the Rurokitan?"

"No."

"The god Hrimshee?"

"Is there a point to your questions, Counselor?" Seven asked, her perturbation rising.

Cambridge had the grace to look wounded. "Isn't there always?" he asked.

"I'm sorry, but right now I haven't the time to engage in useless speculation or trivial banter," Seven replied. "The lives of several of our fellow fleet members may very well rest upon our ability to locate the home of the 'mother' of the Children of the Storm, and it is a task that requires my full concentration."

Cambridge smiled. "Don't be silly. Right now we're flying through space at speeds so epic our sensors can barely compensate. You have nothing to concentrate on other than your wounded pride, and that is one of your least glamorous attributes."

Seven's arms dropped to her sides as she turned, open-mouthed, to face Cambridge.

"Ah, well, now that I have your attention," he quipped.

"Remove yourself from this lab immediately," Seven ordered.

"It's a public space, Seven, or have restrictions recently been placed upon it of which I am unaware?"

Seven turned her flushed face back to the display.

"Look, amusing as it is to tease you, I'm actually serious about this."

"About what?"

"I am currently seeking connections between dozens of ancient races, many of them believed to have originated in the Delta Quadrant."

"Unless one of them is the Children of the Storm, I'm afraid I cannot be of assistance to you," Seven assured him.

"All right," Cambridge said, deflating a little. "I'm sensing reluctance on your part . . ."

Seven's face jerked involuntarily toward Cambridge. "Then I suggest you adjust your sensory perception filters, because they are clearly not functioning optimally."

Cambridge's face broke into a wide smile. "See, that was a little joke. That's progress, Seven. Well done."

Seven's mouth opened again, but he placed a hand over her lips to halt further speech. The gesture had the simultaneous effects of angering her and moving something much deeper and less well understood.

"Let me assist you further before you say something you will no doubt someday regret."

"If one of us should currently possess regrets . . ." she began.

"Uh . . . no, let me finish."

Seven waited in unabated frustration.

"I'm sorry," Cambridge finally said.

"You're what?"

Cambridge sighed. "Don't make me say it again. You have no idea what the first time cost me."

Still flummoxed, Seven grasped for a little dignity.

"For what exactly are you apologizing?" she finally asked.

Cambridge's eyes held hers, and there was no mistaking his sincerity, or the absurd joy he seemed to be taking in the moment.

"It is my belief that several days ago, when you came to my quarters to reschedule our therapy session, you might have misunderstood my preoccupation and taken it personally."

Seven considered his words and said, "I'm still not sure which part of *my* inability to understand your rude and dismissive behavior you are sorry for."

"You've got me there," Cambridge admitted. When Seven continued to allow him to dangle, he made another attempt. "All right, let's try this. I behaved badly."

"You were an ass."

"Were?"

"Are. You are an ass."

"I don't deny it."

"Then your apology is meaningless."

"Not at all. I am, as you no doubt noticed from the first, unable to take the slightest bit of interest in the common formalities that give polite society its pleasant veneer of cohesion. That is something that I don't see changing in the near future or, really, ever. What I regret is that you have somehow taken this weakness on my part personally."

"I assure you, Counselor," Seven replied rigidly, "any discomfort I might have experienced at your hands made only a fleeting impression."

Cambridge's eyes informed her that he didn't believe a word she had just said.

"So we're friends again?" he asked lightly.

A shrill beep from her console alerted Seven to *Voyager's* arrival at their destination. She was briefly torn, but duty seemed like a pleasant escape from the frustration of the conversation.

"Don't let me interrupt," Cambridge said congenially.

Turning to stand beside her and pretending to study the new sensor display, he added, "I can wait."

Chakotay stared at the main viewscreen, showing the undulating mass of gases forming the atmosphere of the planet *Voyager* now orbited. Space was by its nature a cold, inhospitable environment, but usually when gazing upon interstellar bodies there was something intriguing or at least uplifting in the possibility of discovery. It was difficult to understand why the tempestuous mass below made Chakotay feel so utterly empty.

Tearing his eyes away, he directed them toward Ensign Gwyn, who sat absolutely still at her console, her eyes glued ahead.

Preliminary scans were already well under way, so Chakotay decided to fill the time with a question. "Well, Ensign Gwyn, how do you feel about your hunch now?"

There was an expectant pause as Gwyn turned slowly in her chair. Chakotay tensed at the first sight of her face, normally an open catalogue of dozens of thoughts and emotions. The eyes that met his were unusually blank.

"Ensign?" he asked again, his voice tinged with concern.

After a few more seconds, she blinked rapidly, shook her head, and smiled, "Sorry, Captain. I'm not getting anything."

Chakotay sensed a rebuke coming from Eden, but before she could speak, Lasren's replacement at ops, a trim, white-haired ensign named Waters, reported, "Captain, I believe we've found something."

"Can you be more specific?" Eden asked immediately.

"It's definitely a life-form."

"Living in the atmosphere, or is there a surface below?" Chakotay asked.

"I mean the entire body, sir," Waters replied. "The whole thing is a single life-form."

Cambridge studied the display, and for a moment, all thoughts of further tormenting Seven were replaced by unabashed wonder. In a man who felt the universe contained little that could surprise him any longer, it was an unusual sensation.

Seven was busy manipulating a computer-generated schematic of the body. Rows of numbers and scientific notations crawled upward along the right side of the massive screen, but Cambridge preferred the view of the actual planet fixed on the screen's left side.

Grayish brown mists swirled intensely below, forming smaller circles centered by massive black holes that stared up at him like angry eyes. Bright flashes of orange and red plasma crackled intermittently, ripping across the atmosphere with violent brilliance. Although he knew it was only in his imagination, the entire body seemed to wail with cosmic grief.

"The Children of the Storm indeed," he said softly.

Seven raised her hand to her chest to tap her combadge, but before she could do so, a single red flash burst from the surface and floated upward.

"Did you see that?" Cambridge asked, unsure of himself.

"I did," Seven replied softly, quickly tapping on the console, undoubtedly demanding some sort of explanation from the ship's computer.

The spectacle was repeated four more times in the seconds it took for the analysis to complete itself, though the flashes varied greatly in hue, from a pale bluish to sickly yellow and orange.

"What are those?" Cambridge asked.

"We are witnessing birth, Counselor," Seven replied in a hushed tone.

"*Those* are the Children of the Storm?"

"Not as we encountered them," Seven corrected him, "but as they began their existence thousands of years ago."

As Cambridge watched, these tiny specks of light danced ever upward, struggling to free themselves from the tempest below. He found himself involuntarily rooting for them, certain that even the bleakness of space had more in the way of comfort to offer them than the hellish wasteland from which they rose.

"It's no wonder, is it, their propensity for violence?" Cambridge mused.

"What do you mean?"

"Look at their mother."

"I don't believe you possess sufficient data to extrapolate anything about the creature's nature from its outward appearance," Seven suggested.

"Maybe not," Cambridge allowed, "but if that were my home, I'd want to get as far from it as possible."

"They are acting on instinct," Seven advised. "Each individual is expelled from the body with great force and simply continues along an individual trajectory until it has cleared the atmosphere. In this state they are incredibly simple and fragile."

"Like most infants."

"But unlike most, they do not, over time, take on the physical appearance of their parent."

"As far as we know," Cambridge said.

"No," Seven insisted. "They will never possess sufficient mass to aggregate into anything resembling this creature. I'm

not even convinced that they are offspring, as we traditionally think of them."

"Then what are they?" Cambridge asked.

"I cannot . . . that is to say . . ."

Cambridge watched her struggle for a moment, searching
for the right word. It was so unlike her it puzzled him.

"Don't worry about being right, Seven, or even being pre-
cise. Some discoveries are best described by scientists; others,
by poets. What does your heart tell you this is?"

"I believe the life-forms that eventually become the Children of the Storm begin here, as this creature's thoughts,"
Seven finally said.

"Fascinating," Cambridge replied.

Lasren's efforts to reach the Children had left him utterly
exhausted. Although from time to time he was convinced
that some of them had been attempting to connect with him,
either the strength of the psionic field protecting him or the
limits of their abilities had left him no closer to true contact.

Doctor Sharak had finally ordered him to suspend his
work for at least a few hours for some much-needed rest.
As he gently removed the neural scanner from Lasren's forehead, his tricorder, which was patched into a small sensor
array running continuous scans of the sphere, emitted several shrill, sharp beeps.

Lasren immediately silenced the alert and studied the display. Both the resonance strength and the activity level of the
Children encased in the sphere had just risen exponentially.

He immediately tapped his combadge. "Lasren to the
bridge."

"*This is Chakotay, Ensign. Is everything all right down
there?*"

"The activity of the Children has increased beyond anything we have witnessed so far. But I cannot account for it."

"That's all right. We can. We believe we have located the Children's 'mother.' You should report to the briefing room right away."

"With your permission, sir, I'd like to study this a little further."

"Ensign, you are weakened," Sharak interjected calmly.

"It doesn't matter," Lasren insisted. "Captain?"

"Join us as soon as you can, Ensign. We'll await your report," Chakotay replied.

Without bothering to allow Sharak to reconnect the neural scanner, Lasren bolted past him into the cargo bay and stood as near the edge of the psionic field as he dared. Even at the current intensity of the field, strange new sensations began to bombard him. When the sphere was transported aboard, he had been given a small device by Conlon that allowed him to adjust the field's strength on his own. Resolved, he reduced the intensity by the standard three degrees that had, thus far, been absolutely safe.

A wave of emotions crashed over him, but he held his ground. Imaginary wind cried out all around him, buffeting his body. What he was experiencing was too chaotic for him to make sense of it beyond its initial intensity, until he found himself running at impossible speed through the Muoni canyon. His feet didn't even touch the ground. The moment he came within sight of the falls he felt himself fly upward as if desperate to embrace them. Moments later they receded into the distance as he continued to rise above them.

Looking down, he saw the valley far below, a tapestry of vivid greens, blues, and browns more beautiful now than he remembered. Every single blade of grass, every leaf, every twig, every drop of water glowed with its own distinct brilliance until the light overwhelmed him, forcing him to turn away or risk blindness.

And still he soared upward.

Chapter Twenty-four

STARDATE 58463.9
U.S.S. GALEN

As the Doctor ushered B'Elanna and Miral into the quarters they would occupy aboard *Galen,* B'Elanna was both moved and delighted to see that the main area of the Doctor's living space had been transformed into a playroom for Miral. As the entire space, apart from the desk and data terminals linked to the rest of the ship, was a holographic creation, the new configuration hadn't involved a great deal of heavy lifting on the Doctor's part, but tremendous care had obviously gone into every detail of the contents.

A large soft, circular mat embedded with brightly colored letters and numbers lay on the floor. As Miral rushed over them to reach a small climbing dome, B'Elanna noted that a photonic representation of each symbol she touched rose up from the floor and bounced in the air as the computer's voice began a lesson. "*C,*" the computer said as a bright yellow *C* floated at what would have been Miral's eye level had she paused long enough to notice. "'*C*' *is for* 'cat.'" From thin air, a small *a* and *t* rose from the floor and tumbled over to join the *c*, spelling out the simple word. "*Can you say cat, Miral?*" the computer asked.

"Cat!" Miral shouted from the top of the climber, and the computer rewarded her by turning the word *cat* into a small ginger-colored kitten that meowed its congratulations, which was almost but not quite enough excitement to bring Miral down from her perch.

And the mat was only the beginning. Brightly colored blocks and soft balls were piled on one side of the mat, along with a touch-activated easel Miral could use for art or practicing letters and numbers.

Books, puzzles, and other small toys were also strewn about. Turning to the Doctor, her eyes alight, B'Elanna said, "This is absolutely amazing. Thank you so much."

"While we were en route, I prepared a full week of lessons as well as dozens of subject-specific teachers for her," the Doctor enthused. B'Elanna had seen him pleased with himself in the past, but at this moment he might have burst with pride. "I know you are scheduled to report to *Achilles* right away, and I will be working for the next several hours on the surface of the planet with Doctor Sal, but our little Miral will be quite safe in the care of William Shakespeare, who will be providing her morning lessons, and Reg has promised to check in on her in an hour or so."

"That sounds wonderful," B'Elanna admitted, "but we'll have to start the formal lessons tomorrow."

The Doctor's face fell dramatically as he asked, "Why? I assure you she will be perfectly safe and well occupied."

"Oh, it's not that," B'Elanna hurried to assure him. "I just . . . that is, I need her with me today."

"You'll be much too busy to tend to her properly," the Doctor chastised her. "She is an incredibly active young lady, and—"

"I know," B'Elanna interjected. "I'm actually counting on it."

Clearly appalled and disappointed, the Doctor sighed with the passion of one of his operatic divas. "I simply don't understand."

B'Elanna planted a quick peck on his cheek as she placed an arm over his shoulder. "I'll explain tonight. I promise. And please believe me when I tell you, I've never seen anything as wonderful as what you've created here. I'm going to steal all of your programs for our quarters on *Voyager* when we're done here."

This seemed to placate the Doctor's wounded hopes a little. "I don't believe they will function optimally anywhere but here," he noted.

"You're probably right," B'Elanna granted him. "Even when *Voyager* gets back, she should probably plan to spend as much time here as she can."

Finally some of the Doctor's prior luster returned. "Most definitely," he encouraged her.

"Then I guess we'd both best get to our work," B'Elanna said.

The Doctor nodded amiably as B'Elanna crossed the room to collect Miral from the climber.

"Come on, darling," B'Elanna called to her. "You're going to help Mommy with her work today."

In truth, it was the only thing she could have said that would have captured Miral's imagination enough to bring her down from the structure. As B'Elanna took her daughter's hand, a short man dressed in the garb of one of Earth's sixteenth-century nobles appeared in the center of the mat.

"Oh, brave new world, that has such people in't," he proclaimed pompously.

Mindful that the program was probably written to give

the Doctor a detailed report of its interactions, B'Elanna replied, "I'm sorry, William, but you'll have to excuse your pupil for the morning. Hold that thought, though."

She left the program running, though, possibly for the first time ever, at a loss for words.

U.S.S. ACHILLES

Phinn had grown so accustomed to putting one fire out after another during the two weeks *Quirinal* was planet-bound and isolated from the rest of the fleet that the past two days had felt like a dream he never dared believe would come true. Fleet Chief Torres and *Voyager*'s chief engineer, Lieutenant Conlon, had made sure that every resource they could spare were his for the asking. *Achilles* had arrived several hours earlier. A swarm of technicians had descended upon *Quirinal* and had begun the work of clearing wreckage and refuse, along with power restoration to every area of the ship that was functional. The delight on Psilakis's face when Phinn had made his morning report had done much to lighten the lieutenant's spirits, despite the fact that his regular visit with Doctor Sal had confirmed that Captain Farkas remained in critical condition. Phinn hardly dared hope that *Galen*'s arrival would change that, though he'd heard rumors about an amazing holographic doctor stationed aboard who might find something that Sal had missed.

The thought that his captain had sacrificed her life for his was Phinn's heaviest burden to bear. Over the past several days, when the work had been desperately hard, the decisions had been heart-wrenching, or the hours had been mentally and physically withering, Phinn had taken strength from Captain Farkas's resolve in the face of much dimmer odds.

He now lived on the fantasy that one day she would open her eyes and he would be able to report that her engineers had restored her ship to fighting shape. Watching *Voyager*'s and now *Achilles'* crew work, that fantasy seemed closer than ever to becoming reality.

He had boarded *Achilles* almost an hour earlier for a briefing with Commander Drafar to begin discussing repair priorities, fully expecting to meet with Commander Torres at the same time. When she finally arrived, leading a young girl who would never be mistaken for anyone but her daughter by the hand, Phinn assumed that she had been detained by personal needs. He knew *Voyager* had already departed, presumably to determine *Demeter*'s status, and rescue them if possible. It was altogether likely that Commander Torres had been unable to secure child care for the day and had arrived only to check in on the meeting before leaving the work in Commander Drafar's capable, and extremely large, hands.

Commander Torres took her seat after instructing her daughter to sit quietly for a few minutes in a large chair at the end of the table, which, lucky for the little girl, turned on its base and seemed destined to provide hours of entertainment. Turning to Drafar, Torres said lightly, "We're ready to begin."

Drafar had stared at the child from the moment she entered the way Phinn might have stared at something stuck to his shoe. However, the commander didn't miss a beat as he advised Torres that the meeting was already well under way and handed her a padd that undoubtedly contained the revised repair schedule.

Torres had seemed extremely capable but also quite warm and amiable to Phinn, until Drafar addressed her. As her child began making soft whooshing noises to correspond with her chair's spinning, Torres turned a hard face to Drafar and asked, "Why was I not informed that the meeting's start time had been changed?"

"I saw no reason to trouble you, Commander," Drafar replied cheerfully, while casting a dismissive glance at the child. "I was certain you would have other pressing duties to attend to, and after thoroughly reviewing your repair and reconstruction schedule while we were en route to this system, I did not doubt that you would not take issue with the few minor alterations I saw fit to make. I had every intention of briefing you whenever you arrived."

Torres's face softened a bit as she replied perfunctorily, "In the future, I would appreciate being advised of any meeting or schedule changes prior to their implementation, Commander. My first duty is to the fleet, and I do not take the responsibility lightly, nor do I intend to cede that authority to anyone. Do we understand one another?"

"Of course," Drafar replied neutrally.

Torres then took a few moments to review the padd while her daughter managed to spin the chair fast enough to topple it on its side. Phinn expected that most children her age would have cried for comfort after such a fall, but the hardy young girl picked herself up and, after kicking the chair with her little foot for good measure, began the painstaking process of attempting to stand it back up. Torres glanced at her but did nothing to assist her. Drafar's mouth actually opened in apparent alarm at this unruly turn of events.

"You've managed to trim two days off the schedule I had created, Commander," Torres said approvingly.

"My people will work twelve-hour shifts for the next twenty-six days," Drafar said. "And two days is a conservative estimate. I fully expect that once we get under way, we might eliminate another two or three days."

"Who designed this tractor mechanism to right the ship and hold it above ground during the third week of repairs?" Torres asked.

"I did," Drafar replied proudly. In Phinn's estimation, he deserved every bit of praise for it. Phinn had no idea how this most delicate maneuver might be accomplished until he'd seen Drafar's schematics.

"I'm not surprised, Commander," Torres replied, obviously pleased, "but I am concerned about the drain on *Achilles'* power systems."

"It will be a strain, but not unmanageable," Drafar replied.

"Or," Torres offered, "we could supplement the beam with carefully positioned antigravitational units with self-regenerating cells to ease the burden on *Achilles*."

For the first time, Phinn saw shock ripple over Drafar's terribly composed mien.

"Do we possess such units?" he asked.

"We can build them," Torres replied, "though it will add a day to your schedule. For safety's sake, I think it worthwhile."

"I wasn't aware that the Federation had adopted self-regenerating circuitry," Drafar hurried to add.

"It may not be regulation, but I've seen it work before under greater stress than this, and I'm confident it will assist us greatly here," Torres replied evenly.

"Very well," Drafar replied with some reluctance. He seemed ready to say something more, when he was interrupted by a loud banging noise. The child had managed to turn the chair upright, but rather than resuming her twirling game, she was now taking great delight in simply rolling the chair into the wall as hard as she could.

"Miral, stop that," Torres instructed the girl, who cast a disparaging glance her way before giving the chair one last push and searching the room for something else that might be as much fun.

"If there are no further items you wish to discuss, Commander," Drafar said congenially, "Lieutenant Bryce and I can complete our review of the schedule while you tend to your child's amusement."

At this, Torres's face lit with a slight smile. "Actually," she said, "I am prepared to complete the review with you and Lieutenant Bryce, after which Miral and I will accompany both of you to the surface and meet briefly with your team leaders."

"I hardly think *Quirinal,* in its present state, will be a safe place for your child, Commander," Drafar advised her.

"We'll manage," Torres said. "She's a bright child and incredibly curious, but she also understands the meaning of the word *no*. She won't be any trouble, and to be honest, Commander, the last time we met you seemed so distracted by concerns about her proper care I thought you would appreciate a chance to see for yourself how challenging and rewarding her presence can be."

Drafar stiffened in his chair, clearly at a loss. While he would have been well within his rights to scuttle B'Elanna's plans, he seemed to sense the challenge B'Elanna was throwing down.

Finally Drafar seemed to settle the matter in his head. He rose from his seat and in a few long strides crossed to Miral, who was seated on the floor with her legs splayed, still playing with the base of the chair but, as her mother requested, no longer rolling it far enough away to hit the wall.

As Drafar knelt beside her, entering her personal space, Miral looked up at him, her eyes growing wide and her mouth falling open in something resembling awe.

"Good morning, young lady," Drafar said cordially. "Your mother says you are bright. I wonder if you could demonstrate that to me." Reaching for the base of the chair, he grasped a single wheel with one hand and a spindle of the base in another and pointed out a button that released the wheel from the base. He then replaced the wheel and made certain Miral heard it slip and lock into place. "Now you try." He once again separated the wheel from the base and handed it to her. He sat back on his heels as Miral puzzled over the wheel momentarily, then grabbed the spindle and restored the wheel to its place.

Phinn's smile at her success was mirrored on B'Elanna's and Drafar's faces.

"Very good," Drafar said. "Now, if you can manage all four of them, you may resume rolling the chair into the wall if you like." He quickly removed all four wheels and placed them within Miral's reach. Without waiting to check her progress, he rose and returned to his seat at the table.

"Where were we?" he asked perfunctorily. Before Phinn could answer, all three of them heard the sound of the chair rolling across the floor and hitting the wall, followed by a small laugh of delight.

Chapter Twenty-five

STARDATE 58464.5
U.S.S. VOYAGER

Captain Eden was already in sickbay, standing by the still form of Ensign Lasren, when Chakotay arrived. He had been waiting in the conference room with the rest of the senior staff for the briefing when Sharak had called to inform them that Lasren would be unable to join them. Apparently his last contact with the captive Children had finally pushed him well beyond his physical and mental limits. As CMO, Sharak had stepped in and put a halt to the proceedings, very much against Lasren's will, and had confined Lasren to sickbay until he was fully restored to health.

Eden shifted her weight from foot to foot as Sharak gave the details of Lasren's condition. "There should be no permanent damage, Captain," Sharak assured her as Chakotay stepped to her side, "but he will require several days of monitoring. The chemical balance of his brain has shifted, and his electrolytes have diminished beyond safety. He requires undisturbed sleep for his body to begin to repair itself."

"Did he say anything before you sedated him?" Chakotay asked tensely.

Sharak pondered the question. "His words did not follow a logical progression," he finally said. "He talked a great deal about flying and how beautiful it was, but as to what *it* might be, I cannot say."

Eden turned to Chakotay. "He said that our arrival here had affected the Children. We need to know how."

"I agree," Chakotay replied.

"I cannot say for certain that the ensign was in his right mind at the end," Sharak offered.

"What do you mean?" Eden asked.

"He had lowered the intensity of the psionic field. I worry that those he was trying to reach may have lured him too close to danger."

"Were they trying to kill him?" Chakotay demanded.

"These were his actions, not theirs," Sharak replied, obviously struggling to be absolutely clear. "But I do not know that he was fully in control of the situation any longer."

Finally Chakotay posed the next logical question. "Can you revive him, even for a few minutes?" He did not doubt that if doing so posed any danger to Lasren, the doctor would refuse.

Sharak's gaze was hard and inscrutable. "He needs rest," he replied.

"I am aware of that, but it will be dangerous for us to proceed without getting at least a sense of what he learned from the Children."

Sharak bowed his head formally, then took a hypospray from the instrument tray next to the biobed and placed it at Lasren's neck. "A few moments only, I beg you, Captain."

"Of course, Doctor," Chakotay replied.

A dull hiss issued from the hypo and Lasren began to stir. The moment he came to consciousness, his entire body tensed briefly, until he realized where he was. As he proceeded to relax, his eyes held a feverish glow as they shifted back and forth between his two commanding officers.

"You have pushed yourself too far, Ensign," Chakotay said softly, "and will be confined to sickbay until you have recovered."

"No, please, Captain," Lasren pleaded.

"If there is anything you can tell us about what you experienced, please do so now. But try not to upset yourself."

Lasren took several quick, shallow breaths. "They heard me," he began. "They showed me . . . so much."

"What did you see?" Chakotay prodded gently.

"Worlds, so many planets filled with indescribably beautiful life. But not us."

"Not us?" Chakotay asked.

"Not humanoids. The worlds are pristine, untouched by the hands of the destroyers."

Eden and Chakotay shared an uneasy glance.

"The joy they took from these sights, I cannot describe," Lasren went on, clearly growing more agitated.

"Did they tell you anything about the creature we have discovered?"

Lasren shook his head. "I don't know if I was seeing their memories, or hers," he replied. "Only that there was once so much happiness. Until the Borg began to move among them."

Lasren's face contorted in a mixture of pain and rage. "They ripped the life from the land," he said, beginning to weep. "They took what was not theirs. They left nothing but death."

Chakotay look to Sharak and, with a regretful nod, clearly ordered him to once again sedate Lasren.

"Wait," Lasren said, grabbing Sharak's arm with both of his hands.

"You have told us more than enough," Chakotay tried to convince him. "Now you must rest."

"No, Captain," Lasren said, struggling to regain control of himself. "You must free them. They know me. They understand me. They did not hurt me. They will help."

"We can't know that," Chakotay said gently.

"I know it!" Lasren shouted. "Please, free them. Trust them."

Sharak shot Chakotay a fearful look. Chakotay nodded again. "Thank you, Ensign," he said. "Now, rest. That's an order."

"Captain, please," Lasren began again, but Sharak silenced him with another hypospray, and within seconds, he fell into a deep and peaceful sleep.

"Keep me advised of his condition," Chakotay ordered. As Chakotay and Eden began to walk toward the turbolift that would return them to the conference room, Eden folded her hands behind her back.

"What's your sense of this, Chakotay?" she asked.

"I don't believe he was compromised in the same way that the crew of *Quirinal* was," Chakotay offered, "but I'm also not convinced that his analysis can be considered objective."

"Does that make it wrong?" Eden posited as they entered the turbolift, ordering it to deck one.

"It makes it suspect," Chakotay replied.

"Then you believe we should not do as he suggested?"

Chakotay was dumbfounded. As best he could tell, they still had only one ace to play in the game that lay ahead of them, and Eden seemed to be seriously considering throwing it away.

"Halt lift," Chakotay ordered. "I want to be perfectly clear," he began. "It is my belief that we absolutely cannot afford to do what Lasren has suggested. We have no idea if the desire to free them was his or theirs. And we can't know whether or not they might turn on us if we did. I'm not sure they pose much of a threat, but we're not so far from their system that they might not be able to call in reinforcements. Never mind the fact that we might need them to negotiate for *Demeter*'s release."

Eden had listened in stony silence and, once he was finished, said only, "Lift, resume."

"Shall I take your silence as agreement, Captain?" Chakotay asked.

"You have made your position perfectly clear, Chakotay," Eden replied. "I require further information before I can make a decision."

The turbolift doors opened and Eden stepped out, Chakotay on her heels.

"Captain," he said firmly, halting her in her steps just outside the conference room door.

"Something you wish to add?"

Chakotay paused, momentarily unsure how he wished to proceed. Had Kathryn cut him off so abruptly, he would have known that she disagreed with him and was intent on pursuing her own course. He would argue the point with her, however, right up until she gave her orders. Somehow he sensed that Eden was still in conflict. But he couldn't find an argument beyond what he had already said that might bring her more firmly into his camp.

"No," he finally said. "Only that I adamantly believe the risk of releasing them now is much too great to seriously consider."

"Understood."

"Does it matter?" Chakotay asked.

Eden turned on him in genuine surprise. "Of course it does. Right now we have two options, neither of them particularly compelling. I'm hoping that once we receive Seven's report, another may be added to the list. Until then, I plan to keep an open mind."

"Fair enough," Chakotay replied, though in his heart he wasn't sure he believed her.

When they entered the conference room, Eden was shocked to see the entire senior staff crowding the windows of the room to stare down at the organism below. Ensign Gwyn uttered a sharp "Was that one?" to which Seven replied calmly, "Yes."

"Wow" was Gwyn's succinct observation.

Eden cleared her throat, and Paris, Kim, Conlon, Patel and Cambridge quickly moved to take their seats. Gwyn headed immediately for the door, saying, "Apologies, Captain. I've been watching the organism from the bridge and I just wanted to make sure what I thought I was seeing was actually, you know, real."

Eden's lips turned upward as she said, "Take a seat and join us, Ensign."

Gwyn's eyes widened, but she quickly did as ordered.

As everyone settled, Eden turned to Seven and said, "What have you discovered about 'mother'?"

"The organism we are orbiting is, as you already know, not a planet but a single life-form and is unquestionably the origin of the Children of the Storm," Seven began.

"But the Children are not offspring as we traditionally define them," Patel was quick to add.

Unruffled, Seven continued, "The organism is likely tens of thousands of years old, and it did not originate in this system."

"What brought it here?" Eden asked.

"We have no way of knowing," Seven replied. "It is not likely to be disturbed here by any spacefaring species, as there is nothing particularly notable about what remains of the system."

"She wanted a little peace and quiet?" Cambridge asked.

"As I said," Seven replied a little more sharply, "we really have no way of knowing. What we do know, however, is that every few minutes, a new life-form emerges from the atmosphere surrounding the organism. This life-form is an extremely immature version of the species we know as the Children of the Storm. The resonance frequencies of the infants are incredibly weak, compared to their more mature counterparts, and there is little variety in their resonance."

"What does that mean, exactly?" Paris asked.

"We know that the life-form is comprised of two parts, an intelligence that is produced by the organism, and a small extremophile that is then guided into open space."

"But again, 'intelligence' suggests complexity that these creatures do not possess," Patel added.

"We believe each child begins as a single thought, merged with an extremophile," Seven went on. "This is hard for us to relate to because we often carry many distinct thoughts in our minds simultaneously. The creature's thoughts, however—at least those that give rise to the Children—are singular. It is clear that in the past, a wide variety of thoughts emerged from the organism, thoughts of moving through space, of communicating with others, and thoughts of destruction. Over time, these creatures must band together and organize themselves into the configurations we have seen. It is likely they must first, however, survive the journey to find other compatible individuals."

"Is that why Lasren had such a hard time communicating with them?" Conlon asked. "There were only two distinct types of *thoughts* present in the sphere we captured?"

Patel nodded. "Exactly. They need a communicator to talk with us, and probably a highly capable telepath on our end."

"I am also not convinced that many of the life-forms whose birth we have witnessed since we arrived would be classified as 'communicators,'" Seven added.

"Then what are they?" Eden asked.

"I believe they are primarily anger and grief," Seven replied. "I am comparing the frequencies we have already charted from *Quirinal*'s sensors, and from our scans. At best, this is an educated guess."

Eden nodded. She then quickly briefed the others on Lasren's report. When she had finished, Cambridge scratched his head and said, "So essentially, the Children are sent out into the void as single, powerful thoughts that, once collected, become capable of terribly destructive actions?"

"Lasren has confirmed our suspicion that they value simple life-forms," Eden went on. "Clearly they, or their 'mother,' witnessed the Borg moving through this sector and ravaging worlds for their resources. This must have angered the 'mother' greatly, and saddened her."

"And so a war was born," Cambridge added.

"It actually also explains their xenophobia," Patel said. "As long as there were Borg ships in the area, they had a simple purpose. Now, that purpose is gone, but we came along with a ship filled with the one thing that gives them joy."

"The life," Cambridge echoed.

"They understand so little of life as we know it," Patel said, nodding. "And the mother's grief must be unspeakable, especially if she has no knowledge of the Children."

"You think she doesn't know what she's doing?" Kim asked.

"Lasren said that her Children don't know her, though they must have sensed something pretty powerful when we arrived because that allowed them to connect in some new way with him," Eden said. "It is just as likely, given their life cycle, that she does not know them either. Although you would think that their work, clearing the area of the Borg, would have given her some comfort."

"But they could not restore the life to those decimated planets," Cambridge said, "so what is left for her but to mourn?"

"Can we communicate with her at all?" Eden asked.

Seven shook her head. "There might be some telepathic species capable of making a basic connection with her, but in order to avoid risking their possession by the Children, we left all officers that fit that description behind."

"Didn't your catoms allow you to communicate telepathically with the Neyser?" Kim asked.

"Yes," Seven acknowledged, "but they reached out to me and established the connection. I cannot initiate a link on my own."

"Nor should you try," Cambridge added. "Given what little we now know, Captain," he said, addressing himself to Eden, "it is likely that any such contact would be extremely dangerous. This creature's thoughts come to life, and it has had thousands of years now to wallow in its despair. We're not going to correct that kind of depression in a single conversation. Years, perhaps, coupled with evidence that life does remain beyond the systems it watched die, might do the trick, but we're not capable of providing such evidence to it."

Eden sat back in her chair and glanced at Chakotay. After a moment she said, "Lasren told us to release the sphere. He said the children understood him and that they would help us."

"How could he know that without direct communication?" Kim asked.

"How, indeed?" Cambridge added.

"I don't know," Eden confessed. "But he was adamant."

"Why don't we return to the system they inhabit and release them there?" Paris asked. "If they truly want to help us, they need to tell their friends to let our ship go."

"I agree," Chakotay said. "We came here hoping that this 'mother' might have some influence over her Children. Clearly, she does not."

"Then why did our arrival agitate them?" Gwyn asked.

All eyes turned to her and her face reddened visibly.

"Go ahead, Ensign," Eden said.

"I mean, they don't know her, but they obviously recognized something in her."

"It could have been a genetic memory," Cambridge suggested.

"What's that?" Gwyn asked.

"Essentially it is the notion that buried within our DNA is all of the knowledge ever accumulated by anything that contributed to its creation. Sentient life-forms rarely access or use it, though it is thought by some to be the basis for the psychological premise of a collective unconscious." After a moment of thought he went on, "Given the origins of these creatures, their beginnings as simple thoughts, it might be more likely to exist here. They may not understand their connection to their 'mother' but are nonetheless vulnerable to it."

"Does that help us?" Tom asked.

"Lasren is the only one of us who even has a sense of these creatures, let alone their intentions," Gwyn argued. "He's spent days working with them. If he says they can help us, we should let them."

"It's not quite that simple," Chakotay said.

After a moment of uncomfortable silence, all heads turned back to Eden.

"Or maybe it is," Eden finally said.

"Captain?" Chakotay asked sternly.

"Despite our success in locating the organism we were seeking, as it stands now, we are no closer to defending ourselves against an assault from the Children of the Storm like the one that destroyed *Planck*," Eden said evenly. "Ensign

Lasren's work has confirmed their passion for *Demeter*'s cargo, and I believe that they will fight with every weapon available to stop any attempt we make to rescue the ship. While we could certainly formulate an all-out assault that might kill enough of them to allow us to secure *Demeter* and run for our lives, I am willing to countenance such destruction only as a last resort."

"I believe we have reached the end of our options," Chakotay said.

"We have to prove to the Children that we are not what they believe us to be. That is the only way to begin a dialogue that might ultimately result in the release of our people. Ensign Lasren believes we can trust those with whom he has made tentative contact. While I agree that it is impossible to know whether or not that belief came from Lasren or the Children, it is the only option before us that does not include a body count. If it fails, as it might, we still have the more extreme tactical option. But if it succeeds, it will greatly increase our odds of a rescue."

"Even if it does succeed, in some measure," Seven said, "how will we know?"

"Exactly," Tom added. "Are we going to wait for Lasren to recover before we try this? Without him, who will the Children use to reach us?"

"Seven and I should take a nap," Gwyn suggested, and all eyes again turned to her, this time filled with confusion.

"If we're boring you, Ensign—" Kim began.

"No, she's right," Patel cut him off. "The Children may need a telepath for direct communication, but they were able to take over the bodies of many of *Quirinal*'s crew by invading them as they slept. Doctor Sal believes that in a sleep state anyone's mind is vulnerable to them. Both Seven and Gwyn have a greater capacity to be of use to them. We would simply have to modulate the psionic field protecting the ship so that it did not affect the area where they were resting."

"That's what I meant," Gwyn added sheepishly.

"It's an excellent idea, Ensign," Eden confirmed.

"But if it fails?" Chakotay asked.

"Then we will accept it and move on," Eden replied simply. "I believe that we must align our actions with our highest principles. No matter the outcome, we will not have failed if we act from our best intentions."

"The road to hell is paved with good intentions, Captain," Chakotay said with equal certainty.

"So is the road to peace," Cambridge observed.

After a moment of silence, Eden said, "We're going to release the sphere and see what happens. My only question now is, how do we do that?"

It took Lieutenant Conlon almost an hour to figure out a way to safely get the sphere from the cargo bay to the shuttlebay, from which it could safely be released. A path was cleared between the two points, and the psionic field was gradually weakened along the path to draw the sphere toward its freedom. The suppression beam that kept the sphere from exploding was modified so that the sphere would not be free of it until it had cleared *Voyager*.

Eden and Chakotay observed the sphere's progress through the ship from the bridge in tense silence. Eden was convinced that this was the most dangerous part of her plan, and Chakotay agreed. His biggest fear was that once free, the sphere would simply depart the area at maximum speed, leaving them with nothing to exchange for *Demeter*.

Patel had been stationed in astrometrics to observe the

"mother's" response to the emergence of the sphere. Seven and Gwyn had reported to sickbay, where Doctor Sharak had stationed them in the private surgical suite and provided each of them with a mild sleep aid. Conlon would drop the psionic field around that suite once the sphere was free and clear.

It took the sphere six minutes to reach the shuttlebay, but as soon as it was in range of the open door, it increased its speed and flew into open space. Its initial trajectory took it soaring high above the ship, increasing its distance from its "mother."

"Lieutenant Kim, how long will we be able to keep them in sensor range?" Eden asked.

"Unless they alter course and speed, we will need to lay in a pursuit course in two minutes."

"Helm, plot course," Eden ordered Ensign Gleez, Gwyn's gamma-shift replacement.

The clock had almost run out when the sphere abruptly reversed course and dived toward "mother."

"That's more like it," Eden said softly.

The sphere paused several thousand meters from the edge of "mother's" atmosphere and held position. It then moved quickly to another location and again remained stationary for a few minutes.

"What's it doing?" Chakotay asked.

"I have no idea," Eden replied.

A few moments later it began to descend closer to the atmosphere.

"Waters, continue to track the sphere as best you can," Eden ordered as it disappeared from sight.

"Its configuration is so different from the rest of the organism that there is little danger we'll lose it in there," Waters confirmed.

"Be on the lookout for any other incoming signals," Chakotay warned.

"Aye, Captain."

Five minutes passed in silence. Chakotay did his best during that time to quiet his growing doubts and temper his frustration with Eden. For all that she might have doomed his ship and *Demeter* to oblivion, he could not deny after hearing her reasons that she was doing what she absolutely believed was best.

"*Patel to the bridge.*"

"Go ahead, Lieutenant," Chakotay replied.

"*I've been monitoring the sphere within the atmosphere, and I believe it is attempting to collect several of the infant life-forms. Two have already successfully been integrated into it.*"

Chakotay turned a puzzled face to Eden as he asked of Patel, "Do you have any idea why they would do that?"

"*The resonance frequencies of the individuals they have collected are unlike any of the others present in the sphere. Perhaps they may be used to make direct contact with us.*"

"Keep us advised, Devi," Chakotay ordered.

"*Acknowledged.*"

To Eden he said, "How long are you prepared to wait?"

"Longer than five minutes," she replied confidently. "Less than five days," she added in a tone that was considerably lighter.

It took almost half an hour for the sphere to once again emerge from the atmosphere. It flew swiftly toward *Voyager* and held position just off the ship's port bow.

Less than two minutes after that, Sharak's voice called out over the comm. "*Sickbay to Captain Eden. Please report here at once.*"

Eden rose and said briskly, "Mister Paris, the bridge is yours. Captain Chakotay, with me, please."

With a new sense of optimism, Chakotay followed her out, though he kept his own counsel as they walked silently to sickbay.

There, they found Ensign Gwyn seated on her biobed. Seven remained asleep beside her. Sharak said softly, "She awoke of her own accord and asked to speak to our commander."

"Thank you, Doctor," Eden replied, moving to stand as close to the suite as possible without crossing the barrier of the psionic field still protecting her and the rest of the ship.

"You command this vessel?" Gwyn asked, once Eden had settled herself. It was eminently clear from her voice and demeanor that whoever was speaking was not, in fact, the ensign.

"I command the fleet of vessels assigned to this region of space," Eden replied. "I am Captain Afsarah Eden. Captain Chakotay," she added, gesturing to him, "commands this vessel, the Federation *Starship Voyager.*"

"Where is the one who flew with us?" the alien asked.

"Ensign Lasren was weakened by his contact with you and will require rest before he can work with you again, though I am certain he would like the opportunity to speak directly with you."

"You are not destroyers of worlds," the alien said. "You are unlike any we have encountered before. You brought us to a home we never knew existed and to many lost Children. We are grateful."

"It pleases me to hear you say so," Eden replied. "We came in peace, seeking only to better understand you. We believe, however, that you have taken one of our ships captive and we would ask that you help us retrieve it."

"We took the life," the alien replied dispassionately. "We cannot part with it now."

"I understand your passion for the life," Eden replied, "but it is my hope that we might come to a new agreement that would include your ability to continue to enjoy the life, but would also free our people."

"Your people may not have survived," the alien warned.

"Do you know that for a fact?"

"No. We were separated from the others. But they would not have allowed anyone to endanger the life."

"Assuming they are still alive, will you help us?" Eden asked.

After a long pause, the alien replied, "We will."

Chapter Twenty-six

THIRTEEN HOURS EARLIER
U.S.S. DEMETER

Eight days had passed with *Demeter*'s status essentially unchanged, excepting the fact that they were now eight planting cycles, or less than two days, from exhausting their supply of stored seeds. Fife had begun to advise O'Donnell on a regular basis of their diminishing stocks, but the captain had taken the news without a hint of dismay. His continued absence from the bridge and seeming lack of interest in his crew's welfare convinced Fife that either he was working on his supposed plan to "help" the Children, or he was hiding.

The next forty-eight hours would prove critical in more ways than one. O'Donnell's increasing distance from his people had given Fife an easy opening to discuss his fears and plans with Falto and Vincent. Like Url, they had hesitantly agreed to follow his commands should O'Donnell prove unwilling or unable to lead them to safety. Once the supply of seed had run out, the Children would undoubtedly respond, likely with violence. At that point, Fife believed they would have no option other than putting his plan into effect. He had personally prepared the drones for launch and worked with Url to devise the most destructive firing patterns possible and had programmed the phasers to run continuously in the event that the officer manning tactical was compromised in any way.

It was also possible that at any moment, one or more of the other fleet vessels might arrive to aid them. They were now five days past their scheduled rendezvous with the rest of the fleet. Fife assumed that they would be unable to communicate with any of their fellow ships, but he intended by their actions to communicate their desire to escape captivity at any cost, as well as the fact that the Children were still considered hostile enemies.

It came as something of a surprise, then, when bright and early that morning, O'Donnell had broken his silence and ordered a meeting of the senior staff, including their chief engineer, Lieutenant Elkins, at 0800 hours.

Everyone assembled as ordered. Fife would have appreciated it if Url, Falto, and Vincent had attempted to look a little less uncomfortable. They had agreed to aid him, but their uneasiness was palpable, especially once O'Donnell entered and hastily took his seat. Fife knew that they were all capable officers, but they needed a true leader and O'Donnell simply wasn't up to that task. Soon enough, he would no longer be an issue, Fife decided, settling in and greeting the captain with professional cordiality.

For his part, Elkins looked a little lost. He was a plump fellow in his late fifties who had spent the last three weeks assisting with the regular planting cycles and providing maintenance for the overused hydroponic and aeroponic systems. As there was nothing else in his engine room that needed work, Fife assumed he had stepped in with the labs to alleviate boredom. Sometime in the next few hours, Fife would have to brief him on their plan to attempt escape so that he could prepare the slipstream drive.

As O'Donnell spent a moment studying the padd he had brought with him, Fife chose to open the meeting by saying, "Brill has confirmed this morning that we have enough supplies for only eight more planting cycles."

"Doesn't matter," O'Donnell said, brushing aside his concerns. Fife noted the glance of alarm that shot between Url and Falto at this. "All of you, except for Lieutenant Elkins, were here several days ago when I told you that I intended to find a way to help the Children." O'Donnell sighed, and a curious light came into his eyes. "I'm pretty sure we can now do that."

Url straightened in his chair, looking positively relieved. "How, Captain?" he asked.

"Until now, the Children have had to rely on external sources of amusement; namely, us. Their passion for all things botanical is a given. Until now, however, no species has existed that could live in their home, or, more specifically, the atmosphere contained by their energy shells."

"Until now?" Fife asked dubiously. Admittedly he knew next to nothing about botany, but the idea that anything other than the Children themselves could live in the toxic atmosphere they inhabited seemed positively ludicrous.

"Over twenty years ago I began working on a unique hybrid flower I intended to call *Crateva religiosa-Kressari*. The process was incredibly difficult, given the limited amount of genetic material between the Terran and Kressari parent plants that was in any way compatible. I have been assured by many in my field that such a hybrid was impossible. Ironically, our discovery of the Children has finally enabled me to complete this work. The atmosphere contained within the shells is extremely toxic to almost all conceivable life-forms, but it has proven to be the catalyst for a unique mutation that enables *Crateva religiosa-Kressari* to thrive."

"Congratulations, Captain," Url said sincerely.

"Thank you, Lieutenant," O'Donnell replied warmly. "So we now have an opportunity to provide the Children with a botanical life-form that can coexist with them. There's only one problem."

"Only one?" Fife said—a little too sarcastically, as no one else at the table appeared to be amused in the least.

"Yes," O'Donnell replied without taking offense. "We need a delivery system, and for that, I'm looking to you, Lieutenant Elkins."

"Oh, good," Elkins said simply. "I was worried you were going to ask for a miracle. Instead you want something that's just this side of impossible."

"What's the difficulty?" Vincent asked.

"You want to insert this thing inside one of the energy shells, yes?" Elkins asked more seriously.

O'Donnell nodded.

"Then the difficulty is in creating an instrument that can puncture the energy shell and deliver the hybrid cells into it, without destroying the shell. Despite the incredible pressure required to maintain the atmosphere within those shells, they can't even stand up to low-level phaser fire, so a photonic-based tool probably wouldn't be a good idea."

"Agreed," O'Donnell said, nodding.

"Never mind the delivery system," Url said, his earlier enthusiasm dimming a bit, "how are we going to get one of the spheres inside *Demeter* to perform the insertion?"

"We're not," O'Donnell replied.

Url looked lost.

"I'm going out there to deliver the specimen personally. I just need a tool that will allow me to get close enough to a single sphere without killing myself, or damaging the sphere, to inject the genetic material. Once inside, it should begin to grow immediately."

"A subtle knife," Elkins said thoughtfully.

O'Donnell smiled. "Exactly."

"What's that?" Url asked.

"A myth," O'Donnell replied, "but if we had one, it would sure come in handy right now."

"It's an unbreakable knife that supposedly had the ability to cut through space and time," Elkins clarified. "Although, come to think of it, a fine enough slice of benamite might do the trick."

O'Donnell's face lit at the genuine possibility. "It would be hard enough . . ." he began.

"And its crystal form would protect it from the energy shell without altering the shell's harmonics." Elkins sat back in his chair, obviously forging his imaginary knife. "It's worth a try, Captain," he finally agreed. "Probably take most of the day to construct it."

"Begging your pardons, sirs," Fife broke in, "but you can't honestly believe that the Children are going to let you get close enough to any of them to perform this ridiculous procedure."

"I'm hoping one of them will be curious enough to do just that," O'Donnell replied. "And if they don't, it will still have been worth the effort." After a moment he added, "Look at it this way, Atlee. All I've ever wanted was to create new life-forms, and all you've ever wanted is to command a starship. By the end of the day, one of us is going to get our heart's deepest desire. So cheer up."

Elkins chuckled and said, "With your permission, Captain, I've got some work to do."

"Get to it," O'Donnell agreed. "Url and I are going to prepare everything else for my space walk. Let me know as soon as you're ready."

"Aye, sir," Elkins said and hurried from the room.

"I trust there are no other objections?" O'Donnell asked.

No one spoke, but Url, Falto, and Vincent looked at him with respectful awe. Fife cursed silently, realizing that O'Donnell might once again have outmaneuvered him. His only solace was his absolute certainty that once O'Donnell left the ship, the odds of his safe return were infinitesimal.

Fifteen hours later, O'Donnell stood inside *Demeter*'s transporter room. Once he and Url had begun their preparations in earnest, the lieutenant had raised a simple question. Rather than risk the space walk, couldn't O'Donnell attempt to inject his sample into the energy field surrounding the ship? O'Donnell had already considered the possibility, and confirmed that the field did not contain the same atmospheric balance as the individual spheres. His hybrid wouldn't grow there.

The suit was rigged with standard maneuvering thrusters and could withstand the vacuum of space for hours. Of course, no one intended this mission to take anywhere near that long. Transport coordinates had been set for a cluster of nearby spheres just off the starboard bow. If none of them altered course to intercept him once he appeared, it would take fifteen minutes or so for him to get close enough to perform the procedure. Personally, O'Donnell thought he knew the Children well enough by now to believe that as soon as they detected him, one or many spheres would converge on his position. He had packed several of his suit's external pockets with seedlings in small soil containers to hopefully allay their concerns. If the children worked on the seedlings with the same force they applied to every other growing thing on *Demeter* it might be only minutes until those pockets burst and the small buds died of exposure. But if he could get close enough to a single sphere, all he would need was minutes.

Elkins had run as many simulations as he dared with his final "knife." Although the device he had created was more akin to a syringe tipped with a crystal needle, both he and O'Donnell took great pleasure in dubbing it "the subtle knife," settling the invention's name once and for all. O'Donnell did an hour's worth of practice runs with the extensor Elkins had affixed to the knife. Its controls were delicate, and though it was attached directly to O'Donnell's right hand, it took some doing to get used to activating the controls using the bulky fingers of the suit's gloves.

At long last, however, his preparations were complete.

Before assisting the captain into his helmet, Url took a moment to say, "Thank you for this, Captain."

"Are you kidding?" O'Donnell replied. "It's the opportunity of a lifetime."

"I'm not sure I would see it that way if I were headed out there," Url replied honestly.

"That's because you haven't been waiting twenty years for this day, Lieutenant."

Url nodded. "Safe travels, Captain. And if I don't get the chance to say this later—"

"Oh, we're already tempting the fates tonight, Lieutenant," O'Donnell cut him off. "Let's not piss them off entirely by assuming we know their plans."

Url nodded in understanding as O'Donnell climbed up onto the pad.

Once he was set, O'Donnell said simply, "Ready for transport."

As he activated the transporter, Url said softly, "It's been an honor to serve with you, Captain."

Even had he been listening, O'Donnell would not have heard him, so concentrated was he on his own silent last words.

For you, Alana, and for our daughter.

Seconds later, O'Donnell's stomach lurched as he began the process of acclimating to his new environment. He hadn't bothered to share with his crew the fact that he hadn't actually completed a space walk since his days at the Academy. Though it seemed like a lifetime ago, the initial sickening sensation came back to him quickly enough as he struggled to get some sort of bearing. Somewhere, probably behind him, *Demeter* hung in space. Its angle would have made it difficult to orient himself, so he focused instead on what seemed like the incredibly distant sight of a dozen spheres.

Funny, they look bigger from out here, was his first coherent thought.

His breath was coming too rapidly and he took a few moments to attempt to calm himself. The longer he waited, however, the less stable he felt, so he locked his eyes upon a single sphere and gingerly gave his maneuvering thrusters a small burst.

The action sent him rushing forward, much more quickly than he had intended. He tensed his stomach muscles to avoid turning head over heels. After a few more bursts, he was still breathing too heavily, the sound creating a violent whoosh within his helmet, but he was starting to feel like he was getting the hang of his movements.

The intended sphere was closer now, but not nearly close enough. He risked a longer burst, and this time, as he moved forward, the sphere and four of its companions obliged him by closing the distance between them. Once he had settled, he was well within range of his knife, and had only to raise his hand and begin the operation.

He paused, however, at the sight of the spheres beginning to merge together. Fear and adrenaline shot through him. Every time he'd seen this in the past, it had meant only one thing.

No, please, he thought—not for himself, but for the Children, and the precious gift he had brought them.

Within what felt like seconds, the spheres had merged, forming one organism that truly dwarfed him. It moved inexorably toward him and he thought sadly, *It seems I have failed you after all, my beloved.*

As the sphere came to rest before him, he heard Alana's voice again for the first time in weeks.

You haven't, my love. Just breathe.

An incredibly bright flash of light, accompanied by a distinct vibration that shook O'Donnell in his suit, caused him a moment of intense disorientation. When it had passed, he found he was surrounded by light. He took a moment to look around and saw that an energy shell like the one that sustained the sphere had enveloped him. It was not composed of the same atmosphere that the children shared—he could never have survived that. But it seemed as much like an invitation to continue his work as he was likely to get.

Seconds later, an alarm in his helmet began to beep. He checked the display panel on his left arm and noted that the suit's sensors had detected a shift in the atmosphere around him. Whatever it was that filled the space he now occupied, it was slowly beginning to degrade his suit.

You might want to hurry, dearest, Alana warned.

O'Donnell didn't have to be told twice. Steadying himself, he raised his right arm and guided the subtle knife toward the section of the energy shell he now shared with the large sphere. Willing his arm to remain perfectly still, once he had achieved alignment, O'Donnell depressed the release, injecting dozens of living cells of *Crateva religiosa-Kressari* into their new home.

He had no idea how long it might take the Children to realize what he'd done, but he hoped it would be soon. His suit beeped again, alerting him to the fact that the atmosphere that now engulfed him continued to compromise its integrity. He didn't know if he had minutes or hours, but he honestly didn't care. He had done what he came to do, and if he was to die now, at least he was no longer alone.

Fife had watched O'Donnell's progress with the rest of the senior officers and Lieutenant Elkins from *Demeter*'s bridge.

When the spheres had begun to merge, he was certain O'Donnell's misplaced trust was about to be clarified for everyone. He had been shocked by Url's subsequent report that O'Donnell had been enveloped by an energy shell adjacent to the sphere, but was still very much alive.

"It shouldn't be long now," Elkins said.

"When do you think we'll know if it worked?" Url asked.

"As long as he's still alive, there's hope," Elkins replied.

Fife couldn't have disagreed more.

Minutes later, a shrill bleep broke the silence. Fife's head swiveled instantly to face Url.

"What is it?" he demanded.

Url took a moment to check and recheck his display.

"Lieutenant Url!" Fife shouted.

"I'm sorry, sir," Url replied. "I just wanted to be sure. I've got a Federation signal, sir. They're almost a light-year away, just outside the debris ring. But I think . . . no . . . I'm sure . . . it's *Voyager*."

Chapter Twenty-seven

STARDATE 58464.8
U.S.S. VOYAGER

As soon as the warp effect dispersed, Chakotay looked to Ensign B'Kar, who was now standing in for Lasren at ops.

"Status, Ensign?"

"The Children's vessel is on sensors, Captain," B'Kar

replied in his extremely high, nasal voice. "They must have arrived shortly before we did, as they have already cleared the debris ring and are moving into the system."

"Helm, hold position," Chakotay ordered Ensign Gleez. Though Gwyn had awoken from her "nap" feeling quite well, Doctor Sharak had ordered her confined to sickbay for the time being for observation. If all went well, Gwyn would be serving again as a communicator for the Children relatively soon. Eden had remained there with her to be on hand the moment communication again became possible. Seven had already rejoined Patel in astrometrics.

The plan, at least as Chakotay understood it, was quite simple. The sphere they had released had agreed to intercede with the rest of the Children on *Voyager*'s behalf. *Demeter* would not be released immediately, but *Voyager* would be allowed to enter the system and communications would be restored between the two ships to enable Eden to confirm the health and well-being of her people.

Once that was done, Eden would be allowed to discuss possibilities for aiding the Children, and assuming an acceptable conclusion was reached, both ships would be allowed to depart the Children's space in peace.

All Eden and Chakotay awaited now was a signal from the Children that *Voyager* was clear to move through the debris ring and enter the system.

Chakotay hated waiting. But the success of Eden's efforts so far steeled his resolve. The hard work, it seemed, was already done. What remained were really just details.

"Captain," Harry called from tactical, "I'm picking up something really unusual within the system."

"Go ahead," Chakotay ordered, turning to look at Harry over his shoulder.

"*Demeter* is intact, surrounded by a dense energy field," Harry reported.

This much Chakotay had expected. The Children had already explained the means by which they had moved *Demeter* to their system and confirmed the likelihood that if the ship was still intact, it would also still be held by the field.

"Hundreds of alien vessels are within a few hundred kilometers of the ship."

"What's the unusual part?" Chakotay asked.

"One of the spheres nearest *Demeter,* one that is considerably larger than most of the others and of a slightly different configuration, is showing human life signs."

"Is there any way to identify them?" was Chakotay's obvious question.

"I've got a combadge signal," Harry confirmed. "It's Captain O'Donnell."

"How strong are his life signs?" Chakotay asked.

"His heart rate is elevated, along with his respiration, but he's fine for now," Harry replied.

"For now?" Chakotay requested clarification.

Harry shook his head. "I have no idea how long he's been in there, but his suit is degrading fairly rapidly. He's not going to last in there much longer."

"I need a better estimate than that, Harry," Chakotay said.

"I'd give him twenty minutes, on the outside," Harry replied.

"How long did the Children say it would be before we could expect their signal?" Tom asked.

"They didn't specify," Chakotay replied, "but I'd be amazed if it came in the next twenty minutes, if that's your question."

"Harry, calculate the speed with which O'Donnell's suit

is degenerating and, working backward, give me an idea of how long he's been in there," Chakotay ordered.

After a brief pause, Harry said, "I don't think he's been in there more than ten minutes so far."

Chakotay shook his head in dismay, then tapped his combadge, calling out, "Chakotay to Eden."

"*Go ahead, Captain,*" Eden replied.

"We have a problem," Chakotay said, and quickly explained the situation. "So we can assume that as of ten minutes ago, O'Donnell and whoever transported him off *Demeter* were attempting something. It's probably fair to say that he still has someone waiting on his end monitoring the situation and waiting to bring him home."

"*Now who's the optimist?*" Eden replied.

"You know I've had my doubts, Captain," Chakotay said, "but in the last few hours you've made me a believer. We have the beginnings of a peace agreement here. Do you really want to risk blowing it by moving in before the Children invite us?"

Chakotay knew his answer to that question, but he was genuinely curious to learn what hers would be. History suggested Eden would act with caution. Her next question, however, showed she might have finally reached the end of her patience.

"*Can we get a transporter lock on him from here?*" Eden asked.

Chakotay looked to B'Kar, who replied, "No, Captain. If we were to move past the debris field, just to the borders of the system, we could do it, but not from our present position."

"Ensign Gleez, estimated time to get us through that field in one piece?" Chakotay asked.

"Fifteen minutes," Gleez replied.

At this, Tom turned to Chakotay and said, "Gwyn could make it in ten."

Chakotay considered this for a moment, then asked, "What about you?"

Tom's eyes widened in delight at the prospect. "Eight, at maximum impulse, or nine, if you want to take in the sights along the way."

Seconds stretched out as Chakotay waited for Eden to make her decision. Finally her voice came clearly over the com. "*I don't want to risk this, Captain Chakotay, but I think we have to.*"

Chakotay nodded grimly. "So do I."

"Ensign Gleez, you are relieved. Stand down for Mister Paris," Chakotay ordered.

Gleez rose immediately, and Tom moved quickly to take his station.

"Shields to maximum, and take us to Yellow Alert," Chakotay said. "Mister Paris, as soon as you're ready."

"Hang on, everybody," Tom said. "This is going to get a little bumpy."

"Best possible speed, but do try and keep us intact, Commander," Chakotay ordered.

"Yes, sir," Tom replied, slipping seamlessly into the job he would secretly always love best.

As *Voyager* crossed into the debris field, Chakotay sat back, hoping against hope that they were not throwing away all they had so far achieved. It was surprising but satisfying to have learned in the last few minutes that while Eden generally seemed inclined to follow her head, there were obviously times when the demands of her heart weighed infinitely heavier.

•   •   •

The moment Url reported *Voyager*'s appearance, Fife rose from his seat. Url, Falto, and Vincent's eyes were glued to him. Elkins seemed to sense something in their expectant silence, but only looked from one to the other, his face growing more puzzled by the second. Earlier in the afternoon Fife had ordered him to prepare the slipstream drive for initiation at a moment's notice, ostensibly on the chance that O'Donnell's plan worked. Elkins had complied, but Fife had chosen not to disclose his true agenda to the engineer. Something in the man's rapport with O'Donnell had convinced Fife that he would never have been sympathetic to the cause.

"Lieutenant Url, what is the status of our drones?" Fife asked officiously.

"They are prepared for launch," Url replied.

"And our targeting solutions?"

"Locked in."

Fife nodded.

"All hands, this is Commander Fife," he called over the shipwide comm. "*Voyager* has arrived to effect our rescue, and we are going to make sure they have the best possible chance to succeed. In Captain O'Donnell's absence, I am in command of this vessel. Red Alert. Battle stations."

Fife resumed his seat and said calmly, "Lieutenant Url, prepare to launch drones on my mark."

"Shouldn't we retrieve the captain first?" Url asked.

"I don't believe he would want us to do that without confirmation that he has completed his mission," Fife replied.

"Then we have to wait for that confirmation," Elkins said sharply.

"Chief Elkins, your post is the engine room. I suggest you

return there immediately, and bring the slipstream drive on line," Fife replied.

Elkins, however, did not budge.

"Ensign Vincent," Elkins asked, "what is the status of the sphere that engulfed the captain?"

"There is a definite change in its atmospheric density, and a slight change in some of the resonance frequencies within," Vincent reported.

"He's right," Url said. "Commander Fife, the resonance of all of the individuals within the sphere has shifted into a new spectrum entirely. We've never seen this before."

Fife couldn't have cared less, even as the viewscreen before him, still altered to display the frequencies in vibrant colors, showed the clear appearance of dozens of new vivid green points of light.

"The captain's plan is working, Commander," Elkins said authoritatively. "And whatever course of action you are now contemplating was not approved by him before he departed. Think about it, son," Elkins added a little more gently. "We're on the brink of a whole new day in our relations with this species. Don't let an itchy trigger finger get in the way of that."

Fife refused to even glance Elkins's way. "Chief Elkins, you are relieved," Fife replied. "You are ordered to your quarters, and if you refuse to obey that order, you will be subject to court-martial."

Again, Elkins remained rooted to the deck.

"Lieutenant Url, launch the drones and stand by to fire phasers," Fife ordered.

"Don't do it," Elkins pleaded with Url.

Ten seconds of absolute silence passed while Fife waited for Url's confirmation. Finally Url said, "I'm sorry, Commander, but I cannot follow your order."

Refusing to relent, Fife rose and moved to Url's side. "You are relieved," Fife said. "Stand aside."

"I'm afraid I can't do that either, sir," Url replied.

Fife glanced at the faces of his comrades, unable to believe that he was the one they had chosen to betray.

Without hesitating, Fife raised his phaser and pointed it directly at Url, who stepped back involuntarily.

"I understand, but I cannot allow your fear to destroy us all," Fife said as he quickly tapped the tactical console and released the drones into open space.

As he touched the ship's phaser controls, activating a pre-programmed onslaught, a leaden weight slammed into the center of Fife's chest, dropping him to the deck. He never had time to wonder who had stunned him.

Voyager was still thirty seconds from the inner edge of the debris ring when all hell broke loose before them.

As the viewscreen lit up with phaser fire coming from *Demeter* and directed toward multiple spheres in the area, Chakotay immediately ordered the ship to Red Alert, then asked Harry, "What the hell is going on out there?"

"*Demeter* has opened fire," Harry replied.

"That much I can see for myself," Chakotay said. "B'Kar, can we talk to *Demeter* yet?"

"Communications are being jammed, Captain," B'Kar replied.

Chakotay didn't think. He simply settled on the only appropriate course of action and quickly began issuing orders.

"B'Kar, get a lock on Captain O'Donnell and transport him to sickbay. Tom, get us in the middle of this mess now. Put us between the spheres and their fire. Harry, target *Demeter*'s phaser banks and disable them immediately."

Everyone worked in silent efficiency, executing the orders they'd received. As B'Kar and Harry coordinated a quick drop of the shields for O'Donnell's transport, Chakotay watched dozens of spheres destroyed the moment they were struck by phaser fire. Many scattered, attempting to move out of range, but some failed to respond quickly enough or moved inadvertently into danger.

One notable exception to the chaotic activity was the large sphere that held Captain O'Donnell. It remained absolutely still, and as Chakotay clenched the arms of his chair and watched a new barrage of phaser fire head directly for it, two spheres swooped in from nowhere, taking the impact of the phasers and sacrificing themselves in the process.

"B'Kar!" Chakotay called urgently.

Before the ensign answered, however, Chakotay clearly saw O'Donnell's form dematerialize.

"We've got him, Captain," B'Kar reported. "He's in sickbay."

Finally reaching the fray, Tom maneuvered the ship into position to protect a dozen spheres that were targeted by *Demeter*, and the ship shuddered as it took the brunt of the phasers. Spheres swarmed all around *Voyager* and *Demeter*, clearly disturbed by the events, but obviously unable in the first few seconds to form a cohesive attack strategy.

"Shields holding," Harry confirmed as he simultaneously fired a surgical phaser spread that impacted *Demeter*'s phaser banks but left the rest of the ship undamaged.

"*Eden to Chakotay*," the captain's voice came crackling over the comm. "*What the hell is going on up there?*"

Chakotay needed to give his full concentration to the battle but said briskly, "Patch a visual feed to sickbay so the fleet commander can see for herself."

•   •   •

At Chakotay's words, Eden moved to the nearest display panel and saw how quickly her best laid plans had devolved into utter chaos. It was clear that *Demeter* had instigated conflict and that *Voyager* was doing its best to halt it. The only open question was whether or not they would succeed in a timely manner.

"Ensign Gwyn wishes to speak with you, Captain," Sharak said softly over her shoulder.

I don't doubt it, Eden thought bitterly. Turning, she faced the Child's fury registered on Gwyn's face.

"Why have you broken your word?" Gwyn's voice, but clearly not *Gwyn,* asked.

"Please believe me," Eden said, "we intend no harm. We need to communicate with *Demeter* so that I can order them to stand down. We are trying to protect you and our agreement."

Chakotay heard Eden's interaction over the open comm channel. In the tense silence that followed her response to the Children, Harry said, "I'm picking up three robotic drones on an intercept course—" But that was all he had time to say before a massive explosion rocked *Voyager* and destroyed several spheres in its vicinity.

Chakotay didn't have time to give the next logical orders, but thankfully Tom and Harry didn't need to hear them. Tom moved *Voyager* into the small space separating one of the remaining drones from a group of spheres as Harry targeted the other, timing his destruction of the drone as far from its targets as possible while *Voyager* again took the brunt of *Demeter*'s attack in a jolt that sent Tom careening to the floor. Chakotay barely kept his seat, and Harry was pulling himself up off the deck before the exhaust from a ruptured conduit above had cleared. As he resumed his post, Chakotay heard him mutter, "What the hell was in those drones?"

As the crew collected themselves, Gwyn's voice came again over the comm. "*You may speak with your ship,*" she said, "*but if hostilities do not cease immediately, you will be destroyed.*"

"*Understood,*" Eden replied. "*Thank you.*" Chakotay nodded to B'Kar to open a channel, and Eden spoke to *Demeter* from sickbay, saying, "*This is Captain Afsarah Eden, now commanding the Federation fleet. Stand down your attack immediately. Repeat, stand down.*"

A young, hesitant voice replied, "*This is Lieutenant Url, Demeter's tactical officer, Captain. Your orders are acknowledged. And, well, it's good to see you, Voyager.*"

"*Where is Commander Fife?*" Eden demanded.

"*The commander has been relieved of duty, Captain,*" Url replied. "*He was the one who ordered the attack. The rest of us had no choice but to try and stop him.*"

"*Are your remaining weapons systems secured?*" Eden asked.

"*Yes, Captain,*" Url replied, his voice filled with relief.

"*Keep this channel open and await further instructions, Lieutenant,*" Eden replied.

"*Captain Eden,*" Url asked, "*we saw Captain O'Donnell transported out of the sphere. Did you . . . ?*"

"*We have him,*" Eden said. "*Voyager out.*"

Chakotay studied his feed of Harry's tactical display and finally said, "Stand down Red Alert." Now that O'Donnell was safely aboard, he truly hoped he could explain what in the name of all that was holy his people had been thinking.

"Tom, bring us alongside *Demeter,*" Chakotay ordered, as

he watched hundreds of spheres that had been dispersed by the battle regroup, surrounding both vessels. He was confident Eden would do her best to explain this unfortunate turn of events. He only hoped her explanation would placate the Children. If it didn't . . .

This isn't over yet, he realized.

Once the battle had ended, Eden was immediately accosted by Captain O'Donnell, sans helmet, but otherwise still wearing the pressure suit that had obviously just barely saved his life. Its surface was blackened, scarred, and pitted. Sharak hovered behind him, scanning the noncompliant O'Donnell as he grabbed Eden by both arms.

"Was the sphere destroyed?" he demanded.

"Many were," Eden replied, unclear as to the urgency of his request.

"Yes, but I have to know if *my* sphere survived."

"We will scan the area, but I'm not sure how we will be able to distinguish any particular—" Eden began, but was interrupted by Gwyn, who stood in the doorway of the suite. The psionic field separated her from the rest of sickbay.

"The vessel you filled with life survived," she said.

Eden looked quickly to O'Donnell. "You filled with life?" she asked.

"Thank you, Alana," was O'Donnell's inexplicable response as he released Eden from his grasp.

Eden moved to stand directly before Gwyn, O'Donnell at her heels. Gwyn's next words were obviously for him.

"You understood our joy," Gwyn said.

"I shared it," O'Donnell replied, smiling in relief. "I wanted to create a new life-form that could coexist with you inside your vessels."

"Can you provide this new life to all of us?" Gwyn asked.

"Given enough time, absolutely," O'Donnell replied. "But I have also developed a way to seed the fourth planet of this system with life. With your permission, and your assistance, there might soon be hundreds of new species of life for your people to celebrate."

Had this offer not been the only thing that would cement the fragile peace Eden had established between the Federation and the Children of the Storm, she might have dressed O'Donnell down for so grossly overstepping his bounds. As it was, she could have kissed him.

"If this was your intent, why did you also attempt to destroy us?" Gwyn asked.

"*I* didn't," O'Donnell replied. "But I obviously failed to instill in my people a clear understanding of my wishes when I was not on board my vessel. I take responsibility for their actions, of course. They were tragic, and the resulting loss of life is very troubling to me, and I assume to Captain Eden."

"You didn't order the attack?" Eden asked of O'Donnell.

"Absolutely not. It must have been Fife's doing. We have disagreed many times over the last few weeks as to how best to proceed. He was in command in my absence and must have taken your arrival as a cue to attempt to escape. I should have left clear instructions when I departed, but your arrival took all of us by surprise, and, to be honest, my mind was elsewhere."

Eden turned to Gwyn. "We were also taken by surprise and did all we could to protect your people at the risk of our own lives during the attack."

Finally Gwyn said, "You are complex life-forms. You lack cohesive purpose."

"Sometimes," Eden granted her. "But when we are at

our best, we act as one. This has truly been a terrible misunderstanding. But I know that the worst of it is now past and that if you are willing to work with us, what we can achieve together for us and for you will be well worth the effort."

"We met you with deadly force and you responded by giving us two great gifts," Gwyn replied. "We wish to continue to explore the possibilities you have created for us."

"As do we," Eden assured her.

"How do we begin?" Gwyn asked.

Eden turned to O'Donnell, who scratched his head vigorously. "I need to get back to my lab. And to my crew."

Eden nodded. "If you will give us some time to regroup, we will formulate a plan and present it to you as soon as possible."

"That is acceptable," Gwyn replied. "But we have a question for the bringer of life."

Eden lowered her head to hide her smile as O'Donnell stepped forward.

"My name is Liam," he said simply.

"Who is Alana?" Gwyn asked.

Eden was surprised to see tears glisten in O'Donnell's eyes.

"She was my wife," O'Donnell replied. "She died many years ago."

A look of consternation wrinkled Gwyn's brow. "She lives still inside your mind," she said.

O'Donnell nodded. "She does. I keep her there to make her loss easier to bear. And now, part of her will also live forever inside your people as well."

"It was good of you to share her with us."

"The pleasure was mine," O'Donnell replied softly.

Chapter Twenty-eight

STARDATE 58501.0
U.S.S. VOYAGER

"**C**omputer, begin log entry," Eden said as she sat alone at her desk at the end of what had been a string of extremely long days.

"It has been almost two weeks since our work with the Children began. We have focused on two priorities: providing hundreds of the Children's vessels with specimens of Captain O'Donnell's special hybrid, and dispatching planter drones and personnel to the surface of the fourth planet in areas deemed most hospitable to a wide variety of botanical species, which over the next dozen years should create a new and vibrant ecosystem. With the Children's permission, we have named this planet Persephone. At every step along the way, the Children have expressed their happiness and gratitude. I can now state unequivocally that our fleet has made our first true friend in the Delta Quadrant.

"Ensigns Lasren and Gwyn have worked tirelessly to enable constant communication between our species and are to be commended for their sacrifices and their excellent work.

"None of this would have been possible without the efforts of Captain O'Donnell, who was, by nature, the best possible person to have met the challenges posed by this first-contact situation, and whose bravery and ingenuity in the face of daunting odds are equally commendable.

"It became clear shortly after we arrived that Captain O'Donnell's first officer, Commander Atlee Fife, acted both against his captain's intentions and in a manner completely unbecoming a Starfleet officer. Although I disagree with his decision, Captain O'Donnell requested that disciplinary action against Fife be left to him. In truth, it seemed little enough to do for the man who likely saved countless lives on both sides of this encounter, but I hope that his continuing trust in Commander Fife is not misplaced. I will keep a close eye on him in the future, and should he transgress again, or demonstrate in any way that he is not up to the demands of his post, I will relieve him and see him returned to the Alpha Quadrant at the first opportunity. For now, he remains O'Donnell's responsibility.

"O'Donnell has assured me that our work here will be completed by today's end. Prior to regrouping with *Achilles, Galen,* and *Quirinal,* we have one more stop to make, and we will be accompanied on this journey by a number of the Children. Although the entire fleet remains shaken and disturbed by the destruction of *Planck,* it is my sincere hope that the result of this mission will be every bit as successful as our work here over the last two weeks. Once our final journey with the Children is complete, it will be time to begin the process of grieving and mourning those we have lost."

PERSEPHONE

As Captain O'Donnell traipsed across the soft, newly turned earth of the latest seeded plain on the planet's surface, he imagined he could smell the life beginning to bloom all around him. He was wearing a pressure suit, so this was of course, not possible, but he had spent so much time working in the bulky apparatus of late, it had become as comfortable as a second skin.

He carried a few tools in a soft bag slung over his shoulder. As he walked he took in the sight all around him of drones and crewmen tilling soil, planting seeds, and tending delicate new buds. Hovering above many of them were silent spheres, many of whom now glowed with an inner illumination visible through the dense, superhot atmosphere. He had been told this was the result of the joy they now experienced in sharing their habitat with their new "life." To O'Donnell it almost looked like each of his fields was lit by their own personal sun, and it lifted his heart to think that in years to come, so many would take happiness from the work he had begun here.

It had taken some doing, but with Ensign Lasren's help, O'Donnell had convinced the Children that despite the pleasure they took in watching the plants and flowers grow, they must not use their abilities to hasten the seedlings' growth cycles as they had done on *Demeter*. To do so would damage the plants and likely make it impossible for them to continue to thrive once O'Donnell and his people departed. Once in a while O'Donnell had witnessed enhanced growth, and each time had mentally chided any sphere nearby. Though he was never sure they could understand him, and of course, never heard a response, the specimen usually showed no signs of further interference.

Often as he worked a small area of ground on his own, clusters of spheres would descend as if intent on keeping him company. Sometimes they would follow him about, as if curious, and if he turned on them they would quickly disperse. A few brave vessels had become more constant companions.

He was alone today, however, apart from Commander Fife, who trudged silently beside him. The two men had hardly spoken in the last few weeks. Fife had been paired with several trusted crewmen and had done the same hard labor that had brought everyone else great satisfaction on the fourth planet, but it seemed to O'Donnell had done little to lighten his burdens.

Elkins had been almost apoplectic when he, along with Url, Falto, and Vincent, had briefed O'Donnell about what had transpired on the bridge the day *Voyager* had arrived. O'Donnell worried that his choice not to relieve Fife of his position or subsequent duties might actually kill the poor man, but he was determined to try and solve the problem, rather than simply passing it along to someone else.

Once they reached the edge of the plain, O'Donnell dropped to his knees and pulled out a small spade. Fife stood over him until O'Donnell said, "It occurs to me, Atlee, that you and I got off on the wrong foot."

Fife did him the courtesy of not trying to sugarcoat the situation. "I tried to turn the rest of the crew against you, and my actions almost led to your death," he said simply.

O'Donnell looked up—no easy feat in his bulky helmet—and replied, "You're probably not the first man who doubted me or my efforts, and you likely won't be the last." When Fife said nothing further, O'Donnell handed him the spade and said, "Make this hole a little bigger for me."

Fife knelt and did as ordered as O'Donnell retrieved a small specimen container from his sack and gently removed the new plant from its first home.

"This is a simple *Crateva religiosa,* or 'temple plant,'" O'Donnell informed him as he placed the small plant in the ground and scooped the loose soil around it. "Of course, it's been altered for the soil and climate, but I think it will do quite nicely here."

"What is its purpose?" Fife asked.

"It's an ornamental. It doesn't have a purpose other than to be beautiful. In a few months a truly lovely white flower with dozens of delicate white tendrils will bloom. The center of the flower is a pale violet. These were my wife, Alana's, favorites."

"Were?" Fife asked.

"She died many years ago, after a miscarriage."

"I'm sorry to hear that," Fife said softly, and O'Donnell actually believed he meant it.

"Thank you," O'Donnell replied.

Once their task was complete, O'Donnell looked directly at Fife and said, "Do you wish to continue serving as my first officer aboard *Demeter*?"

"I can't believe you'd even consider it," Fife said.

"Are you planning to lead any more mutinies?"

Fife shook his head. "I never really wanted to instigate the first one, but I did not believe you were as concerned with freeing our people as I was, and I honestly thought once *Voyager* arrived that I had no choice but to try and effect our escape."

"I believe you, which is why I'm still content to have you by my side."

"I wouldn't do the same in your place."

"But if I let you go now, that would be all but admitting that I made a mistake, and you can't imagine how that would bother me. Once I've made a choice, I can be pretty stubborn about it. And I know now that we have that much in common."

"What choice do you mean?" Fife ventured.

"Who do you think requested you for this mission?" O'Donnell asked.

"Admiral Batiste."

O'Donnell chuckled. "Batiste gave me a list of ten candidates. You were *my* choice."

Fife seemed genuinely surprised. "May I ask why?"

"You have skills, Atlee. What you need is time and experience to understand where and how best to apply them. You also have courage and strength. It takes something pretty rare to even contemplate what you did. The thing is, the organization you've come up in has been faced with one catastrophic war after another. I'm not surprised by your instincts, but you need to understand that there's much more to Starfleet than battle and enemies, and once you've learned that, I don't think anything will stop you. The only question now is, can I trust you?"

"I could never trust someone who had done what I did," Fife replied honestly.

"People get to make mistakes, Atlee. Do you know what yours was?"

Fife merely shook his head, clearly at a loss.

"You should have told me what you were planning. I wouldn't have agreed with it except as an absolute last resort and, despite your impatience, we weren't there yet. I probably would have ordered you to wait and see what came of my experiment before taking any action, even if the whole fleet had shown up. But I wouldn't have disregarded your opinion. Maybe that wasn't clear from our last conversation on the subject, and that's my fault. I do know, however, that given our relative skill sets, I don't have the luxury of not listening to you."

"I guess neither do I," Fife allowed. "I mean, look at this planet. I would never have believed any of this was possible, given where our relationship with this species began."

"Maybe I've seen too many miracles in my life," O'Donnell

replied. "Or maybe I'm just too stubborn to ever accept defeat. I have this terrible determination to bend the universe to my will. Only once has it ever disappointed me."

"I'll keep that in mind, Captain," Fife replied.

"Then let's get back to work, shall we?"

The two men rose and began to walk slowly back across the plain. Neither of them noticed a small sphere descending to examine the new plant, or the dozens of beautiful white flowers that burst into bloom long before they should have.

U.S.S. VOYAGER

Chakotay felt the same overwhelming sadness he'd associated with his first sight of the Children's "mother" the moment *Voyager* settled into orbit around her. Despite the incredible success of the last few weeks and the accord that had been reached with one of the most *alien* species he had ever encountered, the gloomy tempests and slices of red lightning tearing through the atmosphere of the creature below were visceral reminders that sometimes pain cuts so deeply that certain wounds can never heal.

However, he also knew that it was testament to how much the Children had learned that they were now willing to try and ease the suffering of the creature that had given rise to them. It was also a great honor that they had asked *Voyager* and *Demeter* to make this journey with them and witness their efforts.

"We have achieved orbit," Lasren reported from ops.

It was good to have him back at his post. Something in his experiences with the Children had given the young man a new sense of calm surety. Chakotay planned to speak with

Eden in the coming days about granting him a field promotion to lieutenant. He had more than earned it in what was now almost three years aboard *Voyager*.

"I still can't get used to it," Gwyn said from the helm.

"What's that?" Chakotay asked. As there was nothing for his people to do now but watch and wait, he didn't see any harm in her spontaneous exclamation.

"Seeing all the white lights," Gwyn replied.

Chakotay understood her to mean the computer's display of the various resonance frequencies within the spheres. When their work had first begun, all of the spheres they encountered were filled with varying hues—reds, oranges, blues, and violets—and those colors had been used to identify the positions of the various individuals as well as the likely thoughts from which they had originated. Once O'Donnell had begun to seed them, however, vivid shades of green had been discovered, and many of those had transformed over time into yellows and pure whites.

"We've given them new things to think about," Lasren said.

"Do you really think they'll be able to do the same for her?" Gwyn asked, turning to face him.

"I do," Lasren said, smiling gently.

"There they go," Tom said, and everyone turned back to the viewscreen to watch as dozens of spheres descended into the creature's atmosphere.

Eden, Seven, and Patel were watching the spectacle from astrometrics and were conducting deep sensor scans of the Children's progress. For his part, Chakotay preferred to see what would happen without technology's help. Even if his eyes couldn't detect any change, he knew Lasren—and possibly Gwyn, given her closeness to many of the Children who had spoken through her in the last weeks—might know well before anyone else whether or not the Children had succeeded.

"Are you getting anything, Ensign Lasren?" Chakotay asked while keeping his eyes glued ahead.

"They're excited, sir. Maybe even a little nervous."

"They have every right to be," Tom replied. "Who knows what she'll make of them."

"She should be proud," Chakotay offered. "I just hope it's not too late for her."

A sharp gasp turned Chakotay's head toward ops. Lasren stood still, though his face had flushed and he began to breathe more quickly.

"Are you all right, Ensign?" Chakotay asked.

After a moment, Lasren composed himself and a huge smile spread across his face.

Chakotay looked back to the viewscreen as dozens of flashes of white light tore across the surface of the atmosphere below. Seconds later, countless small white particles burst upward, filling the space around the creature in a heart-stopping spectacle of pure delight. In the past, the birth of new Children had been sporadic and tentative. Now, hundreds spewed forth from every area of the mother's atmosphere, shining sparks whose nature was all too easy to understand.

"*She knows,*" Lasren said simply.

Finally the oppressive gloom that had weighed so heavily upon Chakotay began to recede. As the viewscreen was lit by continuous explosions of white light, Chakotay was able to share in the mother's complete, unadulterated joy.

Chapter Twenty-nine

STARDATE 58505.1
U.S.S. QUIRINAL

P hinn entered *Quirinal*'s sickbay, as he had every
morning since the crash, fully expecting to spend a
few quiet moments with the unconscious form of his
captain before beginning his duties for the day. The first
thing he noticed was that the main bay was unusually quiet
and empty for this time of morning. The second, infinitely
more disturbing thing was that the bed and private room
Captain Farkas had occupied for the last month was empty.

All of the blood left his head and his hands and legs began
to shake uncontrollably.

She's dead, he thought.

She's dead.

Over and over the words raced through his mind, but
they could not find a space to rest, let alone sink in.

A flurry of light laughter came from a room a few doors
down, striking Phinn more forcefully than a slap across the
face. He could not imagine how it was possible that anyone in the vicinity of what was obviously a great tragedy
could be remotely happy right now, let alone find anything
to laugh at.

A medic named Kogdon hurried out of one of the private
exam rooms down the hall, and offered him a wide smile the
moment she saw him.

"Isn't it wonderful?" she asked.

"Isn't what wonderful?" Phinn replied, miffed at her lack of decorum.

"Captain Farkas," Kogdon replied. "She's awake. Go on back and poke your head in. She's already asked to see you. Doctor Sal told her you'd be along any minute now like always."

It was interesting that hearing this amazingly good news had the same physical effect on him as his recent certainty that the captain was dead. Willing his trembling legs to continue to hold him upright, he walked to the end of the hall and, grasping the door frame for support, turned the corner into the room and saw Captain Farkas sitting up on an exam table, surrounded by Doctor Sal and two of her assistants. All of them were chatting breezily, though Phinn noted that Sal's eyes were glistening. He assumed her tears were of joy. He was certain the ones escaping his eyes now were.

"Lieutenant!" Captain Farkas said, a huge smile erupting on her face the moment she saw him.

"I just heard, Captain," Phinn said, hurriedly composing himself and wiping his nose. "I'm so glad to see you awake."

"It's good to be among the living again," Farkas said, nodding.

After a moment, Phinn started to retreat to allow the doctor to finish her work, but Farkas waved him forward and, turning to Sal, said, "Can I have the room for a moment, please?"

"Of course, Captain," Sal said, ushering the nurses out before her and giving Phinn a quick wink as she brushed past him.

As soon as they were alone, Captain Farkas said, "Do you have a report for me?"

"Of course," Phinn said, grateful to have a topic to discuss. "We've been working with Commander Drafar and Commander Torres for the last two weeks, and the repairs to *Quirinal* are on schedule. This morning we'll be activating the antigrav lifts and *Achilles'* tractor beam to haul the ship upright for the next series of repairs on the hull. Seventy percent of our internal systems have been fully restored. Decks one through fifteen are almost ready to house crewmen again, but we're waiting until the external work has been completed before we start adding unnecessary weight to the ship. I'm sure there's more, but those are the high points, anyway," he finished.

"Excellent," Farkas said, obviously pleased. "I've already spoken with Psilakis and Roach, and they have both informed me that you have gone well above and beyond your normal duties."

"Well, since I was the one who brought *Quirinal* down on this planet, I sort of feel responsible for making sure she gets fixed."

"You saved all of us, Lieutenant," Farkas corrected him.

"I . . . well . . . uh . . ." Phinn stammered, finding it difficult to accept the compliment.

"I have something for you," Farkas said with a slight conspiratorial smile.

Phinn's brows dropped in consternation until she reached to a small table beside the biobed and retrieved his chronometer. She extended her hand for him to take it, and he quickly obliged.

"Thank you, Captain," he said, wishing he had a pocket in which to stow it.

"No, thank you, Bryce," Farkas said. "I would have died without it. And while I can't officially condone its existence, I'm thinking you should keep it on you, if only to make sure you get to your new post every morning on time from now on."

"Of course, Captain," Phinn replied before her words had really sunk in.

"My new post?" he asked.

"Lieutenant Ganley has been transferred to *Galen*. His injuries were more severe than mine, given the amount of time he was exposed to the toxins in the air. Both Doctor Sal and *Galen*'s CMO have decided to keep him there until he can be returned to the Alpha Quadrant for an extensive period of recuperation."

"I'm sorry to hear that," Phinn said honestly.

"He's going to be fine," Farkas assured him. "But in his absence, *Quirinal* requires a new chief engineer. As of today I am granting you a field promotion to full lieutenant, and I am assigning you to his post. Congratulations, Lieutenant Bryce," she finished, extending her hand for him to shake it.

Phinn did so, his face flushing again. "I'm not sure I deserve it, Captain," he admitted.

"I am," Farkas said sincerely. "Now get back to work. I expect to see my ship spaceworthy again inside the next two weeks."

"I won't let you down, Captain," Phinn said.

"I know," she replied.

U.S.S. GALEN

Shortly after *Voyager* arrived in orbit, Chakotay granted Tom a few minutes to board *Galen* and see for himself that B'Elanna and Miral were well before beginning his regular duties for the day. Tom half expected to find them waiting for him in the transporter room, but he was met instead by the Doctor.

"Hey, Doc," Tom greeted him cheerily. "How's everything been going?"

"Terrible," the Doctor confided grimly, giving Tom's stomach a turn. In truth he was surprised. His communications with B'Elanna since *Voyager* had bidden farewell to the Children of the Storm had given no indication that anything was wrong. Tom had thought he and B'Elanna were past keeping important secrets, but then again, nowadays that was hard to know for sure.

"I left them finishing breakfast because I wanted to speak to you alone for a few moments," the Doctor went on as they directed their steps toward his quarters.

"What is it?" Tom demanded, growing more concerned by the second.

"You must speak to B'Elanna about Miral's studies," the Doctor said firmly.

"Her *studies*?" Tom asked, wondering if he had heard right.

"Yes." The Doctor nodded. "I have prepared a rigorous curriculum for Miral, as well as a host of holographic instructors perfectly suited to each subject, but in your absence, B'Elanna has insisted on allowing Miral to spend most of her time playing away the day aboard *Achilles* rather than devoting herself to more suitable work."

Tom paused his steps. "Hang on a second," he said. "We are talking about the equivalent of preschool, right?"

"The lessons I have prepared are perfectly age-appropriate," the Doctor huffed, "and will stand her in far better stead than pretending to be a small grease monkey all day."

Tom bit back a smile.

"You must speak to your wife," the Doctor insisted. "Miral's future hangs in the balance."

Tom patted the Doctor gently on the shoulder. "I'll do everything I can," he replied as seriously as he could.

"Thank you," the Doctor said. "I'll leave you to it," he added ominously as they reached the door to his quarters.

Tom entered to find Miral seated on a brightly colored mat, pulling on the tail of what he hoped was a holographic kitten.

"Daddy!" she shouted the moment she saw him. Instantly she released the kitten, which vanished, and rushed to his arms, practically knocking him over.

"Hey, sweetie," he said, gathering her up into a hug as B'Elanna hurried in from her sleeping quarters to join them.

He then shared a wordless but deeply satisfying hug with B'Elanna before releasing the last of his misgivings about their well-being.

"We have to run," B'Elanna said with obvious regret, "but there's some toast left if you're hungry."

"What's the rush?" Tom asked.

"Big day." B'Elanna smiled. "We're lifting *Quirinal* off the surface, and only half a million things could go wrong."

"So, will Miral stay here for the day?" Tom ventured, not at all sure how to address the Doctor's concerns.

"No," B'Elanna replied. "She loves it here. What kid wouldn't?" she added, looking around the room at the variety of toys and educational games, "but Drafar would never forgive me if I left her behind."

Tom was certain he hadn't heard that right.

"I beg your pardon?" he asked.

"It's a long story." B'Elanna smiled wistfully.

"Give me the short version."

B'Elanna shrugged. "Turns out Lendrin males are more than adequate caregivers. In fact, Drafar is exceptional."

Tom's face hardened a little. "B'Elanna, what did you do?" he asked.

She responded with a sheepish smile. "I admit, at first I was just trying to prove a point. I brought her to work with me one day and the two of them really hit it off. Since then, he's had a meter-high shadow following him around everywhere and I can't tell which of them enjoys it more. She's like his mascot, and you'll never believe how much she's learned."

Tom turned to see Miral rummaging in her mother's personal tool kit. "Is that a hydrospanner?" he asked dubiously.

"Don't worry," B'Elanna replied. "She can't turn it on unless I release the safeties."

Tom was glad to hear it the moment he saw the business end of it go into Miral's mouth.

"The Doctor is pretty peeved," Tom said, knowing his was a losing cause.

"I know," B'Elanna said, "and I feel terrible. But as soon as these repairs are done, I've promised him that we'll start more regular studies here with his programs. You know, a few weeks ago I was worried that it was going to be hard to keep her entertained all day between our schedules. Turns out, I'm having to fight off a long list of folks who want her around."

Tom turned again to look at Miral, who was now banging the hydrospanner against a domical metal play structure.

"Can you blame them?" he asked.

"Nope," B'Elanna replied, smiling broadly.

"I still get you both for dinner, right?" Tom asked.

"Of course," B'Elanna replied. "Harry and Nancy are joining us tonight, though," she added.

"I'm serving on the same ship with them," Tom said. "How is it you know this before I do?"

"You've got to start getting up earlier, my love," B'Elanna replied, kissing him gently on the cheek. "I talked with Nancy this morning before she left to meet with Harry on the holo-deck. They've been working out together for a few days, and so far, so good."

"Am I needed here at all?" Tom asked in mock frustration.

"Always," B'Elanna assured him. "Miral, kiss your daddy good-bye. We've got a busy day ahead of us."

"Bye!" Miral said, blowing a kiss from her perch at the top of the play structure.

Not willing to settle for this, Tom crossed to her and gently lifted her in his arms. "Come on, you two," he said. "Let Daddy walk you to the transporter."

U.S.S. VOYAGER

Before heading down to the planet's surface to meet with Captain Farkas, Eden stopped in to see Counselor Cambridge at his request. She found him seated in his usual chair, staring into the distance as his hand played idly with his bottom lip.

"Good morning, Hugh," she greeted him. "You wished to see me?"

"I did," he replied.

"Is something wrong?" she asked, seating herself across from him and leaning forward, elbows on her knees.

"Every spare moment that I've had since you first ex-plained your little problem to me, I've spent researching every conceivable connection between the artifacts you rec-ognized and the resources of the Federation database as well as my own enviable collection."

"And?" she asked, not sure what she was hoping to hear.

"Apart from a momentary flirtation with the certainty

that you were somehow descended from or a member of the Progenitor species, which I have since abandoned . . . And that reminds me, I probably owe an apology to Lieutenant Patel . . ."

"Hugh?" she interrupted, concerned.

"I told her nothing, never fear," he assured her. "But it, like every other path I searched, has led absolutely nowhere. There is clearly something unique and not quite right about your genome," he added, "but as to its significance, I have no idea."

Eden found herself smiling a little.

"You didn't think . . ." she began. "I mean, I've already searched through what little of my uncles' work was ever made public, as well as all Federation sources, and come up empty. Surely you didn't think you would solve something I've been working on my entire life in a matter of weeks, did you?"

"I confess, that's exactly what I thought."

"Oh, Hugh," Eden said warmly. "It's very dear of you."

"Perish the thought."

"Listen. I want your input and I value your abilities, but this is not your problem to solve. And I want you to know something. I was pretty upset the night we first spoke about this, but the last few weeks have taught me beyond a doubt where my priorities are and will always be."

"I'm intensely curious," he went on as if he hadn't heard her, "about these Mikhal Travelers."

"As am I," she admitted.

"Is it possible that our next object of inquiry might include a diversion into their region of space?" he asked.

"No," she replied, "and before you object, let me be absolutely clear. We are here using the Federation's resources and at their bidding. Should we come across something relevant while pursuing their agenda, I would be willing to investigate it as long as it does not become a distraction from our other duties."

"Didn't the Urnatal who presented Dasht with that staff ask us to establish formal relations?" Hugh asked too innocently.

"They did, and that is one avenue I believe we should follow up on. But tempting as it might be to make this mission all about my own little treasure hunt, I'm not going to give in to that temptation, and neither are you."

"I think that's just silly," Hugh said petulantly.

"I'm not surprised," Eden replied congenially. "But that's the way it's going to be," she added more firmly.

"So you're content to leave this to the whims of fate?" he asked incredulously.

"I have to be," she replied. "Otherwise I wouldn't be worthy of this uniform."

"I'm not going to just let this go," he advised her. "It's simply too interesting a subject."

"Don't," she said, "but it will not interfere with your other duties either."

"Understood," Hugh replied. "Most unhappily, I might add."

"And whatever you did to annoy Lieutenant Patel, I suggest you make haste in setting it to rights. I want my senior staff functioning at peak efficiency, unencumbered by petty personal disputes."

"You've met all of your senior staff on numerous occasions now, haven't you?" Hugh teased. "The odds of that happening are only slightly less than the odds we're going to run across your homeworld by accident."

"For what it's worth, I don't think it can possibly be that

simple," Eden said more thoughtfully. "I mean, Tallar and Jobin were never in the Delta Quadrant, at least as far as I know."

"But now in the space of only a few months you have found two artifacts that inarguably originated here and are obviously significant," Hugh argued. "That can't be coincidence."

"It could be, if the common denominator isn't the artifacts, but instead is me."

"I don't follow."

"Perhaps there is no connection between the language written on that staff and the Mikhal map. Maybe my years of exploration with my uncles just made me sensitive to ancient languages, and my ability to translate them is no more than a freakish trick my brain keeps playing on me."

Hugh paused to consider this. Finally he said, "You don't really believe that, do you?"

"No. But it would be nice if it were that simple, wouldn't it?"

"Maybe for you. Personally, I'll wait and hope for better things."

A soft beep from Cambridge's desk pulled them from their musings.

"What's that?" Eden asked.

"Time for my first appointment," Hugh replied.

Eden rose. "Work well," she instructed him.

She left him seated as she had found him. She could only hope that he would take to heart her instructions and determination to avoid confusing the personal and the professional.

Hugh waited five minutes for his patient to arrive before asking the computer to locate Seven. She had notified him, quite unexpectedly, the evening before that she was ready to resume her normal counseling sessions.

"Seven of Nine is on deck six, section three, outside Counselor Cambridge's quarters."

Puzzled, he rose from his chair and poked his head out the door. Seven stood leaning her back against the wall across from him, her hands crossed at her chest.

"Are you coming in, or did you want to conduct your session in a more public place this morning?" he asked.

"I have been reconsidering whether or not I wish to participate in the session," Seven replied.

"Very well," he said, and returned to his chair, the door closing automatically behind him.

A few moments later, Seven entered without announcing herself and crossed to stand beside the chair in which she would normally have sat.

"And what was the verdict?" Cambridge asked evenly.

"You are the most exasperating person I have ever met," Seven said. "And when you consider that this includes every member of the Federation Institute, not to mention the Borg Queen in numerous incarnations, that's saying something."

"You'll get no argument from me," Cambridge replied.

"Do you wish to continue our sessions?" Seven surprised him by asking.

"I believe we still have a great deal of ground to cover," he replied honestly, "but without your voluntary participation . . ."

"Please stand," she said in a tone that brooked no refusal.

Cambridge shocked both of them by rising immediately.

Without further preamble she moved well into his personal space, raised a hand to his face, and firmly pulled his lips to hers.

The kiss was brief, but not without promise. She then stepped back, putting a few paces between them, and said, "The

Meguti once occupied a Class-M planet in sector 191 of the Delta Quadrant and were known for the complexity of their architectural structures, which survived hundreds of thousands of years after they became extinct. The Rurokitan were a migratory race who covered dozens of sectors some sixty thousand light-years from our present location and were last heard from four hundred years ago. Hrimshee was worshipped for two thousand years by the Nov, who waged war in his name with the Veniti and disappeared from all records over a thousand years ago." Without missing a beat she went on, "Given your regard for me, I believe it would be inappropriate for us to continue our relationship as doctor and patient. However, if you are willing to overcome your many shortcomings to explore a relationship of a more personal nature, I would not object."

With that, she turned and left his quarters. Cambridge cleared his throat as his heart began to run a brisk and thready race.

"Damn," he said aloud, wondering exactly when he had lost control of this situation and whether or not his heart would ever again be his to command.

Chapter Thirty

STARDATE 58536.2

Chakotay found it difficult to look for too long at the vast company assembled on the plain below. The evening was cool and would grow colder in an hour, once the sun had set. Most of the area that had housed *Quirinal*'s crew for the last six weeks had been cleared of any sign that they had ever been there. For this brief time, the valley held the entire crew complement of the fleet *Voyager* was leading.

All the ship captains—himself, Glenn, Itak, Farkas, O'Donnell, Dasht, Xin, and Drafar—stood atop a low hill that rose several meters above the field where their crews stood at attention. A space had been cleared in the center, where T'Mar's people should have been.

Behind the captains sat *Quirinal*, atop her landing struts, now completely repaired and ready to rejoin the fleet in the morning. Her massive beauty dwarfed the assembly, while serving as a visceral reminder that sometimes what had been thought lost could rise from the ashes.

Voyager had been dispatched a week earlier to collect the remains of *Planck*. What little they'd retrieved would be stored aboard *Achilles* until the fleet returned to the Alpha Quadrant. The assembly this night was meant to honor the ship and her dead. Another, smaller service would be held in the coming days aboard *Quirinal* to honor the sixty-three men and women who had perished in the attack of the Children of the Storm and during the ship's crash landing.

As he stood at attention, Chakotay found it difficult to shake the shadows of Kathryn's memorial. He was certain that at least this many had been in attendance, and the first few rows of faces he could clearly see were all touched with the somber seriousness of the moment.

Eden stood a few paces in front of the captains, preparing to address the assembly. He did not envy her this task. But any doubt he had harbored in recent weeks that she was suited for the position she held had been banished.

"Good evening," she greeted them, her voice full and

strong. "We gather here to perform our most difficult duty as Starfleet officers. Seventy of our fellows and the ship on which they traveled, the Federation *Starship Planck*, are no longer among us. We honor their service and their sacrifice and vow as we stand here to remember each and every one of them.

"Before I speak of the individuals who died in the performance of their duty, I believe it bears noting that they began this journey with us optimistic about the promise this mission held. Captain T'Mar selected a particularly beautiful quotation for his vessel's dedication plaque: the words of a woman born on the planet Earth long before her people first dared to travel among the stars. Blinded in her infancy, she never looked upon the night sky with any understanding of the majesty it held, but its truth was not beyond her grasp. Her name was Helen Keller, and her words were these: '*No pessimist discovered the secrets of the stars or sailed to an uncharted land or opened a new heaven to the human spirit.*'

"This was the hope of those who served aboard the *Planck*, and indeed the hope with which we each rise daily to begin our duties. We come seeking knowledge of those who share our galaxy as we to continue to expand the horizons of all Federation citizens. We come to bridge the distance between people of goodwill and to bring a better understanding between those who may not yet know what fellowship is possible between those who seek peace.

"This work can only be done by those who maintain a spirit of optimism about our future. When our losses are as great as the ones we suffer now, grief makes it difficult for us to look within ourselves and rekindle this spirit. But we cannot permit our pain, heavy though it is, to diminish us. No one can replace those who have fallen. But it is worth remembering that beyond, and in some measure because of their sacrifice, a new peace has been established between ourselves and a species who now understand that not all who venture into space come to conquer and destroy. Only by looking beyond their cruelty and the devastating consequences of their ignorance was this possible. I would rather still have *Planck* and her crew among us. But I take comfort in the knowledge that her destruction did not turn us inward, where fear and pessimism would have led to even greater losses on both sides.

"Perhaps most difficult of all is the idea that we come here tonight to mourn, but also to celebrate the lives of *Planck*'s crew. Many of you counted dear friends among them. To you I extend my deepest sympathy. For those of you who may not have known them, you have only to look at those standing next to you to know this much of who they were: men and women like yourselves who have come to this distant corner of the galaxy in search of greater knowing."

After a short pause, Eden began the recitation of the names of those who were lost. "Captain Hosc T'Mar, Lieutenant Daniel Tregart, Lieutenant Anthony DeCarlo, Lieutenant Shurl Beldon, Ensign Danan Grim, Ensign Solonor Evet . . ."

As the darkness gathered around the company, Chakotay searched within himself for the patience to accept how much the universe had chosen to take from all of them. It would have been easy to tear at his own wounds, so familiar was the weight of grief all around him. He chose instead to leave them be and to focus on the truth that no one is truly lost when they remain in the hearts and minds of those who love them.

•   •   •

Once the formal ceremony had ended, the space left open in the field was soon filled with officers from every ship in the fleet greeting old comrades and sharing memories of *Planck*'s crew.

B'Elanna held tightly to Tom's free hand. His other arm was wound snugly around Miral, who had fallen asleep with her head on his shoulder. B'Elanna had been meaning for weeks to speak with Captain Eden and had decided suddenly that there would be no better opportunity to address her concerns.

"I need a few minutes," she said softly to Tom.

He nodded, replying, "I'm going to get back up to *Voyager* and put her to bed."

"I'll be there soon, I promise." Before she released him, however, she added, "Wait up for me?"

"Of course," he said, smiling.

B'Elanna then threaded her way through the crowd and climbed the low hill where Eden stood conferring softly with Captain O'Donnell.

Once they had parted, B'Elanna took the opening to say, "May I have a word, Captain?"

"Of course, Commander," Eden said.

Although they were as far from alone as it was possible to get, the sheer size of the crowd made it possible for their words to pass unnoticed by the others.

"What you said up there," B'Elanna began, "about seeking peace, it was lovely."

"Thank you."

"Was it true?" B'Elanna asked frankly.

Eden paused, confusion flashing across her face. "Of course it was," she finally replied.

"Then I have a question," B'Elanna went on. "Why are two

dozen ships that no one could ever mistake as anything but war craft sitting in a classified bay aboard *Achilles*?"

Eden's chin fell and a deep sigh escaped her lips. "I was wondering when you might think to ask about them."

"I've been a little busy," B'Elanna replied. "But it's bothered me ever since I saw them. They're not like any other Starfleet vessels I've ever seen: single-pilot, phaser banks and torpedo launchers, obviously intended for short-range close-combat situations. What possible use could a fleet ostensibly out here to make peace have for ships like that?"

"There are two," Eden replied evenly. "The first is experimental, the second is defensive. Both the Dominion War and the recent Borg invasion have designers at Starfleet reconsidering every single aspect of our armaments. Years of peaceful exploration haven't made the galaxy a safer place, much as we might hope otherwise. We're not looking for any fights, but if they come our way, we must be as prepared as possible to face them with minimal losses on our part. Command has chosen to provide us with these vessels for our use should the need arise. The eight ships that remain in our fleet are certainly imposing, but in a combat situation where sheer numbers would make the difference, our fleet would more than triple in size."

"Am I to understand that these ships would only be used as some sort of last resort?"

"The choices I made over the last month should allay any fears you might have otherwise. I could easily have chosen to launch them, along with the rest of the fleet, and simply attacked the Children of the Storm with every weapon at my disposal. I chose not to do so for many reasons, not the least of which was the fact that we still had other options on the table."

"I want to believe you," B'Elanna said. "But it's difficult. I'm also not sure who would fly them should the need arise."

"*Achilles* has several special operations pilots on board who trained on them before we left the Alpha Quadrant. As I said, I have my doubts that they will ever see use out here, but if we need them, I sleep a little better at night knowing we have them."

B'Elanna considered Eden's words and the sincerity with which they'd been spoken. Finally she asked, "Why does it feel like the Starfleet I was raised respecting, even when I wasn't sure I could be a part of it, doesn't exist anymore? You said we can't let our fears turn us into something other than what we have always professed to be. But what if that's already happened?"

"Starfleet is and always will be worthy of your respect and the best service you can possibly offer it. But like any organization of individuals, some are better than others at upholding its highest principles. Our job is to make sure we are walking every day on the right side of the line, even when the path is difficult to see. Possessing a weapon does not obligate us to use it. But we should not allow everything we have built for generations to fall into oblivion simply because we were unwilling to use every single resource at our disposal in its defense," Eden replied.

"Then why keep them secret?" was B'Elanna's final question.

Eden considered the question. "That was Willem's call."

"Admiral Batiste no longer commands this fleet."

"No, he doesn't," Eden said thoughtfully. "I'll brief the other captains tomorrow," she seemed to decide right then and there. "I'll leave it to them to determine how best to disseminate the knowledge among their crews."

B'Elanna sighed as some of the tension she'd been holding in her shoulders released. "Thank you, Captain. Though maybe I should be more careful what I wish for."

"What do you mean?" Eden asked.

"I don't care who you have ready to fly them, I can think of one former pilot who's not going to sleep peacefully one more night until he's had a chance to test one."

"Thankfully, Commander, *that* is not my problem to solve," Eden said with a knowing smile.

STARDATE 58537.9
U.S.S. QUIRINAL

Regina Farkas had toured every bit of her reconstructed ship in the last week, including the bridge, but as she paused before stepping onto it this morning, she felt the same internal flurry of excitement she had felt the first day she had boarded *Quirinal.*

It's probably just the smell of new starship, she chided herself.

Or maybe it's the fact that you never thought you'd have the chance to do this again, a wiser voice suggested.

It was true that the last coherent memory she had of *Quirinal*'s near destruction was the certainty that she was about to die, and the peace that thought had brought her. Now she wondered how she could ever have entertained the notion. Her unsought reprieve had energized her in a way she could never have expected. If life had seemed precious to her before, it now gleamed with a luster she could not remember ever experiencing.

El'nor had suggested firmly that once they were under way, Regina should avail herself of their counselor's services.

Farkas had suffered a trauma, no matter how pretty a face she tried to put on it now, and she needed to deal with that lest it rear its head when she least expected it. If she'd needed evidence beyond her own troubled reckoning of her last day of consciousness several weeks earlier, she found it in the difficulty some of her people were still having in working as cohesively as they once had. Psilakis and Roach presented the greatest difficulties, as Psilakis had refused to return any of the crew that had been compromised by the Children to active duty until *Voyager* had arrived and Captain Eden had given the order. She understood Psilakis's reticence, but also knew that this particular chapter of their past needed to be put behind all of them. Roach had agreed, but Farkas sensed it would take time until the bonds of trust that had been broken could begin to heal.

Regina had already scheduled a series of appointments for herself, but despite El'nor's well-founded concern, she did not fear . . . well, anything these days. Every day before her was a gift. That was true for everyone, but few took the time to see it that way.

If Regina had made any mistake in the past, it had only been to forget that while, as the Klingons believed, today might be a good day to die, it was an infinitely better one to live.

She had been smiling internally when she stepped onto the bridge, but as her senior staff erupted in a spontaneous round of applause as she moved to take her seat, that smile lit her entire face.

"It's good to see all of you too," she said, settling into her chair. "Status?" she asked of Commander Roach.

"We're ready to depart," he replied.

The rest of the fleet was orbiting the planet, awaiting

Quirinal's launch. She almost envied her fellow captains the view they would have of the next few minutes.

"Helm," Farkas said calmly, even as her insides tingled with pleasure at the thought of all that lay before her, "take us up."

"Aye, Captain," Ensign Hoch replied.

With those words, *Quirinal* lifted from the surface of an unnamed world that by all rights should have been its grave. As dense banks of white clouds cleared and her ship climbed to the heavens, Farkas said a silent prayer of thanks. She had never really doubted her life's choices, even when they led her into darkness. The blackness above now beckoned and in it depths, dotted with distant stars, she felt only hope. Though it might be a pity that few could choose the manner of their death, the greater tragedy by far was in failing to choose a life this filled with promise.

Epilogue

U.S.S. VOYAGER

As usual, Afsarah Eden was having a hard time sleeping. Rather than fight it, she had chosen to spend a few hours alone on the holodeck. Among her personal files was a program she had not run for years. Tonight, however, it beckoned.

Occidon's Parush Desert had once been home to hundreds of nomadic tribes. Its northern edge was bordered by high stone cliffs in which countless caves had been carved and where archeologists had spent years analyzing the illuminated texts that decorated the walls. Most of them were creation stories detailing the romances of Occidon's single sun and the four sisters, or moons visible in the night sky. When Jobin and Tallar had taken her there as a young girl, they had made sure to point out the dozens of different stories contemporary peoples had created to explain the nature of their existence. Unlike many similar civilizations, Parush's inhabitants had been unique in that they seemed perfectly agreeable to disagreeing among themselves about their origin stories. Whereas other cultures at similar stages of their development had usually fought bloody wars meant to prove the supremacy of their beliefs or gods, these people had seemed to accept early on that new ideas could be a source of richness and strength. A story did not necessarily have to be true to be of value, especially when truth was difficult or impossible to know. Above all, these people had cherished the rights of all individuals to their own beliefs, and their ability to embrace this challenging concept meant that thousands of examples of these priceless works of art remained for history to study, despite the fact that those who made them, as well as their descendants, had long ago turned to dust.

Eden loved the caves, and often retreated to them when seeking solitude, but tonight she chose to sit beside one of the many hot springs that still bubbled up from the base of the canyon. An intensely dry heat still came off the desert in waves, even now that night had fallen and the four sisters danced above, but a soft wind whispered through the canyon, chilling the air enough to eliminate the oppressive heat.

As she reflected upon the last several weeks, she found herself emphasizing less than she had for the rest of her people the good they had managed to salvage from this near disastrous turn of events. She did not doubt her actions once the die was cast, but given what had been lost, Eden did wonder at the choice Command had made in ordering the mission in the first place. As commander of the fleet, part of her job was to put the best possible face on their orders for those who served under her. But she'd be damned if she didn't consider their orders a little more carefully in the future, weighing risk against potential reward and bucking Admiral Montgomery or anyone else necessary if she did not feel that there was an appropriate balance between the two.

She was surprised to hear footsteps approaching and worried that duty might be about to call.

"May I join you, Captain?" Chakotay's voice asked as he stepped toward the spring and into a beam of moonlight.

"Please," Eden replied, gesturing for him to take a seat beside her next to the small bubbling pool of water.

"Is anything wrong, Chakotay?"

"No," he replied, shaking his head. "Just restless tonight."

"I know the feeling."

"This place is magnificent," Chakotay said once he'd settled himself cross-legged on the ground.

"You should see it in the daytime," Eden replied. "The caves above are the really amazing part."

"Where are we?"

"The Parush Desert," Eden replied. "Occidon is an uninhabited planet in the Beta Quadrant."

"I've heard of it," Chakotay said, "but never had a chance to see it for myself."

"I was there when I was a child," Eden offered.

A comfortable silence fell between them. The heat and pleasant soft gurgling of water seemed to have the same calming effect on Chakotay that they'd always had on Eden.

"Your remarks last night were very appropriate," Chakotay said, breaking the silence.

Though Eden hadn't really been looking for a review, she was gratified to hear it. "I hope it's the last such gathering of our people for the next few years."

"No argument there," Chakotay agreed.

"Was there something on your mind?" Eden ventured.

Chakotay shrugged. "Not really, although I did want to tell you that I probably didn't give you the benefit of the doubt you deserved."

"Every call we had to make along the way was tough," Eden said. "Things could have gone either way at several points, and I think we were lucky it all worked out the way it did."

"If I'd had my way, we might still be at war with the Children of the Storm right now."

"I doubt it," Eden replied. "I'm pretty sure they could have taken us long before now." After a moment she added, "But that's not why I refused to engage them sooner than we did."

"I know," Chakotay said sincerely. "I had a brief discussion with Hugh a few weeks ago, and he made me realize something I haven't really wanted to face."

"What was that, if I may ask?"

"While we may learn to accept loss, we shouldn't learn to like it. I've had to make peace with too much of it in the last few years. What bothers me is the fact that each time something else is taken, I seem to feel it less."

Eden gazed at him thoughtfully. "There's only so much we can absorb before we become numb."

"But surely that's no way to live."

Eden sighed. "The night before we discovered the Children's mother, I was doing a lot of thinking about exactly what does make life worth living."

"Did you reach any conclusions?"

"The first was that I can *think* a problem to death. The second was that if I'm going to make mistakes, they're going to be big ones from now on, as long as they come from the right place."

"That sounds a little scary," Chakotay admitted.

"My losses most definitely pale in comparison to yours. But that's only because I have risked less in the past, both personally and professionally. I need to trust others more, but to do that, I have to trust myself. Pain is frightening, and unavoidable. Suffering, however, is optional."

Chakotay turned away for a moment, then nodded slowly.

Finally, Eden said, "Even though I helped select all of the officers of this fleet, O'Donnell surprised the living hell out of me in the last few weeks. I don't know how much of his personal history you know, but his tragedies are some I don't even like to think about. And still, he rages against the universe, completely determined to do what others believe impossible. I'm still trying to wrap my brain around the utter gall of a man who can create brand-new life-forms with such seeming ease."

"It's interesting," Chakotay said, "how sometimes the universe puts people exactly where they need to be when they are needed most."

"You think the universe has a plan for all of us?" Eden asked.

"I've seen enough coincidences like this to make me believe it's as reasonable a position as any other," Chakotay replied. "I'm not saying I always like the universe's choices, but over time, they bend toward progress, if not absolute harmony."

"Hm," Eden said. "It's a nice thought."

Chakotay started to rise, and Eden joined him. Before he could offer a polite reason for leaving, she said, "There's another large spring just over there," indicating an area just south of their position. "There are some ancient remains of a public bathing area you might find interesting."

Chakotay smiled. "You've heard of my humble passion for archaeology?" he asked.

"It's one we share," Eden replied as she directed their steps toward the ruins. "Though you come by it more honestly than I."

"How so?"

"I was raised by two men who spent the vast majority of their lives studying such places," she said. "They dragged me from one fascinating planet to the next as a young girl."

"So it's in your blood," Chakotay noted.

"I don't know," Eden replied honestly.

Chakotay turned a puzzled face to hers. "Captain?"

"There's something I'd like to tell you, Chakotay," Eden said, suddenly certain that if she was going to begin to live according to her words, she had to start somewhere. Perhaps it had something to do with her recent admission to Cambridge and the passion with which he'd embraced the hunt. It might also have been B'Elanna's not so subtle reminder the previous night that secrecy had its place, but not necessarily among those who were prepared to live and die by your orders. Or maybe it was simply that Eden wanted to trust others with more of herself than she was accustomed to sharing up to this point. Before Willem, she had felt incredibly alone most of the time and had convinced herself that she liked it that way. Once he had left her she had locked herself away behind her daily duties and responsibilities, unwilling to risk that sort of pain again. It had felt safe.

But it was no way to live.

"Before I do, though," she went on, "I wonder if you could do me a favor?"

"Of course," Chakotay replied.

"Duty is one thing, but when it's just us, you should call me Afsarah," she said.

It was difficult to tell in the dimness if Chakotay's face flushed, but there was no mistaking the sense of relief in his smile.

"Okay, Afsarah," he said. "It's a lovely name, by the way."

"Thank you."

"So what did you want to tell me?"

"It's kind of a long story, and I'm not sure yet how it ends. But it has a lot to do with the reason I accepted command of *Voyager* and, subsequently, the entire fleet."

Chakotay nodded. "Intriguing," he offered.

You have no idea, Eden thought.

"It starts fifty years ago on a planet not that different from this one. You see, when I was a little girl . . ." she began.

The conversation lasted for hours, but Eden had no doubt once it ended that she had chosen well in sharing what she knew of her past with Chakotay. He had embraced the mystery every bit as enthusiastically as Cambridge, along with her determination to allow it to unfold in its own time.

What Eden knew for certain when Chakotay had finally bidden her good night was that the universe had become a significantly less lonely place.

APPENDIX I

THE VOYAGER FLEET
LAUNCHED MAY 2381

U.S.S. Voyager NCC-74656
Intrepid class. Complement: 147

U.S.S. Quirinal NCC-82610
Vesta class. Complement: 681

U.S.S. Esquiline NCC-82614
Vesta class. Complement: 653

U.S.S. Hawking NCC-81897
Merian class. Complement: 75

U.S.S. Planck NCC-81894
Merian class. Complement: 70

U.S.S. Curie NCC-81890
Merian class. Complement: 72

U.S.S. *Galen* NX-86350
Galen class. Complement: 31

U.S.S. *Achilles* NCC-77024
Mulciber class. Complement: 561

U.S.S. *Demeter* NCC-79914
Theophrastus class. Complement: 43

APPENDIX II

FEATURED CREW MEMBERS
U.S.S. VOYAGER

Captain Afsarah Eden
(female) fleet commander

Captain Chakotay
(human male) commanding officer

Lieutenant Commander Tom Paris
(human male) executive officer

Lieutenant Commander B'Elanna Torres
(Klingon-human female) fleet chief engineer

Lieutenant Harry Kim
(human male) second officer, chief security/tactical officer

Lieutenant Nancy Conlon
(human female) chief engineer

Lieutenant Devi Patel
(human female) senior science officer

Lieutenant Hugh Cambridge
(human male) counselor

Doctor Sharak
(Tamarian male) chief medical officer

Ensign Kenth Lasren
(Betazoid male) operations officer

Ensign Aytar Gwyn
(Kriosian-human female) helmsman

Seven of Nine
(human female) mission specialist

U.S.S. QUIRINAL

Captain Regina Farkas
(human female) commanding officer

Commander Malcolm Roach
(human male) executive officer

Lieutenant Commander Gregor Denisov
(human male) chief of security

Lieutenant Commander Julian Psilakis
(human male) third officer

Lieutenant Sienna Kar
(Bajoran female) tactical officer

Lieutenant Preston Ganley
(human male) chief engineer

Doctor El'nor Sal
(human female) chief medical officer

Lieutenant Junior Grade Phinnegan Bryce
(human male) engineer/slipstream specialist

Ensign Jepel Omar
(Bajoran male) operations officer

Ensign Krim Hoch
(human male) helmsman

U.S.S. ESQUILINE

Captain Parimon Dasht
(human male) commanding officer

Lieutenant Derek Waverly
(human male) chief engineer

U.S.S. HAWKING

Captain Bal Itak
(Vulcan male) commanding officer

Lieutenant Vorik
(Vulcan male) chief engineer

Lieutenant Connor Griggs
(human male) chief of security

Lieutenant T'Pena
(Vulcan female) tactical officer

Lieutenant Lern
(Vulcan male) science officer

Doctor Lamar
(Vulcan male) chief medical officer

Ensign Justin Bloom
(human male) operations officer

U.S.S. PLANCK

Captain Hosc T'Mar
(Trill male) commanding officer

Lieutenant Daniel Tregart
(human male) executive officer

Lieutenant Anthony DeCarlo
(human male) tactical officer

Lieutenant Shurl Beldon
(Trill male) chief engineer

Ensign Solonor Evet
(Bajoran male) operations officer

Ensign Danan Grim
(human male) helmsman

U.S.S. CURIE

Captain Xin Chan
(human male) commanding officer

U.S.S. GALEN

Commander Clarissa Glenn
(human female) commanding officer

Lieutenant Reginald Barclay
(human male) engineer/holographic specialist

Lieutenant Ranson Velth
(human male) tactical officer

Lieutenant Cress Benoit
(human male) chief engineer

The Doctor
(holographic male) chief medical officer

Ensign Michael Drur
(human male) operations officer

Ensign Lynne Selah
(human female) science officer

Ensign Benjamin Lawry
(human male) helmsman

U.S.S. ACHILLES

Commander Tillum Drafar
(Lendrin male) commanding officer

Lieutenant Rich Edmonds
(human male) chief engineer

Ensign Illo Mirren
(Deltan male) helmsman

U.S.S. DEMETER

Commander Liam O'Donnell
(human male) commanding officer

Lieutenant Commander Atlee Fife
(human male) executive officer

Lieutenant Url Lask
(Bajoran male) tactical officer

Lieutenant Garvin Elkins
(human male) chief engineer

Doctor Bano Peyman
(human male) chief medical officer

Ensign Thomas Vincent
(human male) operations officer

Ensign Sten Falto
(human male) helmsman

ACKNOWLEDGMENTS

Some books are lonelier to write than others, and this was one of them. That said, those who contributed their vast expertise include Heather Jarman, Mark Rademaker, Christopher Bennett, Kevin Dilmore, Paul Simpson, and Marco Palmieri. A special note of thanks is due to David Mack for his original creation of the Children of the Storm in his marvelous *Mere Mortals.* He'll never know how much pain his semifluid liquid metal hydrogen caused me, but that's probably for the best.

Emotional support during the writing process came largely from my family: Patricia, Matt, Paul, Katherine, Vivian, Donna, Chris, Fred, Marianne, Freddie, and Ollie Jane, whose strength was of particular inspiration. As always, my agent Maura was magnificent. Lynne continues to make every single part of my life possible and can never receive thanks enough.

But the folks who really kept me sane throughout are the mothers, some of whom have been around for years, and some of whom are newer to my life. They include Samantha, Heather (again), Candy, Lynne (again), Julie, Stacey, Jenn, Tina, Amber, Katie, Analisa, Michi, Yuka, and Elizabeth. As much as this book is for them, it is also for their beautiful children: Katey, Maggie, Jack, Sarah, Allison, Rachel, Abigail, Christiana, Carolina, Connor, Sadie, Finn, Vincent, Nathan, Dash, Desi, Elenita, Addy, Erin, Lukas, and Lyla. There's good reason why some of those names might sound familiar if you've already finished the book.

There are, however, exactly three people without whom this book could never have been created. Jamie Costas hired me to write it and gave me a tremendous amount of freedom to push the story to new depths. My husband, David, kept me fed and loved while again listening to every word. And my unspeakably amazing daughter, Anorah, was kind enough to sleep for enough hours each night during the second six months of her life for me to finish the manuscript. More important, however, the new life she has given David and me brought with it a deep well of emotions and ideas that I never dreamed existed before she was born. She is my bean of joy and I love her more than I can ever say.

ABOUT THE AUTHOR

In addition to *Children of the Storm*, Kirsten is the author of its immediate predecessors, *Star Trek: Voyager—Full Circle* and *Star Trek: Voyager—Unworthy*, the last Buffy book ever, *One Thing or Your Mother*, *Star Trek: Voyager, String Theory: Fusion*, and the *Alias APO* novel *Once Lost*, and she contributed the short story "Isabo's Shirt" to the *Distant Shores* anthology as well as the short story "Widow's Weeds" to *Space Grunts*.

Kirsten appeared in Los Angeles productions of *Johnson over Jordan*, *This Old Planet*, and Harold Pinter's *The Hothouse*, which the *L.A. Times* called "unmissable." She also appeared in the Geffen Playhouse's world premiere of *Quills* and has been seen on *General Hospital* and *Passions*, among others.

Kirsten has undergraduate degrees in English literature and theater arts, and a master of fine arts from UCLA. She is currently working on her first original novel.

She lives in Los Angeles with her husband, David, and their daughter, Anorah.